A SPECK OF DARKNESS

C.K. FRANZISKA

ISBN: 979-8-218-04488-6

DEDICATION

To my loving daughters—my sun and my moon. May you always stick together when life is unbearable.

ACKNOWLEDGMENTS

My first debt is to PerkyVisuals Book Covers, my cover and page breaker designer, who made my vision come true after flooding him with more ideas than could ever fit on a book.

Brenda, Lindsay and Rachel, my editors, who went above and beyond untangling my words to give them sense.

My husband, who patiently listened to my crazy ideas and still decided to stay married to me.

And our daughters, for inspiring me to see the world through children's eyes.

PROLOGUE

"Tell me the story again, Mama. Pretty please!" The little girl pleaded, hugging her mother's bony chest and looking at her with big, beautiful eyes.

"Alright, but after that, you go straight to bed."

"Okay."

The mother pulled a strand of hair from the girl's face and snuggled closer to her.

"Before humans were at the top of the food chain, there were mythical creatures that ruled the world. Emmerson was a shapeshifter, and she fell in love with one of the most powerful magicians of her time, Norwin. They were madly in love. Emmerson got banished from her clan, as relationships and reproduction were only allowed between two creatures of the same gifts. The magicians took Emmerson, exiled and carrying Norwin's child, and with this, the demise of mythical creatures began."

"But why did they decide to love each other?" Asked the girl.

"It's not a decision you make. Once you meet your soulmate, your entire world falls into place, and you can't imagine a life without that person."

"That's gross." The girl stuck her tongue out with disgust, and her mother laughed.

"Someday, you will understand."

"Please keep going with the story. I want to hear about the ceremony."

"Okay. But close your eyes.—They got married. Norwin's family saw in Emmerson more than just a shapeshifter and the mother of his child; they saw the potential for a new Crossling. This new hybrid could lead the world with their human mind, animal instincts, and magic. Yet, something was missing: both man and animal were mortal. The magicians needed an immortal leader who could wield the power of infinity in favor of the magicians. That's why they wanted to give Emmerson immortality, as a wedding gift."

"Isn't it boring to live forever? I mean, there are only so many books you can read and coloring pages you can do in a day, and doing it repeatedly seems boring."

"I bet life would get boring without having something to live for."

"Anyway, keep going, please!" The little girl tucked her feet closer and closed her eyes.

"Emmerson accepted the gift of eternal life without knowing the consequences. On her wedding day, they sacrificed two magicians, which gave her immortality. Emmerson bore a son and then eventually a daughter. Her power grew, and the magicians appointed her to take over the world. With several wars under her belt, she was finally on top, with Norwin and her children by her side. As she became more powerful, fear overcame her. Norwin grew older, and the realization of immortality set in—Everyone in her beloved family would eventually face death while she would never age or die. The more she tried protecting her family, the opponents realized she wasn't as invincible as they once thought. Once some realized her weaknesses, they successfully carried out an assignation attempt on Norwin."

"You mean he died?"

"Yes, my child, now hush—Emmerson tried the unthinkable with Norwin—Her instincts told her to give him some of her blood. Her blood healed Norwin, and he became immortal like his wife, or so they thought. Their blood became precious to everyone. Their castle had to be protected, and they could no longer trust their own family. She thought she had passed on her blood to her children; however, Emmerson realized she had exchanged her carefree existence for a life of power, greed, and death. She didn't want that for her children. After their son died of old age and their daughter passed away, Emmerson no longer wanted to be immortal. She asked the magicians for advice, but they had no answers. The parents spent decades with broken hearts after losing their children. After Norwin's passing, it became obvious that he had not become immortal, and Emmerson finally realized her wedding gift was a curse. To end her fate, she returned to her clan and surrendered. They wanted nothing more than to see her dead after her betrayal. They tortured her in horrific ways, but she always returned unharmed. Emmerson was desperate at this point and took her fate into her own hands—She poisoned herself. It turned out that the desire to die outweighed immortality, and her curse was finally broken. Do you remember the two magicians being used for the ceremony?" The child nodded drowsily and fought against sleep.

"After Emmerson gained power, she and Norwin moved into a palace to protect themselves from enemies. They obeyed the rule of never leaving their palace, but their children repeatedly broke it and met with Emmerson's old clan. Taylor, the son, fell in love with another shapeshifter, and he ended up getting another sorceress pregnant. He was afraid of how his mother would react, so he hid it from her. His sister also carried his secret to her grave. The story says that the bloodline still exists today. The magician made Emmerson aware that the only other way to become immortal, without sacrificing two magicians and using the long-lost spell, is to consume the blood from twins of her bloodline."

The mother gently laid her hand on the child's cheek, kissed her, and covered her with a blanket.

"Oh, my dear child, if only you knew some stories hold more truth than we want them to." She sighed, extinguishing the light in her room.

CHAPTER

1

My mother always said I could not lose control if I wanted to stay alive.

"Cassandra, lower your blinds. I don't want the neighbors to see you like that," a voice echoed like a lash of a whip from the kitchen, through the hallway, to my room.

Warm, golden rays of sunshine broke through the window and kept me cozy. I hated my window, because it showed me a world I would never fit into.

Day in, day out, I saw people passing under my window on the second floor of our tiny house.

I could hear children scream outside and even catch a glimpse of them sometimes. How carelessly they played catch or soccer, not realizing that they were in the best time of their lives. The mothers dressed the children in dirty clothes, no longer good enough for school, and only used outdoors. Often I heard them screaming with joy. Sometimes I listened to the little things they were arguing about until their mothers roared out the window that they should get along or there would be no television before bedtime.

This world was so foreign to me. My brother and I had spent little time outside when we were younger. The piercing fear of showing my true face was too intense.

I spent most of my childhood in the courtyard of our house, hidden from curious eyes. Several times, I had fallen down the slippery wooden stairs on my way down to the yard after it had rained. But every time my parents heard the rumbling sound of my fall and came to check on me, I denied it out of shame and tried to hide the new bruises on my legs and arms.

The cold stone walls of the courtyard gave me a feeling of security that I had never felt when I was out with the neighborhood children. As if by instinct, I knew playing amongst them without accidentally revealing my gift was an impossible task. Down there, in the safety of my courtyard, I could play ball, ride my bicycle, cover the stone floor with chalk—alone, of course—and even conjure up a picnic for my parents and brother if I felt like it.

Sometimes I tried to brew magical potions—with my imagination—from my mother's plants, which were neatly placed in the house and on the porch.

Then, when I was five years old, I had turned my parents' room upside down in search of more chocolate. I knew my mother was hiding the candy from me somewhere, but I couldn't figure out where. So instead of chocolate, I found an old book bound in leather, decorated with the moon's cycle and various plants. From time to time, I tried to imitate a potion or a spell, but not a single one succeeded, and soon I lost interest in the book.

Sometimes I even imagined I could talk to Fairies, but they didn't exist either—at least that's what my brother told me. Those were just children's games, and there were no potions or Fairies. I was aware of that now.

Yet there had to be more than just humans in this life. I wished there was more—no, there HAD to be more. I needed there to be more than just the primitive life in this insignificant village.

By now, I was no longer a child, and the fantasy world I had lived in was extinct. Meanwhile, there were homework assignments and my books, and I still preferred to avoid other teenagers.

I continued to look at the street and watch the old yet well-kept houses in front of me and heard my parents whisper. My big brother Lex kept running from the bathroom to his room and back, slamming the doors loudly.

I could see the wind brushing through the trees, which grew more assertive. I could feel the air changing every morning—getting cooler—when I stepped out of the house for school. My favorite season was about to begin, autumn, and my birthday was creeping up on me in just a couple more days.

After this dry summer, which had been hotter than the last, I couldn't wait for the temperature to drop. Finally, the beauty of autumn was about to unfold. I wished for the colorful leaves to cover the streets and meadows.

My room was still uncomfortably warm because our AC failed in the middle of the year's hottest week that summer. Unfortunately, my father wasn't a handyperson, and getting an appointment for someone to look at it was even more challenging than watching my father trying to fix it himself.

My mother, Amber, put a lot of effort into decorating my room because I spent most of my time alone here. A large four-poster bed, buried under many cuddly stuffed animals and pillows, stood in front of me.

I knew how ridiculous the stuffed animals looked in a teenager's room, but I didn't care. I loved the black cat I got from my parents after my first hunt. Or the wolf my brother Lex gave me after our parents decided we were too old to share a room. The wolf helped me not to feel alone at night.

On the weekend, I hardly dared to get out of bed. While Lex was busy meeting friends, going to the cinema, and strolling through the nearby town, I jumped into my bed with a book and closed the thick curtains to disconnect from the rest of the world.

A wardrobe stood beside the bed, crammed with clean piles of clothes. A large, heavy wooden desk occupied one wall, covered with sketches, writing utensils, and school notebooks. I wrote notes from the books there. Hundreds of books, ranging from fantasy to poetry, were neatly classified on the bookshelf that stood on top of my desk. Although I have searched through the books daily to find answers to my question, almost all of them were still in their original state. I was still hoping to find an explanation. But after researching hundreds of books, I still had no answer.

My parents always avoided the question, saying there were only a few people of our kind. But that wasn't enough for me. If my parents didn't want to tell me why I was different from the other children my age, I had to find out on my own.

I heard the doors slamming again, and I knew full well that Lex had to be dissatisfied with his outfit. Every time he wanted to look at himself in the mirror, he had to go to the bathroom, which was down the hall and next to the dining room. Lex never left the house without the perfect appearance.

In contrast to my brother's walls, which were hung with

posters, pictures of sports teams, and actresses, mine only had a vast mirror hanging next to the door. But this mirror was my enemy. It kept showing me a reflection I didn't want to see. A stranger I couldn't control as much as I tried.

I stretched my arms out on my squeaky chair and looked around my room.

Is this going to be the sight for the rest of my life? I asked myself.

I was now almost 18 years old and had never left the village.

My parents feared someone would notice what was happening behind our closed doors. What if someone saw me when I lost control? The neighbors would call the police and probably run away as quickly as possible. Perhaps they would wonder how they had noticed nothing wrong with our family in the last seventeen years—since we, the Kaysers, moved into this house with a one-year-old child and a newborn.

By now, we had become good at maintaining the appearance of a typical family.

The open window let the golden sun rays dance over my body. In just one hour, the sun would disappear behind the houses in front of me, and the night would allow a glimpse into my illuminated room.

I quickly jumped up, ran to the window to lower the blinds, and took a deep breath.

"Cas? How often do I have to tell you to lower your blinds before it gets dark outside?" My mother's voice rang through the house.

How could I be so foolish and make the blinds pop loudly onto the windowsill? I slapped my hand on my forehead.

Of course, my mother would hear it because her ears perceived noises renounced to humans.

My hair stood up, but I was used to the tingling. I hated

getting mad because that gave me insane goosebumps every time.

With a quiet squeak, the door opened. Usually, my hearing was so good that I could hear my parents' footsteps from afar, but I was far too busy fighting the tingling of my pores.

"I'm sorry," I said, trying to avoid my mother's piercing gaze.

Amber Kayser, my mother, was an elegant woman with an oval face and thick, wavy, reddish-brown hair. Her cat-like eyes were green with a hint of blue, and her skin tanned from the long days of summer. But what I admired most about her were her curves and the suppleness and calm she radiated when she entered a room. Her face was still as supple as it was years ago, almost as if she weren't aging.

"We're about to leave. Please try to get yourself under control and get dressed," my mother said, still looking down at me, but the corners of her mouth curled in a loving smile. She slipped out of my room without waiting for an answer.

I didn't like to be scolded. But to be honest, what child did? It's as if I had not heard the same thing a hundred, maybe even thousands of times. I could take my life into my own hands, being almost legally an adult.

You're an extraordinary girl with a special gift, my mother's voice said in my head; that's something she would say often.

What does that even mean: *extraordinary*? All I wanted to be was an ordinary girl with average grades and friends. But my brother lived the life my heart longed for.

Something warm and fluffy touched my arm and distracted me.

Self-control was the most crucial rule in my life if I wanted to blend in with the crowd and stay alive. But nothing about my family was normal, and having no self-control made me an outsider. For example, I had to brush my clothes daily so no one in class would see me covered with cat hair. My excuse was my fluffy Maine coon cat Damous, who looked more like an overly used broom. He had only come into the house to explain the hair.

But for me, Damous was more than just a cat. He spent hours curled up next to me on the bed, and from time to time, when I felt the need to leave the house outside of school to lie and read in the garden under a tree, he was always at my side.

Damous had been with our family for two years, and he had become irreplaceable to me.

Slowly, I got up and went to my mirror to see if the transformation was finally complete. No, it wasn't that fast this time. I looked at my reflection and wondered how I would ever find a boyfriend without telling him the family secret, as I had sworn my parents never to tell.

Like my mother, I could switch between my human and feline forms. But the books I had rummaged through over the years depicted it as a mythical figure or fictional being, not a factually documented thing.

My transformation mainly was uncontrolled—when my mood swung from one second to the other. Every little emotion seemed to make the cat take over. Years of training with my parents and self-discipline didn't seem to have helped me.

Sparkling green eyes in a fur-covered face with a red-brown nose, black whiskers, and a beard looked back at me. The big cat ears protruded like towers from my head, with fine hair at the ends. Fur covered my whole body, and a short, bushy tail unconsciously moved back and forth behind me. The black coat was short but thick; if you looked closely, you could see dark gray spots. When I opened my mouth, white, pointed teeth flashed out.

The only difference between a typical cat and me was that I could walk upright like a human and kept my height. But, to be more precise, I resembled a lynx, which didn't make this remarkable transformation any better.

I knew no one of our kind besides my family and another clan. For years I had hoped to meet other family members or shapeshifters my age who didn't have the same heritage as me, but I was always disappointed. Both of my parents were single children. Lex and I had hoped to hug our grandparents at some point—but they had all died before we were even born. The weird thing was that we never visited their graves, and that made me wonder.

There were no pictures or stories from my parents' past, nor did they ever talk about the time before they became parents. They also avoided answering why we were shapeshifters—able to change between human and animal forms. And the more I tried to figure out why we could change, the more silent my parents became.

After my distrust got ignored and my parents continued to make me believe we were just an extraordinary family, I gave up.

Although I had tried to convince myself with the belief that there were only four of us and another clan of two people, I stopped asking questions. Well, mostly. The curiosity about my family tree was still burning inside of me.

Okay, I thought, *my brother wasn't better off.*

But unlike me, Lex had the upper hand over his wolf and only turned if he wanted to.

Lex had inherited the self-control and form of a wolf from our father, Zino. In addition, he was popular at school because he didn't have to fight against his transformation. His classmates worshiped him, and he belonged to the table of pretty, hip teenagers, while I was careful not to let other students near me.

It had been months since the last classmate tried to sit next to me in the cafeteria, only to discover that I wouldn't even look at her. Then, as the school bell rang for the next lesson, she gave me a compassionate, awkward smile and disappeared into the crowd of students.

Of course, I was sorry about ignoring other children since the beginning of first grade, but how could I build a friendship if I couldn't show anyone my true face?

Slowly, my ears retreated. Long dark blond hair fell over my shoulder to my chest, my fur grew back into my skin, my eyes turned back to pupils instead of slits, and my teeth became smaller. My face was round and surrounded by messy hair. The only things I kept were my excellent hearing, sense of sight, and smell.

I couldn't decide whether I liked or hated my human skin. Cold air surrounded me like an icy blanket. Without my fur, I had to cover myself up with clothes. I never froze with my lynx coat! But hair spread wherever I went, and I didn't have that problem with human skin.

The only warm thing on my body was the big moonstone I always wore around my neck—usually buried under a shirt or in my fur. It had been a gift from my mother, and since I got the pendant ten years ago, I could count on one hand how many times I had taken it off.

"How long do you need?" Lex said with his clear and determined voice as he stormed into my room and stared at me.

Again, I noticed how different we were. Lex drove one hand through his blond, short hair while pushing the other into his narrow hip. I had to look up to see his dark brown eyes; he was always wearing something trendy. His blue sweatshirt stood out, the loose leggings made him look athletic, and the cream-colored collar under his shirt emphasized his tanned skin. He knew how charming yet lethal he was.

"I'll be right there!" I answered, trying to cover my body as much as possible with my hands.

I hurried to my wardrobe, pulling out a pair of jeans and a crumpled shirt.

"What are you looking at? Can I help you with something?" Irritation arose in me, and I could feel my pores preparing to let the cat fur through.

Then I thought about the trip our family wanted to make and could distract me from the transformation.

CHAPTER

2

Family trips were the highlight of my week. It was the only thing for which I voluntarily left my room and could hardly wait to sit in the car.

"You really need to learn how to handle yourself better, or do you want to be afraid your whole life?" Lex said under his breath. Of course, he only wanted to be friendly, but he knew how hard it was for me to contain my feelings.

Again and again, he had been at my side when I stormed out of class to hide in a toilet stall so that no one would see me. Lex was always defending me from his friends or inviting me to celebrate with him—which I kindly refused.

Every time I couldn't control my emotions, my brother rushed to the rescue, and he knew how grateful I was for him, although I could never say it out loud.

"I'm trying," I replied, pushing myself past him into the hallway.

Family photos hung in the hallway, of course in our human form, because our parents often had guests over to preserve the appearance of an average family. We found this ridiculous, but we couldn't stop our parents. So annual family pictures were in our house rules, and there was the same yearly dissociation.

It wasn't as if we didn't like the family pictures. But the portraits only show what everyone should see—a small happy family who burst with happiness and joy—not who we actually were.

But it wasn't like that.

The feeling of being the black sheep in the neighborhood, even in the entire village, came over me every time I left the house.

As we walked through the hallway, the floorboards creaked under our feet. Finally, we slipped into our worn-out shoes, which waited for us next to the kitchen door.

"Give me a moment. I forgot something," my brother said and disappeared into his room.

"She's not ready," I hear my mother whisper through the crack in the door.

"But we have to tell her. It's only a matter of time before it starts—"

My mother cut my father off. "Nothing will be the same as before. It will turn her world upside down."

"I know." My father cleared his throat.

"And yet you want us to explain it to her?"

"We have no choice," my father pleaded.

"Of course we have. That's why we left it all behind." Her voice darkened.

"But you know as well as I do that the day of her finding out the truth is getting closer, and we know we can't run away from it forever."

"And until that day comes, we will be silent." My mother's voice grew quieter. The tremor in her tone revealed she was in pain.

I didn't want to eavesdrop on my parents, but my body

froze in place. It would have been more sensible to reveal my presence, but inside of me, a box had opened, in which I had packed all my questions about their past and our family, and now opened, I couldn't close it again.

"She knows something is wrong," my father continued quietly.

"Okay, I'll talk to her, but remember, I warned you. There is no going back after it." My mother couldn't get any further because Lex had stormed past me and came to a halt in front of the dining table—full of anticipation of the hunt.

I tried to make a smooth move out of the jump—which I had made over my brother's sudden appearance—so that my parents didn't notice that I had been listening to them.

What did they have to explain? And the more pressing question was: to whom?

Were my parents talking about me? Or was there a dark secret from their past that they wanted to cover up all these years, and now it was about to come out? Who was the mysterious 'she'?

I entered the kitchen, stumbling and clumsy. Our parents sat at the wooden kitchen table and pretended to go over the route for the hunt.

Lex slurped his long legs over the stones beneath us. Old bricks covered the floor, the kitchen was forged of heavy black iron, cast irons decorated the walls, and plants seemed to protrude from the ceiling. The room seemed huge compared to the other rooms in the house.

It was our mother's favorite room. She cooked daily and sometimes spent hours processing meat, so she put a lot of emphasis on a lot of space.

Like every week, we planned to go hunting as a family. Of course, we didn't eat the animals raw. Instead, we brought home the captured prey, dismantled them, and cooked the meat. My mother thought it was more economical than going shopping every week. In her opinion, supermarkets couldn't be trusted anymore because everything was full of pesticides and chemicals.

We killed no prey on some hunting nights and released them after capture. Our parents introduced that idea so we could sharpen our hunting techniques to feed our own families eventually. But I couldn't imagine explaining to my future husband—who would be one hundred percent human—that I had captured an animal alone, without a weapon and with my bare hands, without betraying myself.

"There you are at last! I thought we had to go alone," said my father as he looked up for a moment. He seemed unfazed by the entire conversation with my mother.

The sofa he was sitting on was far too small for him. With his black, short hair and terrifying eyes, he looked dangerous. As a result, people tended to avoid Zion, who wasn't only large physically but also very muscular.

But I could look behind his facade and knew my father had more heart in his chest than all the people in the world together. He cared graciously for our family, and I could always count on him.

Of course, he was the family's pack leader and led us safely through the hunts. He was also responsible for catching enough food for us when the rest couldn't.

"Cas' hair stood up again," Lex teased, laughing, thrusting his elbow into my side.

"You're not funny at all!" I turned away from him and looked expectantly at our parents, but neither Amber nor Zino admonished him. I was used to being teased by my brother, but that didn't mean that it would later go unpunished.

My father got up to get his car keys, and a piece of paper

fell off the table. Maybe this paper would give me a clue about what our parents had been whispering. I picked it up.

It was a newspaper article with an accident pictured on it. I read the caption out loud:

Fire Devil still on the loose

Then I looked up to my father, who had not noticed that something had fallen off the smooth wooden surface he had brushed against when he walked away.

Last night, another burnt wreck was pulled out of a ditch. There is still no sign of the driver Hector Alicen (42), the passenger Lucy Alicen (41), and their two sons Rowan Alicen (19) and Draven Alicen (18). The Alicens family was last seen in the restaurant 'Zum Adler'. After that, the family was on their way home, according to the restaurant's server. Neither relatives nor friends could reach the family on their mobile phones. A link between the previous victims has not yet been confirmed. If you hear or see anything from the Alicen family, please contact the local police.

Below the newspaper article was a picture of two boys. They were standing next to each other, and the taller one had his arm wrapped around the smaller one.

I shuddered as I looked into the little brother's black, lifeless eyes, which stood out because of his light pigmentation. Although the picture was in black and white, I was sure he avoided direct sunlight whenever he could. Dark, long hair partially covered one eye; I would have preferred it not to be visible. A severe and clumsy smile shaped his face into an unusual grimace—he looked tormented.

The taller boy was the exact opposite of him. He had

short, light hair, a distinctive face, friendly facial features, and radiant eyes. A contrast arose between the skin colors of the boys, and I imagined his sun-kissed skin.

The article said they were siblings, but I immediately doubted it. Then I remembered how different Lex and I were and tried to swallow my accusation. Why wouldn't they be siblings?

My father jerked the newspaper clipping out of my hand. He glared at me, crumpled the paper into a little ball, and threw it into the trash can next to him.

"Why is the article cut out?" I asked, and both my brother and mother looked at us.

Lex hadn't noticed that I had picked up the paper off the floor because he was mesmerized by examining his shoes.

My mother surveyed me and looked at her husband. "Sometimes, there are things you don't understand yet. I tried to trace the family down, but I couldn't find them. After the hunt, I will continue my search because I know the parents," he replied narrowly and went to the door.

Did the whispering have anything to do with this family?

"What's the matter?" Lex looked at us questioningly, but he got ignored.

"Why didn't you tell us about the *Fire Devil?* And why have you been hiding that you are searching for them? This article is already five weeks old." I had read the date above the newspaper clipping before my father snatched the paper from me. I knew they could probably recognize my fear through my posture, but I didn't care.

"What Fire Devil?" Lex asked, confused, and ran to the trash can to retrieve the paper. Unfortunately, our father blocked his way before getting close to the can.

"Your mother and I didn't want to scare you. I thought someone had already stowed away the newspaper article in our room— " He glared at his wife. "But your mom must have forgotten about it."

"They have a right to know why we are worried. The secret is out now, and they will find out eventually," Amber whispered.

This was their secret—they wanted to protect us from the cruel deeds of the Fire Devil. But they had whispered about a female person and not of an entire family. Was there more to it than they wanted to tell us?

Admonishing, he looked at Amber but gave in. He walked into the next room and returned with an old wooden box, which I knew was my mother's jewelry box. Zino slowly opened the lid and pulled out several newspaper clippings, which he distributed on the table. Each article showed a picture of at least one teenager and a picture of a burned car.

My heart hurt as I ran my fingers over the cutouts. I couldn't imagine how terrible it must have been for the members of these families. I tried to memorize the faces of the children, just in case I saw them on the street on my way to school, so I could inform the police if I saw one of them.

"The first incident occurred nine weeks ago when a burned car was found in a forest, leaving no trace of the family. Since then, they have found eleven more cars in the area, and seventeen children and their parents are missing. At first, I suspected it had nothing to do with us, but after friends from my childhood disappeared, I started looking into it. All missing parents are members of our Monday table. I think someone is trying to erase this regular's table to the ground. I just can't figure out why."

My parents went out to dinner with friends every Monday. They called it the regular's table and never asked us to accompany them. Everything I knew of those

Mondays, our parents had never missed one. They hired a young lady to care for us while they were away.

Katie was sympathetic and one of the few people who knew our family secret and kept it to herself. Probably just because she was constantly typing or making phone calls on her phone instead of paying attention to us. At first, I assumed she was too scared of what my parents could do to her if she revealed our secret, but then I realized she wasn't smart enough to imagine this consequence. She literally got paid to play on her phone.

"That's terrible! I didn't know!" Lex said nervously, waving his hands as if trying to shake off an annoying beetle. I rolled my eyes and turned back to my father.

Silence settled in the kitchen—nobody knew what to say. The uneasy feeling that our parents knew more than they admitted upset me, but I didn't have enough courage to ask more questions about the articles or the mysterious *she*-person.

After a few seconds, my mother cleared her throat, stood up, and hugged us. "But that can't happen to us. We're different from the regular's table. Your father and I will make sure that nothing happens to you!" I could see my father giving her a crushing look in the corner of my eye. "And now it's finally time for the hunt. My stomach is growling."

My mother smiled and linked her arms around ours. We strolled past our father, who held the door open for us.

As soon as we had stepped out of the door, Lex sped up his pace to be the first by the car. Even though we weren't kids anymore, he still couldn't resist playing this childish game. I ignored him as he hastily stumbled over the uneven stone slabs through the front yard.

I turned to my mother and snuggled up to her. "But I still don't understand why you kept this from us."

"Everyone has secrets. Sometimes those are unpleasant topics; sometimes, you try to protect someone. I'm not saying it's right, but we knew we had to hide it from you. You're very curious. Am I wrong?" My mother smiled at me, and we walked down the narrow path through the garden to the car.

I looked up at her briefly and shook my head. "I still have so many questions, like—"

My mother interrupted me before I could ask the question. "And I don't have any answers for you right now. But it's time for your father and me to sit down with you and talk about something else. We need to discuss a few things, but it must wait until after the hunt. Now we have to find food and help him out. You know how much I hate buying pre-packaged meat."

My stomach tightened. My mother's tone had changed for a second—I knew the conversation after the hunt would be severe.

I still looked into her eyes—full of confidence that she would lead me safely to the car—and tried to read her emotions. My mother was many years ahead of me in controlling her feelings, but for a fraction of a second, she let her guard down, and sadness flickered in her eyes. Then the moment was gone. I wasn't sure what to think but had no choice but to wait; I knew that my mother's patience was infinite, and starting an argument would be unpleasant, primarily for me.

The night broke in. The sky turned dark red, and the smell of freshly cut grass lingered in the air.

The narrow stone path led past our house to the garage. My father's old Bronco parked in front of it as well as my mother's cute little Beetle. The fact that the truck was still running surprised me daily. He reminded us periodically that it was a family heirloom from our grandfather and would be passed down to us at some point.

Lex didn't care about the heirloom. He was still hoping to wake up, walk out of the front door and see a nice and expensive mustang standing in front of the garage if he passed his driver's test in a few weeks. I knew this dream would never come true, but I couldn't tell him.

I could hardly wait to drive the truck or the Beetle one day.

We got into the Bronco, and my body shook. The thrill of the hunt spread through my body. Only a few more minutes until I could let my true nature run wild.

CHAPTER
3

The ride only lasted ten minutes, but the silence made it seem like an infinity. I could feel the adrenaline of each person in the car.

We drove into the forest and parked at the edge of the trees next to a small abyss. It gave us a better overview of the trees in front of us.

As we got out of the truck, I could no longer suppress the desire to transform myself. In a split second, hair grew from every pore of my body. A bushy tail drilled through my jeans into the open, and my ears and nails grew.

"She will never learn how to be patient," Lex said, who was taking off his clothes except for the long undershirt he always wore under his shirts.

"Stop picking at your sister," our father said to him, and I gave my brother a satisfying look.

Furious, Lex also transformed, his hair growing with dark brown fur that had a gray undercoat. His ears elongated and formed into pointed wolf's ears, his face replaced by a muzzle with whiskers. Sharp claws drove out of his paws.

While we were getting rid of our clothes, our parents changed. Our father was a bigger version of Lex. His reddish hair was ruffled and yet looked beautiful. His paws were twice the size of my brother's, and when he was standing next to Lex, you could see the difference between the adolescent and the adult wolf.

I removed the shredded clothes, and my gaze fell on my mother's shining, fluffy fur. It was longer than mine and pitch black, her blue-green eyes taking my breath away every time I saw her. Supple and with the elegance of a cat, she peeled herself out of her clothes and shook out her fur.

We went over the plan my father had worked out for the hunt. He ensured that we hunted in a distinct part of the forest or the mountains every week. He didn't want to attract the hunter's attention.

We understood our tasks without a word.

I remembered my first hunt when my father had chosen a little hare as prey. But instead of catching and killing it, I had only thrown it through the air and played with it until the rabbit grabbed a convenient second and hopped away. My father had a lot of fun watching me, which was one of the best memories I could remember with him. But as the years went by, my playfulness mellowed, and I learned what hunting really meant. My hunting instinct grew and grew with each year, my prey got more extensive, and my tactics better.

While my father was very proud of me and spoke praises, something seemed to worry him. I couldn't figure out what was on his mind each time his worried gaze met mine.

The battle plan was always the same: we divided into two teams. A lynx and a wolf had to work together because the wolves' sense of smell was better trained to pick up a track, but the cats were faster, more flexible, and could hunt both on the ground and in the trees. After a team caught something, we met again at the car, and the two shapeshifters with the most prey could choose the body parts of the next meal.

Of course, Lex and I knew our parents had only created this rule so we could bring more prey home. However, it was an incentive for us, and as sibling love is, we couldn't turn down a healthy competition.

Lex was hunting with me this time. At first, I wanted to protest because he had annoyed me all day, but then I changed my mind. We were a good team. We had learned that we could beat our parents by working together. It didn't happen often, but it felt terrific the few times it worked out. Maybe a hunt would help stop his teasing for the day.

My father let himself down on all fours and picked up a trail. The forest yawned pitch-black in contrast to the moon-lit sky. The smell of damp moss rose into my nose, and my fur stood up—how I had missed this smell! We had been hunting in the mountains the week before, but this time we were back in the forest where it all started—it was MY forest!

We switched locations to make sure that no one could find us. They probably wouldn't believe their eyes if they saw oversized predators in the wild. But if they did, it could spread fear. And fear could turn into action, and before we knew it, people would hunt us—to make their forest safer and study us. People had a desire for knowledge, which I knew all too well because my human side was curious. I still tried to figure out what gave us the ability to change shape, and I knew other humans wouldn't leave us alone until they found an explanation.

The quiet rustling of leaves and the fresh scent felt like a second home. I lived for these sounds. The forest was my pulse, like a mother's heartbeat to her newborn, and it calmed me down.

My father's loud howling made an icy shiver run down my spine—it was the call of the hunt, and it brought death with it. Lex and I ran straight into the forest while our parents ran along the edge of the tree line to get deeper into the woods from the opposite side. They were faster than us because, unlike us, they were adult animals and we were still in the juvenile phase. I didn't feel like a kit, but I knew my full-grown form would be completed after my twentieth birthday. With my eighteenth birthday approaching, two more years still seemed like a long time.

The scent of a hare lingered in the air. Unfortunately, the rabbit wasn't big enough to keep the family afloat for several days, so I ignored the aroma of the small rodent.

I made sure to land on soft moss every time I jumped forward, which helped me stay silent and undiscovered. The wind whipped thin branches back and forth above me, and I could see moonlight making its way through the treetops and illuminating the ground below me. There was nothing better than hunting at night when the moon showed the forest at its best. Hungry animals filled the woods at night, which usually stayed unseen during the day.

An owl hooted when I passed an enormous tree. I could hear the warning it sent to the other animals in the forest.

I looked over at Lex, who found a better scent. He told me with eye contact that a bigger animal was just a few steps ahead of us. We slowed, the smell of a wild boar penetrating my nostrils. Every cell in my body was tense, and I pressed myself against the floor to minimize my size.

My animal instincts took over every brain cell. My claws

dug into the ground, my tail twitched, and my pupils enlarged to take up every little movement of the animal. In the middle of a clearing, separated from us only from a small bush, stood a wild boar and her piglet. They were busy slurping mushrooms off the ground, not noticing the lurking predators.

I gave Lex a signal by looking at the tree beside me, and he knew what to do. Quietly, he stalked around the clearing and positioned himself on the other side of the prey—we surrounded them. Then, without a sound, I drove my deadly claws into the tree's bark and climbed until I reached a large branch just above the eating animals. I had missed the feeling of wood under my paws and the adrenaline of stalking!

I looked down. The pigs had not noticed our presence and continued filling their bellies. Finally, Lex looked up at me and I knew he was ready and waiting for my signal.

With a silent movement, I let myself fall off the branch and landed on the big sow while Lex ran after the startled fawn and rammed his teeth into the juicy neck fold. Lex pulled the fawn to the side with a violent jerk that immediately broke its neck. I tried to do the same with my prey, but the wild boar was too strong. While I was holding it on the ground, it was screaming and kicking with its legs, Lex came to my aid. Together, we applied pressure on the neck until it gave in.

Our parents taught us not to let the prey suffer and to kill immediately. The first animals had been problematic for us. First, neither of us had been strong enough, and second, our animal instinct had not been mature enough to consider the killing of animals normal.

There were nights when I laid sleepless in bed, tormented by the sounds of the panicked cries of the animals. But years had passed since my first hunt, and now

I could find peace with it. My father treated each animal respectfully, leaving only the bones behind after processing it.

"Finally! And I thought we'd never catch something. Well, which body part do you choose?" Lex asked and dug his fangs into the sow.

"What a dumb question. Of course, I will choose the bacon. I think we have a fair chance against our parents. Let's go back to the truck," I said happily, looking at the slain pig. I bit the fawn into the neck to take it with us.

Next to each other, we went with the hunted prey in the car's direction until a loud cracking sound behind us attracted my attention. In a fraction of a second, we pressed ourselves against the lifeless bodies, looking at our surroundings.

I couldn't shake the feeling of being watched. Something threatening hung in the air; no animal was stupid enough to approach a lynx and wolf. At least, I thought they wouldn't be. Was it perhaps the hunter who took care of this forest? Had he finally caught us? My father described him as fearless.

I suppressed a loud hiss that formed in my throat, which was painfully tight. But after a few breaths, the threat seemed to move away, and the tension in the air subsided.

"What was that?" I asked quietly.

"Smells like a dog."

"I think the hunter is back in the woods," I breathed, after remaining in position for a few more minutes, to make sure we were alone again before continuing our way.

We arrived at the car where our parents were already waiting for us in their human forms and dressed. "And? What did you catch?" Our father asked although he could see it.

We passed them without saying a word and went to

throw the pigs into the trunk when I saw in amazement that they had only killed a deer. Usually, the back of the car was filled with bodies, but there was no hare, elk, or bear to eat this time. It was just a puny deer.

"Looks like we won," I said, throwing the piglet into the trunk.

"While hunting, we remembered that we still have some meat in the freezer. And there's something your mother and I have to tell you two."

I looked at my father, and joy bubbled up in me, hoping it was finally time to learn more about our ability. Or did it have something to do with their whispering? It could also be about the burned cars, but he interrupted me before I could imagine any further possibilities.

"We can sit down at the back of the canyon?" It was more of a command than a question as he said it.

Lex and I turned back into our human form, squeezed into the clothes we had left behind, and followed our parents, who were already huddled on the floor, dangling their legs into the abyss.

I stopped for a moment—an ice-cold shudder ran through my body, but the feeling was gone the next moment. I couldn't sense any danger. Apart from my family, there was no one around us. I was probably just cold in my human skin, and the mysterious cracking in the forest had made me paranoid.

Irritated, I shook my head and continued my way to the gorge. With a groan, I dropped next to my mother and looked down the embankment.

"Your father and I have something to tell you. We have tried to keep it away from you as long as possible, but we think, as Cas is almost of age, it's time." Our mother paused and pressed our father's hand tighter. "It was exactly eighteen years ago that Zino and I faced a hard decision—" but she didn't get any further.

Close to us, I could hear a breath that wasn't part of my family. It was quiet and grew louder and louder. A terrible smell of sulfur polluted the sweet, moist forest air.

My mother jumped up and transformed. My father followed her example and looked down the slope into the gorge as if he was looking for a way out. Startled, I looked at my parents and jumped up hastily.

"What's wrong?" I whispered to my parents and stood between them for protection. They taught us over the years to keep calm and generate as little attention as possible in tense moments like this one.

"We have to go!" My father walked towards the truck without further explanation, and we darted after him wordlessly.

The wind seemed to stand still, and the foul sulfur smell that turned my stomach upside down drowned the scent of moss out. I could feel the threat in my neck, but I still couldn't find the cause.

The first time I had this feeling, we had been hunting in another clan's territory, and it was a very unpleasant affair between the family leaders. However, they had talked it out among themselves, and the clans were friends now for several years. To be honest, they were friends with my parents. They had no children, and I could count on one hand how many times I had seen them afterward.

The current tension was different. The stench was new, and a dark atmosphere hung over the forest, making the environment seem like a still life. Could it be the same person? It had to be a person because I could still hear the quiet human breath.

"Quick!" my father hissed through his teeth and was already in the car.

The engine tore apart the forest's silence and echoed

back from the nearby trees. While the rest of us tried to jump into the car, he drove off, even though I had not yet closed the door properly.

"What is going on?" Lex screamed hysterically and looked out through the rear window, where we had just sat a minute ago. He calmed down instantly. "I think it was just the hunter," he said.

I almost threw my upper body over the back seat to see with my own eyes what drew his attention. Behind the tree, next to where the car had stood a few seconds ago, was a tall but slim figure with a hooded cape and a black hunting dog. They stood there motionless. I couldn't see the face in the hood's shadow, although all my senses were on high alert.

Our parents looked into the rear-view mirror, and the tension we had been feeling for minutes dissipated. I reached for the blankets we stowed in the trunk for emergencies, threw one at my brother, and wrapped myself in a blanket—while I didn't let the hunter out of my sight.

Just as my father lifted his foot off the gas pedal, the hound charged after us. While the dog was chasing the car, I thought it was an ordinary hunting dog, till it became bigger and bigger and increased in speed. Finally, it transformed into a massive fire, shaped like a gigantic hound!

"Drive!" I screamed and couldn't tear my eyes away from the flaming creature. I rubbed my eyes just to make sure my vision wasn't failing. But when I opened them again, the demonic being was only a few feet away from us. I had never seen such an animal.

The car made a gigantic leap forward as my father pushed the pedal with full force down, and I tried to look at the person I had seen standing next to the tree. The clearing was empty.

The next few seconds lasted an eternity.

The abrupt stop of the car threw me against the driver's seat, and I hit my head on something hard. A metallic smell hung in the air, and I could feel blood running down my temple.

Lex started screaming. As I was trying to fish for him, I heard a muted impact, and his scream fell silent. The car rolled over. The weight of my brother's lifeless body pressed me against the side of the vehicle. Shortly afterward, the noises around me fell silent, and the pain in my throbbing temple disappeared. I blacked out.

I drove into consciousness as if I had fallen off a swing in a dream. My body shook, and I could barely breathe under my brother's weight.

Please be a dream. Please be a dream, I thought with a pained face.

With the last drop of strength, I opened my eyes to a small gap, the hooded figure standing in front of the truck on the path. The car had landed on the roof, and I could see my parents lying unconscious in front of me.

My father must have tried to dodge the person who had appeared before us. Unfortunately, we had been too busy trying to escape the flaming hound that he hadn't paid attention to the road. So when he tried to swerve around the person, he had lost control of the car.

Petite feet became visible through the broken window. I tried to reach for them to beg for help, but my vision darkened and the world around me went quiet.

CHAPTER
4

I fell onto my back, hard.

I gasp for air, desperately grabbing my throat. I opened my eyes, but my surroundings looked blurred and colored red. Tiny red spots glowed above me. I rubbed my eyes, and the red veil wore off a little. These weren't red dots; those were stars in the night sky.

My stomach throbbed, and my limbs burned with pain. Panting, I turned to my side and could finally take a long breath. Freezing air penetrated my lungs and made me cough—the cold burning in my trachea.

I didn't know how much more my body could take.

My hands blindly drove over a stony surface until I got a hold of a large rock next to my head. I was sure I was nowhere near the woods anymore because clean, cold air replaced the smell of bark and leaves.

Memories shot through my head, but I couldn't sort them out properly. I could hear screams and the threatening crackling of a fire. I slapped my hands on my ears to end the noises—but in vain.

Rolling into a ball and hugging my knees, I tried to protect myself from the beast. I knew that the evil dog must have found me. Trembling, I waited for the dog's bite, but nothing happened; the air fell silent.

During my struggle, I almost missed my brother's genuine cry. His voice sounded close; he couldn't be far from me.

"Lex?"

I heaved myself onto my hands and knees with a sudden energy surge. My vision became more apparent with every blink. I was on my feet quickly, but my wobbly legs made me stagger around. I prayed my knees wouldn't cave in underneath me.

In the distance, I could see the lights of a small village, and it seemed as if a black veil hung over the buildings. I stood on an enormous cliff, surrounded by a rocky landscape.

"Cas? Where are you?" Lex's voice called, and I tried to follow the sound.

"Over here!"

My eyes were burning, and just a few steps away, I could see something dark on the floor, which had to be Lex. I let myself fall to the ground beside the shadow, hoping it was really my brother and not another horror figure.

"Is that you?" I asked softly, rubbing my eyes.

"Who else would it be?" He barked, and my mouth curled up with joy. He had certainly not lost his charm.

"You are alive!" I said with delight and exhaled.

I blinked a few more times until I could recognize him. His lower lip was swollen, and I could spot scratches on the right side of his face. He struggled to sit up. His pained look told me he was as miserable as I was—but we were alive. That's all that mattered.

"Where are we?" He rubbed his temples.

"I don't know."

My eyes drove over our surroundings, trying to find something I could recognize which would give our location away. But apart from the lights in the distance and the stone structures around us, nothing looked familiar.

"What the hell happened? Why are we here? Where are mom and dad, and why is your face full of blood?" His voice trembled.

I could see fear in his eyes. A lump began spreading in my throat. I suppressed the tears that were gathering in my eyes.

"I don't know," I answered, trying to make my voice sound soft to calm him. But that was apparently not the answer he had been waiting for, and he suddenly sat up, his breath whistling.

More memories shot through my head, and I closed my eyes to see the pictures more clearly. I saw a dark figure, but as much as I tried to focus on the face lying in the hood's shadow, it became more blurred. That image was followed by blazing flames and two red eyeballs floating in the raging fire.

After the painful thoughts had subsided, I relaxed and opened my eyes. I looked into the reddened eyes of my brother, who was shaking.

"What's the matter?" He asked anxiously.

"Memories plague me, but they are very blurry, and I can't understand the context. So why are Mom and Dad not here? They were with us, weren't they?"

"I can't even tell where we are right now, so how am I supposed to know where our parents are? We need to get back to the forest and find them. I'm sure they have an explanation of what's going on."

"We have to find out where we are first. We could be miles away from them."

Lex nodded silently, got up with a loud growl, and extended his hand to help me. Just as I was about to grab his hand, the pain of memories made me cringe—the cracks in the film filled in before my eyes. My stomach turned, and I had to fight the lump in my gut that felt like a stone. He helped me up, and I could see sadness flickering in his eyes.

"Can you remember what happened before I found you?" I asked and could see from his helpless expression that he didn't know. "We were hunting in the woods with our parents when we caught a dangerous scent. I remember sitting in the car and being chased by a dog in flames controlled by a dark figure in the shadow of a tree. Dad tried to dodge something and lost control of the car. I can remember the fire dog and the hooded figure."

Silence filled the air. Lex looked at me, stunned. I couldn't tell by his facial expression whether it surprised him at what had happened or whether he remembered all of it and had to process it.

"Are you out of your mind?" Lex snarled and let go of my hand. "You want me to believe that an animal that only lives in your imagination hunted us? Cassandra! There is no such thing as a fire dog!"

I shook my head. I knew what I had seen. It wasn't a mythical creature that I had come up with. How could he not believe me when we depended on each other? Then again, I wouldn't have believed it if I hadn't seen it.

If he couldn't remember the accident, the dog's memory probably didn't exist either.

"Believe me! Can't you remember? Are you trying to suppress it?"

Our eyes met, and my pores itched. He seemed as anxious about our situation as I was, but I had to stay calm. After all, I was the only one who could remember the hunt—where we had been hunted.

I played the last minutes in our truck again in my mind, and then it hit me. The muffled sound I had heard in the car just before Lex's scream turned silent must have been the impact of his head hitting the car. That was probably the reason he remembered nothing. He must have suffered a concussion. It was my job to make a logical decision for us.

"I can't deal with this any longer! I'm going to look for our parents. Do whatever you want!" His face was red with rage.

He turned away from me; my brother had never used this tone in my direction. Of course, we had minor disputes here and there, but this behavior was new to me.

I tried to grab his hand, but Lex escaped from my grasp. "We have to stay together. The best decision would be to seek shelter and wait until dawn. Who knows what else is waiting for us out there?"

"Our parents are waiting out there! They are probably worried sick because they can't find us. So either you will come with me, or our ways will part now."

I gasped. "We don't even know which way to go. How do you know where they are?" I had tried to stay calm, knowing my brother must have an injury to his head, but my cheeks glowed, and I could no longer suppress my anger.

"There is something in this forest that wants to harm us! I can't risk losing you too! We have to stay together! We—" A sound silenced me.

"What was that?" Lex stopped abruptly and threw his hand into the air to keep me from answering.

It sounded like someone had stepped on a pebble, which leaped softly over the rocky ground. I brushed it off. It must have been an animal, for no man would dare to climb the slope of a mountain at night.

"It's the safest if we stick together and look for a hiding place. We will start searching for them first thing in the morning," I whispered, and continued to peer into the darkness. Although my animal instincts were sharpened, I couldn't find the source of the sound.

"Hiding is for sissies. I will certainly not stay here," Lex hissed and set himself into motion.

I looked helplessly after my brother. I wanted to run after him and beg him not to leave. Grab him by the arm and tell him he wasn't clear-headed and was making the wrong decision; that I wanted to find our parents as much as he did—but I couldn't move. Something inside of me stopped me and held me in place.

"Lex! Come back... please," I whispered the last word to myself, knowing that my pleading was useless.

Why couldn't I follow him? Why didn't my limbs respond to my orders? I only had a few moments until I would lose him, too. I had to hurry.

But darkness had devoured his body, and there was only me and the moon left, who threw its silver rays over the landscape.

A wave of sadness swallowed me whole. I had lost both my parents and my brother within a few minutes. It had been my job to take care of my wounded sibling, and all I did was watch him walk away.

Then, a lovely sound rang in my ears; I could hear a woman's sweet voice singing in the distance but couldn't tell from which direction it came or what language it was. The music wrapped around my body like a warm blanket. I absorbed every word, hoping the song would never end, but the sound became quieter until it fell completely silent.

Something followed that I had only read about in books: emptiness.

All emotions, painful memories, and thoughts were simply gone. I felt no pain when I thought about my parents and no anger at my brother, who had just left me. Instead, I felt numb—numbed by too many indescribable events at once.

What's wrong with me?

As much as I tried to fill the emptiness with the thought of my family to feel something—it didn't work.

I tried to cry, but my eyes stayed dry. A few moments ago, sadness had almost torn me to pieces, but now I couldn't even produce a tear or scream in anger.

Emotionless, I strolled to the mountain's slope and sat down cross-legged.

Without a racing mind, I sat up there and looked down through the darkness at the lights of the houses in the valley.

How did the inhabitants of these neatly lined buildings feel comfortable with their perfect gardens? Did they sleep peacefully, knowing that their families were well? Or did they numb their boredom with electronic devices to escape reality? Maybe they flipped through books that I had already read. There were millions of possibilities.

But my only reality was that I was alone. Without family, a plan, not knowing where I was and how I got here, and with no human soul within reach, I could ask for help.

A sweet smell lingered in the air. I tried to figure out what it was, but I had never smelled that aroma before. Before I could turn around to follow the note, somebody pressed something damp onto my mouth and nose.

I didn't resist the hands that appeared out of nowhere and pressed the ammonia-soaked cloth to my face. No fear or panic arose in me. I knew I should fight back, but my body didn't move. Without fear, I inhaled the smell of ammonia until I became dizzy, and the world around me slowly faded.

CHAPTER
5

The smell of fresh wood surrounded me, and I could feel something soft beneath me. Before I could open my eyes, I stroked my fingers over the smooth surface and felt a soft fabric slipping through my hands.

At first, I thought I was lying in my bed at home and finally waking up from a terrible nightmare. But the fabric under me was smooth and delicate, not even close to the fluffy yet overused blanket in my bed, which now seemed like the nodes of my unbrushed cat.

"Cassandra?" An unknown voice entered my consciousness, and I slowly opened my eyes. I calmly looked into the face of a strange woman who seemed to float directly above me. "And I thought you wouldn't wake up. How are you?"

"Mm…" It was all I could get out. My head was buzzing, and my throat was burning, but otherwise, I seemed unhurt.

I sat up, and the stranger sat down on a chair that stood next to me. When I looked down at myself, I saw somebody had dressed me in a cream-colored dress. Where were my t-shirt and jeans? But who had changed my clothes, and who was this smiling woman watching me?

Light fabrics hung between the woman and me. Then, as if she had read my thoughts, she stood up and pulled back the thin curtains fastened between the four posts of a bed.

A colossal mirror appeared to my right, covering almost the entire wall. Next to the mirror was a large window with two double doors framed by a Victorian arch.

It was too dark outside to see where I was. I let my eyes wander over the rest of the room.

The walls were painted white, and a massive wooden chest with drawers and a wooden cabinet covered the wall opposite me. Behind the woman, who had returned to the chair, were two large wooden hinged doors with cast iron embedded in the stone wall.

"My name is Syryn Megia, but you can call me Miss Syryn or just Syryn. Can you remember what happened before you woke up here?" The stranger asked and looked at me compassionately.

Her skin was flawless, and her grey-silver eyes ate into my consciousness. Her face was narrow and caressed by her long, dark brown hair reaching over her hips.

"I know…" she continued, "millions of thoughts must shoot through your head, but you're safe. There's nothing to be afraid of here." Miss Syryn stood up smiling and sank onto the soft bed beside me. A breathtaking smell misted my senses.

I inspected her. Although she wore a simple, skintight, no-frills, black dress, it brought out her slim figure and all her beauty. I immediately realized that Miss Syryn was the most beautiful woman I had ever seen. The closer I looked at her, the more inhuman she seemed to me.

I wanted to say something, but the words got stuck in my throat.

"How rude of me to just leave you here without information." She made a casual but exquisite gesture. "Ok, let's just start at the beginning to help your memory. Your family had been hunting in the woods when an Oblitus attacked you. You and Lex escaped, but your parents fell victim to it, and we're still looking for them. After you escaped the Oblitus, Miss Zea called attention to your accident, and I sent two trainees to bring you here. I have to apologize for the use of ammonia. I assumed you wouldn't voluntarily go with strangers, and I couldn't risk losing another child. Your brother Lex is in the room next to us."

She spoke the last sentence so casually as if it was a fact that he was here. I stared at her and tried to sort my thoughts.

The clear images of the dog and the shadow figure penetrated back into my consciousness. Then, my parents' lifeless bodies were lying in front of me, and my brother, who had just left me standing on the mountain.

"My brother is here?" I brought it out with a croak.

"We found him wounded. A healer took care of his injuries, and he's fine now." Her voice sounded like tender butter on a warm summer day.

I grabbed at my temple, where I had previously felt the wound of the impact with the window… but it was gone. I stared at Miss Syryn and kept driving over my head to ensure I didn't imagine the injury.

Was my mind playing games with me? Didn't Lex ask me where the blood on my face had come from? Maybe I was still dreaming.

"Oh no, my dear," Miss Syryn began as if she had heard my question before I could ask it. "Your wounds were real, but we didn't have to heal you. Your wounds must have healed before we could discover them."

"What about our parents? Why didn't you save them if you knew what was going on? And what is an Ob—" I tried to remember the strange name she had thrown at me.

"An Oblitus?"

"What is it?"

"You don't seem to know much about our world," she answered softly, rubbing her flawless chin.

"Your world?"

"How about—" but before Miss Syryn could make a suggestion, I interrupted her, my head aching with questions.

"Where are our parents? And where are we? Why did you bring us here?" The questions gushed out of me without control.

Were my parents still alive?—I didn't dare say it out loud. Of course, they had to be alive; after all, they were...my parents!

I didn't want their unconscious bodies to be the last picture I had of them. I looked at Miss Syryn in shock. Instead of answering, she put her hand on my shoulder, and for a moment, I felt that all the pain that stuck to me like a thorn had disappeared. But of course, that was just an illusion because no one could make emotions just disappear.

"Take me to my brother, please. I have to make sure that he is well," I said in a firm voice, determined that I had already wasted enough time.

"On the way there, I will answer your questions." Miss Syryn rose elegantly from the bed and reached out to me. I pretended not to have noticed her gesture, swung my legs over the edge of the bed, and jumped to my feet.

I prepared myself to feel the pain of the accident and

the rough landing, but as much as I stretched out my limbs to remember what I had been through in the last few hours, the pain wasn't there.

"Can you explain why my brother and I woke up on an unknown mountain, far away from our car?"

"I promise you I will answer all your questions. Let me see if I remember your first questions, and let's start there." She took a strand of her long, dark hair in her hand and wrapped it around her finger as if it would help her focus. Then, with a quick movement, she turned towards the door. I followed her hastily to understand every word.

"Unfortunately, I couldn't save your parents in pursuit of an Oblitus. I cannot enter an event of the Mortal World without disrupting the balance of their and our world. Oblitus are Shadow Creatures. They are creatures cast out of the human and this world and trapped between our two worlds."

My mouth opened. *Shadow Creatures?* And she had repeated it—*our world.* After hundreds of books, I could confidently say there was only one world—the Human World.

She went on without paying attention to my confusion. "I had you two brought here so the Shadow Creatures wouldn't get their hands on you. They wouldn't have let go until they found you. Unfortunately, the teleportation from the car to the mountain wasn't in my hands, but an instructor will explain everything to you tomorrow, and we are here. This is your brother's door."

Miss Syryn had led me through a large corridor. White, high walls surrounded us, and mighty silver statues lined up to our left. Massive chandeliers hung from the ceiling, illuminating the stone floor's red carpet. Finally, we came to a halt in front of a mighty wooden door.

"In about thirty minutes, I will send an instructor to

pick you up for dinner, and then I can answer further questions." Without another word, Miss Syryn knocked on the door and walked away.

"Wait! You can't leave me here. There must be a misunderstanding. There are no Shadow Creatures in our world. I have to find my family," I said, but as much as I tried to get the attention of the mysterious woman, the farther she moved away from me without looking back.

My head was throbbing with pain; I had more unanswered questions than answers. Where the hell was I? And where was my family? Why couldn't I wake up from this nightmare?

"Who's there?" My brother's familiar voice pierced my ears, my heart leaping and bursting with joy.

"It's me, Cas."

The massive door opened in front of me, and before I could step over the threshold, Lex ran into my arms. I pressed him as hard as I could and hoped that this moment would never end. I had found him, and he was fine!

"I'm so glad to see you here. A crazy woman was here and told me about an accident, and that something was after us. We have to get out of here," Lex said, releasing the hug. He attempted to push past me, but I blocked his way.

Miss Syryn had not lied. She had found my brother and brought him here. I examined him; he was unharmed. The scraped wound in his face had disappeared, leaving his eyes filled with fighting spirit and energy.

"What's wrong with you?" He looked at me incredulously and paused.

"I think it's best if we stay. Miss Syryn had visited me also," I replied, looking at Lex attentively.

How could he still deny the accident? Whatever the woman had done to heal him so quickly, she didn't seem to have been able to help his memory.

"You don't believe her, do you?"

"I saw it with my own eyes. We need her help to find our parents."

Every fiber of my body urged me to leave this place as soon as possible, but my mind resisted. Miss Syryn had the answers to my questions about why we were attacked and where our parents might be. She had spoken of Shadow Creatures and her world, and I just had to find out what she was talking about. Was there a world I didn't know? An explanation for being a shapeshifter? It would also increase our chances of having an adult by our side to find our parents.

"And what about me? Or Damous? He will rot in our house if we don't return. We have to go home, NOW. Maybe our parents are already waiting for us?"

"Lex," I tried to reassure him. "If you had seen what was chasing us, you'd believe me. We can't do anything for Mom and Dad right now. They're gone or even dead, and the same fate awaits us when we return home. Damous has the cat flap. He'll be fine until we get home. I won't help you escape." I walked to the bed in his room and sat down on it.

His room had the exact dimensions of the room I had woken up in. But instead of silver metal, the furniture were made of solid dark wood, and the walls were painted light gray.

"What is going on with you? You're acting strange." Lex dropped onto the bed next to me and looked depressed. His belligerent eyes changed, now reflecting sadness.

"We have to find our parents, but we won't be able to do it alone. I want to tell you they are fine, but I can't do that." I took a deep breath. "This woman can help us find them."

I could explain what was going on with me. I loved my parents and would do anything to be reunited with them again. But I also wanted to find out what this other world was all about because it could be an answer to the questions that had plagued me since my childhood. That reason made me change my mind.

"I can't let you down. I'll stay with you because someone has to take care of my little sister." Lex smiled back and put his arm around my shoulder.

We sat on the soft bed and stared at the floor before us until a knock sounded on the door. I didn't know how long we had been sitting there without saying a word, but it didn't seem like thirty minutes to me.

"Yes?" We shouted together, and the door jumped open.

"Miss Syryn gave me the instructions to pick you up for dinner. Welcome to Teviena."

We looked up at a boy who was now standing in the doorway. He wore black clothes, his bright, honey-colored eyes stood out, his brown-styled hair looked a bit ruffled, and his confident smile pierced in our direction.

"She told me she would send an instructor, not a boy. So what is *Teviena*?" I asked him and slowly got up from the bed while Lex was busy examining him with a dreadful look.

He seemed so familiar to me. I was sure I had seen him before. But through the events of the last hours, I couldn't remember where.

"Don't be so cold to him. I'm sure there's a reason she sent him. What's your name?" Lex interfered and walked past me to give him his hand. Lex tried to look taller next to the stranger with his puffy chest.

Then it hit me.

"You are the boy from the newspaper article," I said in

surprise.

"Which newspaper article?" The stranger's eyebrows drew together.

"You know, about the Fire Devil." He tilted his head in confusion and raised a brow. "The article about your family." Then I noticed he couldn't have seen the article because the paragraphs about his family had been a missing person report. "It said that you disappeared without a trace and left only a burned-out car in a ditch," I summarized the article to help him.

My ears glowed with shame. How could I assume he had seen it? And what did he think about me, that I had memorized his face?

"I didn't know there was an article about us," he said hastily, and his eyes surveyed me.

"You must be Draven then, right?" Lex threw in and kept trying to look more muscular than he was. I wondered how my brother knew his name. I could have sworn he hadn't seen the clipping after my father threw it away.

"Rowan. My brother's name is Draven. Soon you'll get all the answers you need. Please follow me." Without even looking at Lex, Rowan turned around on the doorstep and started moving.

"What are you waiting for? It has been a wise decision to stay here," Lex said, throwing a cheeky grin at me.

"We're not here, so you can prove your dominance. Just because he is good-looking and taller than you doesn't mean you have to stand up against him." I walked past Lex and followed Rowan, who didn't stop for us.

"Come on, Cas. I've never seen you around a mysterious boy before. And you have to admit…" He took a dramatic break, "I look much better than him."

"Whatever you have to tell yourself to sleep peacefully at night." I couldn't help but smile. I forgot all the grief that gnawed at me for a few moments. "The only reason I didn't leave is that I want to find our parents. I won't stand in your way if you want to get your fingers dirty the first night!"

I should have known that the urgency of the search was now playing in the background for him. Lex was too distracted to measure his strength with Rowan and didn't even notice his competitive behavior.

But that was also an advantage because it would give me time to learn more about these Shadow Creatures and why they were targeting us.

"You're a spoilsport!" His laughter echoed through the corridor, and my heart filled with warmth. At least he hadn't lost his sense of humor. He would need it.

I sped up to keep up with Rowan, who was about to turn right at the end of the corridor.

CHAPTER
6

Rowan led us through the corridor I had used to get to Lex. But he guided us further away from the room where I had woken up.

As we turned around the corner, I stopped. A mighty hall lay before us; I could see its splendor through the floor-to-ceiling doors. Eleven large arched windows provided light in the hall during the day, but I could only see all-consuming darkness. Dozens of 19-armed candlesticks lit up the hall with candlelight.

More silver sculptures covered the walls, representing every mythical imaginable creature—from a proud Unicorn to a Fairy, a Werewolf, and many other animals whose names I didn't know.

The largest table I had ever seen occupied most of the hall. It was round, and a big hole yawned in the middle. Around the table were about forty to fifty chairs. In the center of the table stood another small round table, which was equipped with nine massive wooden chairs, and between them stood a throne.

Miss Syryn sat on it. Even though she didn't fill the throne with her petite figure, it looked like it was made just for her. The moment I saw her, she looked at me, and the noise in the room died.

When I finally took my eyes off the throne, I saw that children and teenagers occupied almost every chair.

I look into the eyes of a little boy who couldn't be older than six. Next to him was a girl—I estimated her around my age. She put her arm protectively over the shoulders of the boy.

My gaze wandered over other faces—some young, some fearful, some full of fighting spirit, and some keeping their head bowed to the ground.

Had all these children lost their parents? Had Miss Syryn also saved them from a Shadow Creature?

I had assumed that Lex and I were the only ones who had suffered this fate. But now, I looked into dozens of eyes and knew we were all in the same boat. We all had no parents and depended on a stranger who sat on a throne.

"Welcome our newcomers, Cassandra and Lex, who, like many of you, lost their parents tonight. Miss Zea made me aware of their situation, and I had them brought to safety. We are still actively looking for your parents. The Oblitus are getting stronger, and we must start preparing for battle. Tomorrow morning, the training will finally begin! It would be wonderful if someone could take our newcomers under their wing. And now, I hope everyone is hungry."

The rambling started again, and Rowan took us to two free chairs at the very end of the hall. I could feel the eyes of the other children and quickly sat down on a chair to escape the curious gazes.

"What do you think the new ones are?"

"Can't you smell it?"

"Oh, you think they're shapeshifters?"

"Just ask them!"

"Go ask yourself!" Two girls near us whispered, and I tried not to pay attention to them, but it was difficult for me with my excellent hearing.

How were there other people who knew about shapeshifters? I couldn't find anything about it in all the books piled up in my room and the library.

Did our parents know about this place? They must have known. Was that what they wanted to tell us about at the gorge? That we weren't as extraordinary as they wanted us to believe?

It made little sense. I knew they would have never kept this place from us if they had known about it.

"Miss Syryn and the other instructors will introduce you to our training for magical gifts later." Rowan pulled me out of my thoughts, and I looked up at him. I forgot he was standing next to us.

"Maybe you can already tell us something about this training, so we don't have to bother Miss Syryn," Lex replied with a smile, unable to turn his eyes away from me. I gave my brother a warning look.

I knew what he was trying to do. It wasn't the first time he had wanted to tease me with a boy.

"Miss Syryn will visit you later," he answered narrowly. Then, without getting further involved in a conversation with Lex, he looked at me, bowed slightly, and walked away to the opposite side of the table to a section filled with other boys.

I had to admit, unlike my brother, Rowan acted like a gentleman. He had not responded to my brother's game, made sure we had made it to our chairs and the bow—he could have left without a word. It was a gesture that no boy my age had ever done. I looked after him and saw how the boys overwhelmed him with questions.

My ears glowed with shame as he looked over his shoulder in my direction—smiling. A pair of green-blue eyes were in front of my face as I turned my head away. I jumped back and almost fell off the chair but came to a halt when I bumped into Lex, who was sitting beside me. I had not noticed the girl sitting next to me while observing Rowan.

"Hello, my name is Amara Hazen. I'm sorry to hear about your parents. I lost my family six days ago. Can I keep you company?"

Amara was very tall for a girl, and though she sat, she towered over me, her long, wavy, dark blonde hair falling to her shoulders. Like every other student, she wore a cream-colored dress, which seemed too big for her slim figure.

"Ok." My answer sounded more like a question. She had surprised me, giving me no time to reject her offer like I usually did when someone approached me.

Lex recognized my situation and jumped in. "My name is Lex Kayser, and this is my sister Cassandra."

I looked at her in amazement. I could have sworn she was radiating something that drew me to her, like catnip for a cat. However, I couldn't tell if it was because of her cheerful and open nature or because she was the only one trying to start a conversation with us.

"What are you, if I may ask?" The question gushed out so quickly that I only understood it after it had left my lips.

I just had to know if there were other shapeshifters or if I just imagined it all. After all, I didn't want to believe that my parents were liars and that they had deliberately concealed it from us.

"You mean besides my human nature? Unfortunately, we can only show our gift during lessons and training, and

I am not as spectacular as the other trainees here." I held my breath. The moment I had been waiting for so long was finally here. "I am a sorceress. What are you?"

Emotions I had suppressed since I was a little girl rushed through my body and made me tremble. I wasn't crazy. There was another person like us—perhaps not a shapeshifter, but she was more than just a human.

My hands shook with excitement, and I couldn't utter a word while Lex pretended to have known all of this for years.

"Shapeshifter," Lex said narrowly, looking at Rowan, who was still entertaining the boys.

"What kind of shapeshifter are you?"

"There are several forms of shapeshifters? I knew it!" I replied, perplexed, and almost jumped off the chair. "Well, I can turn into a lynx and Lex into a wolf. Our parents never really talked about other people like us."

My throat became dry at the thought of our parents, and the feelings of joy and curiosity ebbed away.

"Mm, this is extraordinary. I thought that only the same form of shapeshifters could produce offspring." Amara paused for a moment to think, but then she continued. "That is very interesting. Yes, there are hundreds of forms a shapeshifter can be. You thought there were only wolves and lynx?" Amara pulled her brows up in surprise.

"We've never met other shapeshifters except for a clan of wolves. So what do you mean that only the same shapeshifters can have children?" I asked curiously.

Since first grade, I had avoided every child who dared to come near me. But Amara was sitting next to me, and it felt like my soul had been waiting for this one person who understood what it was like to be different. I didn't have to deny my ability to transform in front of her; it felt so good.

"I lived in a village where many shapeshifters,

magicians, and mythical creatures lived together. But I have never seen two different shapeshifters as siblings."

"Apparently you don't know everything about shapeshifters," Lex casually threw in, and I stared over at him, eyes narrowing so that only he got my message to behave.

"There is an entire village full—" I faltered, not knowing what to call these people.

"—full of people with gifts?" Amara helped, and I nodded eagerly. "Of course there is. I'm surprised you don't come from a magical village."

"I didn't know there were such villages. We grew up in one surrounded by ordinary people," I replied and could tell from her facial expression that she was surprised.

"What kind of gift does the boy who brought us here have?" asked Lex, who was still watching Rowan.

"Rowan? Nobody knows what he is. He keeps it a secret. But if you find out, please tell me. Some trainees believe he is something ugly, like a frog or maybe a troll. He's not one of the talkative kind," Amara answered, her gaze hanging on Rowan. "I can assure you it can't be ordinary because we've never seen his brother. He doesn't dare to leave his room."

I thought of the article again and the boy who suffered under the weight of his brother's arm. His eyes had given me the chills.

A movement in the corner of my eye made me look at the hall's entrance. Without a sound, the vast wing doors of the hall opened, and dining carts rolled in silently—but humans did not push the carts. Instead, a soft whirring echoed in my ears. I looked closely at a food cart coming by our table, and I could see tiny figures of white smoke behind it. They looked like little Fairies. I blinked and tried to understand what was happening. Was everyone able to see these miniature figures, or had I finally lost my mind?

Speechless, I looked at my brother and Amara, who was just waiting to see our puzzled faces.

"It took me two days to figure out what these smoking figures are. At first, I thought they were little Fairies, but I've never heard of a Smoke Fairy. It's much more interesting than that. Miss Syryn uses drops of water and turns them into condensation. And everyone knows that water has memory—she stores a task in every drop of water as she evaporates it. So, Viola, now she has hundreds of Steam Fairies. I don't know if that's really their name, but I can tell you that this isn't a simple spell." Amara sounded proud of herself.

On the dining carts were turkeys, pigs, fruit salads, vegetables, cheeses, sauces, sweets, and other food carried by the Steam Fairies through the air and placed on the table. After only a few minutes, delicacies covered the wooden surface before us.

"There is no such thing as Steam Fairies or magicians," Lex growled, and half the table looked at him. "What?" He barked back. "Do you think I'm a fool?"

I hadn't expected this reaction from him. After all, he had sat next to us for minutes and listened attentively to Amara while not letting Rowan out of sight.

I also found it difficult to process this statement and consider his feelings valid. But we were shapeshifters—meaning there was more than just the Human World.

Someone cleared his throat behind Lex, and we turned around abruptly. Miss Syryn stood behind us, smiling lovingly at Lex. A sweet smell found its way back into my nose.

"Could we talk, Lex?" Miss Syryn asked, holding her hand out to help him up.

"Okay," Lex replied, still angry, pushed his chair back

loudly and looked straight into her eyes.

Just as I was about to get up, Miss Syryn glanced at me, and I knew she wanted to talk to him alone. At first, I wondered if I should resist her request. He was the only thing I had left, and I couldn't let anything happen to him.

But before I could open my mouth, Miss Syryn said, "He's in excellent hands. I'll bring him back to you."

They left the hall together, and the children at the table circled back to their conversations.

My stomach turned inwardly. I should have fought it and insisted on going with them. But I had no energy left, and every attempt to make him remember had failed. Miss Syryn might have been able to help him.

"I don't mean to say anything, but if you could see you two side by side, you'd never think you are siblings."

Amara wasn't the first person to tell me that. We didn't look alike, and our personalities couldn't be more different, but whenever someone said something about my brother, I felt assaulted. I had to protect him, as he had done for me countless times.

"He isn't usually like this. Too much has happened in the last few hours, and I just can't imagine our parents being missing or even dead. They would never abandon us without fighting. I have so many questions, and no one seems to have a correct answer," I said.

The thought we would probably never see our parents again made the room spin. Or maybe our parents had made it out of the car and were now looking for us; I wanted to hold on to that belief.

While Amara was listening, she loaded her plate full of food and ate.

"You don't have to protect Lex. Everyone at this table has been through the same. We all have lost our parents and siblings and have unanswered questions. I just stayed to find out how to find my parents and be strong for my brother," said Amara, looking at a boy who was busy laughing with other children.

"I didn't know you had a brother." I looked at the boy, who must have been much younger than Amara. "That must be so hard for him. But, luckily, he has a strong sister like you."

"He is the youngest of my brothers. Our older siblings have disappeared with our parents," her voice trembles, her gaze fixed on her brother.

"Your older siblings disappeared too?" I couldn't believe it. The disappearance of our parents had shattered me, but I couldn't imagine losing my brother too.

Amara nodded silently and looked at me, her eyes flooded with tears. "Can I tell you the story another time?"

"Of course. I didn't mean to be tactless. I'm so sorry," I lowered my head. Amara gave me a sad smile.

The wound was also too fresh for me. I wanted nothing more than to hug my parents, but the thought that it would never happen blazed within me.

"Tomorrow, we will finally have our first lesson, and I hope that we at least learn why we are here."

Startled, I looked up at Amara. I had already forgotten about the lesson, but it gave me hope.

I filled my plate with food. My stomach growled, but when I wanted to eat, I noticed it wasn't hunger, only nausea.

I tried to remember the last seconds in the car. It must have been our parents who pulled Lex and me out of the wreck and brought us to safety. The Oblitus would certainly not have spared us and let us go. But that still didn't explain how we woke up on a mountain miles away from the car. None of our parents would have been strong enough to transport us so far. There had to be a clue somewhere in my memory, and I just had to make myself remember.

"It will get better."

I looked up and into Amara's warm, green-blue eyes, radiating something familiar.

"What do you mean?"

"The first few days without your parents will be the most difficult. But we have a goal in mind. It gets easier from day to day, I promise."

"I don't know if I can ever get over this pain." I grabbed my chest and tried to calm my heart down. "It's getting late, and I'm tired. I should probably go to bed. See you tomorrow?"

"I hope I didn't upset you and your brother. I'll save you a seat tomorrow. Good night."

"Hopefully, by tomorrow, the world looks different again. I firmly believe I will just wake up from this nightmare, and everything is fine."

"If you need anything, pull the golden cord in your room, and an instructor will visit you," she said.

My room. My heart ached at the thought. It wasn't *my* room. It was just a room where I had woken up in a nightmare, and soon I would wake up again and find myself in my real one at home.

I got up and looked around again before waving to Amara. The other children talked cheerfully and stuffed their mouths full of food. I walked to the big-winged door alongside the table and looked over my shoulder.

How could a nightmare seem so real?

The surrounding sounds echoed loudly from the walls. I could smell the juicy food and feel the warmth of the people surrounding me.

The walls began to close in on me. I had to escape from all these noises and impressions. I could no longer bear the laughter of the other children. How could they sit here, eat and continue their lives as if nothing had happened?

Silently, I walked down the corridor, paying no attention to the statues on the wall. My steps made a loud, muffled sound as I walked across the red carpet, and I could still hear the clinking of cutlery. After a few steps, I picked up the speed until I ran, my door just in front of me. I quickly pushed the handle down and slammed it shut behind me.

Silence.

Nothing and no one was in this room except me and my heartbeat.

After I dropped into bed, groaning, I stared into the mirror and saw my reflection. I didn't know how long I was looking at myself. I threw my legs over the edge of the bed and walked toward the mirror.

My green eyes glared at me, and I noticed what had changed. My facial features had hardened, and I looked like a younger version of my mother.

The smell of fresh wood was still in the room, and the bed looked inviting. So without worrying about the accident, Lex or my parents, I slipped under the duvet.

Tiredness dragged at me, my eyes becoming heavy, and I let myself fall into the void.

CHAPTER
7

My head was throbbing. I could hear the soft sound of water and desperately tried to get up, but I was too exhausted.

I remembered the dream; the nightmare. We were out hunting in the woods, and there was a hooded figure and a dog that went up in flames. Somebody had taken my brother and me to an unusual place and told us our parents had disappeared.

I grabbed my humming skull.

"Finally, you are awake. I knocked and heard a scream, so I gave myself access to your room."

I tried to focus on the voice that still sounded far away. Slowly, my vision became more apparent, and I could see Rowan's face hovering over me. I had seen him in my dream.

"Excuse me?" I whispered and shook my head.

"It sounded like you were in danger, so I entered your room to see if you were okay."

If Rowan was standing before me, it hadn't been a

nightmare that woke me up—it was reality. I turned to the side to avoid him seeing my panicked expression.

"Why can't anyone leave me alone? I just want to sleep," I barked, hoping he would leave.

"Okay, I'm going, but before I do, I have to tell you something. Our first lesson is in a few minutes, and I'm pretty sure you don't want to miss it."

I turned and looked at him, knowing that he was just trying to help me. It took me a few breaths to let reality sink in. I couldn't miss the first lesson, no matter how much my head hurt.

"No one told me when and where the lesson would take place. I don't even know where I'm supposed to go," I said, trying to sound as lovely as possible.

Rowan was my only option to get to the lesson in time, so I couldn't scare him away.

He grinned at me. "Of course, I can help you. Miss Syryn released the room number and time yesterday after dinner, but you were nowhere to be found."

I tried to suppress an eye roll. Of course, I had missed her speech. I had left the hall earlier than anyone else because I didn't know Miss Syryn would address us again.

"Give me five minutes, and we can go. Please be so kind as to wait outside," I replied quickly and tried to sit up, but I felt dizzy.

"Let me help you."

He grabbed my shoulders and gently pulled me into a sitting position. His freezing hands sent a shiver down my spine.

"I don't need any help! Please wait outside," I hissed but was glad for his help, anyway. "You should pay more attention to the circulation in your hands. They are freezing."

He quickly pulled his hands back and rubbed them

against his jeans, looking out the window, embarrassed.

"It's a family disease," he mumbled under his breath. "You have five minutes." Rowan hurried out of the room, and I was finally alone again.

I slit my feet carefully over the edge of the bed. In front of me was the window from which I could see nothing but yawning darkness the night before. A new day colored the horizon with a breathtaking sunrise—the sky was bright red, and the sun's rays danced across the bed.

With wobbly legs, I stood up and walked over the old wooden floor to the window. I pushed myself against the handle, and the glass door sprang open, presenting a stone-covered balcony in front of me. The side railing was the only barrier between me and the abyss while the fresh wind blew through my hair.

The sound of turbulent water masses had become louder, and I held onto the railing to look down. Below me were three more floors with balconies, and the exterior facade had green algae in the cracks of the rock. Terraces surrounded me—to my right, left, and above me.

The building seemed to float above a waterfall, with millions of gallons of water flowing into a large circular lake. An oval-shaped island surrounded it. Six large stone buildings towered around the lake. Behind the buildings, I could see a high stone wall that served as a separation between even more water and a forest landscape with mountains.

What buildings were they?

I closed my eyes for a few heartbeats and let the water carry my thoughts away. A quiet knock on the door brought me back.

"I'm coming!"

I ran into the room, slammed the window shut behind me, and hurried to the closet. About twenty dresses, one more hideous than the next, hung in front of me.

The last dress I had worn was for a school performance in third grade. Since then, I have resisted wearing the ones my mother brought home from shopping. With a dress, I had to be careful how I sat down or if the wind would take hold of it, showing more than I liked. Plus, I didn't want to attract attention, so my jeans, shirts, and sweaters were the perfect disguises.

I rummaged through the closet and, to my surprise, found a pair of jeans and a simple beige t-shirt. Full of relief, I slipped into the clothes.

I was on my way to the door when I realized I wasn't wearing any shoes. Under the closet was a selection of different shoes I hadn't noticed the night before. I quickly grabbed a pair of sneakers hidden behind high-heeled boots and opened the door.

As I tried to get out, I ran right into Rowan. He was bigger and stronger than I expected, and I bounced back.

"Oh, I'm sorry," I apologized and pushed past him, walking down the corridor, my ears glowing with shame. I tried to speed up my pace until Rowan's throat-clearing stopped me in my tracks.

"What?" I turned to him, throwing my hands in the air.

"I admire your determination, but Room 301 is this way. Of course, we can take the detour you are about to take, but then we will probably arrive at the end of the lesson."

"I just wanted to get my brother," I lied and tried to turn away from him, but he cleared his throat again.

"What is it now? I want to offer you a cough drop, but unfortunately, my belongings weren't included when I was involuntarily brought here."

He chuckled. "I like your sense of humor, especially the involuntary part, but his new friends have already picked him up." His emphasis was on new friends, and I could hear his amusement but ignored his comment. "You're the last one missing, so they sent me to get you. We have to hurry."

I caught up to him quickly, peering at him, and noticed that he was still grinning. "Why are you smiling? Did I say something wrong? And why did Miss Syryn pick you as her errand boy?"

"Do you always ask this many questions? Do you even know where we are?" Rowan looked at me and could probably see in my helpless eyes that I didn't know.

I couldn't remember much from yesterday's conversations, but the name stuck to me. I knew this place was called Teviena.

"I assumed Miss Syryn had informed you. Of course, I want to tell you everything down to the smallest detail, but we are here."

We stopped at the door at the end of the corridor, and he opened it. I didn't notice how we had made it through a staircase to the third floor.

Rowan pushed me into the room without warning. More windows than I could count filled the room. I raised my hand to protect my eyes from the bright sunlight flooding the room. It took me a few seconds to get used to the brightness. Whispering overstrained my hearing, and the dusty smell of old books irritated my nostrils. I wasn't sure if the aroma made my eyes watery or if it was the light.

Finally, I lowered my hand and looked around. The hall was furnished with dozens of chairs, standing in a semicircle in front of a podium like a grandstand. Two stairs led down between the rows of seats. On the walls stood tall bookshelves filled with hundreds of dusty books, just waiting to be picked up again.

I searched the rows for Lex, but my gaze got stuck on

Amara, who threw a smile with an energetic hand wave in my direction.

Several people turned around, and I looked next to me, where Rowan had just stood and realized I was alone. Where had he gone so fast?

I had to go alone to the place that Amara had reserved for me. Frantically, I hurried down the stairs and threw myself next to Amara to escape the prying eyes.

"I thought you weren't coming anymore." Amara smiled warmly before pulling out a notebook and several pens from a bag tucked under her chair.

"Yeah, I slept a little tighter than I thought. Rowan helped me find the hall. Without him, I wouldn't have made it in time. Did I miss something?"

"As you can see, Miss Syryn isn't here yet." She shrugged her shoulders. "But I am prepared for everything." She pulled out a bag from under her chair and showed me some sandwiches she had taken from breakfast.

"I can see that," I laughed and leaned against Amara, giggling, until I realized how strange that must have been for her. I slid back into my chair and looked around.

Dozens of children sat together in groups and talked. I tried to find my brother's face in the crowd—without success.

Next to the podium, a door opened, and a small, heavyset man, who tried way too hard to hold on to the little hair he had left and thick horn-rimmed glasses, entered the room.

Suddenly, the hall fell silent, and all eyes fell onto him, who quickly stepped towards the desk. With a loud bang, he threw a thick leather bag on the table, opened it, and pulled out a piece of chalk. Then he went behind the desk, pressed with his foot a small lever recessed into the floor, and a black blackboard shot up past him.

"I hoped to meet all of you under different circumstances, but unfortunately, the different clans must come together in critical times like this one to protect our youth. My name is Jovan Amaeral. Welcome to Teviena, a training place for magical beings. Look around you."

He paused for a moment to give us time to examine our neighbors.

"Everyone sitting here today has lost their parents in recent weeks. Many of you wonder why it happened, why you survived, and where your parents are. Unfortunately, your families fell victim to the Shadow World. So far, we still have no clue where your families are and what the Oblitus are planning to do with them, but I can assure you, we are working very hard to get them back. Oblitus are Shadow Creatures who have been excluded from the magical or the Mortal World."

While Mr. Amaeral continued, he drew two curved lines overlapping in the middle and pointed to the upper area above the lines.

"This part represents the Mortal World, and here, below the lines, is the Magical World." He pointed to the area below the lines. "Shadow Creatures, also known as Oblitus or the Forgotten, occupy the small part in between. We are talking about all the people or beings who used black magic or were classified as dangerous and are now trapped between the two worlds in Bridlio. The only way to regain their freedom is to destroy one of these worlds. Therefore, the path between the worlds would break and open a way for the Shadow Creatures to leave captivity. Some of you might wonder why they are trying to break free. The most powerful wizard of all time created Bridlio. However, every magic spell has a loophole, and one of the Shadow Creatures must have found it. Someone in the

Shadow World was powerful enough to break the spell and brought accomplices from the Shadow World with them. We don't know how many of them escaped, but it must be a powerful magician as a leader who knows about black magic."

He took a long breath and looked over the shoulder in our direction.

"And so the hunt for us, the magical beings, has begun because there is much less magic than humans on this planet. And now to the question of why you are here. I am sure every one of you knows the saying that cats have seven lives. Almost the same applies to you. We have given each of you puppy protection, but unlike cats, you only have one more life. The puppy protection was cast with the spell to create the Shadow World. Any magical being under 21 will be teleported to a safe place when threatened. Yes, you heard that right; this puppy protection protected you at the last second from falling victim to an Oblitus. It's the reason you guys can sit here today and make plans. We must get rid of the Shadow World once and for all and find your families."

My head was spinning just as I thought the new reality I was being pushed into couldn't get any worse. Did I understand him correctly?

Amara was busy scribbling in her notebook. I gazed at the sheet of paper in front of her.

Oblitus

Shadow World-Bridlio

Black Magic

Where are our families?

Mr. Amaeral had turned to face us, and my eyes rested on a girl's hand frantically waving in the air.

"Yes?" He said.

"Why do we have to fight? Isn't it better to let older

generations take care of it? Haven't we suffered enough?"

A loud murmur went through the rows. Several children agreed with her, and Mr. Amaeral raised his finger to silence us.

"Excellent question. First, the youngest generation learns the fastest and can be trained more efficiently because your gifts can still be formed. The older you get, the more difficult it becomes for you to master your gift. Each of you has an extraordinary gift, and together we can form an army that the Oblitus cannot foresee. And second, most magical beings over 21 years old have been abducted, so our hope lies in your generation."

"So we are practically served to the Oblitus as an appetizer?" A boy asked, his eyes sparkling with anger.

"No, I wouldn't see it that way. We give you a choice to be among those preparing for battle and being trained to fight for survival. Or you can choose to get up, leave this room, and be taken to the next magical orphanage until we hopefully find your parents and siblings. No one will blame you if you leave now."

Several kids stood up, looked around, and left the room. Only a fraction of the young people walked out of the hall, but the empty seats were yawning like black holes between us.

I had promised Lex I'd only stay here to get answers. Now that I had them, I could have stood up and walked out, but I stayed seated.

This room was filled with people who were just like us. There were other shapeshifters and magicians. This place was the answer to my question I had been carrying around since I could walk. There was a Magical World—a world where I wasn't a freak of nature.

"Why can no one cast a spell to protect us from the Shadow World and send them back to where they came from?" Cried another boy from the row below me.

"These two solutions have already been considered. Miss Syryn, the most powerful sorceress since Norwin, took on this task personally and failed. If she cannot protect us, then we have no choice but to fight the Shadow World with common strength," Mr. Amaeral said, without taking his eyes off the boy.

"How are we supposed to protect ourselves against black magic?" A young girl called into the hall. She looked no older than ten years, and I could see the fear on her face.

"I know you must have more questions. We will assign each of you to a group so that we have a wide range of different beings and gifts in each group. You will receive a note with the name of an instructor and the place and time of the first training. I keep every instructor updated so they can answer any of your questions. And now, without further ado, I'm releasing you for lunch."

Mr. Amaeral bowed to the offspring and was about to leave the room when a young fellow called. "We're supposed to waste our time eating? I thought they could attack us at any second?"

"I wouldn't recommend that you exercise on an empty stomach. I can say from experience that a balanced meal makes it a lot easier." Mr. Amaeral giggled and left the hall through the door from which he had come.

"That's it?" I asked irritatedly and looked at Amara, who was still busy scribbling into her notebook.

"I also expected a little more of it, but I had a lot of time the last few days to read through the library of Teviena and learned some things that can be very useful to us. Let's eat. I can show you my notes when we get there," Amara answered, slammed shut her notebook, grabbed her bag, and got up.

"I have the feeling I have more questions now than before. Oh, wait, I should probably find my brother and see how he's doing. It's not even twenty-four hours since—"

"I understand. We can still walk together to the dining room if you like?" Amara asked.

I agreed.

CHAPTER
8

I couldn't see Lex anywhere between the young people who had gotten up and tried to push themselves out the door.

I noticed that almost all the girls wore dresses, and the boys wore black pants and shirts in different colors. I had decided against the dresses waiting for me in my closet, now regretting it.

Together, we tried to find a way through the door, and after a few minutes, we finally arrived in the corridor. The crowd pushed us over the red carpet. Amara tried to talk to me, but the surrounding chatter was too. Finally, without exchanging a word, we arrived in the dining room, where the Steam Fairies were waiting for us.

The noise spread throughout the room and made it easier to have a conversation.

"I wonder where Miss Syryn is? According to yesterday's statement, I assumed she would teach the first lesson." I looked around. "And she isn't here either."

"She has a lot on her plate and comes, as her

circumstances permit. And besides, she's busy picking up more kids worldwide, which must be exhausting." Amara had a good explanation.

"My parents did a good job keeping this Magical World from us. Until yesterday, I assumed that there were only two kinds of shapeshifters, and today there are hundreds of them, magicians and Oblitus. Deep down, I always knew there had to be more to our secret, but this—" I let my eyes wander over the various children who were busy filling their stomachs. "I need a crash course to understand what this world offers besides Oblitus."

Amara looked at me with a pitiful expression, her eyebrows tightening as if she was thinking. "How about I get all my notes from the room after lunch, and then I can tell you more about the story of magical beings? I can't imagine what it's like to be thrown into the deep end. Your parents must have had a good reason to keep this information from you guys."

"There is no logical reason to let your children believe they are abnormal and that there are only a handful of people who share the same fate with you," I whispered, looking for Lex.

At the end of the dining room, on the other side of the round table, I could see his blond hair. It must have taken him some time to style it that flawlessly. He was in a deep conversation with two boys.

"Wait a moment," I said briefly and ran over to him.

"Lex, I was looking for you. Why didn't you wake me up this morning?" I asked and put my hand on his shoulder.

"Hey, Cas. I didn't want to wake you too early. Do you want to join us?" He answered. I could feel the derogatory looks of the other boys sitting next to him.

I was used to being looked at like I didn't fit in. So, of

course, I should have expected to get strange looks when I decided against the clothes in the closet and was now the only girl in jeans and a t-shirt. Or maybe it was also my wild hair, which stood up in all directions.

"I wanted to ask you if you want to sit with Amara and me?"

Lex laughed hysterically and looked around. "You're kidding me, aren't you?" He examined Amara across the table. "She had her nose in her notebook during the whole lecture. So it wouldn't surprise me if she were one of the people to ask a stupid question." The boys laughed, but I remained calm.

I knew this power game all too well. Lex tried to look cool in front of his new friends and carried it out on the back of the outsiders—as he called them. But he forgot that I—his sister—was an outsider, too.

"So you saw me at the meeting and didn't think it was necessary to come over? I was worried about you! But you don't care how I'm doing. I wish you and your mindless followers a good day." Enraged, I turned away from them, but Lex grabbed my wrist and pulled me closer.

"I'm trying to help you. How about you choose the side that sits on the longer lever once in your life? No one here knows you. It's like a fresh start," he whispered to me. I couldn't believe what he had just said.

"The longer lever? You don't think you can take on Shadow Creatures alone, do you? Can you tell me what magical beings your friends are? Or can you tell me one good quality of them?" He looked helplessly at his new friends and shrugged. "You are so superficial. And now let go of my arm!" I pulled out of his grip and strutted away.

Lex made no further effort to stop me. Instead, he just shook his head in confusion before turning back to the others.

Never in my life had I turned against my brother in public. But since they had teleported us on the mountain, our connection had somehow been broken. Or maybe it was me who had changed too quickly in the last few hours.

I ran back to my seat with a throbbing heart. Amara, who had watched the whole spectacle from her seat, gave me a tortured smile.

"I don't want to get involved, but it didn't look like you, and your brother agreed," Amara said, filling her plate with roast, potatoes, and bacon.

"It was the first time I had told my brother what I think of his behavior," I replied, settling down beside her in sorrow.

I had imagined that I would feel better after I had told him my opinion, but I felt the opposite. My guilty conscience plagued me. I shouldn't have talked to him that way.

"We've never really fought until we got here. My parents always told us we have to stick together and that there is a reason we are brother and sister," I added and examined the food in front of us. I knew I had to eat, but the confrontation with Lex still upset my stomach.

"Maybe," Amara grunted through a full mouth. She looked like a hamster about to bury his collected nuts.

"My brother thinks I should join his group so I have a chance of survival."

"Well, that would be fun. How can you tell someone that this is about teamwork and not who looks the best?"

"My words." I couldn't suppress a smile.

My last meal had been at noon in the Human World the day before. My stomach growled for everyone to hear as I led the fork with a thick piece of roast towards my mouth. This was precisely what I was missing. Everyone in the family knew I was obnoxious with an empty stomach. My father had even distributed small snacks all over the house so he could throw food at me if I got hungry.

We shoveled so much food into our mouths until we felt like we were bursting. After finishing our plates, we stood up silently to go to our rooms. We came to a halt at the door to a staircase, which I had already noticed the previous night.

"I have to go downstairs. Where's your room?" Amara asked.

"If you turn left here, my room is on the left. I think it's the fourth door from the dining room, or maybe it's the third? I'm not sure anymore." I tried to remember the many doors between me and the dining room.

"I'll find you," Amara replied, running down the stairs.

For the first time since I got up, I felt alone. I inspected the silver statues on the way to my room. They looked massive and heavy; the details were impressive, and the proportions of each animal were just right.

The door handle was within reach as footsteps sounded behind me.

"Cassandra?" Rowan called loudly, and I cringed.

So much for rest. Privacy didn't seem to be a thing in Teviena.

"Would have been too nice if I could enjoy a few minutes alone," I said but smiled, so he stepped closer.

"I didn't mean to dump you earlier. We had little time left, and I wanted to ensure we didn't miss anything during the lecture. What do you think if I tell you later a little more about Teviena and the Oblitus?" Rowan asked and paused. He looked at me like a dog, eagerly waiting for me to throw his ball.

"Don't you have something better to do?" It sounded more unfriendly than I intended it to.

"I just want to make sure everyone here is on the same

page. You and Lex are the last to arrive here in Teviena. Let's hope it stays that way."

"Amara, the girl who was with me today, is coming soon."

I knew he tried his best to welcome us here, but it was too much for me. I wasn't used to being approached by so many people. The urge to go home, lie next to Damous with a book, and hear my parents' laughter from the next room pulled on me.

A piece of paper attached to my door caught my attention. I tore it off and looked at the text.

"What group are you in?" Rowan asked tensely and tried to look at the note in my hand.

"It says with Mrs. Nerol. My first training is tonight at six in Room 401."

"What a coincidence. I have Mrs. Nerol, too."

His words startled me. I wanted to hold a pillow in front of my mouth and scream; of course, fate had put him in my group.

"Wait, aren't you coming from the dining hall? You didn't have time to get to your room and see the note." I thought I had gone too far to call him a liar. I grimaced and hoped he would ignore my comment.

"There are pros and cons to being Miss Syryn's errand boy. The advantage is that I usually know everything before they pass it on to the trainees."

"I have to apologize for my behavior. I didn't want to portray you as a liar. It's difficult for me to make friends. My parents have disappeared. Lex isn't acting like himself, and you seem to follow me," I explained shyly and tried to grab the door handle to escape the conversation.

"You don't have to explain yourself. I understand. I don't know what you guys have planned, but how about we meet after training?" asked Rowan.

I wanted to say no, but I couldn't spontaneously think of an excuse to serve him. I nodded in silence.

"Ok, I'll see you later." He walked past me, his footsteps disappearing in the distance.

Why was he so persistent? Was I the only one who didn't know what was going on? How did Lex know everything already in such a short time? Maybe I should see Miss Syryn to have a conversation with her alone. Then, perhaps I wouldn't be the only one left in the dark.

Finally, I pushed the door open and dropped myself on the bed.

Silence.

No people were talking to me and trying to tell me that Oblitus existed. No one attempted to bomber me with more information, which I wanted to know, but it was way too much at once—no noises from other people and no smell that overstimulated my senses.

I just wanted to curl up into a ball and let the warmth of the sunlight fill the empty space in my heart.

CHAPTER
9

I didn't know how much time had passed when Amara knocked on the door.

"Come in," I shouted, and she stepped in, entirely out of breath.

"Unfortunately, we don't have as much time as I thought, but we will make it work. I have to go to my training with Mrs. Nerol at 6 o'clock," she exclaimed.

I couldn't see her face behind the pile of books. "You're kidding me, right?"

"No, why?"

"You are also in the same group as me," I answered and was ecstatic to have her by my side.

"That's the best news I've heard in days, but what do you mean by *also?*"

"Rowan is in our group."

"How do you know?"

"He intercepted me in the corridor and offered his help," I said casually.

"How come he only offers you his help?" Amara was

visibly amused; she lowered her arms, and I could see her sparkling green-blue eyes.

"He's just trying to keep me posted. He said that Lex and I were the last to be found."

"But still… since I've been here, I haven't heard from anyone that Rowan—the messenger of Miss Syryn—personally takes care of a newcomer."

I was running out of explanations. I didn't know him well enough to know that he rarely dealt with other trainees.

"He just wants to be nice."

"You could say that." Amara grinned, and I threw a pillow at her. Amara pulled her hands protectively in front of her face, sending the books flying high in the air. As one of them threatened to land on her head, the pillow and books stopped mid-flight.

"Wow! How do you do that?" My mouth stood open; a handful of books and the pillow hovered in front of me, at eye level.

"I'm still a sorceress, remember? Not as good as my parents, but I can do some simple spells," she reminded me. "And now we must start learning a bit of the story before going on to the training. So—" Amara let the objects, still floating in the air, down to the bed where they piled up neatly.

"This is madness! What would I give to use magic," I said, driving my hand across the books to make sure they weren't wrapped with a fishing line to show that trick.

"Unfortunately, it looks more spectacular than it is," Amara muttered sadly.

"I would never use my hands to carry anything again if I had magic. What else can you do? Can you make things disappear or conjure up everything you want?" I asked and had to realize there were no cords.

"Yes, but it tugs at my energy. Every time a spell is used, a certain amount of energy is required by a magician. The more complex the spell, the more energy is needed. We can use pentagrams and wands, but my parents couldn't teach me before they disappeared."

I looked up and saw that her eyes were filled with tears.

"Oh no, don't cry. I didn't want to recall those memories in you. How about you tell me everything about magical beings?" I tried to cheer her up, and to my relief, she agreed, and her tears disappeared.

"Okay. They taught us that the extinction of dinosaurs was the beginning of humanity, but there were also beings living among them. Each one of them had a gift. Many will probably sound familiar, like Magicians, Vampires, Unicorns, Basilisks, Nymphs, Titans, Werewolves, Griffins, and Ghosts. But there are many more, such as Sirens, Lamia, Chimaira, Manticores, and so on. It was a very carefree time until babies without gifts were born. In the beginning, giftless humans and magical beings lived among each other, but the more civilized the humans became, the faster they stopped believing in magic. They called us supernatural beings, mythical creatures, legends, and fantasies, and the less they believed in us, the more we disappeared before their eyes. Nowadays, people are already so far that they can only perceive our human form because the faith is missing to see the beauty in our magical form."

"Are you trying to tell me that people can't see us in our magical form? I don't think so. Of course, they can see us." I interrupted and shook my head.

"People no longer believe in magical beings. Before you came here, you also thought that wolf and lynx shapeshifters were the only ones that exist, right? It's the same with people; their imagination is no longer wild enough to believe in us. They are too caught up researching new technologies, creating offspring, and going to work every day that they have no place for miracles like us," Amara explained.

"I don't know what to say. It's normal for you, but it shook my world when this weird dog chased us in the woods," I sighed. "And now you're telling me I've been hiding from human eyes for years that couldn't see me to begin with?"

I tried to sort through all this information and make sense of it, but it all sounded so bizarre that it couldn't be true. My parents would have pointed it out to me.

"What dog are you talking about?" Amara asked, interrupting my train of thought.

"My parents, Lex, and I had been hunting in the woods when we got a bad feeling. Suddenly, a hooded figure stood next to a tree with a dog. When my father wanted to leave, the dog chased after us, and his eyes were glowing red. And I know you probably won't believe me, but he caught fire and got bigger and faster." I could hear the screams of my brother in my head, followed by the muted impact of his head on the window.

"That's strange."

"Of course, it's strange. It was a burning dog that ran behind our car," I stressed, knowing she would doubt my credibility.

Amara flipped through a book she had brought with her. The old pages were a bit torn from handling.

"Here." She pointed to a picture. "The Klushund, a demonic animal. Traitors, who have to walk forever as large black dogs, are usually described with large, red shining eyes. An encounter with the menacing beast brings illness, suffering, or plague in the legends. Eyewitnesses reported that they spotted one in a very dark and dreaded forest area."

Amara held out the book, and next to the definition she had just read, there was a picture of the beast. A black dog with bright red eyes, his teeth clenched and his posture tense, ready to jump.

"The dog I saw looked very similar to this one. Is there a connection with fire?" Goosebumps ran over my body as I continued to look into the big, threatening eyes.

"I've read this book hundreds of times. There is nothing about fire, but maybe we are lucky and find an explanation in the library books," Amara added. "But before we dive into this topic, I'd like to tell you more about the different beings you can meet here in Teviena. "

"How about you just lend me your books? Then I can read them, and if I have questions, I will ask you?" I cleared my throat. "Speaking of my parents... how did you end up here?"

I knew I was moving on thin ice. It had not been easy for me to think again about the previous night, and I knew Amara plaited the same sadness every time she talked about her parents. But I wanted to help her. Although it was the most painful memory of my life, it was good to talk to someone about it.

Had they also been hunted? Apparently not by a demonic dog.

"My family was on the way to our neighbors a week ago. They were a pixie family, so they were a mix between Fairies and Goblins. A few days before, they invited us to a barbecue. Everything seemed normal, so we went to the kitchen when we arrived. Our mothers were preparing the food when someone knocked on the door. The knocking turned into hammering, so our fathers went to the entrance to open the door. They had just walked through the kitchen door as the front door shot through the hallway in splinters. I could hear my father screaming, and my mother took my friend and me by the hand and pushed us into the small guest toilet next to the living room. My older brother Ravinder had not been with us that day, but my other siblings were. Cora and Taymon were downstairs playing board games. Barb's mother barely made it into the room with us when my mother closed the door and sealed it with a spell." She wiped a tear from her cheek while she paused.

"We had to be quiet because we could hear the footsteps of the intruders. But Barb couldn't suppress her anxious whining, so they quickly knew where we were. They couldn't open the door, but that didn't stop them from trying to kill us; they set the house on fire. I could hear my siblings screaming for help, and slowly we lost consciousness caused by the smoke coming out from under the door. My mother tried to save us with her magic, but she was the first to faint. It was horrible. The heat of the fire had melted the doorknob, and I couldn't open it to help my siblings. I still remember the silence between my cough as her screams fell silent. Barb had just turned 21, so she was no longer protected by the puppy protection. The next thing I remember is Miss Syryn. She sat next to me and explained what had happened. Shortly afterward, my little brother Taymon arrived here, and we have been waiting for Ravinder and Cora since then. Unfortunately, both are beyond the age of puppy protection, so I don't think they made it here." Amara's voice trembled, and tears rolled down her cheeks.

I wanted to hug her, support her, and show her she wasn't alone. I didn't care if she thought it was weird that we didn't even know each other for over twenty-four hours. But, after entrusting me with her most tremendous trauma, a hug was the least I could do to comfort her.

"I shouldn't have asked you." I lowered my head.

"It's okay," Amara replied, wiping the tears with the tip of her dress. "You're the first one I told my story to, and it feels good. When I talk about my parents and siblings, I feel like I still have them with me. I know we're supposed to find them, but my gut tells me something terrible happened to them. I cannot bring them back with the help of my brother alone, so I stayed."

"I want to help you."

She shook her head, and her eyes went through the foggy room. Her emotions had unleashed magic in her, which flowed uncontrollably through the room. Loose objects and furniture floated in the air. Amara shook her head again, and the floating objects hit the ground, and the fog cleared.

"I can't control my magic, and since my parents are gone, I don't have an anchor point. The more I try to control my magic, the less it seems to work." Amara looked embarrassed at the duvet and tugged at it as if removing hair from it.

I stretched out my hand and flinched as my fingers touched her cold skin. Fortunately, she had been too busy removing imaginary hair and wasn't aware of my sudden reaction.

"I'm not a good shapeshifter, either. My brother can transform whenever he wants, and I...it's a good day if I only turned a few times into a lynx against my will." She looked up at me. "You're not alone. Can you explain to me what an anchor point is? Maybe I can help you. I know nothing about magic, but I'm always ready to learn something new."

It was a lie. I hated trying new things. My human routine was set in stone. School, reading books, taking notes, playing with Damous, reading more, and then going to bed. In the meantime, there were meals, but even these were never a surprise. It was the same menu weekly, both at school and home. I refused to do something unfamiliar, fearing that I would like it, and I had to step among people for it.

But everyone in this building was as abnormal as I was.

The cold of her hands burned on my skin, and although I wanted to keep comforting her, I removed my hands and pressed them against my thighs to warm them.

"Excuse my icy hands. My magic pulls at my energy." She rubbed her palms together, which immediately turned reddish. "Many magicians and magical beings use an anchor point to get their emotions and power under control. Every time I got mad and wanted to use my magic to let my feelings run wild, I could hear my mother's voice in my head. She was my anchor, a connection that worked against my magic and helped me restrain it. But the pain of loss I've been carrying around for days is gnawing at me. Being a sorceress has many advantages, but it's also a balancing act between white and dark magic."

"Your siblings and parents are still with you. They continue to live inside of you. But that's probably not the answer you wanted to hear from me. Can I serve as your anchor point?"

"Anyone can be an anchor point if the connection between the two people is right. I'm my little brother's anchor, but he's also a magician. I can't explain how it works, so I'm unsure if you can help me." Amara stood up, sighing, and picked up the bedside lamp that had fallen to the floor because of her wild magic. "But that's not your responsibility. Let's get back to our lecture."

I admired how quickly she had caught herself, but I was still worried. Although I had only met Amara the day before, I wanted to do my best to help her as she had helped me.

"Humans cannot see our supernatural form. So my family and our entire village could live a relatively normal life." Amara raised a finger as if something had just occurred to her. "Children are another story. Most kids can see us, which has something to do with their imagination, so be careful. Oh, no…" She looked at her bare arm as if she was wearing a watch. "Time has passed faster than I expected. We have to go."

My legs trembled with excitement. I couldn't wait to see other gifts, plus the training would help Amara push the memory of her family out of her mind.

I was glad not to have to sit around anymore. My entire world seemed to have only one purpose: to hunt these Oblitus and send them back to where they came from.

I was still unsure if I wanted to stay in Teviena after the training or go home to look for our parents with Lex—but I would have to make this decision after the training.

"Let's go," I said, jumping off the bed.

Amara tried to scoop up her books from the bed. I could see that the magic consumed her energy as she struggled to pick them up.

"Please lend me your books. I want to learn more about this world, and I think it's easier if I read it myself." I winked at her.

"Are you sure? That's a lot of books. I have no problem bringing them back to my room," she replied.

Even before she could grab another book, I piled the remaining books on top of each other and placed them on the bedside table, which looked like it would collapse at any moment under the weight.

"Your notes are in safe hands. Reading was the primary hobby before I came to Teviena." The name still felt funny on my tongue. "Because of my self-control, I spent little time outside the house," I admitted and walked towards the door.

If my parents had explained that human eyes couldn't see our gifts, my life would have been very different. But I didn't want to think about that.

"You are more than welcome to keep them," said Amara, and her eyes sparkled with joy that someone was interested in her hard work.

"Do you know how to get to Room 329?" I asked in confusion as we stood in the corridor. I tried to decide if we should turn right or left.

"Of course. Didn't anyone explain how Teviena is divided and how you recognize the room numbers?" Amara walked towards the statue that stood directly on the wall in front of us.

"I have the feeling there is a lot I don't know yet," I admitted and shrugged.

"This is a Wedo," Amara explained, pointing to the silver statue right in front of her.

A colossal wolf with raised front paws and a wide mouth looked down at me as if it were snapping something from the air. I had not noticed how frightening this statue was. Of course, wolves were no stranger to me because both Lex and my father could turn into one. But this silver colossus in front of me was decorated with peacock feathers on his neck and tail, and two folded wings protruded from its shoulder blades. I put my hand on the cold metal and examined the detail.

"They're our protectors, and if we ever get attacked, this beautiful Simargl will hopefully save your butt. But until then—" Amara pointed to the Simargl's paw, and a number poked into my eye. "It will just guard your room."

"Now I see it. That means my room number is 407. But what exactly does a Wedo do?" I raked back and lifted my hand. I couldn't imagine this massive piece of metal as a protector. After all, I looked into the blank eyes of a lifeless magical creature.

"I'd like to tell you, but then I'd have to kill you," Amara said in a harsh voice and couldn't help but laugh. "Fun aside. If they ever attacked us, the Wedos will come to life—each statue protecting the room and the person of their room number. Every Wedo is a powerful creature. So let's hope they never come to life."

I had noticed the statues before, but I had only seen them as decoration. Now that I knew what they were capable of, I saw them in a new light. I looked down the corridor and saw a mighty centaur outside my brother's door.

Amara turned away from me and walked in the opposite direction of his room. I could see more Wedos alongside the wall. A Pegasus was protecting the next room. I caught the room number walking by.

405?

"Where's number 406? And what kind of Wedo do you have?" I asked as my steps synced with Amaras.

"All the rooms with the even numbers are looking out to the courtyard of Teviena. The staircases separate our rooms from theirs. And my Wedo is a Griffin."

"When was Teviena built?" I asked, running my fingers over the uneven stone wall between a Wedo that looked like a mighty tree with a face and a troll statue.

"A very long time ago, however, people previously inhabited this building. After there was no longer any use for this building, they shut it down. To probably answer your next question—No, it wasn't previously used by magical beings to train *fighters*," Amara pronounced the word with caution. "They used it as a training center for many magical beings, and my parents met here."

My skin started tingling, and I wondered if my parents

knew about this place. But if they knew about Teviena, what good reason was there to hide it from us?

"They couldn't have known about this place," I whispered, and Amara looked at me.

"Maybe they kept it from you because of the incident." Her voice grew quieter, and I moved closer to understand her better. "A few years ago, there was an accident bad enough to close the doors of Teviena forever. I am not sure what had happened either; my parents unconsciously discussed it and forgot that I was doing my homework at the dining table. They just called it an incident."

I opened my mouth to ask more questions, but Amara cut me off. Finally, we reached a standstill in front of a dragon statue with the number 401.

CHAPTER
10

"Let's do this," said Amara, pushing herself through the door next to the Wedo.

This hall was filled with steps and benches, as well as a podium and a blackboard, which lay at the end of the room. In front of the platform stood a more prominent woman with robust black curls, dressed in tight black clothing and a stern look.

"You must be the last ones," said Mrs. Nerol with a firm voice, pointing with a wooden stick at two seats. "Take a seat. I don't want to waste a second."

This woman was the complete opposite of Miss Syryn. I wasn't sure what kind of instructor I had expected, but she certainly wasn't it.

On tiptoes, we hurried to the only empty chairs left. But, unfortunately, they were in the front row by the podium, and as much as we tried not to attract attention, all eyes were directed at us.

I was never late in the Human World, so why was it so hard to be on time?

"As you could read on the note, I am Mrs. Nerol. You can also call me Mrs. Nerol."

She paused, and I heard a few children laughing. After a few seconds, however, it subsided when they realized it was still her formal name.

"I am one of the best sorceresses of our age and have voluntarily applied for a job as an instructor. Some of you might have seen me in the corridor or during meals in the dining hall. Since I am not a woman of many words and have little time to prepare you guys against the Shadow World, I will keep it short and sweet. May your gift be your guide."

With a loud bang, she clapped her hands together, and the room flooded with white light. I closed my eyes.

I wanted to slap my hands in front of my face to protect my eyes from the light source, but my instinct told me not to cover them. I had to see what was happening. As I opened them, I let myself fall off the chair onto all fours in terror.

The hall had turned into a jungle landscape in just a few heartbeats. I was alone. The chair I was sitting on was the only thing that reminded me I wasn't hallucinating.

A sharp smell of earth and plants rose in my nose. The humidity and heat were overwhelming. In front of me stood tall rain trees, with ferns overhanging and small bushes sticking out of the wet earth. But before I could explore my surroundings, I heard a branch crack.

There was no time to ask questions about how I ended up here.

Within seconds, I had turned into a lynx and ran toward

the next colossal tree in front of me. I rammed my claws deep into the bark in pain to get up the tree. The bark was firmer than the surface I was used to in my forest. I could see the treetop above me and wanted to climb to get a better view of my surroundings, but then I stopped.

I held my breath and tried to figure out where the sound of the branch had come from. My sensitive hearing and sharp eyes couldn't pinpoint the cause of the cracking. A loud throbbing rushed through my body, and my ears and tail twitched with tension, my heart racing.

My pointed ears moved back and forth, the fine hair at the end moved in the light wind—I heard something—a growing whistle. Quickly I bent down, and with a loud impact, an arrow drilled itself into the place of the tree where my head had just been.

I realized how serious the situation was. I had to act quickly.

The arrow had surprised me, and I knew the attacker must have been the trigger for the cracking.

I had to get off the tree, so I wasn't a vast target. Skillfully, I jumped on a branch that lay on the back of the arrow and let myself fall from branch to branch onto the floor. Effortlessly, I fell on my paws.

As I desperately tried to come up with a plan and assess the situation, I remembered my mother's words: *"Cas, remember, you can't be an excellent hunter if you just rely on common sense. People are no longer dependent on it to survive in the wild. Your shapeshifter senses are much more precise, and your instincts will guide you. But never forget who you really are. When your shapeshifter takes over and pushes your humanity aside, there is no turning back. The lynx in you will win."*

I remembered my father, who always devised a precise hunting plan. But I had never hunted without my pack, and now I had to rely on myself—this time, I was the prey. I was trying to think what he would have done if he were here.

There was a shooter and me. I was in an unfamiliar landscape, but it was basically the same as at home.

May your gift be your guide—Mrs. Nerol's words were simple.

For a split second, I thought about how I would approach the threat as a human, but after I realized that fleeing wasn't a solution, I relied on my animal instincts.

I instinctively knew what to do, and instead of hiding or running away, the hunting instinct awakened an entirely different tactic. There was only one way to escape this attack—I had to face the shooter.

As if on velvet paws, I crept through the bushes in front of me, the wet leaves were sticking to my fur, but I paid no attention to it. The smell of sweat rose into my nose, and the further I crept through the undergrowth, the stronger it became.

As my heartbeat slowed down, I could sense another one, which was quiet and rhythmic. The shooter knew about hunting because the slow heartbeat gave no sign of thrill. I focused on the sound and saw him. A figure covered with a black hooded cape stood in the middle of the clearing with a stretched bow.

My heart stopped for a moment. The figure reminded me of the night of our accident, but I had no time for that. So instead, I pressed my human feelings aside and focused on the mission—destroy.

My common sense tried to make itself back into my head again because I had never attacked a person in my life. But there was simply no other option. I had to do something.

Silently, I pressed all my weight on the floor to jump, my body tense, every muscle ready.

The shadowy figure continued to look around with a taut arrow as I took this opportunity to my advantage. My puffy tail waved silently behind me, and as the shadow figure turned its back on me, I jumped. I felt my claws retract. But instead of drilling them into the enemy's flesh, I landed on the damp ground with a powerful impact.

Surprised, I tried to avoid turning my back on the shooter but had to realize the earth had swallowed him up. Then, even before I knew what had happened, the surroundings lit up again with the bright light.

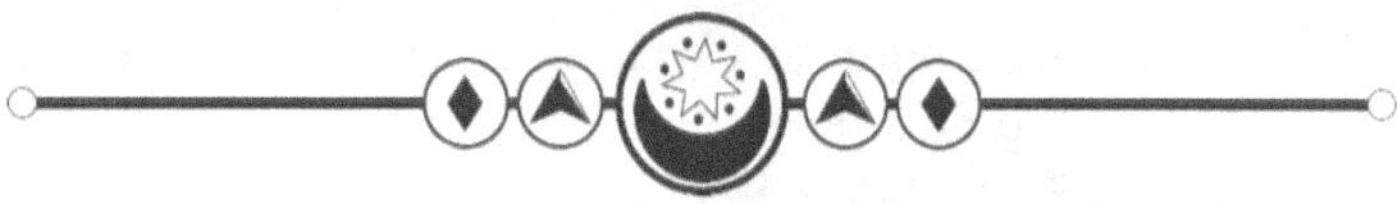

I was back in Room 401, next to Amara, when I opened my eyes. I didn't know what to think, and Amara also seemed confused.

A loud noise brought my attention to the desk, where Mrs. Nerol stood, clapping her hands. A broad grin was visible on her face, and she walked towards the row of seats to my left.

"I have to say; It quite disappointed me that only one person in this room could protect his mind from me. But you all did much better than I expected. Each of you received the same mission. With the help of a spell, I have sent your subconscious on a journey to test your quick-wittedness, dexterity, logical thinking, skills, and actions. I have to admit that it was probably not as easy as with another instructor, but when I'm done with you, each of you will be able to defend yourself against an attack."

Mrs. Nerol walked from one seat to another, touching the hands of the children as she walked by. I looked at her in disbelief.

What the hell had just happened? Had my mission been

to attack a human being? I looked into the faces of the other children.

"My goal is for all my trainees to come out of this fight alive, but for that, I need your complete trust and attention." She was standing in front of me and was about to touch my hand, which was lying on the table in front of her, as I pulled it away.

"With all due respect. How can we trust you if you enter our subconscious without asking us and allow us to be threatened by a person?" I hissed, my voice sounding harsher than I had intended.

"I like you." A faint smile crossed her lips. "Not only did you resist the terrible dress code—" She pointed to my jeans and shirt, "but you also dared to speak without permission. "You— " Mrs. Nerol paused and waved her hand through the air with a questioning gesture.

"Cassandra."

She dropped her hand. "You are also bold enough to question an instructor. I appreciate your opinion, Cassandra, but this spell cannot hurt you. Do you think you would have behaved the same way during your mission if you had known about it before? The Oblitus must have a powerful magician at their side to escape the Shadow World. If I can get into your consciousness, it will be a piece of cake for the magician to hinder you with a single spell."

A lump spread in my throat. Until yesterday, I didn't even know magic was real—just as real as my shapeshifting ability. And now I was told that a spell—which Mrs. Nerol had done without effort—could bring us down. How should I be able to defend myself against such an attack? Shapeshifting wasn't even close to being as powerful as magic.

"Of course, I would have acted the same way. But you

just threw us under the bus," I replied, and a soft murmur flitted through the rows of seats around me.

"Still, I don't assume that an Oblitus will announce itself before attacking you. To be prepared for this battle, I need to know everything about you; your gift and strengths and your weaknesses and fears. And who in this room would like to tell me voluntarily about his fears?" Mrs. Nerol looked around. Most teenagers pretended not to hear her while the rest were busy examining their nails or tables. "That's what I thought. But, Cassandra, if you can't trust me, there's no one here in Teviena who can help you get over your loss and bring out the potential of your gift."

I looked at Amara, hoping to read an approval on her face that I was doing the right thing. She just nodded silently, and her gaze rested on my hand.

"Okay, but what do you need my hand for?"

Mrs. Nerol laughed softly, and the corners of her mouth curled. "I only had a few students like you in my life. I will assign a Signum to each of you. There are five different Signa. Each Signum divides you into a phase of your training based on how you mastered your first mission. You have the chance to ascend a phase by proving your gift and abilities daily. This applies mainly to those who are dissatisfied with their rating. These Signa are valid only during the training period and can be dissolved by me anytime. You will probably have something to complain about that—" She looked at me with raised eyebrows. "Students with lower Signa are humiliated. But that's why each of you can only see the Signa assigned to your phase."

The teenagers next to me inspected the inside of their wrists. I couldn't see what a Signum was, but curiosity gripped me. Slowly, I stretched out my hand, and with a gentle touch, Mrs. Nerol ran over the back of my hand.

At that exact moment, a voice entered my

consciousness. When I looked up at her, I saw her lips weren't moving, but I heard her voice. *"I'm not sure if you're naturally brave or draw that energy out of your fear; both are deeply intertwined. But be careful. In a tense time like this, with hundreds of magical beings under one roof, you can't allow yourself to get into the crossfire of other beings with your firm opinion. If you trust me, I will teach you stuff you didn't even know you could do."*

My gaze rested on her dark brown eyes, and I nodded silently. How had she spoken to me without opening her mouth? Had she penetrated my subconscious again?

Without another word, Mrs. Nerol turned to Amara. Now I could finally see what she had been talking about and what the others had already seen before me.

A turquoise circle, as if painted with watercolor, was depicted on the inside of my wrist. The ring was drawn with streaks and enclosed a drawing that looked almost exactly like Mr. Amaeral's drawing on the blackboard of the human and Magical World surrounding the Shadow World. Two black circles were visible in the turquoise Signum, the circles overlapping and forming an empty space in the middle. In the upper circle was an outline of a diamond in which two equilateral arrowheads met in the middle; a small diamond framed the point of contact of the arrowheads. In the lower circle was a waxing moon with a seven-pointed star above it, and the star was decorated with small dots.

The meaning of this Signum was foreign to me. I ran my finger over the new color on my skin. It felt soft and was painless.

"Now that I'm done with the question-and-answer game," she looked back at me, "I can now tell you something about the Signa. The symbols in the middle of the circle indicate which gift of magical beings you belong to. By the pressure of the ring, you can see what stage you are in."

Five different circles appeared on the board.

"If it is an almost transparent circle, you are in the first phase. If your ring is strong and even, you have reached the highest phase, phase five. Five people wear a turquoise ring instead of the usual black color in this room. That means that you are the group leader for your particular phase." Mrs. Nerol strolled comfortably from one person to another. "At the end of our training, I will distribute a grimoire to everyone. The grimoire will match your symbol in the Signum. By tomorrow, you will have read this book to understand what each of you is capable of. Of course, you will also find new clothes in your wardrobes adapted to your abilities. And—" but before Mrs. Nerol could finish her sentence, a loud knock shook the door.

Everyone turned around and noticed that Miss Syryn was standing in the doorway.

"I just wanted to see how you are doing, Alysa," she breathed, sliding down the hall's steps.

There it was again, the sweet smell. The previous day, I could not determine what it was, but now, I smelled the aroma of vanilla and sandalwood. I tried to suppress the urge to take a deep breath to suck in her perfume.

"I have assigned the Signa to them, and our first training is now over. I still have to distribute the grimoire, and then I'll be available," Mrs. Nerol replied, who had just gotten back to her desk.

"You were a lot faster than the others," said Miss Syryn and walked along the three rows of seats in the room.

"Please come, one by one, to the desk to pick up your grimoire." Mrs. Nerol walked towards the blackboard, and I noticed a piled-up stack of books next to the desk on the floor. I could have sworn it hadn't been there before.

"I don't want to disturb you," said Miss Syryn after she

had finished her round through the hall and disappeared again through the door.

I pulled my brows together. Where did she have to go in such a hurry? She hadn't even stayed with us for five minutes.

"The book will look empty at first sight, but if you drive your Signum over the book's cover or ribbon, you can read the content. A person with the same Signum can only read this book, so it won't allow you to read the book of another gift. We will continue our training after breakfast tomorrow, and you will receive your next mission." Mrs. Nerol sat down on the chair behind the desk.

Amara had been faster than me and stood a few paces away from me. She strolled past me, a book pressed against her chest, and grinned.

After a few minutes, it was my turn. Nerol handed me a thick book, and the smell of leather lingered in the air. Without further words, I copied from the previous children and drove my Signum over the cover. The Signum that adorned my wrist appeared on the edge of the book. I ran my hand over the uneven yet soft leather and tried to memorize every scratch. As I turned my gaze away from the book, Mrs. Nerol looked at me with wide eyes and grabbed my arm before I could turn away.

"Your Signum is special. I have only seen it twice in my life so far. First, I thought it was a mistake, but now I'm not sure anymore. I suggest you don't tell anyone about your Signum until I figure out what it means. Unfortunately, there is no book with the information about your specific Signum, but this grimoire will help you learn more about your shapeshifting. That's also the gift the other children should only know about for now." Her voice was serious. She let go of me.

It would have been too easy if my Signum had been

normal. It wasn't like I didn't have enough trouble getting used to this new world.

"We should leave," Amara said with a joyful grin. I followed her silently.

Silence reigned between us as we made our way back to our rooms. While I was thinking about what my Signum could mean, Amara kept looking at me from the side. None of us dared to say anything.

After a few minutes, I couldn't deal with the quietness anymore. "Mrs. Nerol said these Signa wouldn't put us in categories, but I don't even know if it's okay to ask you about your level." I slowed my step.

"I'm wondering the same thing, but I don't think we're committing a crime. I'm in phase four, and of course, a sorceress," Amara giggled high-pitched, and I looked at her in surprise. Her reaction sounded unusual, but I brushed it aside.

"I'm in phase three and a shapeshifter," I replied, but I couldn't look her in the eye.

I had never been good at lying and tried not to let it show that I kept the essential part of my Signum to myself. It was wrong to lie to a new friend, but was Amara already a friend? Was it possible to build a friendship that quickly? I wasn't familiar with this subject because I had fled from every child in the Human World who had dared to look in my direction.

"I would be interested to know which of the others is so advanced that the person could simply block the subconscious spell. And did you see Mrs. Nerol? She conjured the spell without blinking an eye. That spell costs enormous energy," Amara said.

"Unfortunately, I know little about magic. I only know that I shouldn't have challenged her like that. She will probably make my stay here a living hell."

I dreaded the next training session. If a hunt was the first mission, what could she have in store for the next training? A fight to the death?

"My parents used to talk about Mrs. Nerol when Teviena was a training center for Magical Beings. They tried to separate humans and magical beings from each other so that no one showed his gift in the Mortal World. They had to learn how to keep their gifts under control before returning as young adults to the Human World. My parents were trained here, and your parents must have, too. Nerol was my parents' teacher. She is strict, mighty, and an excellent instructor. My parents would be so proud of me if they could see how well I did on my first mission."

My fingers started tingling, and I tried to remember all my parents' conversations, but none of them included Teviena.

"Do you know more about her?" I asked and pointed with a head movement to Room 401 from which we had come.

"Not right now, but I can do some research. I can hardly wait to read my grimoire." Amara held the book under my nose, and I tried to look at her Signum, but Amara waved it so fast that it was blurred.

"I'm going to my room to catch some air. The magic took way more energy than I expected. Let me know if you find anything interesting, or I'll see you tomorrow at breakfast."

We said goodbye to each other. Amara turned around, walked down the corridor to the staircase, and disappeared. I was happy to have Amara by my side. She was like the subtitles of a foreign movie, but we were trapped in a different world and not a film.

I needed a break from people, a break from my frantic thoughts. A time-out from the blazing feeling that I will never see my parents again. Never!

Again, I looked down at the book in my hand. A door fell loudly into the lock, and I almost dropped the grimoire in surprise. Footsteps arose behind me, and an uncomfortable feeling befell me; I sharpened my ears but couldn't hear another sound.

Then, just as I arrived at my door and thought I had made it to safety, I looked over my shoulder, and my knees almost gave in.

"I thought you forgot our date." Rowan smiled at me, and his warm, amber eyes sparkled.

CHAPTER
11

How could I have forgotten him? I knew he must have been in the same room as I was during the training, but it didn't occur to me to look for him.

"No, I didn't. I just wanted to go to my room to drop my grimoire off." I looked embarrassed at the thick leather book in my hand.

Yes, I had completely forgotten the date. I had been so busy thinking about my Signum and the mission that the arrangement had escaped me.

"May I come in?" he asked, amused, and followed me through the door.

"Actually, I could need a little alone time, which has nothing to do with you. I am not used to having so many people around me," I replied, rushing towards the bed to store away the grimoire.

"Didn't you go to school in the Mortal World?" He raised an eyebrow.

I paused. "Of course, I went to school. But my personality isn't made to make friends," I admitted and

107

tried to make my bed, which I had left unmade, while he looked around.

"I don't think you should be alone with all your questions. Of course, you learn a lot from Amara, but maybe I can show and tell you a few things she doesn't know about."

I weighed my options. Either I could browse the grimoire alone and learn about my gift, or I could accept Rowan's offer and widen my horizon about the Magical World. My curiosity was greater about the unknown than something I had known since I was born.

"I hope it's important enough that it can't wait until tomorrow," I replied. "However, I must go back in time to read this monster." I ran my hand over the book's old material again and turned to Rowan.

"You will be back before you know it." He led the way to the stairwell. "There's something I want to show you."

"I can hardly wait," I said, unable to suppress the sarcasm in my voice.

"I'm curious to see if you're still on such a high horse when we're done."

Side by side, we walked up floor by floor.

"Where are we going?" I asked, alarmed, as we arrived on the sixth floor.

My legs shook uncontrollably. I weighed up how well I had assessed Rowan. He was a stranger, and without thinking, I had agreed to go with him to an unknown place without telling Lex about it. What if Rowan wasn't the friendly neighbor boy I thought he was? What if—I interrupted that train of thought. Miss Syryn wouldn't trust him if he were dangerous.

"To the attic. Don't be afraid. I won't hurt you," Rowan encouraged me, and we finally reached the end of the staircase.

A wooden door was embedded in the ceiling. Rowan climbed up a rickety metal ladder anchored in the wall and swung the door open with a mighty push that landed on the wooden floor with a loud bang. He disappeared into the hole above me.

I knew it wasn't a good idea to follow him, that I should turn around and run away. I rubbed my sweaty hands against my pants and was ready to leave when his face appeared above me in the square in the ceiling.

"Come on." He held his hand out to me.

I hesitated and looked over my shoulder, down the stairs, and up to him again. I grabbed the cold metal of the ladder and started climbing.

The attic looked like an ordinary storage room under a roof. I had expected dust or cobwebs, but the room was clean and empty, too clean for my taste. The only object in this room was a light bulb that illuminated my surroundings.

"This room hasn't been used for years. I don't know if it will ever find use again. But now, back to what I wanted to show you."

Rowan walked past me and stood in the middle of the room after closing the door behind him.

"Teviena is a former asylum. That's why I had to laugh when you said they put you here involuntarily on the way to our first meeting. But fun aside. Magical beings and humans have lived side by side for centuries. Our advantage was that humans idolized us initially and then stopped believing in us. Norwin was one of the most powerful magicians ever, and we consider his bloodline the most powerful among the beings. His story ended tragically, but he was the magician who wanted to protect our gifts from the people and conjured up a parallel world next to the Mortal World. He used this world as a refuge when his family was threatened and people became skeptical of their gifts. Humans were looking for the trigger for diseases, plagues, and unfathomable events, and who could be blamed better than something they didn't understand? Miss Syryn picked this place. And for double security, she reactivated Norwin's parallel world to protect us from people's curiosity. It is no longer safe for us to live in the Human World right now. The disappearance of dozens of families has caused turmoil."

I tried to absorb this information. "But what exactly is a parallel world?"

Rowan only grinned and walked toward me. He grabbed my arm, closed his eyes, and muttered something. His icy hands burned into my skin, and I noticed for the first time that he wore a silver ring on his right ring finger. A large dark blue stone with gold was embedded in the silver.

"Trust me," Rowan whispered, "Close your eyes."

It was the second time someone had asked for my trust that day. My hands were shaking. "It would be more pleasant if your hands weren't freezing," I replied, trying to wiggle myself out of his grip, but he strengthened it.

I had no choice. Resistance seemed futile, and slowly I closed my eyes. A cold gust of wind ran over my body and through my hair. I gasped.

"You can open your eyes now."

I had not noticed that Rowan had let go of me, and when I opened my eyes, I stared into the yawning darkness. Within seconds, my eyes got used to the light, and I realized we were still in the same attic, but the room had changed. Inches of dust rested on the floor, furniture, and objects around us. Rattling metal beds, mattresses, night bowls, and other utensils were scattered throughout the room. The window was smashed, and many roof tiles were missing, so I could see the night sky. The moon shone through the roof, making it easier for me to see. This is what I had imagined a room to look like that hadn't been used in years.

"Norwin's spell created a duplicate of this world."

His words startled me. My first instinct was to transform, but I could get myself under control just in time to prevent the transformation.

"We can use everything that people have built in the parallel world. However, we cannot build new buildings as this would attract attention. What looks like a pile of rubble and ashes to humans can become one of the most important buildings for us with just a little magic. Teviena, for example, is habitable at first sight, but the spell makes it livable for us."

"So just to clarify it. Right now, we're in the Mortal World. But Teviena is in a parallel world? This building exists in both the human and the Magical World, and a spell protects us from human eyes?" I repeated. "I thought people couldn't see us."

"In a nutshell, yes. Even if people lived here, they couldn't see us; we are on a parallel plane. We can see people, but we are strictly forbidden from contacting them. Humans will look like faded ghosts to us, and they can't see us, but they can feel us, so be warned."

Was that the reason so many people thought ghosts haunted their house? Have magical beings been living under the same roof as them in the parallel world?

I looked around the room and thought about all the horror stories told by asylums. "But I thought they couldn't see us even without a parallel world. So why do we need this spell?"

"With all the incidents of families disappearing, we are risking them seeing us again. That's why we need to protect ourselves. We had to ensure that we remained undetected. It would have been only a matter of time before a person with the belief in magic would see one of us."

I rubbed my palm over my face. He had promised to tell me more about Teviena, and he didn't disappoint. But I hadn't assumed that everything in the Magical World was so complicated.

"Okay, I think I have enough for today," I said, exhausted, and turned to Rowan.

"I forgot you know nothing about your real background. Let's head back." He walked toward me and grabbed my arm. While Rowan murmured the same sentence again, I kept my eyes wide open this time.

I watched as the room turned. The beds, mattresses, and dust swirled around until they dissolved into thin air. The attic was now flooded again by the light of the single bulb I had previously discovered. Rowan released his icy hands and wanted to turn away from me to return to our rooms when my question made him pause.

"Are you a magician?"

Rowan laughed to himself but looked at me harshly. His laugh was sharp, and the sparkle in his eyes had disappeared. I took a step back.

"Why do you think I'm a magician?"

"What you just did to the room is indescribable. And it seems as if your magic is pulling the blood and warmth out of your hands just like Amara's," I said hesitantly.

"I don't understand why everyone here is trying to figure out what gift I have. Believe me, Cassandra, I'm not a magician, and if you knew what I am, you wouldn't be so calm. My ancestors are not from a cute picture book story. I know how people and magical beings react to my kind, and I'm glad you met me and not my brother. Unlike him, I can control my gift," his voice was angry and his eyes dark. "Miss Syryn taught me how to jump back and forth between two parallels so I can save newcomers like you."

Without another word, he went to the door, opened it, and disappeared down the ladder. His shoes made a soft metallic sound with each step until it fell silent.

"No reason to be unfriendly," I called after him and scratched my head.

"Some people would be happy if they could choose their gift. I thought you were different." His voice was quiet but loud enough that I could hear it.

His behavior surprised me. First, he followed me everywhere and tried to tell me everything about Teviena. And now he just left me hanging. I waited a few more minutes, hoping that Rowan would come back, but I realized I was on my own.

Mrs. Nerol had warned me I should dial down my temper and questions, and within a few hours, I had disregarded her advice.

I looked into the yawning darkness of the trapdoor.

Why was he so sensitive about his gift? It couldn't be that bad.

I climbed down the ladder into the stairwell—a loud cough echoing from the corridor on the sixth floor. My blood froze in my veins, and I stopped.

CHAPTER
12

"Hello?" My voice trembled.

I focused on my surroundings; there were no footsteps or heartbeat.

Just as I had seized the courage to continue my way to the room, I heard a noise coming from the corridor next to me. My instinct advised me to leave, but my father had taught me never to turn my back on a threat.

I took a deep breath and walked towards the doorframe of the sixth floor, peering around the corner.

Darkness obscured my vision. Light reflected off three silver statues lit by the candlelight of a chandelier. The mythical creatures pointed out that this corridor had only three doors.

"Hello?" I shouted anxiously through the hallway, and my voice echoed back.

I must have been wrong. I waited for a second, and just as I was about to turn around on the heel, a movement drew all my senses in.

A long shadow ran across the dark corners of the

corridor opposite me. I tried to focus my eyes on the corner because I thought I could see something and took a step towards the niche—as he walked out of the darkness.

My heart stopped.

At first, I could see his black boots, followed by burgundy pants, and the sound of heavy fabric made me cringe. Suddenly, a cloak was pulled out of the darkness and caressed the prominent figure in front of me. Shiny black embroideries were embedded both in the cape and a muscular chest. Now the stranger's face came to light, and I knew exactly who I was dealing with.

My heart started racing.

"Who do we have here?" He asked with a growl and stepped closer.

My breath stopped. I stepped back to increase the distance between us, but he had recognized my intention.

"Stay," he said sweetly with an amused grin, and I involuntarily stopped in the middle of the movement.

My legs seemed to be embedded in concrete and held me in place. Invisible hands closed around me, and as much as I tried to free myself from them, I couldn't move.

Frightened, I looked up at the slender figure, which was only a few steps away from me. His skin was white as paper, his facial features were more bestial than human, and his raven-black eyes looked at me. His lips were closed, one corner of his mouth raised, and both his mouth and eyes reflected a dominant smile.

He stood right in front of me, ran his fingers through one of my strands of hair hanging over my face, and held it in front of his nose.

If I had been able to, I would have screamed in fear.

He smelled at my strand, like an animal his prey.

Panic eros in me. I wanted to run; it didn't matter where,

but as far away from him as possible.

"My brother smells like you," he whispered beside my ear, dropping my hair.

I continued to fight against the invisible power that held me against my will. Maybe I had only imagined it, but I felt able to move my fingers a little.

"Well.. Look at that." He snapped his tongue, walking around me as he was sizing me. I could feel his gaze drilling into my shoulder blades. "You're pretty strong. I can see why he takes a liking to you." He was now standing in front of me, and I wanted to jump at his throat, but my body was still frozen.

"Relax," he said, and the invisible hands around me disappeared. I stumbled forward and was about to bump into him as he grabbed me by the shoulders and stopped my fall.

"Not so hasty, my little one. We should get to know each other first before it comes to a hug." He sounded amused, but a dark undertone made me shiver.

"Never touch me again!" I growled, disgusted, and wanted to turn away from him, but his soft laughter made me stop. "What?" I raised my eyebrows and looked at him hatefully.

"For a shapeshifter—" Once again, he sniffed in my direction and closed his eyes as if he were a child who had just smelled cookies. "You're a cat—"

"Lynx," I corrected him angrily and tiptoed back a few steps to bring a safe distance between us.

"Cat, lynx, lion… They all have fur, whiskers, and seven lives. You do have seven lives, right?" He scratched his chin and looked at the ceiling as if he could read the answer up there.

"Don't be ridiculous," I replied. His arrogance made me boil inside. "I wish I could say it is finally nice to meet you,

Draven, but that would be a lie." I spit out his name as if it were poison.

Draven was Rowan's brother. I remembered the newspaper article that showed the photo of the two brothers. In the photo, he looked small, grumpy, and awkward. But now, a full-grown young man with curly, night-black hair and a striking face stood in front of me. I had to tilt my head up to look into his eyes, which looked like soot.

Could it really be the same boy? His hair had been straight and long, and his face was... had been the face of a boy in the photograph. But this boy right in front of me looked closer to my age. How old had the photo in the newspaper been?

"I see my reputation pursuing me. But, of course, you can only have heard good things about me," he growled with a smile, and his eyes flickered.

"Don't flatter yourself," I said narrowly, trying to hold his amused gaze, and after a few seconds, I caved in.

"I expected more from my brother, but that doesn't matter. I'll make sure it doesn't happen again," he replied, grinning, analyzing me again, and walking past me. "If I were you, I'd stay away from the darkness. You never know which monsters could hide in their shadows," he said casually over his shoulder as if it wasn't a warning, but I understood.

"You mean a monster like you?" I asked and looked after him.

"You have no idea what I am capable of," he replied cheekily and made no effort to stop.

I grabbed my chest and tried to calm my heart, which was pounding wildly.

Rowan had been right when he warned me about his brother. He was much worse than I could have ever imagined.

I watched him disappear into the stairwell. I could finally breathe again. My hands were sweaty, and my breath was uneven.

What did he mean by I didn't know what he was capable of? Rowan still hadn't told me what gift he had, but I had learned from Draven that mind control was a fraction of their gift. Draven's mind control was as easy as breathing for me. I shuddered when I thought about what else he could do.

Without another stop, I quickly went into my room and locked it from the inside.

Draven's dark voice echoed through my head. He had called me *his little one*. No one was allowed to give me a nickname except my family. I knew he had only done it to humiliate me, but for what? I had done nothing wrong.

I stalked from one side of my room to the other, my head threatening to burst.

What was Draven thinking about treating me like that? And why had Rowan just left me standing, knowing that the way to my room alone could be dangerous when his brother was at large? I took off my shoe and threw it into the corner, noticing the Signum that Mrs. Nerol had given me.

It reminded me I was supposed to be reading my grimoire, but the rage brewing inside me decided against it.

I wanted to visit Lex and tell him about my encounter with Draven, but then I remembered Mrs. Nerol's words that I should keep myself out of the crossfire of other beings. Starting a fight against Draven with my brother would probably lead me to oppose any further advice from her.

My feet hurt from pounding on the stone floor, and I

threw myself on my bed.

After our argument, Rowan wouldn't talk to me anyway, and that was a good thing. I had experienced what Draven was capable of on my own skin, and I was no longer out to know what gift the brothers had.

They were dangerous, that much I knew.

How could Rowan have deceived me? He had been so kind and caring. But if the same darkness I felt when Draven told me to stand still also blazed in him, then it was better to ignore him.

I had to join my forces with Lex so that such an incident would never happen again.

With this plan, I reached for my bedside lamp to get some sleep, but the thought of darkness made me shudder, and I let the light burn. Even before I knew it, I sank into a deep sleep.

CHAPTER
13

Within a second, I was on all fours on the bed and looked around. Conversations echoed through the locked door. I stared at the same wooden wing door in Teviena.

For a moment, I had hoped to be back in my room at home, but reality set in fast.

Slowly my tension subsided, and I sat down on the edge of the bed—memories of the day before shot through my head.

I had to find my brother and talk to him.

With an enormous leap, I stood in the middle of the room and wanted to run out the door, but something stopped me. I looked around until I caught my reflection in the large mirror behind the bed and slowly walked towards it. The jeans and t-shirt I wore showed slight stains from the last day. My hair was a frizzy mess, and I had light black edges under my eyes.

Although I had slept—I wasn't sure how long—it hadn't been enough for my body.

Before I stepped out of the room, I grabbed a new pair of jeans and a t-shirt, went to the dresser, and opened the first drawer, hoping to find a hairbrush. My intuition was correct. Next to a few neatly folded towels was a brush. Hastily, I ran it through my hair and threw it back in the drawer.

"Not bad," I said to my reflection, and my gaze remained on my pants.

Didn't Mrs. Nerol say we were going to be given unique clothes? I opened the closet, surprised to find something I hadn't noticed before. A robe hung neatly on a coat hanger. I pulled it out and put it on the bed. What should I do with it?

In front of me was a black robe, with a long cloak attached to the shoulders, running over the arms. The chest was embroidered with vertical braided cords, each with a small moonstone in the middle. Smaller stones attached the strings to each side. A golden embroidered belt was at the waist and held the garment together by the slit that reached the floor. Both the collar, the forearms, the lower half of the robe, and a visible strip on the edge of the cape were decorated with golden seams, and on closer inspection, I could see a thin strip of emerald green in it.

Draven had worn a similar outfit the night before, but his had been dark red with black embroidery.

How could this outfit be more helpful than what I was wearing? The cloak would be in my way while moving, and the robe would pull over the ground while stalking. I raised the hem of the robe and noticed that under the skirt was a black pair of trousers. At least I didn't have to worry about showing too much.

I mumbled under my breath as I put on the new garment and fished black boots out of the wardrobe, which completed my look. The robe and cape made me look more elegant than I was used to, but my hair looked more like a bird's nest as I examined myself in the mirror. At least there was one thing I could always count on to stick out.

What am I doing? I shook my head.

I decided I would wear these clothes during training, and if I hated them as much as I imagined, I could put them back into the closet and slip into my cozy clothes again.

I opened the door. People passed by my room without paying attention to me. Within a few steps, I had reached Lex's door and hesitated momentarily. What should I tell him? That Rowan's brother had harassed me, knowing how Lex would react? He would protect me and teach Draven a lesson, and even though I wanted him to, I couldn't dare. Lex would create a scene that would likely upset Rowan even more and could cause us to be banished from Teviena. But I had to come up with something because I didn't want to run into Draven again unexpectedly.

Not even a heartbeat had passed when the door was opened, and Lex looked at me in amazement.

"There you are," he said.

He also wore a black, long-sleeved vest with the same cape, black trousers, and a long-sleeved vest wrapped around his chest. The cape's hem, collar, the chest area of the vest, and belt were embroidered with silver instead of gold.

This outfit was made for him, and he knew it.

"Did you expect me?" Even before I got an answer, Lex stepped into the corridor and strolled with a smile towards the hall, his cloak loudly waving at the speed of his stride.

"Actually, I was just about to come to you, but apparently, you were faster. How are you?" He looked at me. "I see you also got your new clothes."

I felt like an imposter beside my brother. I tried to focus my thoughts on his question.

"It could be better," I murmured and followed him. "How are you?"

"Don't I look great?" Lex replied, making a turn.

My mouth opened with disbelief, and I stopped. Lex had always been the emotional one of us, and now he acted as if nothing had happened. The only thing that interested him at the moment was his new clothes.

I tried to calm down. Something was wrong with him. I knew he could be superficial, but the Lex who was now walking next to me behaved differently than the brother I knew.

Lex also came to a standstill and looked over at me. "What's wrong?" He sounded irritated.

"How can you be so—" But I fell silent before I could unleash all my emotions on my brother's, which had accumulated in the last two days. His eyebrows tightened. "Nothing," I murmured and walked past Lex.

I didn't want to argue with my brother because I needed him. I tried to convince myself that his behavior had something to do with the impact of his head during the accident. How else could he walk through the corridor so relaxed?

"You know you can trust me. I want to help you." Lex hooked his arm into mine and pulled me with him.

"It's nothing."

Silently, we strolled next to each other, and I could feel his burning gaze on my face.

"If you don't tell me what's wrong with you, I can't help you. Miss Syryn helped me; maybe you should take the step and talk to her."

Why couldn't he see I was struggling after losing our parents? Could he really pretend from one day to the next as if they never existed? Didn't he have that burning pain in his chest that almost took his breath away when he thought about the events of the last days? That pain was pulling me into the darkness.

But when I looked into his face, I didn't see the sadness that had spread within me.

"When I'm ready, I'll talk to you, but I can't right now." I lowered my head and tried to suppress the tears that flooded my eyes.

I wanted to tell him how much grief gnawed at me and that I needed him. He just had to realize that I needed help without mentioning it; after all, he was my brother.

"Cassandra!" My name echoed through the corridor like a loudspeaker in the store. We looked up at the stairwell door before he could see my tears.

"Good morning Amara," I said, forcing a smile onto my lips. She had arrived at the right time to interrupt the awkward conversation with Lex.

Amara was like a breath of fresh air. She wore the same robe as mine, but hers was emerald green instead of black and decorated with the same golden embroidery.

"I'm so glad to see you here. I learned so many interesting things from my grimoire, and I can't wait to tell you all about it." Amara's voice trembled with joy as she stopped in front of me. "Oh hey, Lex." She looked at her boots. "I've heard a lot about you."

Her cheeks blushed with this lie. I hadn't told her much about Lex. She moved shyly to the other side of me. These were the few seconds of distraction I needed to dry my tears.

Then I remembered the grimoire. I have had no time to open the book at all.

"Um, I haven't started mine yet," I choked out, and Amara looked at me in horror.

"But that was our task until today. So maybe you can glance at it after breakfast before the training starts."

I didn't know her well, but in that short time, I noticed she was always overly prepared for everything and that missing a reading task was indescribable.

"Which grimoire?" Lex threw in and looked at Amara from the side.

"We received a book from Mrs. Nerol to help us understand our gifts better. Our task was to read it until today, but I was busy yesterday." I knew that both of them wanted to know what had been so vital that I had not even looked at it. "I was exhausted and fell asleep with the book in my hand," I said quickly and sped up.

I wanted to tell them the truth, that Rowan had dumped me, and Draven had held me against my will; it was on my tongue—but I closed my mouth.

"You must still be in shock. It took me days after my family disappeared until I could eat again," Amara quickly objected. "If I didn't have Taymon by my side, I probably would have gone crazy."

Lex looked at me questioningly.

"Taymon is her brother," I said narrowly.

Although it hurt me that Amara had lost her parents and siblings, it felt good to hear that I wasn't alone with my uncontrollable emotions. I waited for a reaction from Lex, but his expression didn't change.

"Is he younger?" He asked.

"Yes, he is the baby of the family." Amara smiled, and her eyes lit up for a moment.

I knew that feeling—that joy when I thought of Lex— but right now, he made it hard for me to like him.

"I have Mr. Adrian, and we haven't received a book from him. But he let us compete against each other, and I have to say that, unlike some others, I am doing well as a shapeshifter," Lex explained without going further into detail.

The wooden doors of the hall stood open. I walked through the hall and sat down in a free spot near where I had met Amara the first night. I knew Lex wouldn't follow me. He lived in a light-hearted world, and I needed to distance myself from him.

"Is everything okay?" Amara put her hand gently on mine.

"I don't know—my brother's acting weird. I expected him to miss our parents, too, but somehow it passed him by. And then there was the brief fight with Rowan. I'm not sure what happened," I sighed and examined the breakfast in front of us. I didn't dare to tell her about Draven.

I reached for a loaf of bread, a few slices of cheese and ham, a hard-boiled egg, and a pancake.

"Not everyone mourns the same way. Perhaps it will take him a few more days to understand what happened. Perhaps this behavior helps him to hold on to the hope that we will find it. If I were you, I'd still try to talk to him. I would be glad if I could talk to Taymon about it, but I must be strong for him." She reached for the bread and bit into it.

"How is he?" I was ashamed that I hadn't inquired about him.

"The first day was the worst. Miss Syryn pulled him aside and talked to him; since then, he has been better. I don't know what she told him, but his feelings turned a hundred and eighty degrees, and I'm glad." She reached for a piece of cake and stuffed it into her mouth. "What do you mean you had a brief fight with Rowan?" Her eyebrows raised.

"If annoying people were a sport, I would get a gold medal." I drilled my knife into the soft butter in front of me. "I lied when I said I went straight to bed. Instead, I was up with Rowan. One minute he told me the story about Teviena, and the next minute he got angry and stormed away. I thought he was a magician like you, and apparently, this accusation hurt him."

And if you had seen what his brother was capable of, you would know that he was far more dangerous than a magician—but I kept that part to myself.

I drilled around in my food, Amara quietly smacking her lips.

"I didn't expect Rowan to have a problem with his gift. But I grew up in a village with many unique gifts, so for me, it's as natural as breathing. Should I talk to him?"

I shook my head vigorously. "Don't worry. I think I have to take care of this mess myself. I'll talk to him."

Amara looked over at me, and her mouth curled.

"Excuse me. Your name is Cassandra, right?" A dark voice almost pulled me off the chair.

My pores tingled, but I calmed down in time before the transformation could begin. My eyes wandered to a boy and a girl standing behind us. Relieved, I exhaled. The deep voice had catapulted me back into the darkness of the sixth floor.

"You scared me," I replied, grabbing my chest. I couldn't stop grinning in shame at my reaction, and he also seemed embarrassed that he startled me.

A medium-sized, skinny boy stood behind me. He grabbed his neck with one hand, scratched himself, then ran his hand through his brown, ruffled hair. His clothes were the same as Lex's, but the primary color was black and patterned with blue, green, and golden embroidery. His blue eyes pierced right through me until he couldn't keep eye contact any longer and looked at the ground.

"My name is Niam Franzier, and this is my girlfriend,

Ella." During the introduction, he pointed to himself and then to the girl beside him.

Ella was a very petite person with a calm smile. Small dimples appeared on her cheeks as she smiled. There was no breeze in the hall, but her long blond hair moved like there was. Her golden eyes radiated the same calmness as her smile. Her robe and cloak were white with gold embroidery.

"Well, she's not my girlfriend. We are just friends…well…we haven't known each other long, but—" Before Niam could continue to stammer, Ella interrupted him.

"I think they know what you mean," Ella said calmly, gently reaching for his arm. "I am Ella Baltrus. We wanted to introduce ourselves because we are also in Mrs. Nerol's group. We were very enthusiastic about your exchange of words with Mrs. Nerol."

I was speechless. The conversation I had with the instructor had attracted the attention of others.

I hesitated and waited for them to go on, but both just stared at us. Apparently, it was my turn to introduce myself.

"As you already know, my name is Cassandra Kayser, and this is Amara—" I realized I had no idea what her last name was.

"Amara Hazen," she added.

"—Hazen. I must confess that I didn't notice you guys yesterday. I'm sorry. Do you want to join us?" I pointed to the empty places beside me. I sincerely hoped that they would understand my empty gesture.

Niam reached for the next chair beside Amara without hesitation while Ella gently grabbed a seat next to me.

"Okay. I have to ask you. What gift do you have? Ella and I have spent all morning guessing what it could be, but I think she's wrong. Please tell me you are a shapeshifter, and you can turn into a dragon." His eyes couldn't get any bigger while he waited for me to reveal the secret.

"Um...until now, I didn't know that shapeshifters could turn into dragons. Yes, I am a shapeshifter, but my form isn't nearly as exciting. I can turn into a lynx."

Niam lingered, his grin getting wider. "They say that cats are very rebellious, no matter how big or small, which makes so much sense." While Niam was busy figuring out where his error had been, Ella cleared her throat quietly—but not quietly enough for my sensitive hearing.

"Yes?"

"Niam couldn't stop guessing what you could be. It's a little game he plays to withdraw from reality. I'm a Light Fairy, if you haven't guessed it yet." Her dainty smile and golden eyes seemed to shine.

"I knew it!" said Amara loudly, and I started laughing.

"Am I the only one who knows nothing about Dragons and Fairies?" I shrugged my shoulders. "Being a Light Fairy suits you. Your radiance is as calm as the sun on a warm spring day. Niam, what gift do you have?" I asked hesitantly because I feared getting the same unpleasant reaction from Niam that Rowan had given me.

"You won't be able to guess my gift. My human form is the best camouflage." He leaned over the table in excitement.

"Believe me. You don't want me to guess. All these gifts are still new to me."

"What do you mean, *new*? In which village did you grow up?" Niam must have realized in my sad eyes that I didn't know what he was talking about. "You had no contact with other magical beings? Never?"

"So... We knew another pack of wolves with whom we occasionally went hunting, but otherwise, I didn't know there were other magical beings out there. I always thought the creatures in picture books were fictional." I glanced at the still full plate to avoid their surprised expressions.

"It's not your fault." Niam waved his hand. "I can't imagine not knowing anything about the Magical World. But wait, didn't you say you could turn into a lynx? So why do you spend time with wolves? Aren't you rivals like dogs and cats?"

"My mother is also a lynx, and my father and brother are wolves."

Niam's chin dropped.

"I've already explained to her it's impossible. Or maybe it's just a rumor that we can only reproduce within our gift. Who knows?" Amara shrugged her shoulders.

I swallowed. Why did no one believe me that it was possible to have different shapeshifters as parents? My family couldn't be the only one.

"It doesn't matter who your parents are and if you are a Crossling or not. The important thing is that the sparkle in your eyes is still there. Unfortunately, that light has disappeared in many children. Some of us will never get over this trauma. Others will hopefully rediscover their light when it's time," Ella applied, her calm voice smoothing my tension.

I don't know what she was talking about. I looked around at the children and teenagers surrounding us.

While I was busy healing my own mental wounds, I had not noticed that other children were struggling with loss.

A little girl with black curly, short hair and thick glasses sat close to us, and just like me, she was just playing with her food. Next to her sat a massive boy, armed with two spoons, pushing as much food as possible into his mouth as if he had not had a meal for days.

I realized what Ella meant. The light that was supposed to shine in many of these children's eyes was gone. Some children laughed, but it looked painful, and only a few seemed to have overcome the heartbreak and talked happily.

"Maybe I should accept Miss Syryn's offer and speak with her," I said.

"Trust me. She'll find you when you're ready to talk. She has already helped some children, as I have observed in the last few days. I don't know how she helps them, but it seems to work. Niam and I arrived here five days ago, and we were told we could talk to a trusted person if we needed help, or Miss Syryn would visit us personally. The last five days seem like an eternity." Ella loaded her plate. "You're a sorceress, aren't you?" She asked Amara.

"How did you know?" She sounded surprised, the corners of her mouth smiling from ear to ear.

"I've met many magicians, and the sparkle at your fingertips makes it easy to recognize you." Amara and I looked at her hands, but none of us could see the sparkle Ella had been talking about. "You probably can't see it. I always forget that only Light Fairies can see energy. As a toddler, I couldn't stand to perceive my surroundings and energies as light, but the older I get, the easier it becomes to deal with my gift and use it to my advantage."

I tried to imagine what it would be like to see energy as light. How many children in this room were glowing for her like little lightning bugs?

"Do you only see life energy and magic, or is there more?" Ella's gift fascinated Amara, and she bounced on her chair. "I read in a book that Light Fairies can turn light into objects, change colors and even create light. Are you also able to fly?"

Ella laughed, amused, put down the fork, and held her hand, with the palm-side up, in front of Amara. Out of nowhere, a small, radiant spot formed in the middle of her hand and enlarged. The point bounced in her palm. Then it stretched and swirled around her arm like a snake until the ray of light disappeared back into Ella's skin without hurting her.

"She's great, isn't she? I could watch her play with light all day." Although Niam had seen some of her tricks before, he couldn't turn his eyes away from her. "You guys have to wait a little longer to witness my gift. Maybe we should go outside after our training, and then I can show you what I'm capable of."

"I didn't know we could go outside. I would be thrilled to get some fresh air," I said.

Finally, there was something besides the training that I was looking forward to.

"Of course, we can go outside. We aren't in Bridlio."

I remembered that name. Bridlio was the prison of the Shadow Creatures, as Mr. Amaeral had explained.

I had mastered strangling down a few bites, and although the food smelled great, it tasted like paper. But I had to keep eating because I needed the energy. I stuffed my mouth full of bread and got up. "I don't want to be rude, but I must get back to my room to prepare for the training."

"We have to get going in a few minutes. How about we meet on the ground floor in 3 hours?" Niam asked and was busy piling up a sandwich made of six slices of bread.

Amara looked at me questioningly, and I nodded.

"We'll see you after training in three hours." Amara pulled on my arm.

Not long after we were out of the reach of Niam and Ella, the words just bubbled out of Amara. "Did you see the ball of light coming out of her hand? And she just smiled! How come it didn't pull on her energy? I can feel the energy draining out of me every time I use magic. It weakens me, but it looks like child's play to her."

I could fully understand her enthusiasm for Ella's gift. It was the first time I had seen someone use a gift, except for Amara and Draven. How many other kinds of gifts were out there?

"I didn't know there were people who could produce light. It was fascinating and so elegant. Now I'm curious what Niam is."

Amaras face got serious. "You know you don't have enough time to go to your room to read your grimoire. We only have 15 minutes left."

I would have had enough time to at least open the book to fly over the text if Ella and Niam hadn't shown up. But I couldn't change that. I had to go to practice and hope that Mrs. Nerol didn't get wind of it. I knew what I could do when I turned. Unlike Amara, I had no spells to memorize.

"Their interruption took longer than I expected. But I can do it. It can't get worse than the last training."

How wrong I had been with this statement.

CHAPTER
14

We stepped through the door of Hall 401, guarded by a great dragon Wedo. This time we were one of the first. Mrs. Nerol was nowhere to be seen, but a brown head of hair caught my attention, which was even more conspicuous by the light of the morning sun.

My heart started racing. It was Rowan.

I could see the rich dark red color of the new cape, which was embroidered with black. I was unsure if I should go to him to apologize for my behavior the day before or just pretend I didn't see him. But at that very moment, Rowan turned in our direction and looked straight into my eyes. Did he know what his brother had done?

"I'll be right back," I muttered to Amara, and she followed my gaze.

Stiffly, I made my way to Rowan.

"I need to apologize for my behavior yesterday—"

But Rowan interrupted me with a gesture. "You don't have to. I'm sorry I reacted so harshly. I should have known you are a newcomer to the Magical World and have many questions."

My body relaxed. I had assumed that my unnecessary speculation had started an endless quarrel.

I looked into his warm eyes, which were the opposite of his brother's dark, feral eyes.

He wore the same clothes as his brother, but his behavior was different. He gave me no reason to be afraid of him or ignore him for his brother's deed.

It couldn't hurt to have him as an ally. He knew his brother better than anyone and could probably help me.

"No, I HAVE to apologize. If I had known how sensitive the subject of gifts can be, I would never have put you in the corner like that."

Rowan's eyes flitted across my face, and a radiant smile appeared on his lips.

"What's so amusing?"

"Oh, Cassandra Kayser. There aren't many other trainees like you. Whenever I think I've figured you out, you surprise me."

My cheeks got hot, and I looked away. "Me?" I asked, puzzled, and ran my hand over my Signum, which stood out under the sleeve.

"Even though you are fighting against your own shadows, you have the power to make sure that the surrounding people are doing well. Unfortunately, most children here are so preoccupied with themselves that they completely ignore other people's feelings."

My stomach turned. He thought I apologized because I thought it was the right thing to do. But my apology was more a ticket to safety. I wanted to find out if he knew what had happened after his disappearance in the attic, plus I had no more energy to maintain this dispute.

He drove his hand through his hair. "We all have the same fate. No home to return to, and we are being trained to protect ourselves. If we don't stick together, we'll never be able to get rid of the Shadow Creatures." He stretches his arms out. "You must have had a bunch of friends at home," Rowan teased.

My skin tingled with shame. "Let's put it this way... I read many books in my spare time, whereas Lex—" I fell silent, and Rowan looked at me enthusiastically.

For a fraction of a second, images from the past appeared in my mind. I saw Lex bring his friends to our home, and they laughed loudly as our mother stood in the kitchen and cooked for everyone. Our father sat on the couch reading a newspaper while trying to ignore the loud noises. Again, I felt this numbing pain in my chest.

My gaze fell back to Rowan. "It's not important. I'm more of a loner."

"I met Lex again this morning. He seems like a pretty cool guy."

Now that we were talking about siblings, it was the perfect moment to tell him about his brother, but a loud knock stopped me. I closed my mouth.

Mrs. Nerol's narrowed eyes glanced at us as she tapped the desk with her knuckles.

"We don't meet here to chat."

I scurried between the other children, who were as disorganized as I was looking for their place, and settled down next to Amara.

"It looks like everything is fine now. But, I told you, a conversation always helps," Amara muttered with her head lowered so that Mrs. Nerol wouldn't catch her talking.

"Thank you!" I couldn't say more because Mrs. Nerol stood in front of our table.

"You all look great in your new clothes." Mrs. Nerol paused for a few seconds to look around the room and then cleared her throat. "Let's get started. First, I wanted to divide you all into your levels, but I was thinking, how about we figure out how much you learned from your grimoire?"

My mouth opened with indignation. I wanted to say something but didn't get the chance. Instead, Mrs. Nerol clapped her hands in front of her, and light flooded the room, followed by darkness.

I was prepared for the hard impact this time. Frantically, I tried to open my eyes before hitting the ground, and to my surprise, I landed gently on my paws. Unintentionally, I had shape-shifted between the loud bang of Mrs. Nerol's hands and the arrival in the dream world.

My paws were burning.

Finally, I could open my eyes, but a glare burned on my retina, so I had to blink again to get used to the brightness.

As my vision cleared, I could see dunes of red-brown sand stretch out in front of me. Grains of sand whipped around my ears, leaving me with a stabbing pain. High dunes stood out from the blue sky as far as my eyes could see.

Confused, I looked around in search of a threat or the meaning of the mission. Meanwhile, I tried to keep my hot paws out of the sand, one by one, to cool them.

Why had Mrs. Nerol sent me to a desert? I could see no danger far and wide.

Slowly, I staggered forward, my paws digging painfully into the hot sand. To my surprise, the new robe and cape had disappeared. However, they would have helped give me some shade.

My black fur seemed to absorb the high sun. I felt like

a blot on the red-brown background. I had to find a shelter because I was an easy target in the middle of the desert.

I would have preferred the rainforest with the shooter instead of fighting the sandy wind and burning my paws. Aimlessly I climbed up a dune with long jumps, but at the top, I realized that my effort had been in vain. Sand stretched for miles before me with no sign of other life or vegetation.

As if Mrs. Nerol could hear me, I screamed into the sky. "What do I have to do?" I waited for an answer or a sign, but nothing happened. I was helpless, and the heat bothered me.

One thing I knew, I couldn't stay here because the sun would take me out faster than any attacker.

With a pained face, I walked on. I would have loved to curl up in a ball instead of burying my paws in the hot sand. Instead, the sun burned my body from above, and the stored heat of the sand seemed to boil me from underneath alive.

I continued to move laboriously until I felt something under my extended claws—it was hard and gave resistance. Then, abruptly, I stopped and tried to feel the thing beneath me. Could it be a piece of stone? I pushed my paw over the rough surface to catch a glimpse of the find. A small spot was now freed from the sand, and I breathed a sigh of relief; it was a stone.

Could this be my salvation? Were there any other stones burning under me from which I could build a hiding place?

With a few vigorous movements, I dug out the stone. I stood against the slope and began digging out the sand under it. At first, I thought the stone would slide in my direction as I scraped out the sand that served as a foundation. But I was lucky; the more I exposed the stone, the greater my joy became. Finally, the rock revealed itself as a stone slab resting on two more.

I breathed a sigh of relief.

Only a few strong scratches and I had enough space to get under the stone slab to safety. My breath was uneven, and my mouth was dry. My head spun, and dizziness spread through my body. Just as I thought I would collapse from heat and effort, I pushed myself between the exposed stone slabs and settled on the cooler sand in the shadow of my new hideout. Relieved, I closed my eyes, and when I opened them again, I saw Mrs. Nerol standing before me.

I was back in Room 401. Surprised, I looked around and saw that some were still sitting on their chairs with their eyes closed while others were busy digesting their mission.

Only a few places next to me, I recognized Ella and Niam. Ella looked happy while Niam was still deep in his mission.

My head was throbbing, and my body was aching. I had assumed that the training was only taking place in our heads, but when I saw my hands, I knew that the subconscious spell was much more.

My hands were red and pulsing. I thought everything that happened in my subconscious wouldn't affect my body, but that wasn't the case.

"Are you alright?" Amara asked from the side and looked at my reddened hands.

"I wasn't aware that we could get hurt in the missions. I thought it was like a simulation."

Amara embraced my hands and cooled them with her palms.

"I realized it after our first mission. You know why my hands are so cold—the more magic I use, the cooler they get."

Amara's hands felt like ice on my warm skin. Within a few minutes, our hands had reached their average temperature, and Amara pulled her hands back.

"Thank you. My hands would still glow without you. You don't have cold feet by chance because mine could use some refreshment?" I couldn't resist a loud laugh, and Amara was amused.

In the corner of my eye, I could see Mrs. Nerol, still walking up and down in front of her desk, observing her group. "I have the feeling that not everyone has read the grimoire I handed out. May everyone who hasn't been able to complete the task I gave rise."

The whispers between the children fell silent, and I could hear the surrounding heartbeats.

No one stood up. Was I the only one who hadn't opened the book? For a few seconds, I struggled with the decision of whether I should tell the truth or stay quiet, but then I knew I had no other choice. I pushed my chair back and stood up. The whisper returned, and my ears were running warm.

I was standing there, all alone, with all pairs of eyes on me.

It didn't take long, and someone pushed a second chair loudly over the wooden floor. I didn't dare to turn around to see the second person, but my curiosity was more significant than my shame. A familiar face grinned at me.

Oh, Rowan.

Of course, he hadn't had time to read the book because he had been with me. Two more chairs were audible, and a little girl with brown hair and a blond curly boy looked anxiously at Mrs. Nerol.

Mrs. Nerol leaned against the desk. "I didn't give you the task because I wanted to punish you. I need you to learn more about your powers. We can only win the upcoming battle if we work as a team, and everyone needs to have their gift under control. Just one mistake or hesitation can cost you your life. Is that what you want?" Mrs. Nerol's gaze passed to me, then to the two children I didn't know yet, and she ended her long break while her eyes remained on Rowan. "That's what I thought. So please take it to heart that you read your grimoires. It could save your life."

The girl cleared her throat. "I started the book, but I didn't make it to the end," she whispered shyly.

"I didn't ask you to get up to make an example of you, Zarah. I want you to understand that everyone has to participate in our training and work on their gift without supervision. It can take days, weeks, or even months until we have to fight back against the Shadow World. No one knows when it will happen. But I know we can only do it as a team. Each of you has an irreplaceable gift that we will need to win. It's not about everyone fighting for themselves. You have to be able to work together as a team to be stronger. Together, you will be unbeatable."

The girl tried to avoid eye contact with Mrs. Nerol. She could be older than ten, and I tried to put myself in her position. She was one of the youngest kids I have seen in Teviena. Losing her family and trying to keep up with older children couldn't be easy.

Mrs. Nerol spoke again: "Your subconscious has shown you an environment unsuitable for your gift. This time, it was your job to get to safety by using your mind and the environment's resources. The goal of this mission was to show you that you cannot always use your gifts under ideal circumstances, as in yesterday's mission. Your powers may be useless, and you have to rethink quickly." Mrs. Nerol paused and let her words work for a few seconds.

I had not noticed that the environment had been perfect for my transformation the day before. Trees to climb, bushes to hide, and leaves on the ground to hear attackers from afar. The forest was one of the few environments where I was superior.

The desert was the opposite of what I was used to. But, until now, I hadn't considered that the place of the fight would matter.

A hand flew into the air to my left.

"Jonathan?"

"I have learned so much about my gift in the last few days, and I am glad that you are preparing us for the fight, but could you at least explain the mission to us next time before you put a spell on our subconscious?"

Jonathan was a small, skinny boy with bristly, black hair. I had seen him in the dining hall before, but I had not noticed that we were in the same group.

"I can understand the inconvenience. Of course, I would prefer to slow down your training, but unfortunately, none of us knows when we need to be ready. I am expected to prepare you as much as possible, and I have sworn that each of you will sit at the table alive at the end of the battle, so we can all celebrate together."

Mrs. Nerol had sat down in her chair and waited to see if there was an objection to her actions, but no one dared to say anything.

"I will release you now. Please take the extra time to look into your books if you haven't already. If you want to continue your training, you can find me on the first floor in the training hall. There you can prove your gifts without a spell. And if you want to compete against a person with the same gift as you, look at the color of the cape. We have given each trainee new clothing that adapts to their gift and makes it easier for you to see who you're fighting. Amara, for example, is a sorceress. You can tell by the emerald green color of her cloak. Jonathan is a shapeshifter with his black cloak. Fairies are dressed in white. There are other colors, but I won't list them all. In addition, your Signum has changed after today's mission. If there are questions, come find me in the training room, or I'll see you back tomorrow morning at the same time here."

I held my breath, hardly daring to look at my wrist. I hadn't read the grimoire, nor had I done well in the desert, but would Mrs. Nerol really demote me for that?

I exhaled when I saw the turquoise circle with the symbols. Somehow, I managed to stay at the same level and was still the group leader. I turned joyfully toward Amara, who sat silently beside me.

"Are you okay?"

Amara didn't move at first, but then she seemed to awake from a trance.

"Can you imagine living in a world where you can't use your gift? I never imagined how people can live without magic, and that's what my mission showed me. I couldn't use my magic." Amara stared into the void, and I shook my head.

"I burned my paws, literally. How can you live in the desert without trees and shadows?"

Amara looked at me and smiled.

"She sent you to the desert? And I thought my world without magic was cruel. Maybe we'll have time to check out the gym before meeting Ella and Niam."

Amara shot in the air and walked around the table until she stopped in front of Ella and Niam, who were standing expectantly in front of us.

CHAPTER
15

"What are your plans for right now?" Amara asked Ella and Niam.

I had not expected to see them again so quickly, even though I knew we were sitting in the same room during the training.

My eyes flew over their new clothes. Ellas stood out in white and gold. The golden embroidery reflected her gift as a Light Fairy well. Niam wore black and had to be a shapeshifter, but I couldn't figure out what the blue, green, and golden embroidery meant.

"We wanted to ask you the same. But, now that we have more time than we thought, should we go outside already?" Niam could hardly hide his excitement.

"I wanted to read my grimoire finally, and I also need to find my brother," I said, my eyes fixed on his colorful stitch work.

"You want to go outside?" I immediately recognized the voice and turned to Rowan, who was hidden behind Ella.

I froze. "We wanted to meet later, but maybe I can get excited about reading afterward."

Seeing him changed my mind. I didn't feel like talking to my brother, reading the book, or getting into another unpleasant situation with Rowan. I knew everything was fine between us after my apology, but his rapid mood changes scared me.

"If it's okay for you, I'd like to join?"

I looked around and hoped Niam or Ella would object, but both nodded joyfully.

"The more, the merrier," Niam said, turning to Rowan. He smiled back at him and avoided the outstretched hand Niam held out to him.

I took a deep breath. Maybe it was an opportunity to get to know Rowan better without being alone with him.

"I remember you two very well. On the day you arrived in Teviena, I was there. They sent me out to retrieve most trainees. I'm Rowan."

Niam slowly lowered his hand after he noticed Rowan wouldn't grab it. "Unfortunately, I can't recall my arrival. I only remember waking up to Miss Syryn's voice. But let's not talk about that. I need fresh air."

Niam went ahead, followed by Ella, Rowan, and Amara, and I hurried to stay close to them. We walked down the corridor, into the stairwell, to the first floor.

A large hall appeared in front of us. The interior was vast, and the ceiling was twice as high as any other floor I had seen. Ornate arches that covered a path behind them occupied two walls. Above these arches was a kind of terrace forming a second floor. But all I could see were more arches and locked doors. The wall to our right was made of hundreds of small rectangular windows that let sunlight in. I walked through the room and felt small.

"This room used to be the activity room. Down here,

the patients could play games or enjoy the sunlight through the many windows. And on the upper floor were the guards who could watch everything from above from their rooms," Rowan explained.

"How do you know so much about this building?" Ella asked tenderly, and I was glad someone had grabbed the question out of my mouth.

"My parents were very interested in old buildings, and I never thought I could use this knowledge at some point. Besides, Miss Syryn often talks about the layout of Teviena."

This hall was everything I imagined an asylum entrance would have looked like in the past and more. It reminded me of a ballroom in a castle.

A large wooden door lay in front of us as we arrived at the end of the hall. Thick iron hinges held the wood upright.

With a loud squeak, Ella opened a door leaf and stepped out into the bright sunlight. My heart jumped. I couldn't wait to smell the outdoors again. Although I had a balcony that gave me a beautiful view of the lake and the surrounding buildings, I lacked the sight of grass and trees.

I was the last to step through the door, and as the warm wind blew through my hair; I looked around contentedly.

In front of us were two staircases, which bent 180 degrees and almost touched in the middle of a courtyard. Behind the steps was a pebbled path surrounding a large fountain. A bronze statue of a woman in a long robe towered in the middle of the water. She extended her arms to both sides and held her relaxed face towards the sky with her eyes closed.

The path led back together behind the fountain, followed by a mighty tree growing into the sky.

A garden, which was separated by a few bushes and

trees as a barrier, covered the rest of the courtyard.

As I thought I had seen everything, my gaze fell on a glass greenhouse to our right.

"Now, we can show you what we discovered two days ago. But you have to promise it will stay between us," Niam whispered and walked down the stone staircase into the courtyard.

"I have no one to tell it to," I said because apart from Lex, there was no one else here I knew enough to exchange secrets with.

"I didn't even tell my sisters about it. They are here too, but too occupied with training. Did you tell anyone, Ella?" Niam turned to her, but she just shook her head.

"Unlike you, I have no siblings," Ella replied. "Don't you have a brother, Rowan?"

A gurgling sound escaped him. I realized how uncomfortable the subject was to him, and my reaction was the same as his. I could feel my hands sweating, and my mouth became dry.

"Yes, my brother Draven, but you won't see much of him because he is currently getting private training. He has a little trouble controlling his gift."

I had been in the wrong place at the wrong time. It didn't seem to me that he didn't have his gift under control because he had been quite precise when he used it on me. But it reassured me he wasn't walking around freely in Teviena.

"Looks like I could use a few private lessons myself," I said, laughing softly. "Unlike my brother, I don't have my gift under control, either," I tried to distract from the conversation about Draven.

I didn't want to think about him. Just because Draven scared me didn't mean Rowan was a ticking time bomb, just like him.

I looked at him. His amber eyes shone warm in the sunshine, while Draven's were darker than the night sky without stars. His hearty smile didn't resemble his brother's nasty grin.

I couldn't let Draven be the reason to exclude Rowan. Draven's behavior had not been his fault, and in the last few days, Rowan had proved that the well-being of the other trainees was everything to him.

"I'll join you for extra training. My siblings also know how to use their gift, and I can't even do the simplest spells." Amara added, her cheeks turning red.

"There are so many magical beings who can no longer control their gift fully. I still remember the stories of my parents when they were taught here in Teviena. They still had to protect themselves from human eyes because they still believed in magic. Nowadays, no one believes that something as powerful as me exists!" With a giant leap, Niam jumped into the air, and my breath stopped.

While Niam seemed to hang in the air, his appearance changed. His head turned into a mighty dragon's head, while his arms and legs stretched into a snake-like body. Green, blue and golden scales covered his body, and two enormous wings unfolded from his back and protruded to both sides. The tail end and the back of the head were equipped with colored feathers. Niam's sharp teeth gleamed hungrily, and his scales reflected the sun and threw small dots of light on the walls of Teviena.

I looked up at Niam, mouth wide open, who stood a good seven feet above us.

"Are you kidding me? I thought my transformation was fascinating, and now you show up, and you can turn into a winged-dragon-worm? How can you compare my gift to yours? Of course, you're much stronger than me," I screamed, hoping I was loud enough for Niam to hear me.

As soon as he had shifted back, he stood before us. "Ouch! Winged-dragon-worm? Really? Have you never heard of a Feathered Serpent?" Niam raised his eyebrows, but he could tell from my expression that I was overwhelmed. "I keep forgetting that this is all new to you."

I couldn't turn my gaze away from Niam until Amara started talking. "I have already experienced all kinds of gifts and shapeshifters, but this was something I will never forget." She also seemed to struggle to take her eyes off of him.

"Well, I hope we can keep it between us. I promised my sisters that I wouldn't turn outside the meetings, but I just couldn't suppress it to see your faces." He strutted on with a satisfied grin.

"And it's forbidden," added Ella quietly.

"It's not like you haven't broken that rule a few times to play with light," he giggled back, and I remembered the dancing ball of light in her hand.

"I can understand now why you love your gift so much," I replied, fascinated, and joined him at the fountain.

The gentle footsteps of Ella and Amara followed behind us, but another pair of feet was missing. I turned and saw that Rowan hadn't moved and was watching us.

"What are you waiting for?" I shouted in his direction and waved my hand to say he should come along.

He caught up with us in just a few steps. "I didn't expect a Feathered Serpent. I was so sure he was a gnome," Rowan whispered, laughing.

I thought for a few breaths about whether I should say it or remain silent, then I found the courage. "Now, we are the only ones who haven't shown their gifts."

My heart pounded wildly. I should have kept my mouth

shut.

Rowan's face darkened, and I regretted my decision immediately. Then his expression changed to a smirk. "Let's hope a lot of time goes by before we have to use them."

I smiled and was glad of his reaction. Of course, I wanted to know what gift he had after his brother gave me a taste of their abilities.

What gift hid behind their red color with the black embroidery? I shook my head. His gift wasn't the most important thing; he was a good person, and that was the only thing that mattered.

"Come on now! We want to show you our find," Niam cried, who was standing in front of the glass building in the courtyard.

From the entrance of Teviena, the greenhouse didn't look impressive, but I realized it had to be the same size as the hall on the first floor.

A glass dome towered in the middle of the oval metal structure. The glass was frosted, and the frame was made of bronze-colored metal.

We walked through the glass swing door and found ourselves in a room full of plants. When I entered the room, it felt like I was walking through an invisible fog. The humidity was overwhelming, and in a short time, my clothes felt damp.

Hundreds of different colored and sized flower pots filled the room. I recognized some flowers from my mother's garden, such as opium poppy, nightshade, and belladonna, but all the others were new to me.

"Welcome to the headlock. This building is called Flora, but after a few trainees couldn't stand the humidity and heat and passed out, we renamed it," Niam said, who drew the new air into his lungs with outstretched arms.

Thunder shook my eardrums, and the greenhouse seemed to get smaller. I jumped backward out of the door in one movement and landed on my paws.

"You don't have to be afraid. Flora is a very tender soul, of course, not when someone insults her." Ella gave Niam an admonishing look and extended her hand to me. "Don't listen to him. You're the best florist I've ever known and Cassandra, may I introduce... Flora. Isn't she beautiful? This greenhouse has its own soul. It takes care of the plants, waters them, and can grow almost anything you dream of."

Everyone looked at me. Fortunately, no one could see my glowing cheeks under the fur. Ashamed, I looked at the ground and grabbed Ella's hand, which led me back into the greenhouse.

"If no one else is going to say it. You look cool! When you said lynx, I imagined something small and cute, but I didn't expect you to be so big!" Niam said, and the boiling heat of shame slowly subsided.

"Says the wing-dragon-worm." I let go of Ella's hand, and everyone laughed; I could feel Rowan's piercing gaze, but he remained silent.

I shook myself, and I was back in my human form in no time. I slowly got better at turning from a lynx back to a human. And the new clothes were amazing. Not only did they disappear when I shifted, but they also came back when I turned into a human again.

"But we must hurry before someone sees us," Ella said.

Flora had calmed down. A quiet breath was audible, and I could see the movements of each window, moving them in unison with each breath.

"Two days ago, I was looking for some holly apples when Niam struggled to wait patiently on the bench." Ella pointed to a metal bench at the end of the greenhouse, surrounded by plants. "While he was sitting on the bench, he tapped his fingers on the metal bars, and to our surprise—"

Ella gently ran her hand over the metal bars of the seat and tapped on the first, third, and fifth bars, then on the fourth and again on the fifth. She took a step back, and the ground under it gave way. Then the bench turned, and the metal frame slowly sank into the ground until it was entirely swallowed.

I rubbed my eyes and walked towards the sinkhole, where a spiral stone staircase was hidden and covered in damp moss. The end of the spiral staircase was just a few feet below us. My first thought led me back to the slippery wooden staircase in the courtyard of my home. How many people had slipped on the moss and plunged into the hole's depths?

"We found a secret passage. We don't know how many trainees know about it, but it gets even better inside."

Amara clung to me, trembling. "My mother always told me about the many hiding places of Teviena, but I never thought I would ever find one of them."

The same excitement that Amara felt went through me. What could be at the end of this staircase? How many thrills could I endure in a day? Ever since I opened my eyes, the magic of a world had engulfed me.

I followed Ella, who walked down the stairs—the steps weren't slippery, to my relief. I looked into the tunnel's darkness, and at the end of the corridor, I could see blue rays of light dancing on the walls.

"What's behind this tunnel?" Amara whispered excitedly.

The bench ascended silently behind us and blocked the way to the outside and the light supply. Niam was the first to venture into the tunnel. The same discomfort that had invaded me when Rowan wanted to show me the attic rose in me again. My feline eyes had gotten used to the darkness, but I couldn't see what triggered the blue light that flooded the tunnel.

"Well, I don't want to lie. We panicked when the bench passed us for the first time and blocked the hole above us. But what we're going to show you now is the real find," Niam said, and with a loud *Tada*, he stepped out of my sight and presented a room.

It was twice as large as the room I stayed in, with moss covering the thick stone walls. Old bookshelves filled with leather-bound books stood on one wall, and an old yellowed couch with a table stood in the center of the room.

Above me was the fountain. I could see the base of the statue. How was that possible? The water, which flowed calmly and rippled over us, replaced the ceiling, but not a single drop fell on us. Instead, the sunlight reflected through the liquid and colored the room blue.

"This is breathtaking!" Amara and I said at the same time. I saw her open mouth and had to laugh.

"Right? That's what we thought, and the cool thing is that no one on the outside can hear or see us. We tested it. Ella threw rays of light at the ceiling as I tried to look through the water from above, and I could see nothing but water. Ella, however, could see and hear me. Isn't that sensational?" Niam said, dropping loudly on the sofa, stirring up dust, and coughed.

"It's so beautiful," I choked out and could finally tear my eyes away from the ceiling.

As I turned around, I could see Amara already deciphering the book's edges, and Ella quietly settled next to Niam. My eyes fell on Rowan, who had not said a single word since the courtyard.

"Is everything alright with you?" I asked softly.

The corners of his mouth went up. "Of course. There was just nothing to talk about. I had never been good at filling the silence with words." Rowan turned away from me and inspected the room.

Everything indicated no one had used this hiding place for years. A thick layer of dust covered the books on the shelves and the furniture. Next, I discovered a red carpet, which lay spread out under the table and couch.

"Look at this," Amara squealed, and before I could turn to her, she ran into me full force.

She had fished an enormous pile of books from the shelves and tried to navigate to the table. The stack blocked her sight. Amara quickly found her balance without dropping a book on the ground. She slowly lowered the books onto the table and picked up the first one.

"These are both grimoires of magicians and books about different shapeshifters. I have never seen a collection with so much knowledge. We have to show it to Miss Syryn!" Amara said, jittery to have so much spiritual capital in her hands.

I grabbed the next book and opened it carefully because the yellowed pages seemed fragile. The book was filled with various pentagrams, drawings of plants, mushrooms, and candles. It reminded me of the book I had found in my mother's room years ago.

"Although I think you are on to something, but I think we should wait. Have you wondered why these books aren't in the library? Someone deliberately left them here. Let's find out first why these books are hidden and not displayed to the public," Rowan replied soberly, looking over my shoulder at the book's contents.

"Maybe you're right. There must be a reason these books are stored here. Give us a few days to study their content, and we promise you we will hand them over to Miss Syryn afterward," Ella added, and she, too, had picked up a book and flipped through it.

"But you have to promise me we'll take good care of them," Amara replied, and everyone nodded.

Ella and Niam must not have noticed these books' value when they discovered the room. I was surprised. It wouldn't have been my first thought to check the books, either.

"I hate to interrupt, but I have to go back. How about we start reading them tomorrow? I still have to read my grimoire before Mrs. Nerol's training," I interrupted and put the book back on the table.

"I have to go back, too, to check on my sisters. But first, we should strengthen our bodies with a full plate of food," Niam said and set himself in motion.

CHAPTER
16

There were no surprises this time on the way back to Teviena, like Niam's shapeshifting or Flora's snapped breathing that made the glass structure rattle. I decided to meet up with them again in the dining hall after reading my book.

I hurried into my room and finally had time to look at my grimoire, but it wasn't as informative as I had imagined. I had hoped to find pages of the origin and the unique characteristics of the transformation, plus a complete list of my powers. But instead, it explained which senses were hypersensitive, how to hunt, and in which situations it was more skillful to master as a lynx or as a human being.

The only exciting thing about the book was that the last half was empty. I was surprised to open blank pages, but then I thought that the blank pages would fill over time because my gift had not yet fully developed.

Disappointed, I hid the book under my pillow and headed to the dining hall. Niam and Ella had taken their seats next to Amaras. I couldn't find Lex, Rowan, or Miss

Syryn, but the other instructors had joined us for dinner and sat at the round table, where the throne rested and encircled by the trainees' table.

I knew Mrs. Nerol and Mr. Amaeral, but the other faces were new.

I plopped down beside Amara. "Anyone has any idea who the other instructors are?" I whispered as I observed every movement of the strangers in the room.

"The gentleman over there with the long beard is Bertger Adrian, the oldest magician I know personally. Many students say he is 139 years old, but according to my calculations, he must be at least 167. He is a bookkeeper and deals with the history of magical gifts and beings." Amara murmured, pointing at a medium-sized man with a brown cloak. His long white hair reached his shoulder, and a white mustache danced on his face when he took a bite.

"He can't possibly be 167," I mumbled and examined him more closely. "Yes, his hair might be gray and white, but look at his face. He doesn't look older than 60."

"Believe her," Ella admitted. "I know he taught at least three generations of my family here in Teviena, and I wouldn't be surprised if there were more. The woman next to him is Chara Joyal. Be honored if you ever see her in action. The tragic story of a Qilin is that there can only ever be one of them. The second a new Qilin is born, the birthing mother dies. But that makes them even stronger," Ella said through her hand over Niam and looked at a petite woman in front of us with long, dark brown hair and a charming smile.

"I don't know what a Qilin is," I admitted.

"My mother used to describe her when I was little. She said she has a body like a deer covered in scales and has a dragon head with large antlers and blue flames as mane and tail. She said she has never seen a more beautiful being in her life than a Qilin." Niam answered while he stuffed his mouth with meat.

I almost lost my appetite as I watched him sink another fork into his mouth without swallowing.

"This sounds magical. Maybe we will see her as a Qilin one day." I tried to imagine the creature, but it didn't go well together as much as I tried to mate a deer with a dragon's head and fire.

"And that leaves us with the last instructor, Erebus Lafon, who is the opposite of Joyal. He's a Nightmare." Amara faltered. I could see goosebumps running down her arms.

"What do you mean, *Nightmare*? Is he that mean?" My eyes pierced into the profile of a young man with black, short hair and a stone-cold expression.

"No, he's *literally* a Nightmare. He can turn into a black stallion in flames," Amara explained. "My father said that his mere sight was enough to be plagued by nightmares."

With this description, the memory of the Klushund was called back into my head, which had appeared on the night of my parents' disappearance.

"Can he turn into another animal?" I asked.

If he was a shapeshifter, perhaps I was only a few feet away from the person who had harmed my family.

"I know what you're getting at, but the answer is no. He can't turn into a Klushund," Amara added. Niam and Ella looked at us with narrowed eyes.

With a derogatory gesture, I tried to stop them from asking questions about a Klushund.

"My sister Adria told me he was an inmate in Bridlio before," said Niam.

My skin began to tingle.

"That's absurd! The Saperians would never let anyone from Bridlio train the new generation. I can't imagine that's true," Amara said in horror, giving Niam a stern look.

"That's what I told her, but she was so convinced that it sounded believable," he muttered, trying to hide behind Ella to escape Amara's angry gaze.

"What are you talking about? What exactly is Bridlio, and what are Saperians?" I asked softly. All the unfamiliar words overwhelmed my brain.

"Bridlio is supposed to lie somewhere in the depths of the earth, and a powerful spell protects it so that the Oblitus can't break out. And the Saperians are the four wise men. For centuries, they have been in charge of maintaining the balance between the human and Magical World. A man, a magician, a shapeshifter, and a fortune teller. Together, they determine who is classified as an Oblitus through the magic rules and training centers. They are why everything has been so harmonious over the last few hundred years. The Saperians would never allow an Oblitus from Bridlio to be sent as an instructor," Amara muttered angrily.

"But if they are so wise, how come the Oblitus broke out?" Niam asked innocently, with a cheeky smile.

"What are you laughing about? Don't you care about the lives of our families?" Amara yelled at him and jumped from her chair. "They probably couldn't foresee it. They wouldn't let this happen on purpose! So there must be a good reason for all of this."

"A reason?" Niam pulled back his chair in anger and stood up. "Maybe they just failed? Maybe the protection spell wasn't strong enough anymore? Or maybe no one is to blame except the Shadow Creature, who was strong enough to break out of Bridlio and release other Oblitus on the way out. So where are your wise men now?"

Amara didn't like his provocation, walked up to him, and both stood forehead to forehead in front of each other.

"I think that's enough for today," said a deep, loud voice, and both Amara and Niam took a step back.

Their loud argument had attracted the attention of the whole hall. I had tried to silence them by clearing my throat loudly, but they were too agitated to notice. Finally, Amara lowered her head, and Niam tried to squeeze into his chair as he looked into Mr. Lafon's eyes with an anxious look.

It was quiet enough in the room to hear my heart beating.

"We are very sorry," Amara choked out, and she also sat down in the chair next to me without lifting her eyes from her plate.

Niam didn't dare to speak at all and continued to look into the reddish pupils of Mr. Lafon.

"After such a performance, I would have expected more backbone from you, Mr. Franzier, and I am quite surprised by you, Miss Hazen. I didn't assume you had the temper for an altercation with a shapeshifter." His crisp voice went through us like a machete.

Amara's nostrils trembled with rage. I couldn't tell if she was still mad at Niam or if Mr. Lafon's speech had made her upset.

"It won't happen again," Niam said, his voice shaking.

"You better hope it won't." Mr. Lafon smiled and looked down at me. "I thought you'd be able to control your friends better, Miss Keyzer. After all, I have heard that you are the shapeshifter with the temperament."

My cheeks flushed, and my stomach turned.

How did he know my name, and why did he assume I was the hothead? Until a few minutes ago, I didn't even know he existed.

My skin itched, and I fought against my transformation with all my strength. I couldn't let him win. If I changed now, it would support his statement.

"That's enough, Erebus," said Mrs. Nerol, standing next to him. "I don't believe these poor children need a scolding after all they've been through in the last weeks."

Mr. Lafon strutted back and forth in front of us; then, he walked back to the small opening in the table to get to his chair. "You used to understand fun, Alysa. These kids make you soft." He sat in his chair with a broad smile plastered over his face and returned to his plate.

"Next time, it would be wise for you not to carry out your discussions in public," Mrs. Nerol said to Amara and Niam before walking off.

My fingers hurt. I had drilled my fingernails into the chair to escape my transformation by the breadth of a hair.

I had lost my appetite once and for all. We stormed out of the hall without looking back.

"I'm sorry, Amara," Niam apologized. "I shouldn't have reacted so impulsively and challenged you."

Amara's cheeks were still red, and she didn't dare to look up.

"It wasn't your fault. I am going to crawl into my bed now and leave this day behind. Tomorrow is a new day with a fresh start," Amara said and strolled past us to get to her room.

"Should I come with you?" I called after her, but she just shook her head and disappeared into the door to the stairwell.

"Seriously, Niam? What were you thinking?" Ella frowned, but her voice was tender and loving even as she tried to sound upset.

"I didn't know she would react like that. I had so much tension built up, and I didn't intend to let it out on her. The last few weeks have been the hardest of my life. Every day I have to explain to my sisters that we will find our parents, and I am not even sure if this day will ever come. But if I don't take our current situation with a pinch of humor, I won't be able to look into the sad eyes of Kira and Adria and tell them that everything will be fine."

Tears formed in his eyes. The grief he felt was the same that was seething in me. This emotion brought us together and made me feel like I had known Niam much longer.

"I'm so sorry about your parents. Do you want to talk about it?" I said, but I was sure that this vulnerable moment was only short-lived if I assessed him correctly.

"I am okay, just worn out. Thank you, though. I'll see you tomorrow, and you better don't tell anyone that I was close to tears. Winged-dragon-worms don't cry," Niam replied, laughing as he used his new nickname.

"We all should rest. We will straighten everything with Amara tomorrow. What a day! I will see you guys tomorrow morning," said Ella as she walked away.

She was right: *What a day!*

I didn't notice how I got to my room and into my bed in pajamas.

As the event from the last few hours rushed through my head, I hoped Lex would still knock on the door. I waited for his arrival for some time and didn't notice how my eyes slowly closed until sleep overwhelmed me.

CHAPTER
17

The first thought that ran through my mind when I opened my eyes was that I had missed Lex's knock. I rushed to get ready for the day and hammered at his door.

"Come in," cried his familiar voice, and I entered. "I didn't expect you to be here this early." He looked past me to see if I was alone, and disappointment ran over his face. "How is it going?"

His usual smile raised the corner of his mouth. I had missed that expression more than I wanted to admit. Never had I seen my brother so grown up as I did at that moment. He wore his new vest and cape with pride and reminded me of our father.

"I feel better. I see you are doing well. How's your training going?"

My legs were still tired from the last training session. Finally, I dropped onto a chair that stood next to the bed.

Lex stopped in the middle of the room. "Mr. Adrian is pretty good. I thought it would be boring because he is about two hundred years old, but now I feel he is the best instructor. He let us fight yesterday. You should have seen me, Cas."

He spread his legs and raised his hands as if fighting a ghost.

"Mr. Adrian muttered a few words, and suddenly our doppelgängers were standing in front of us, and I had to compete against myself! Do you know how hard it is to fight someone who knows all your tactics and has the same strengths as you?" He punched into the air and threw his hands up in victory.

"That sounds pretty hard, if not impossible. I hope I don't have to do that," I admitted, trying to imagine my chances of fighting myself.

"But I've heard Mr. Lafon is very strict with his trainees. It would be fascinating to have him as an instructor," Lex added, and an icy shiver ran over my body.

Did Lex mean the same Lafon I met at dinner? The man with the stone-cold face and who can go up in flames?

"Have you met him before?" I asked.

"I met him casually in the hallway. A guy from my clique, Anders, has him as an instructor, and he said that yesterday, in the middle of the night, he appeared in his room as a Nightmare, and Anders had to fight him before he could continue sleeping. Isn't that a terrific idea? I would have torn him to pieces."

I was stunned. "Terrific? I would have been frozen in fear. His transformation sounds dark."

Our eyes met, and his excitement subsided when he saw my facial expression. He strolled towards me, pulled me to my feet, and hugged me.

"What did I do to deserve this?" I tried to resist his embrace, but it felt good. That's exactly what I needed.

"I know you, Cas. I hope you know I'm always here for you. Soon we will be strong enough to take up the fight against the Oblitus and bring our parents back. We'll find them, I promise you," Lex murmured, and I embraced the hug, warmth rising inside me.

This was the brother I knew—the caring big brother who always supported me.

I opened my mouth to tell him about the encounter with Draven, but a loud bang interrupted me. We jumped into the air and landed in our animal forms on the floor. Someone had knocked the door open, and it had slammed against the wall with full force. It stood wide open and showed the bewildered faces of the three boys.

I recognized two of them immediately. They had been standing next to Lex during our argument at breakfast a few days before. Both were muscular and tall. A loud laugh escaped my throat as I looked into their faces. You didn't have to be a genius to see that both had only muscles and no brain.

The right boy stood a little bent forward, and his arms hung limply down as if they were too heavy for him. The boy's posture to his left was the exact opposite. He looked fluffed up as if he was expecting to be involved in a fight at any moment. The third boy standing behind them didn't seem to fit into the picture. He was half a head taller than the other two and made a bright impression. His limbs seemed to be neither limp nor under constant tension.

"Did we disturb you?" The boy to the right asked with a hollow voice.

"What are you talking about, Mono?" Lex replied angrily, turning back into his human form. "You're talking about my sister here!"

Mono pulled his head in and looked at the ceiling while the other boy continued to ram his elbow into his side like he didn't understand what Lex had said.

"Wipe that stupid smile off your face, Erik! Don't you

remember my sister?" Lex asked the boy with his exaggerated posture.

"You could have told us she was your sister. I thought she would be another wolf and not a lion," said Erik, and I couldn't stop laughing.

"A lion? Have you ever opened an animal book? She's not a lioness! Can't you see that she's a lynx?" Lex cried in horror and pointed at me with both hands. I leaned over the chair, chuckling, and was about to fall to the floor laughing.

"I didn't know there is a difference between a lioness and a lynx. I assumed that all big cats are called lions."

"You thought that all big cats were called lions? You have far greater problems than preparing for a fight." Lex shook his head and turned to me. "I wanted to introduce you to some of my new friends differently, but here they are. May I introduce to you Anders, Mono, and Erik. Anders has hit the jackpot and has to fight Mr. Lafon, isn't that right?" Lex drove around and looked at him in a challenging manner.

"Believe me, Lex, it's not as great as you make it sound. I could hardly sleep last night because I had the feeling that he would come back to my room. Luckily, I don't need much sleep as a gargoyle, but I'm pretty upset," the boy behind Mono replied, stepping forward.

His black outfit and the cape were now visible, which were covered with gray embroidery. Mono wore the same emerald color as Amara, while Erik was dressed in gray with brown.

"Don't butter it down. Who wouldn't want to compete with his instructor to see what you can do?" Lex said, and everyone looked at him in amazement. "I mean, we are here to learn something. That won't happen if we have to compete against weaker children all the time."

I shook my head vigorously as I pressed my hands against my cape. I could list hundreds, no, thousands of things I would rather do than fight Mrs. Nerol.

With a confident smile, Lex pushed past his friends into the hallway. "If anyone wants to join me, food is this way."

The boys joined his pack leader without hesitation, but I stopped. "I'll be right there!" I screamed after him and waited for an answer that never came.

CHAPTER
18

I I stayed in his room for a while because I couldn't decide if I should go to breakfast to see my new friends or sneak back to my room to take a few more minutes before Mrs. Nerol unleashed the next training on me.

Then I had an idea.

I hurried through the corridor into the stairwell, stumbled down the stairs to the first floor, and ran through the immense reception hall without seeing another soul. Once outside, I breathed. The sun threw warm rays of light in my direction.

I made my way to Flora. The gravel crunched under my boots, and I could hear the water rushing from the fountain. I had almost arrived at the greenhouse when I stopped.

"What are you doing out here so early in the morning? Shouldn't you be sitting in the dining room?" A voice said from afar.

I turned, but there was no one. Then, finally, something

moved under the tree beside the fountain.

"I could ask you the same thing," I replied, smiling as Rowan approached me.

How could I have compared him to Draven?

His brown hair wasn't styled and waved in the wind. He fixed me with his warm eyes, and my cheeks glowed. Where was my fur to cover up my embarrassment when I needed it?

"Judging by your grumbling stomach, you can't tell me you ate already."

With this detail, I knew his hearing was as precise as mine.

"It has more to do with my sensitive stomach than hunger," I replied quietly and looked into his honey-colored eyes. "How did you know I could hear you from the tree?" I asked in surprise.

"It was more suspicion than knowledge. Everyone knows that a lynx has good hearing," Rowan answered, circling me. I knew this behavior, sneaking around like I was prey.

"Apparently, good hearing is a trait we both possess."

Rowan paused. I could see in his face that he was punishing himself for his mistake. He shouldn't have heard me being so far away, but he did.

"I wanted to go into the hiding place to see if there was a book about Bridlio, the Oblitus, or the Saperians. Since I didn't grow up in the Magical World, I still have a lot to learn," I said. "What brings you here? We missed you at dinner last night."

I wasn't sure if the others had missed him, but I had noticed his absence and that of Lex and Miss Syryn.

"I come here every morning. The sun reminds me how much some people take it for granted that they can feel it. I wanted to come to dinner last night, but my brother needed me."

When he spoke about his brother, I jerked involuntarily. His eyebrows tightened, and he looked at me questioningly.

"You know him?"

Panic broke out in me, and my voice trembled. "Umm… I have seen him in the newspaper's photograph back at home." An innocent smile spread across my lips to cover my lie.

I tried to stay as close to the truth as possible. I had seen Draven in the picture, but it didn't look like him anymore.

"You are afraid," he breathed, his gaze clinging to my eyes.

"I'm not," I replied, trying to resist his gaze.

"Then why is your heart racing?"

I grabbed my chest as if I could stop my heartbeat with my bare hands.

Rowan knew something was wrong. I couldn't keep it a secret any longer.

"I met him in the hallway when you left me in the attic," I said hesitantly, waiting for his reaction.

His face developed from a joyful smile to a questioning expression to a grim shake of his head.

"Why didn't you tell me about it?"

"I was scared," I admitted, and my body relaxed. Finally, I could tell someone about it. It had gnawed on me like a mouse on cheese.

"Did he do anything to you?" He asked, his eyes sparkling angrily, but his voice was soft and worried.

I thought for a moment. Physically, no, besides touching my hair, but mentally he had left his trace in my consciousness.

"He frightened me," I said cautiously.

His nostrils flared. This was the moment I could tell

Rowan everything about the night. The stalking, the manipulation of my consciousness, his threat that I should stay away from shadows. But I decided against it. It was something between Draven and me, and I wanted to do everything to keep Rowan out of it.

Rowan was a good person—deep inside, I knew that.

"Would you rather continue to enjoy the sun or help me find some answers?" I asked slowly.

"Are you sure you want me there?" His voice was in pain.

"Of course!" I smiled at him and turned toward Flora.

After a few breaths, I looked over my shoulder and saw him following me. We walked through the glass door together and greeted Flora, who quietly hummed back at us.

"Can I help you with your brother?" I was determined that I had to bury my fear of him. Draven was just a trainee, like all of us.

"Draven? Thanks for asking, but you can't help me with him. He's just in a difficult phase of his life right now. I promise he'll never get close to you again," Rowan murmured as we arrived at the bench.

The bad feeling that I could be the trigger for a fight between the siblings pulled me down. I didn't want to tell on Draven, but it was his own fault. He had crossed a line that was inexcusable.

I closed my eyes, took a deep breath, and focused on what I was trying to do. Then, with steady hands, I pressed on the metal bars Ella had used the day before, and the bench opened the passage into the deep.

"What are you doing?"

I startled around and looked into the piercing blue eyes of a girl. Her black, long hair was tied to a braid. She was shorter than me by almost a head.

"It's not what it looks like," I said, not knowing how I could explain to this girl why we were now standing in front of a sinkhole in the greenhouse.

"It looks like a secret passage to me. Where does it lead?" The girl peered past Rowan and me into the darkness below us.

"You're Viera, aren't you?" Rowan asked calmly, trying to block her view.

"Viera Fosmire, seventeen years old, and I assume you lost your parents just like I did," Viera said, continuing to examine the ground.

I frowned. I have never heard anyone introducing themselves with their age included. It reminded me of speed dating; not that I had ever done anything like that, but that's how I had seen it on a TV show.

"You startled me!" I tried to find an excuse, but the dark hole behind me made it difficult. How are we supposed to talk our way out of this?

I could hear the bench behind me that had given up waiting for us moving back to its rightful place.

"I know Teviena has secret passages, and I also know that my gift is useless against the Oblitus. That's why I've been trying to find a good hiding place for the fight. You probably think I'm a coward, but I am the opposite. I just can't fight." Viera talked so fast that I had trouble understanding her.

Rowan smiled. "I don't think you're a coward. How about you show Cassandra what your gift is?" He said, stepping away from us.

Viera reached her hand out to me, and I retreated anxiously. I tried to remember Mrs. Nerol's words about the colors of the cloaks, but she had not mentioned navy blue with turquoise embroidery.

With a swift motion, Viera grabbed my wrist and stared

at me. I held her eye contact and waited for something to happen—Nothing.

"Well… I am not sure what we are waiting for. I don't know what your gift is. Why don't you grab Rowan's hand and show it to us? But actually, I don't want you to touch him because—" I snatched my arm away and slammed my hands on my mouth.

I looked at Viera in horror, who shrugged her shoulders. A heat surge rushed through my body, flushing my face. My eyes raced over Rowan's face, and his amused grin and my hope that he hadn't heard my last sentence evaporated.

"I know, I know. It's not easy to deal with this gift. Unfortunately, not everyone can handle the truth," Viera explained and put on turquoise gloves, which she had removed from a bag of her cloak.

"You can only tell the truth?" I asked in shock and rubbed the spot on my wrist where Viera's hand had rested a few seconds ago. "But it's not contagious, is it?"

"Of course not." Viera laughed. "But it wouldn't be so bad if it were. Imagine a life without lies? Doesn't that sound great? If everyone had to speak the truth, there would be no secrets. I am an open book. You can ask me anything, and I must answer truthfully. I can also make other people speak the truth through physical contact."

Did a girl who can not lie catch us taking a secret tunnel? How would the others react if they found out about it?

"You knew about her gift?" I asked Rowan in disbelief.

"As I said, I've attended the introduction of most of the trainees. Many don't remember me, but I never forget a face."

"Why didn't you tell me she was in the room before I revealed this?" I pointed at the bench in front of us.

"In his defense, I must confess that I saw you all disappear into this tunnel yesterday, but I didn't know how to address you," said Viera before Rowan could speak.

At least it wasn't my fault that someone else knew about the tunnel. But I had to tell the others anyway because there was the danger that Viera could expose our special room.

"You don't have to be afraid. Your secret is in good hands with me. I know I can only tell the truth, but I can twist the truth to my desire. And I can assure you that I'm good at saying what's going through my head without going into answering a question. I don't have a filter, so to speak. Speaking of which, did I just catch you two doing something nobody should know about?"

The grin on her face widened. I didn't know what she was referring to. Then it hit me.

"Oh, no! We didn't sneak out of Teviena to be alone! We just happened to meet in the courtyard, and then we wanted to—" I stopped in the middle of the sentence because I didn't want to reveal what was in this secret passage.

My cheeks glowed, and I tried to avoid Rowan's gaze. How did I put myself in an uncomfortable position again? It shouldn't be hard for me to tell her he isn't even a friend. He is just a boy who tried to help me understand the Magical World, no more and no less.

"So you're telling me he is still available? That's good to know." Viera turned to Rowan, who was still watching me as I tried to get out of this mess.

I wanted to know what made him smile. Had it been my statement that I didn't want a stranger to touch him, or was it about my attempt to keep our hiding place secret, although both of us knew she had watched us the day before?

"Why aren't you helping me?" I asked desperately and threw my hands up in the air.

"Because it's much more exciting to watch you," he replied. "How about we go back inside and talk to the others? Which instructor do you have?" He addressed his last question to Viera while we moved towards the entrance hall.

"At first, I had Mr. Lafon, but after it turned out that my gift didn't make me a fighter, I got Miss Joyal. I could have told him right away that it wasn't a good idea to accommodate me with shapeshifters. After touching two children, they expressed their fears loudly in front of the entire group and then sat in their seats like a pile of misery. Mr. Lafon had difficulty finding a suitable opponent after that. Shapeshifters and their fear of failure," Viera shook her head and saw my unpleasant facial expression, "Darn. You also wear a black robe, so you're one of them. I didn't mean that all shapeshifters are wimps." She held her breath.

I squeezed a smile on my lips and hoped that I had not just betrayed myself. The fear of failure was an enormous part of me. Viera wasn't wrong with her assumption that I had concerns about my shapeshifting. But it would destroy me if everyone in our group knew about my fear.

"By the way, I am Cassandra." I thought about adding my age as she had done before, but it seemed strange to me, so I left it out. "Weren't you afraid of Mr. Lafon?"

"You mean because he's a Nightmare? Why should I be afraid of him? Of course, I have a lot of respect for him because he could harm me within seconds with his hooves, but everyone in Teviena could defeat me, so it's not worth worrying about who could be dangerous."

Viera had a point. She couldn't protect herself with her gift, but maybe there was a solution.

"I don't know if you were there when Mr. Amaeral gave us the lecture on the Shadow World. But he said that some trainees could have another gift. My friend Amara is very well-read. Maybe she can help you so that you aren't defenseless," I said, wondering what Amara would think of including Viera in our group. Maybe that would distract her from the fact that she had seen our hiding place.

She tilted her head. "Miss Joyal started teaching me tricks with a long stick, but I'm not very talented. I'm pretty sure I don't have a second gift."

"How do you know about Mr. Lafon?" Rowan cut in, and his gaze rested on me.

"It's a long story, but yesterday at dinner, there was an argument between Amara and Niam, which was interrupted by Mr. Lafon. He made no secret that he knows each of us by name," I explained briefly, and the red eyes of the instructor appeared before my eyes. I shook my head to shake the image away.

"You just asked Viera if she fears him. Are you afraid of him?" Rowan continued and kicked some pebbles out of the way as he walked towards the steps of Teviena.

"I was told that a Nightmare is a black stallion with flames. So, of course, that sounds a little scary." I kept silent about the part where his shapeshifter form reminded me of the Klushund and caused the feeling of panic and fear in me. "It sounds dark in contrast to the other shapeshifters I have met so far."

Rowan just nodded, and we went up the stairs and into the entrance hall.

What was he referring to? Was there a connection between Mr. Lafon's and his gift? Were he and Draven Nightmares too, and his brother's abilities were just a tiny facet of the gift?

"Not every shapeshifter you meet will be as beautiful as

Niam. Prepare yourself for the fact that there are also threatening creatures with good hearts. Maybe you shouldn't listen to people who put such nonsense in your head." Rowan's eyebrows were scrunched together, and I knew this conversation was no longer about Mr. Lafon.

"I don't want to interrupt you, but it's very unpleasant to listen to you guys as the third wheel," Viera said.

I had forgotten that Viera was our problem that we had to solve. "I'm sorry," I replied narrowly because I was still trying to figure out why Rowan didn't just tell me what it was all about.

"Where can we find this, Amara?"

I scratched my chin. "That's a good question. Let's try it in her room. Promise us you won't tell anyone about what you saw in the greenhouse," I begged her. I wasn't sure if we would find Amara in her room, but it was my best guess.

"I can't promise it 100 percent, but I will do my best," Viera replied and stretched out her gloved hand at me to shake on it, and hesitantly I grabbed it and shook it gently.

Rowan walked silently next to us, stopped, looked up at the ceiling, and sped up. "I have to go. Hopefully, we'll see each other later, Viera and—" he shouted over his shoulder as he disappeared into the stairwell.

"We just assume that he meant Viera and Cassandra," Viera added, looking at me.

"Certainly," I replied in confusion because I wanted to know the rest of the sentence. "What do you call your gift? There must be something shorter than a person-who-can-only-tell-the-truth?" I asked to distract from the subject of Rowan.

"I'm a fortune teller, and of course, the people who tell the future say the same about their gift. So we're both fortune tellers in that aspect. But I am called a Soothsayer, while the others are called Diviners," Viera explained as we climbed the stairs to the fifth floor.

"I didn't know there were two kinds of fortune tellers, but I can't be used as a yardstick for magical knowledge, anyway. Amara should know."

Silver statues were distributed in front of the doors. Amara had shown me where to look for the room numbers, and I remembered her number was 507. I scanned the Wedos until I stopped in front of a Griffin.

The eagle's head looked directly at the door in front of it, while the lion's body was ready to jump with its wings pressed close to it.

"Ok, no matter what happens, please give me a few minutes to explain to Amara what is going on before you talk," I warned Viera.

"I'll do my best."

What if Viera went ahead of me and revealed that she knew about the secret hiding place? Actually, she knew nothing about the hiding place; she only knew that there was a hidden staircase in the greenhouse, nothing more. But that was bad enough.

I held my breath and walked toward the door.

CHAPTER
19

My heart was racing as I knocked on the wooden door. It opened with a squeak, and I entered. It was the first time I saw Amara's room.

A thick mist lingered in the room. I walked on flat grey stone, and I could see the chalk markings of a pentagram. Besides the bed stood a chest of drawers, a wardrobe, and a small table covered with plants, herbs, and candles, and of course, two filled bookshelves were on one wall.

Amara sat on the floor in the middle of the fog, concentrating on a book with Ella and Niam.

My heart almost jumped out of my chest. I had assumed Amara was alone and that I only had to explain to her the betrayal of the hiding place, and then we would tell the others about it together. But now, all three looked in my direction. There was no going back.

"Where were you at breakfast today, and who's that behind you?" Niam asked in surprise, jumped on his legs, and tried to wipe the chalk from his cloak.

"I didn't expect you all to be here. Well… it's a funny

story... When I wanted to make my way to breakfast, I changed my mind and instead—"

Viera interrupted my trembling voice. "I watched you all disappear into a hole in the greenhouse yesterday, and this morning Cassandra and her handsome boyfriend were trying to sneak back down there."

I threw my hands into the air and moaned. Viera had put these sentences down so quickly that I hadn't even had the chance to object. What happened to the plan that I would explain the situation? What should I say to make it better?

Amara blinked in disbelief, while Ella smiled kindly. Niam was already on his way in our direction to get a better view of Viera.

"You didn't show up for breakfast because you secretly met with Rowan?" Ella asked with a grin.

"What makes you think Rowan is the handsome friend?" Niam asked her, and his mouth turned down. He dropped his shoulders when he saw the scolding look of Ella, who didn't go further into detail.

"We didn't sneak around, and I didn't meet him secretly. I met Rowan in the courtyard as I tried to get some fresh air. Unfortunately, Viera caught us while we were opening the tunnel. I'm so sorry," I replied, looking at my boots.

"I am Viera!" She waved innocently at the others. I tried to suppress an eye roll. Her timing was something she had to work on.

"Um... I don't think it will be a problem if another person knows about it. But Viera, promise us not to tell anyone," Amara said after a long break.

"Viera is a fortune teller," I burst out.

"How cool is that? You can see the future?" Niam was still making circles around her, who tried to ignore him.

"I'm not a diviner. I'm a soothsayer. Keeping my words to myself is tough, and I can't lie."

Silence set in.

That was the moment I had been waiting for, the realization that our secret space would soon be less of a secret if she spilled the beans.

"You can't lie? Not at all? Not even a little lie like, I didn't watch you yesterday?" Amara inquired and drew closer.

"I totally watched you one hundred percent yesterday," Viera replied.

I could hear the wild heartbeats in the room.

"But she can do something cool. Show them," I begged Viera, pointing to her hands.

Reluctantly, Viera took off a glove and put her hand on Amara's shoulder, who didn't dare to step away. "And now what?" Amara asked, tapping her foot on the ground.

"Amara, what is your greatest fear?" I murmured, and we didn't have to wait long for the words to gush out of Amara.

"Heights, of course! Have you ever looked from your balcony into the depths of the waterfall? Who wouldn't be afraid? I've been avoiding the balcony for days. And the open sea. Just the thought of all the undiscovered creatures lurking in the water, not to mention crabs, with their long, spider-like legs. Oh…" Her eyebrows tightened, and she stopped talking. "You can make other people tell the truth?" Amara withdrew from the hand that was resting on her shoulder. "How about we all forget what I just said and start over? I have no fears."

Laughter rang through the room. For a few seconds, everyone forgot about the elephant in the room.

"Oh, how rude of us. We forgot to introduce ourselves. I'm Amara, and these are our friends Ella and Niam. Do you have any siblings here?"

My heart calmed down—Viera's gift guided us further away from the hiding place matter.

"Could you imagine what it would be like if more children here had my gift? It's difficult to make friends if you aren't able to lie or keep your mouth shut." Her voice was shaking. "I won't be a thorn in your eyes. I promise I will try to keep your secret."

"You can stay with us, right?" I searched their faces for an answer.

Although I initially wanted to get rid of Viera, I felt sorry for her. It took me seventeen years to find friends that accepted me for who I am. I had never had friends or a boyfriend, but that was my choice in the Human World. It wasn't Viera's fault for her loneliness. I could change her situation and offer her my friendship.

"I brought Viera here, not because I wanted to know your darkest secrets, but because we need your help," I said to Amara. "Viera has no way to protect herself from an Oblitus other than to tell the truth. So I thought you could help her figure out if she might have another gift she doesn't know about yet?"

Amara wrinkled her forehead. "I've read in a book that they tested the former trainees in four categories to find out if they had more than one gift before being assigned to a Quarter here in Teviena. Transformation, magic, elementary science, and dark magic. They tested magic with magic spells and potions. Elementary sciences include the gifts of the elements: fire, water, earth, and air. Ella is an obvious example of an elemental gift. Dark magic was a tightrope walk. Many beings such as the Nightmare, Vampires, Werewolves, Sirens, and more have been called dark. All of them had to pass a test of good-naturedness in order to be classified as harmless. But some couldn't master it and were classified as dangerous. The worst of the worst are in Bridlio; others could be guided on a righteous path with the right training. I see no problem with why we can't test Viera. But I won't touch dark magic," said Amara, trying to find the right book on her shelf. "Here it is!" She grabbed a thick book and found the right page in no time. "As I have already said, it should be easy to find out if Viera has another gift."

I grabbed the book and looked over the delicate handwriting.

"Don't you think we should discuss it with an instructor? After all, it's their job to prepare us," Niam objected hesitantly.

He had a good point. Unfortunately, I got lost in the idea that we had to master everything on our own, that I had completely forgotten that there were instructors who could help us.

"How about we ask Mrs. Nerol after our training? Maybe those tests still existed when she used to be an instructor," I thought aloud and laid down the book.

"Can you imagine how terrible it must have been when a trainee took the test and it came out that he had dark magic?" Ella said, clinging to her heart.

"Do you think there are trainees here right now who have dark magic? We could be sitting in a room with them during our training, not even knowing." Niam looked at each of us.

No, this thought had not occurred to me because until a few days ago, I was unaware that there was a completely different world besides my everyday life. Would Syryn allow children with black magic to live under this roof?

"None of us have dark magic, and so far, I have met no one who shows any signs of it," Amara muttered, deep in thought.

I swallowed. What if I had dark magic and didn't know about it? Is that why my parents kept me away from the Magical World so I wouldn't end up in Bridlio? But I couldn't remember anything that pointed out that I could be evil. I had always followed all the rules and had done nothing wrong. Maybe telling a little lie here and there, but that was it.

Did Draven have black magic? It certainly matched his character, but I pushed the thought aside.

Viera reeled me back in. "Amara is right. Miss Syryn would never allow it. And to come back to your idea, we could ask Mrs. Nerol. Worst-case scenario, I have no other gift, and then I can hide in your tunnel if it comes to a fight," said Viera and turned towards the door. "I'd love to keep talking to you guys, but I can't be late for my training with Miss Joyal. My room number is 511 if you want to find me later. I can already tell you that my room is boring compared to this one." Even before we could say goodbye to her, she had already slipped out of the door.

"I like her," said Ella, looking for her boots, which she had spread on the floor.

"I am still very sorry that I gave away our hiding place. I hope it will remain a secret. But, luckily for us, she doesn't know what's under the bench." The feeling of guilt rose again in me and made my heart race.

"It wasn't your fault. Viera saw us all yesterday, activating the bench. Don't worry. There could also be other people already knowing about it before we even found it. We stumbled over it by chance," Niam replied, and a stone fell from my heart; they weren't angry with me.

"We'll find a way to help her. The idea of being completely helpless despite being gifted is scary," added Ella as she slipped into her boots. "But we also have to get going to avoid being late. Come on, come on!"

CHAPTER
20

Mrs. Nerol was waiting impatiently for us as we stepped through the door of Room 401.

"I am glad you have decided to join us," she growled.

I looked at an old wall clock. We were one minute late. One!

"As some of you already know, I had the privilege of training some of your parents before Teviena was closed. To be accepted to attend Teviena, each person had to pass several tests. Now that I know your strengths and weaknesses, we must consider that some of you might have another gift."

It couldn't be a coincidence that Mrs. Nerol spoke of the tests a few minutes after I heard about them for the first time. Did someone eavesdrop on our conversation?

Frightened, I looked at Amara and could read the discomfort in her face, apparently experiencing the same uncomfortable feeling.

"That's why I decided today's training will consist of testing each of you. So, who wants to start?" Mrs. Nerol looked through the rows of children, but no one moved.

"No volunteers? Then I'll start here." She looked at a little boy I had previously noticed passing by in a corridor. His hands trembled as he tried to smooth out his white pants after getting up.

If I was right, his color indicated that he was a Fairy. From the blue embroidery, I was pretty sure that his element must be water, but I could be wrong.

"I've asked Miss Syryn to keep you company so you don't get bored. Please behave!"

Mrs. Nerol stepped out of the room with the distressed boy, who kept looking back at us.

Just as the door locked behind them, Miss Syryn stepped out of a dark corner into the light. "What a beautiful morning." She looked through the window into the blue sky. "Today, I have the honor of testing you personally. I've heard a lot about each of you. A few weeks ago, I was chosen by the Saperians as head of the Teviena Training Center to prepare you for the battle against the Shadow World. Today you will learn two important things: First, Mrs. Nerol will determine if you have more than one gift, and second, you will learn how to compete against your own abilities. Every Oblitus has an extraordinary gift like you, and just like your gifts, it differs from person to person. Many Oblitus will have a gift combined with dark magic as they have been classified as dangerous. The training against the dark magic will follow in a few days. Until then, you will be busy perfecting your gifts so that you are well prepared. I will use a subconscious spell for this training. Your job is to defeat your doppelgänger."

Lex's words shot through my head. Mr. Adrian had also let him compete against his doppelgänger. When Lex told me about it, it sounded so easy. But it was my turn to face a version of myself. I felt sick to my stomach.

Miss Syryn grabbed a large black stone tied around her neck with a silver necklace. Bright rainbow colors radiated from it. The stone seemed to glow, and before I could inspect it, I stood in a forest.

I was getting better at this. This time, I didn't fall off my chair or on all fours to catch myself.

I picked up the sweet smell of pine needles and the sound of a woodpecker. A scratching noise made me turn around in a flash, and I could feel the hair sliding through my pores. Then, even before I could transform, something heavy fell onto my shoulders and pushed me to the ground. The impact of my back on the root-covered ground made me cry out in pain.

Frantically, I tried to push the weight off my body and open my tear-covered eyes. Finally, I got a hold of something fluffy and pulled on it, my teeth crunching with effort.

I forcefully opened my eyes and stared into two green, glowing dots. Black fur surrounded the eyes, and white pointed fangs sparked bloodthirsty above me. Large claws dug into my chest and made me groan in pain.

I crossed my arms over my chest to brace myself against the beast that was about to bite my throat.

Then something unexpected happened.

The crushing weight disappeared when I was convinced to feel a firm bite on my tender neck. I had shape-shifted, but my transformation had given me a kind of energy surge that hurled the attacker a few feet into the air, away from me. I took this opportunity to bring myself to all fours and looked after the black fur ball, which landed gently on velvet paws in front of me.

There it was—my doppelgänger!

I recognized in the black, dilated eyes that my opponent was weighing out every step I made. The thick, black fur was ruffled from the unexpected flight through the air. The bushy tail twitched involuntarily behind the doppelgänger, and the ears were folded backward. I knew that I only had a few seconds to come up with a plan because the slitted eyes of Cassandra 2.0 expanded, again and again, focusing on my every move. Then, finally, it was ready to attack.

How should I defeat myself? My doppelgänger had the same hunting tactics as me because falling from a tree onto the prey was my number one trick in hunting.

I tried to look at my surroundings, trying not to turn my eyes away from the predator, who was just waiting for an opportunity to shred me into pieces.

Trees, little bushes, and some patches of grass surrounded us. A familiar noise sounded in the distance.

I had an idea.

With all my strength, I resisted my instinct to retreat to get a better vantage point or to puff up menacingly to prove my strength and hope that my doppelgänger was intimidated.

I chose the opposite.

With a mighty leap, I jumped towards the huge lynx, which made a big step backward in surprise. Then, with two more big jumps, I got past my opponent.

The rushing of water grew louder with each leap. My doppelgänger had fallen for my surprise attack and pursued me. Just want I wanted it to do.

The thought of another shapeshifter chasing me made me shudder, and I was astonished that I had considered this method. But I knew I had no chance against myself when I used my daily maneuvers.

The edge of the ravine was now visible in front of me. I followed the sound of water. Everything was falling into place.

The time had come.

I stopped in my tracks. It only took a couple of seconds to feel the claws drilling painfully into my hip. Through the impact, we overturned and were catapulted even closer to the abyss. The sharp claws let go of me as we were thrown over the hard ground. I curled up to absorb the impact and landed on my back again, where I came to a hold.

My doppelgänger flew towards me, claws extended, and it wanted to finish what it had started. It opened the mouth and gave a view of the sharp incisors. But before my opponent could bury the teeth in my flesh, I dug my claws into the shoulder blades of the doppelgänger, pulled my legs in, pressed hard against the belly of the other lynx, and let my claws retract again. Then, with a powerful kick, my opponent flew over my head.

I looked at it as it tried to turn around in the middle of the air to land on its paws, but only the front paws found a hold on the smooth stones of the gorge, while the rear end hung over the abyss.

A flicker of panic and despair rushed over my opponent's eyes as it desperately tried to climb up the rocks. I was so close to offering my help, but then I remembered it was my mission to defeat myself.

Exhausted, I rolled to the side without losing sight of the enemy. For a moment, I thought the doppelgänger would lift itself up without my help—but I was wrong. I could hear the scratching of the claws on the stone ground, and then it gave way. Where the head could just be seen just a moment ago, the abyss yawned.

I crept closer to the gorge to see if I could find the body in the rushing floods. I had just arrived at the canyon and looked over the abyss as two huge paws snapped in my direction, throwing themselves around my neck and pulling me down.

In shock, I woke up in my chair, the loud throbbing of my heart booming in my ears and sweat running down my neck.

It took me a few seconds to understand what had happened. In the relief of defeating my doppelgänger, I hadn't considered that my opponent could have found a foothold on the stones. Unfortunately, my curiosity and arrogance had let me down, so I allowed my doppelgänger to pull me into the depths with it.

"It looks like there's a draw between you and your doppelgänger. You did well," said Miss Syryn, and I looked into her cool but beautiful eyes.

"I was sure that I had won," I replied, dazed, and tried to imagine how the fight would have continued if I hadn't been so naïve as to look into the abyss.

"A draw is still better than a defeat. Learn from your mistake. That's why you're here," Miss Syryn answered with a smile and went to a boy who woke up panicked from his dream.

She held the stone in her right hand, and her knuckles were pale as chalk from the pressure she put on it.

"Looks like it's your turn, Cassandra. You can return to your room after Mrs. Nerol is done with you to get some rest." Miss Syryn looked at the doorway.

"Take your time," Mrs. Nerol exclaimed impatiently through the rows of children still in a trance.

Amara had her eyes closed. She was still competing

against her doppelgänger, and I wondered if it had been her turn already to get tested.

"I'm coming!" I shouted and hurried after Mrs. Nerol.

CHAPTER
21

I closed the door behind me as I stepped out of Room 401 and tried to keep up with my instructor, who walked silently down the corridor towards the staircase.

"How was your fight against your doppelgänger?" Mrs. Nerol asked.

I cringed. "Just when I thought I had won, my doppelgänger pulled me into the depths of a ravine. Miss Syryn said it was a draw, but it felt more like a defeat to me," I grumbled and couldn't stop replaying the last seconds of the fight in my head.

"You remind me of your mother. She was a very ambitious trainee. Your father was her best friend while they were together here in Teviena. But I could never have imagined they would become a couple and go against the rules. You and your brother are exceptional. I can imagine why she wanted to keep you away from the Magical World. The Saperians strictly forbid the reproduction of different beings, and being a Crossling can even lead to a stay in Bridlio," replied Mrs. Nerol and led us to the first floors.

I looked at her. I had wondered if my parents had ever set foot in Teviena, and she had answered my question. I didn't know that my parents were trained here, nor that it wasn't just uncommon but forbidden to reproduce.

Why had they never spoken of their time in the Magical World? Were they afraid of being locked up for breaking a rule?

I didn't understand why everyone made such a big deal. I couldn't imagine a life without my brother as a wolf. It made me smirk thinking about him as a lynx made me.

"I didn't know you knew my parents," I said. "But why is it forbidden? After all, Lex and I are harmless."

"You may not be dangerous, but imagine a gifted magician and a strong shapeshifter giving birth to a child, and it's a hybrid. And this hybrid would then reproduce with another hybrid. Can you imagine what powers the third, fourth, or fifth generation could have? A whole family could be stronger than an army of normal magical beings like us," Nerol explained.

"A hybrid?"

"It is a being with two gifts."

"So it isn't impossible for a cross between magical beings, as everyone thinks? It is just forbidden to maintain peace between the beings and to divide the gifts fairly," I murmured loud enough for Mrs. Nerol to hear.

"I wouldn't say that all gifts have the same strength, but taking everything into account, the security of the Magical World is more important than anything else. This regulation has worked for centuries. Of course, there were some Crosslings here and there, but these mistakes were fixed."

"Mistakes? You think children like us are mistakes?" Her words struck me like a sword and made me stop in my tracks.

I couldn't believe she had the audacity to call me a mistake. No wonder our parents didn't want to introduce us to this world.

Mrs. Nerol shook her head. "I didn't mean it like that. I'm certain you're not a hybrid. And the Saperians tested the hybrids, which were secretly produced, and they classified most of them as harmless. But, of course, a handful used their gifts for horrible deeds. Amber left Teviena at night nineteen years ago. A few days later, another teenager was banished to Bridlio because of her terrible acts as a hybrid and—" Mrs. Nerol's breath stopped. It was almost as if someone had squeezed the air out of her lungs. Then she caught herself again "—and my daughter Brianna died. I always assumed that your mother had run off with my daughter's killer because he, too, had disappeared that night."

My mouth opened wide.

"I searched all the continents for Orion but never found him. So then, the night you and your brother showed up here, I realized that your mother couldn't have anything to do with Brianna's death, and it was just an unfortunate time of her disappearance. But, unlike her, your father finished his last year here in Teviena before rejoining your mother."

I looked into the sad yet angry eyes of my instructor. The pain in her heart filled the room and almost suffocated me.

"My parents were here at the same time as your daughter? Why do you assume that my mother had something to do with her death?"

What had happened to Brianna, and why did I not know about my mother's dark past? Was that what she wanted to tell us on the night of the Klushund? Had she escaped the Magical World because she was involved in a murder? Was Mrs. Nerol the anonymous person who my parents had been whispering about? Did my mother want to visit her to confess to her?

"They weren't all in the same training year, but your parents knew Brianna and Orion, and they spent a lot of time together. Orion came from an Amarok family. He was brilliant, strong, and, unlike the rest of his family, very good-natured. As you already know, your father is also a wolf, but he could never have taken on Orion. An Amarok is almost twice the size of a normal wolf, and both wolves courted your mother. I never thought your mother would choose Zino. He was her best friend, but the chemistry was between her and Orion. Pandora also belonged to this group and was a hybrid of a Siren and a magician, banished to Bridlio for her actions. Brianna was your mother's best friend, so I learned quite a lot about your parents from her. I gave up looking for Amber and Orion a few years ago. I just wanted to know what happened that night when I last saw my Brianna alive." A small tear rolled over her cheek, which she quickly wiped off.

She couldn't be talking about my mother. The woman who was always quietly humming in the kitchen, preparing meals for the whole family; who sat on the chair in front of my teachers every year and listened to how well educated her children were; who stroked my little fur-covered back for hours to calm me down and help me turn back. She had to be wrong. My mother couldn't hurt anyone as much as kill someone and then build a new life based on lies.

"How are you sure this Amber is my mother?" I stuttered.

"How many Kaysers with the gift of turning into a lynx can there be?"

A lump spread in my throat.

I didn't want to believe her. My mother was no saint,

but she couldn't have anything to do with a murder.

My mouth was dry. Then I shook my head and straightened up.

Mrs. Nerol looked down at me and gave me a sad smile. "We can't change the past. We can only shape the future. And believe me when I tell you, I enjoyed having your father and mother in my training."

Confused, I shook my head. Nothing she said made sense.

"We need to focus on your tests."

I tried to ask further questions, but from the stern facial expression, I could see that Mrs. Nerol had already revealed much more of herself than she had liked.

In this conversation, I had learned more about my parents than in all the years living under the same roof.

Of course, I now understood why they wanted to protect us from the Magical World. How would my life have been if the Saperians had learned that I was more than a Crossling? But wait… What if I was a Crossling? A hybrid? Could I have another gift I didn't know about? What would the Saperians do to me if I did?

Fear and panic spread through my body.

Mrs. Nerol walked quickly towards a door in front of us I had not noticed before on the first floor. A small wooden door was inserted opposite the front door between the arches on the same side of the house as my room. Nerol murmured something, opened the door, and pushed me through the door frame.

In front of us was a room carved in black stone. There was nothing in this room, not even a window, except a large, white glowing crystal rising from the floor to the ceiling. Nerol walked towards it.

An unpleasant silence overwhelmed me, and the stone seemed to absorb all the sounds. I took a step forward, awaiting the click of my heel on the stone ground; there was silence as my boot touched the floor.

"This is the life source of the magic in Teviena." Pointing to the crystal in front of us. "Just like your parents, you have to pass three tests today. Since we already know that you have the gift of shapeshifting, we don't have to test you for it. Let's start with the first test."

Her stern look silenced me as I opened my mouth to object. I didn't want to know if I had another gift. I didn't want to be a Crossling, much less a hybrid. I only needed my brother and an escape route to get out of here—I had to get out of here.

I looked around for a way out, but the door behind me had melted into the wall. My hands trembled.

"Focus on the crystal and look closely at the white light. Imagine your body merging with the crystal as if you were an element. Now focus on the crystal and try to change the color of the light. Let the crystal feel your emotions. Focus."

Did Mrs. Nerol think I could change the color of this massive stone? I stared at the smooth, transparent surface of the crystal and tried to become one with it, but all my effort was in vain.

I couldn't concentrate. My mind wandered to the prison where I would soon live if I were a hybrid.

"I guess we can assume that you aren't a sorceress. If you were, the crystal would have helped you. Ok, now the second test." Mrs. Nerol waved her arms through the air, and four thin colorful strands emerged out of the crystal and swirled towards me. "Don't worry. This will test whether a basic element is anchored in your body. Stretch out your hands, but do not touch the elements. If you have the gift of an element, it will come to you."

Hesitantly, I stretched out my arms. I could see the

colors red for fire, blue for water, brown for earth, and white for air. I couldn't turn my eyes away from the bright streaks floating toward me. Shortly before my hand, the strains curled into balls of light and stopped, their energy penetrating my body. The pulsation of the elements gave me goosebumps. Finally, there were just inches between them, and I left. The balls started circling my hands, and for a moment, I could feel Ella's proud feeling when she controlled the light.

Just as I hoped an element would choose me, they shot back at the crystal and disappeared. A feeling of sadness came over me.

"We can also exclude the gift of an element. Now the last test. Please step towards the crystal and touch it."

I frowned. The last task was to touch the crystal? This had to be the most straightforward test I ever had to pass.

I knew which test was missing. This was the moment when I would find out if I had black magic.

I stumbled to the crystal, which was three times my size. Uncertain, I touched the icy surface, which burned under my skin. I could feel the crystal vibrate slightly, but nothing else happened. Mrs. Nerol was fixed on the spot where my skin met the stone. Her face didn't give away what the result was.

Her eyes warmed up for a split second. "You passed the test of good-naturedness. I expected nothing else from you," said Mrs. Nerol loudly and walked towards the door.

I took my hand off the cold surface and followed her.

"That's it? It's that easy to tell if someone has another gift or dark magic?" I was surprised because I assumed I had to master more tasks before the result.

"There aren't many hybrids, so the chance of being one is minimal. And testing for black magic only takes a few seconds." She closed the door behind us, which locked loudly. "Are you not satisfied with your result? It's difficult to be a hybrid—you would have two unique powers to train daily to gain control over."

I thought for a moment. In the last few days, I improved at getting my transformation under control. But I still hadn't perfected my gift, and If I had a second one—that would undoubtedly be catastrophic.

I shook my head.

"What happens if you fail the last test?"

"The crystal turns red or black. The red color shows the person's tendency toward darkness, but most trainees can be redirected to the right path with the appropriate training. Black means that the darkness is deeply rooted in the heart and cannot be saved with love and training. Fortunately, I only knew three children personally who didn't pass this test. Two of them are now in Bridlio, but one of them has turned away from the path of dark magic."

I already knew a person who ended up in Bridlio from her story, and that person, Aurora, had been in my parents' circle of friends. Had Orion been the other person? Mrs. Nerol had said that Orion was good-natured, so I didn't think she meant him.

"But my parents had not been among those who didn't pass the test, had they?" I asked tentatively.

"Of course not. I shouldn't have revived the past. No matter what you learned about them today, never doubt their kindness. Both were excellent trainees, and there must have been a reason your mother turned away from Teviena and raised you outside the Magical World," said Mrs. Nerol with a strict undertone. "What happened to Brianna was a tragedy—one I will never forget. But that's the burden of the older generation, not yours. You need to focus on perfecting your gift."

Talking about my parents' past weighed heavily on my

shoulders, but I had to hide the guilt that my mother might have something to do with Brianna's death. And if we could find them after we defeated the Oblitus, then I could find out the truth.

"I will do my best," I promised when we arrived at the door of Room 401.

Mrs. Nerol stopped for a moment before grabbing the door handle. "I know I have to be neutral to my trainees as your instructor, but believe me when I tell you—I'm glad to have you in my group. You remind me of my daughter. Although the memory is still painful, you are raising a new hope in me I haven't felt in years," said Mrs. Nerol, without looking away from the door handle, and she disappeared.

CHAPTER
22

Lost in thought, I walked down the corridor, not knowing what to do with all that knowledge. The idea of going to my room to sit around made me redirect my path to the courtyard. I needed fresh air.

I tried to make sense of everything. I tried to understand what made my mother disappear from a place like this. But the more I tried to puzzle my mother's past back together, the more unclear the picture became.

I had to find out what happened to Brianna and why my mother had fled Teviena. Somehow, the story made little sense.

For a second, I thought about telling my brother about the new secret I had just revealed about our parents, but then I changed my mind. Lex probably wouldn't believe a word. He would probably think that I was being eaten up by grief. He wasn't wrong, but unlike him, I couldn't stop thinking about them.

Then came the thought that I hadn't considered yet. There must have been a reason Mrs. Nerol had suspected my mother and why she escaped and hid us. Did our mother want to protect us because we are Crosslings, afraid that the Saperians would test us and lock us up? Were we still in danger? Had the tests proved I wasn't a threat or had they only attracted the attention of the Saperians?

I had arrived on the first floor, only a few feet away from the entrance door, when I stopped in my tracks.

I had to warn my brother that we had to get out of here as soon as possible.

It turned out that I wasn't a hybrid, but the thought that we could land in Bridlio as Crosslings made me shiver.

I had to return to my room to pack my belongings, but then I remembered I had been brought here with nothing but my dirty clothes, and not even that was still in my possession.

Within a few heartbeats, I had reached the stairwell and leaned against the icy wall. I needed a break, a moment to catch my breath. So much information has been drilled into my head in the last couple of days that I no longer knew what was real and what wasn't.

This Magical World had devoured me without me being aware of it. For years I had dreamed of a world like this, and now that I have arrived here, I found out why I didn't fit into this world either.

I shouldn't have persuaded Lex to stay here when he tried to escape the first night. I should have supported him. It was my fault that we had been drawn into all this.

"I'm sorry to interrupt your panic attack, but if you don't restrain your thoughts a little, then soon everyone will know that your mother is a murderer and you are a Crossling," a deep voice growled from the darkness above me.

My blood froze.

Draven stepped out of the shadow of a dark corner, his

black eyes fixed on me. I didn't know how long he had been watching me because I had been too busy wrestling with myself.

I looked at him in shock. I was about to turn around and run to the courtyard to escape him, but I paused. "What did you say?"

"You heard me," he said grumpily, strolling down the stairs closer to me.

The coldness that had broken out in me turned into a raging fire, leaving my ears glowing with rage. This time, he had gone too far. I stepped up to him and held his gaze, my body shaking.

"Of course, you can read minds," I said sarcastically, laughing loudly.

Draven was only one step away from me. I climbed the next step and stopped, chest to chest, in front of him.

"You think you can do whatever you want with your gift? That you can intimidate girls whenever you like. You surprised me the first time we met, but you can't frighten me this time," I growled.

He smirked as if he considered leaving me alone or whether my anger was the reason to continue.

"You have no idea what you're talking about," I continued as he held his index finger in the air.

"You mean the death of Brianna? The daughter of an instructor who was found lifeless by the lake?" He asked mockingly, turned away from me, and slowly ascended the staircase.

How did he know about Brianna? Had he overheard the conversation between my instructor and me? Mrs. Nerol had disclosed no information about her death, only that she had died.

"How do you know about her?" I asked and stumbled the stairs up behind him.

"Suddenly, you want to talk," amusement rang in his voice as he climbed on, ignoring me.

"What do you know?" I asked again and forgot for a moment who I was dealing with.

"It was the reason Teviena was closed and why it was no longer safe to train here," he said briefly and had now arrived on the second floor. "But that's something my brother could have told you because he knows every detail about Teviena. It's his wild obsession."

"What happened to her?"

The corner of his mouth pulled upwards, revealing pearly white incisors, his eyes sparkling with mischief.

"Who would have thought you were questioning me— the brother of the model child—and not him?"

I clenched my fists to keep myself from jumping at his neck. But he was right. It would have been much easier to find Rowan and ask what had happened to Brianna. But I couldn't bring myself to ask him about it. I didn't want him to think that my mother was involved.

Draven, on the other hand... I was sure that he had no heart or soul, and he wasn't afraid that he probably faced the daughter of a murderer. No, that thought of death even seemed to amuse him.

"On one condition." He paused for a moment.

I wanted to say *whatever you wanted*, but I held my breath, hoping he wouldn't force me to beg.

"You can't tell my brother about our encounter. He was pretty upset when he heard about our last one."

That was it? That I didn't tell him about this conversation? I wouldn't have told Rowan how I had squeezed the information out of his brother anyway.

"Agreed." My lungs burned from the effort to keep up with him. I looked at my boots to make sure I didn't step beside a stair and didn't notice his outreaching hand in my direction.

I slammed against it and looked at him in irritation.

"You want to shake on it?" I stuttered.

This gesture seemed too much for such a minor condition, but he looked at his hand and then at me. I shrugged, not thinking why it was so important to him, and grabbed his cold, soft hand.

"You still have so much to learn." The corners of his mouth drew to a mischievous smile, and he stepped higher. "Why are you so interested in this tragedy?"

I paused for a moment. "It's none of your business." My body was glowing. I wasn't sure if it was because of the effort to keep up with him or that I hated asking him for more information.

"I'm just asking." He pulled his eyebrows up and shrugged his head. "According to reports, Brianna was found at the lake by the Quarters." He looked at me casually and saw that I didn't know what he was talking about by my tightly contracted eyebrows. He sighed. "You know—the lake on the west side. The surrounding houses are called Quarters. The trainees who occupied them claimed Orion knelt over Brianna's lifeless body and disappeared into the night right after that."

I waited for him to continue, but Draven whistled and examined his fingernails.

"You made me promise for that? I already knew that Orion had something to do with it," I snarled, and he turned to me.

"What exactly do you want to know? If your mother killed her?"

His ignorance made my pores tingle. "How do you know about my mother?"

The corners of his mouth went up and showed his teeth. "Amber? Everyone knew your mother. She was a model trainee, and then…" he made a dramatic break, "She just vanished into thin air."

How did he know Amber was my mother? He must have been listening to Mrs. Nerol's conversation because I had not given him any information about my family.

"I didn't listen to you." He raised his index finger again and pointed at my forehead. I cringed. "You make it too easy to get into your mind. You're like an open book, and your questions and emotions are way too…" he was fishing for the right word, "…nerve-wracking."

I cleared my throat and tried to ward off the thoughts in my head. "How do you do that?"

"As you said—I can read minds, and yours is the loudest and most annoying one in this building." He turned away from me.

I needed more from him. More answers. "What are you?"

Sneering laughter echoed through the stairwell, my hands getting cold with discomfort.

"Did my precious brother still not tell you what we are?"

"I wouldn't ask you if I knew."

"Believe me. You don't want to know!"

I stomped my foot, he swirled around, and my icy gaze hit him.

"I don't feel like secrecy anymore! I may be on the verge of being locked up because I'm a Crossling. Until today, I didn't even know it was punishable, and then I was told that my mother might have been involved in a death. She deliberately kept us away from this place, this world, but why?"

I was so angry that I could feel the fine hair raising on my skin. My breath was uneven, and my ankles hurt from running up the stairs.

Draven looked at me and smiled. "You think they'll put you away because you're a Crossling? Don't be silly. The Saperians have much more important things to do than to take care of an ordinary shapeshifter. And this place is safer for you right now than any spot in the Mortal World. I can assure you that your mother had nothing to do with the death of Brianna."

"Why are you so sure?" I looked deep into his flickering eyes.

"Because I was there."

I opened my mouth to let out a loud laugh, but where Draven had just stood, there was only a dark swath of smoke.

What in the world? Where did he go?

I frantically looked around, grabbing my head. I looked over my shoulder and back at where he had just stood, but even the smoke had cleared.

The list of his abilities expanded. He could read minds, and—I couldn't figure out whether he could move extremely fast or teleport—he basically dissolved into thin air.

After a few seconds, my surprise subsided over his quick disappearance as the memory of his last sentence shot back into my head.

Because I was there.

What did he mean by *being there*? That was impossible. According to the newspaper article, he only had to be one year older than me. Maybe he was a baby, and his mother had been a trainee, and he said he was in Teviena at the same time, but even that made no sense. As a one-year-old, he would never have been able to remember the incident.

Dozens of possibilities rushed through my head, but none sounded right.

I wanted to make my way to find and confront him, but

then I realized I didn't know his room number. I had to talk to Rowan and ask him if he could take me to his brother.

You can't tell my brother about our encounter. Those were Draven's words.

He had known that I would turn to Rowan. For a moment, I wondered if I could make an exception. I knew it was a promise I made, but Draven wasn't the most trustworthy person, and if he were in my shoes, he would have probably already betrayed me.

But my respect for him stopped me. Maybe I couldn't trust him—after all, it was the second time he had entered my consciousness and read my thoughts—but he was my only chance besides Rowan, who could help me learn more about my parents. Whether he was present as a baby at the time or not, he knew the story.

I had promised him I wouldn't say anything about him, but that didn't mean I wasn't allowed to ask Rowan if he knew anything about my parents.

As I walked through the next doorframe, I was surprised to see the silver dragon in front of Room 401. Draven had stopped in front of my corridor.

I wanted to head for Rowan's room and tried to remember if he had ever given it to me. But, as much as I tried to remember, I was sure he had never said his room number aloud. I had the opportunity to go knocking door to door until it was the right one, but I had no energy left.

Today I met Viera, gave away our hiding place, failed during my training, mastered the tests, and was pulled into the wormhole of the past. I was exhausted.

I stomped to my door, threw it open, and slammed it behind me.

Tomorrow.

Tomorrow I would find out what had happened, but at

that moment, my body and mind had enough.

# CHAPTER
23

I spent the rest of the day in my room without being disturbed. I waited for one of my friends to knock on the door to keep me company but was disappointed.

The more I tried to convince myself that I needed a break, the greater the urge grew to visit one of them and talk about my parents' past.

I wanted to talk to Lex and tell him every little detail about my knowledge—but it had to wait. I needed to know the entire story, not just small pieces with no logic. There were too many loose ends. I didn't even know what connection Orion had to my parents. Maybe all of this had nothing to do with my mother. Just because Orion was a friend didn't mean they were in this together.

After a few minutes that felt like hours, I forced myself to deviate from the subject of Brianna and let it rest for the night.

I withdrew from the past and tried to find myself in the presence.

I knew I was a Crossling, not a hybrid, which was an

advantage. But what if one of my friends was a hybrid, or someone didn't pass the good-naturedness test?

No, that can't be.

None of them had black magic; I would have noticed.

Lost in thought, I flipped through my grimoire. Perhaps there was something I didn't know about my transformation and had skipped that part while reading, but I was also disappointed. The second half of the book was still empty.

Did the Grimoire of Amara and the others also have bare pages?

I hadn't noticed how tired I was, and before I knew it, I opened my sleepy eyes. The sky was bathed in red, and I knew I had slept through the night.

My stomach growled loudly, and I decided it was time to see if there was breakfast. I walked past my brother's door on the way to the dining room. His centaur Wedo stood protectively, with room number 409 engraved on the pedestal opposite the door.

I listened and hoped to hear a noise from his door to have an excuse to knock, but there was silence. Then I concluded he wasn't in his room.

It wasn't long before I reached the dining room, the sound of loud voices and laughter rushing through the air.

Well, I got lucky. It was time to eat. I couldn't stand this hunger any longer.

I could see Amara in the same place she was sitting the day before, with Ella and Niam beside her and Viera and Rowan sitting next to them.

It was strange to see them all together at breakfast

without me. For a few seconds, I watched the interactions between my friends before I started moving toward them. The seat next to Ella was occupied, but Rowan, who had just discovered my presence, waved at me to make me aware that the chair beside him was still available.

When I saw him, I remembered I had to find a suitable moment to find out if he knew anything about my parents or Brianna. But it had to wait.

"There you are!" Amara exclaimed as I passed her.

"We've been here for days, and I still don't remember the meal times. Usually, you remind me every time it's time to eat," I said to Amara, laughing, and sat down next to Rowan.

"You didn't miss much," Rowan added, pushing a full plate of ham towards me.

"I'm so hungry, I could swallow a whole pig," I replied, regretting my choice of words. I threw my hands in front of my mouth, but it was already too late.

"You think you said something bad about your shapeshifter form and a pig?" Rowan couldn't stop laughing.

"I'm not used to talking to people who don't belong to my family. This saying was a classic at our dining table."

"You don't have to apologize for that," Rowan replied, still smiling; his pearly teeth flashed out from behind his lips.

"And Cassandra, how did your test go? I heard you were all tested yesterday," Viera called over Rowan's plate. Her voice was too loud for the environment, and some children turned to her.

"Would I still be here if I didn't pass?" I asked. I didn't want to give her a straightforward answer while the other children watched us.

"Oh, I hope Miss Joyal will test us soon. I hope it turns

out that I have a second gift with which I can defend myself against the Oblitus," Viera replied, turning her attention back to her half-full plate.

Did Viera know hybrids weren't well regarded in the Magical World? I had been so afraid of being locked up as a Crossling or hybrid that I tried to run away the day before.

"What happened to the trainees who didn't pass the test in the past?" I turned to Rowan, who was poking at his food.

"When the crystal lights up in red, they placed the person in the Dark Magic Quarters. They continued to be trained like any other child with a gift. They were usually also hybrids and could move freely in Teviena. But their training focused on turning black magic into good energy. They were tested regularly to see if the crystal continued to discolor or remained bright white. However, if the crystal turned black, the Saperians were immediately alerted. Hearsay says that the person was immediately banished to Bridlio," Rowan casually explained, pushing around a piece of meat on his plate.

"Do you know anyone who has dark magic?" I looked into the strange faces of the children sitting around us. Maybe there was someone in this room who could use dark magic, and I didn't even know it.

"Why is it so important to you to know if someone has black magic? Just because the crystal finds black magic in a person does not mean the person is evil or dangerous. Everyone deserves a chance to become a better person," replied Ella, who had eavesdropped on our conversation.

"I don't want to come over as insensitive. It's just that Mrs. Nerol told me something about my parents' past, and now I can't stop thinking about it. Apparently, one of their friends got banished after an incident." I lowered my voice with every word.

"Your parents were here when Pandora was banished?" Niam asked with wide eyes.

"What do you know about Pandora? I heard this story for the first time yesterday and—" But I didn't get any further.

Something cold wrapped around my wrist, and as I looked up in shock, I saw Rowan standing before me. He pulled me up from the chair, and I let him do it.

His face was chalk white, and something uncomfortable flickered in his eyes. I couldn't determine what had spooked him but realized it had to be something important.

"I have to show you something," Rowan said, pulling impatiently at my arm.

"Can I at least take my plate?" I asked him because my stomach started making loud gurgling noises.

"Sure."

"Where are you going?" Ella asked, surprised when she saw Rowan walking past her, me with my plate in tow.

"Come with us," Rowan hissed, but he didn't slow down to wait for her.

The scratching of chair legs across the floor made me cringe, followed by quick steps.

"Do you have to drag her behind you like that?" Amara asked, who had arrived at my side.

"Oh, I'm sorry." Then, as Rowan turned to me, he removed his firm grip and looked at me compassionately. My arm burned where our skin had met as if snow had kissed me for too long. "You want to see this, trust me."

I tilted my head. "Ok." It sounded more like a question than an answer. I was hungry, confused, and not really in the mood for more secrets.

"Where are we going?" Niam called through the

corridor, gasping loudly beside Ella.

"To the hiding place," Rowan whispered.

"I know a shortcut," Amara shouted enthusiastically and ran past Rowan to take the lead, navigating us into her room. We looked at each other in surprise as we entered the room.

"Oh, wait a minute…" Amara rummaged through a brown velvet bag and pulled out a small bow made of braided wooden sticks. "This morning, I was bored, so I thought about how we could make it easier to get into our hiding place. Then I remembered that my family used these arches to visit each other and called them Fores. It works as long as at least two Fores have been placed in different places and have a carving of the same symbol at the arch's highest point. Then, you can teleport back and forth between the arches. I put the second arch under the fountain. Usually, I use them to sneak into the library so no one would notice, but I felt that a shortcut to the hiding place would be better," Amara explained, tugging at the sleeve of her coat.

"You are exceptional!" Viera hugged Amara vigorously.

"But how are we supposed to fit through this little arch?" asked Niam, puzzled, looking at the Fores, which was no bigger than Amara's palm.

"I shrunk it so I can transport it better." Amara put the tiny arch on the floor behind her bed and whispered something. The wooden branches shot in the air and came to a standstill above her head.

"Follow me."

Nothing indicated that the Fores was a portal to another arch. Instead, we stood in front of a few large branches braided into a bow. But when Amara took a step closer to the arch to the wall and was about to crash into it, she was already gone.

"Who wants to follow her first?" Niam asked and backed away from it.

The thought of walking into the wall head first made my hands tingle. But then I couldn't stand the curiosity anymore. After all, Amara did it, and she made it look too easy.

"I will probably never get used to magic," I murmured, taking a long breath and stepping through the arch.

Amara clapped her hands.

"What did I tell you? Isn't it incredible? My relatives always show up unannounced this way." Amara's voice was shrill.

"I must admit, these Fores are handy." I saw Viera, followed by Rowan, walking through the arch. Niam and Ella arrived hand in hand.

"She asked me to hold her hand," Niam replied with red cheeks, letting go of her hand and looking away.

"As if!" Ella laughed and nudged him with her shoulder.

"We made it! Thank you, Amara. This passage will make it much easier for us to sneak out of Teviena." Rowan ran his hand over the braided wood as if trying to understand how this magic worked. "The last time we were here, you put a stack of books on the table. Do you remember?" He walked towards the table where the books were still neatly stacked. "I noticed a grimoire was named Pandora."

Niam interrupted him. "You mean Pandora, like in Pandora's box?"

"I was thinking the same until Cassandra told me about her conversation with Mrs. Nerol. Pandora was a hybrid of a magician and Siren, and possessed black magic. Unfortunately, the instructors couldn't direct her to the right path, and she was banished to Bridlio. So what if this book..." Rowan pulled the thick leather-bound, equipped with the name Pandora, out of the stack and held it high, "...is the grimoire of Pandora? This might help us figure out what abilities a being with black magic has. Of course, it would only be a fraction of the capabilities we're going to face, but it could help us, right?"

"But I thought we couldn't read the grimoires of other gifts?" I asked carefully and looked at the book more closely.

"Not every grimoire is enchanted," Viera replied, stepping from one leg to the other. "Am I the only one who thinks this isn't a good idea?" Her voice sounded uncertain, and she looked at the book as if it was the devil himself. "What if these grimoires were hidden down here for a good reason? Maybe they shouldn't be found. We can't risk learning about black magic."

"Who said anything about learning? We would only find out what an Oblitus is capable of. Of course, we won't use the grimoire to train with it. We would just study it," assured Amara, and curiosity bubbled up in me.

"I think it's a bad idea. There must be a reason someone hid this grimoire with the others down here," Ella repeated, emphasizing the seriousness of the situation.

Her fear wasn't unfounded. But if this grimoire really belonged to Pandora, my parents' friend in Teviena, then this book might prove my mother's innocence.

"I understand your fear, but I am also in favor of us taking a quick look at it, and then we can still decide whether it should be hidden down here, far away from prying eyes," I objected.

Ella nodded slowly.

"Is everyone ready?" Rowan asked and looked spellbound at the dusty book as if it would grow teeth at any moment and bite him. Finally, he opened the cover with a jerky motion, and we held our breath.

I saw a beautiful, italic font in black ink on the first page. I tried to decipher the first words, but reading the letters upside down was difficult.

Rowan cleared his throat and started reading.

Pandora Asra-17 years old.

Today was my first day in Teviena. My parents used to tell me about this place, but I never thought I'd be accepted because of their past. But I made it.

I had to pass some tests before they assigned me to a Quarter and my new room. My test results were:

Shapeshifting—Siren,
Magic—present,
Elemental magic—no,
Dark magic—present.
Conclusion: Hybrid with black magic.

I am still not sure if this result is good or bad. They placed me in the Black Magic Quarters because of these findings. Hopefully, I'll find some friends soon, because I'm not used to being without my family.

Tomorrow can only be better.

Rowan stopped reading and flipped through hundreds of pages written in the same neatly cursive handwriting.

"It's a diary," Viera said enthusiastically, trying to decipher a few more sentences.

"It looks like it. Maybe Pandora wrote something about my parents or what happened to Brianna," I thought aloud and tried to grab the book.

"I don't think it's a good idea to get into the mind of an Oblitus. You know we could fall victim to it at any time as well as I do, even though we currently have no signs of black magic. Just a small step in the wrong direction, and we find ourselves in Bridlio." Ella's voice was slightly raised, and she tried to close the book, but Rowan held it open with a firm grip.

"It's just a few letters on a piece of paper," Niam replied, pushing Ella out of the way. "We will certainly not fall for black magic because of a book. This grimoire could give us an advantage over the Oblitus. So I am in favor of reading it." He pulled his hand up as if a vote was going on between us.

"I am in favor, too," I added, hoping to learn more about the events that led to my mother's escape.

Amara also raised her hand reluctantly. "There is still the possibility that we might face her soon. What if she also escaped from Bridlio?" She added, and we knew she had a reasonable explanation for her decision.

I tried to imagine facing my mother's friend. Would Pandora recognize me and spare me? After all, I was the spitting image of my mother.

"I also vote for us to read it," Viera said with a firm voice.

"All right!" Ella threw her hands up and settled down on the couch. "Don't tell me later that I didn't warn you."

CHAPTER
24

Just as we were about to sit on the floor in front of the table to read the next page of Pandora's diary, the sound of steps made me stop. I concentrated on my surroundings.

"Do you hear that?" I asked, and an unpleasant silence settled in the hiding place.

With every second step, pebbles were kicked away as if the person didn't have enough strength to lift both feet at the same height while walking. I looked up to the ceiling and through the blue water into the courtyard of Teviena.

A dark shadow appeared at the fountain's edge, and a large hood blocked my view of the face. The rest of the body was wrapped in a deep red coat. At first, I thought it had to be another trainee because the color resembled Rowan's cape. But on closer inspection, I couldn't see any embroidery on the front of the cloak or sleeves.

An old, wrinkled hand writhed out of the sleeve and touched the water, and the liquid began to discolor at the touch. At first, it took on a pink tone, but it quickly turned red.

Ella screamed. Rowan leaped into the air with a graceful motion, pressing his hand to her mouth to silence the outcry.

"No one can hear us here," Niam assured in a whisper, but based on the volume of his voice, he didn't seem to be sure about it anymore.

It felt like little spiders were running over my skin.

"Who is it?" Amara muttered and slowly got up.

"He didn't come from the entrance hall but the garden," Viera replied with a quivering voice.

"It's an Oblitus!" Rowan growled, removing his hand from Ella's mouth, who kept her mouth open but muted.

"How do you know that?" Amara pressed herself against me.

"I can feel it." His gaze was directed at the hooded figure.

"Quickly, let's go through the Fores and let Miss Syryn know!" screamed Viera and made her way to the wooden arch, but my body resisted her plan.

I didn't want to run away anymore. I didn't want to hide. Nobody could assure me that the Oblitus was still there when we returned with Miss Syryn. He couldn't get away from me again.

I looked into the frightened faces of my friends, walked one step towards the Fores, swung around in one quick movement, and ran towards the tunnel.

I could hear them screaming after me and trying to stop me, but they weren't fast enough. The bench from the greenhouse was waiting in front of me at the end of the tunnel and opened the way to the outside world.

A loud gasp sounded behind me. No one would stop me from avenging my parents. The anger I had been trying to suppress for days was back, and I couldn't think clearly.

I didn't know how to take on an Oblitus and what gift he had, but I knew I couldn't let him go unpunished.

I stumbled over the last step into the greenhouse, my bones groaning, and leaped feverishly towards the exit. But Flora had something else in mind. A powerful gust of wind threw me on my butt. It took me by surprise.

I was so angry that I shifted. With all my strength, I buried my claws into the sandy ground to stand against Flora's wind. Behind me, I heard my friends fighting the same gust that seemed to roar down all the way into the tunnel.

Only a few steps to the exit, and I was free.

Amara's worried voice penetrated my ears. "Don't do it, Cas!"

The sound of my name turned my stomach. Only three people called me Cas, and two of them had disappeared. I shook my head and let it bounce off me.

One step and I made it into the courtyard and had assumed that the Oblitus was already waiting for me after all the turmoil, but he was still standing with his hand in the water at the fountain.

I aimed toward the hooded figure with long jumps when I was jerked back. Hissing, I turned and looked into Rowan's angry eyes. I tried to resist his grip, which held me in place with his arms around my waist. He was too strong.

As I looked at the fountain, I saw the Shadow Creature being aware of my struggle. Although I couldn't see his eyes, I felt like I was being watched.

I knew it was only a matter of seconds until the Oblitus took advantage and attacked us both. The loud footsteps of Ella, Viera, Amara, and Niam sounded behind us. The Creature stepped back and whirled with his right hand in the air. A black, smoking circle appeared in front of him, and before he stepped in, he waved his left hand in our direction and disappeared into the smoke.

"What the hell has gotten into you? You could have died!" Amara yelled, shaking me.

Rowan let go of me and crossed his arms behind his back, head down.

"You didn't have to follow me! That was my fight!" I yelled back, and the energy that the anger had released in me disappeared as quickly as it had come.

Like a sack of potatoes, I slumped to the ground, but Rowan held me upright while I slowly turned back into my human form. He led me to the fountain's stone wall and sat me down. I looked at my trembling legs, and my cheeks blushed.

What was I thinking? Had I assumed I would survive a fight against an Oblitus if I couldn't even beat my doppelgänger.

"We really should go back inside. If it was that easy for this Oblitus to show up and disappear again, he could come back and even bring reinforcement. We have to make Miss Syryn aware of this incident," Niam said calmly and helped me up.

"We should get out of here," Ella agreed, looking around as if another Oblitus was just waiting for us to be careless.

Niam and Amara pressed their shoulders under my arms and carried me up the stairs into the hall. I had no strength to stand on my own.

I let the Oblitus disappear again.

"How could a Shadow Creature get through our protective spell?" Amara's voice was low.

No one answered. Amara was well-read in spells; after all, it was her gift. But if she didn't know, then only an instructor could help.

"They found us," Ella said quietly, staring into the void.

"Does anyone have any idea where we can find Miss Syryn?" Amara groaned under my weight.

"She's probably in a training session. I think it's best if we go to find any instructor, and they will let her know," Rowan replied and led us to the first floor.

Just as we headed through the corridor to Room 101, Miss Syryn came running toward us in a hurry.

"What happened?" She asked in horror.

"We were outside—" Amara said but paused as if she had to search for the right words. "And suddenly an Oblitus appeared at the fountain and turned the water red. Cassandra tried to defend us. But, through the effort, she lost a lot of strength." Her cheeks blushed.

I knew she wanted to keep our hiding place secret and therefore had lied, but this lie gnawed at her like a mouse on cheese.

"That shouldn't have happened. It's still far too early," Miss Syryn replied in thought, looking away from us, then she turned her attention back to us. "Is the Oblitus still in the courtyard?"

I raised my head and looked into her surprised face. Of course, it was way too early. I had only one fight under my belt, which was a defeat. I knew that every day without an attack was a blessing, but I had expected that we still had weeks to prepare.

"What do you mean, *it's too soon?*" Rowan asked, grabbing my arm to take the load from Amara's shoulders, who gasped loudly.

"I assumed we had more time. Please bring Cassandra to her room so she can rest. I will send a healer to her and take care of the matter with the Oblitus."

She had mentioned a healer the night I arrived. Lex had claimed her help, but apparently, my injuries hadn't been severe enough.

Miss Syryn stormed past us with a blowing cloak and disappeared into the stairwell.

"And now? Shouldn't we all be resting together in the same room? They could attack us any minute. They know where we are now. It is only a matter of time until the Oblitus returns with his friends, and then I would prefer not to be alone." Viera's voice trembled.

I had forgotten entirely that her gift wouldn't protect her. We have spent our time reading an old diary instead of testing Viera.

"It's probably forbidden, but we should try to get to the crystal to run the tests alone. We have little time until more Oblitus shows up here. Of course, you won't be able to master a new gift in this short time, but if we have a few more days to train, we'll know that you can fight back if they find you in hiding," I choked out.

My limbs hurt, and my head was throbbing. I was still powerless. I didn't know how I would stay on my feet during this quest, but it was our only chance. We had to take it at all costs.

"You're not going anywhere in your condition," Viera said tenderly, throwing a warm smile at me.

"I may be able to help," Ella said. "I've never tried it, but I've watched my mother once. Maybe I can turn light into energy, and if I do it right, I can fix Cassandra with a little energy." She sounded insecure.

"And you're telling us now after we've dragged her up an entire floor?" Niam asked dryly, but he grinned.

"What if it goes wrong? What happens then?" Amara inquired cautiously.

"Mm... I haven't dealt with that yet. Let's just assume it works."

Amara and Rowan were about to disagree as Ella put her palms on my shoulders and closed her eyes. The fire of the torches on the wall and the sun's rays falling through a window flickered, and Ella's skin began to glow. She kept getting warmer and brighter until her skin turned into something I had never seen before.

I was looking at a substance resembling glass. Ella was almost see-through. Her whole body had changed from her hair to her feet and even her clothes. She looked like a glass figure illuminated from the inside by something yellow. The yellow ray of light burned in her chest, snaking through her arm and over her wrist into my shoulder.

Warmth spread through my body, and a feeling of peace and relaxation. The warm feeling went through every cell of my body and wrapped around me like a warm blanket on a cold winter's day. When Ella withdrew her hand, I wanted to hold on to her to taste more of her energy, but I decided against it. She had given enough.

"Ah… You are shining," Niam stammered, apparently as surprised by her gift as anyone else in this corridor.

Ella slowly opened her eyes, but they were also of the same substance as her body, so that I couldn't recognize her pupils.

"You don't know how proud my parents would be! It's something extraordinary when your element chooses you. I had always been able to manipulate light, but it never happened before that the light chose me to serve as its source," Ella replied with a thick and strong voice. A small golden tear of joy ran down her cheek.

"We might not be your parents, but we are very proud of you," I said and wanted to hug her, but her glass-like figure looked too fragile to be touched. "Thank you so much, Ella, for using your gift to heal me." I paused for a moment to find the right words. "And thank you, Light, for finding me worthy of being healed," I added.

It seemed strange to me to thank something I couldn't

see, but the light wasn't just an element for Ella. It was her life energy, and how she described the light, it was even more.

"You are the most beautiful thing I have ever seen," said Viera, and I could see Niam's insulted expression.

"My whole life led up to this moment. Without you, the light would probably have taken weeks, months, or years to choose me. Some Elementals, or Fairies, as you call us, never get chosen by their element. The light chose my mother, but my father is still waiting for it." As Ella spoke, the light in her slowly faded, flickered, and she turned back to her human form.

"Then let's hope that we find our parents soon unharmed and your father will also be chosen. Can your mother control this energy? I mean... daily every minute?" Amara asked with wide-open eyes.

"Once an element has chosen you as worthy and gives you the power to metamorphose, you can fall back on your element any minute and perform a metamorphosis. So yes, she could," Ella squealed happily. None of us had ever experienced Ella in an outburst of feelings, let alone an unexpected burst of energy.

Niam was frightened and grabbed Ella's arm anxiously because he thought she might have suffered from the side effects of metamorphosis. "What is it?" He asked, looking around, and continued to hold her.

Ella laughed loudly and put her hand gently on his.

"I just become aware that I can now also metamorphose! I've always dreamed of it, but I never expected it to happen," Ella replied with delight, grinning from ear to ear.

The calm, gentle Ella, who I had only known for a few hours, had changed abruptly. The light had changed her energy from within; a spark had been breathed into her.

And just this spark had been enough that Ella could feel overwhelming emotions. A few minutes ago, she would have reacted calmly to this situation, but now she could no longer hide her excitement.

"Are you sure you're okay?" Amara asked because she, too, was surprised by her reaction.

"It will probably take me a few days to get used to the new potential of my gift," Ella replied with encouragement, shaking Niam with excitement.

"I don't want to be a spoilsport, but we probably won't have days. I'm thrilled for you, but we're under time pressure. If we want to find out if Viera has another gift before we are attacked, we need to get going," Rowan threw in, and the mood in the corridor suddenly changed.

"It would have been too nice if we could have a break," sighed Viera, her gaze falling on me. "How are you feeling?"

"Like born again! We can't waste any more time and must ensure no one catches us."

"Isn't it easier to ask an instructor for help?" Ella inquired, who had returned to her sober, calm manner.

"I don't think they want to spend their time testing more children if the Oblitus could fall with the door into the house at any moment," Rowan replied, sounding plausible. "And now let's go before we take root here."

With a burst of fresh energy, I ran down the stairs behind my friends until we arrived in the large hall on the first floor.

CHAPTER
25

"It's this door," I whispered, pointing at the same door I had used with Mrs. Nerol. "Does anyone know the spell to open it?"

"I do," Amara said hesitantly. "I tried not to listen, but my brain was soaking up the spell when Mrs. Nerol was using it." She scratched one foot across the floor.

"You don't have to be embarrassed. Without your comprehension, we would end up in the library," Viera answered and patted Amara proudly on the shoulder.

"Library?" I was puzzled.

"Do you see the fine font carved into the door frame?" Amara asked and made me aware of the small writing, which I had not recognized without pressing my nose almost against the wood. "Those sentences turn this door into a portal. But it also serves as a protective spell to repel uninvited guests. We used this door as an entrance to the library without casting a spell. Only a few can read this spell in the old language and pronounce it correctly to activate it. I will do my best not to disappoint you."

"Disappoint? Even if the spell doesn't work, you're the only one of us who can help me. Even if we don't make it into the room, I'm just glad we tried." Viera's voice was warm as she looked at Amara.

"I favor Viera and Amara going in alone, and the rest of us can stand guard. It will hopefully only take a few minutes," said Rowan, who was already facing the entrance hall.

"I'll take over the stairwell, and Ella and Cassandra will stay at the door. If we see something, we will knock three times, and you have to get out immediately," Niam added, positioning himself in front of the staircase.

"Can I come to support you?" I asked.

"That's fine with me," Amara replied with delight, closed her eyes, and mumbled a chant.

The runes in the doorway glowed. Her spell lasted much longer than Mrs. Nerol's, but it seemed to work. Amara pressed the door handle down and opened the view of the crystal.

"Quick," Amara breathed, pushing Viera into the room first.

Amara closely followed her. Just as I was about to set my foot on the floor of the Crystal Room, the room swirled around itself and changed. Stunned, I looked around and at Amara's horrified facial expression.

Viera, who had just stood before me, had now disappeared, just like the crystal. Crowded bookshelves were reaching to the ceiling. I could see a few desks covered with unfamiliar objects and maps of foreign lands on the walls.

We turned to the door to get back into the entrance hall to find Viera, but the door slammed shut behind us. As much as we tried to shake the doorknob, it didn't give in— the door remained locked.

"I caught you red-handed," said a scratching voice behind us, and I drove around.

"Mr. Adrian," Amara said and started to relax. "I'm not sure what you mean. Cassandra and I were looking for a friend and came here by chance."

From her friendly tone, I figured Amara knew Mr. Adrian well. I had seen him at the dinner table before Mr. Lafon made us run for the hills. The name also seemed familiar to me for another reason. Then I remembered Lex had told me about Mr. Adrian.

"Miss Hazen." He shook his head. "I didn't think you would hold a well-read man like me as a fool. I know exactly why you landed here. You tried to open the door to the crystal. I'm not sure yet why you needed it, but we can discuss all this over a cup of tea as I think about whether I have to inform Miss Syryn about your little adventure or if I pretend I haven't seen you here," said the small skinny man, whose face was covered by a long beard. His voice was raspy as if the dust of the books slowly rubbed on his vocal cords. His brown cloak flapped as he walked toward us.

"How about we start with your name?" Mr. Adrian asked while a dozen Steam Fairies brought a small table, three stools, a steaming teapot, cups, and saucers.

"We don't have time to explain. Our friend has probably gone into the crystal room and can't get out without our help," I explained and turned back to the door to help Viera, but the knob was still locked.

"The longer you take to explain to me why you broke into the crystal room, the longer you will have to stay here," said Mr. Adrian, still in the same calm tone.

"My name is Cassandra Kayser," I said in a slightly quivering voice.

"Oh, you're the sister of Lex Kayser. He talks a lot

about you," he replied, settling down on a stool. "Please sit down. Amara, you already know that time in this library differs from the rest of Teviena."

She looked at me. "A few hours in the library are the same as a few minutes outside this room. The first time I spent over four hours here—books are my refuge in difficult times—but those four hours here weren't even an hour for outsiders. Time behaves differently here,"

"Why do you know my brother so well?" I asked because the feeling of time pressure to save Viera had dissolved.

"He comes every night to learn more about his transformation. I'm surprised you're not interested. It can't be easy being a wolf after losing half of our pack." He poured us tea, the sweet smell of chamomile calming my mind.

"I'm not a wolf," I said casually.

Mr. Adrian's eyebrows tightened, and his eyes met mine for the first time. "Normally, I miss nothing, but you surprised me. So you must be a Crossling. Are you also a shapeshifter, or do you have a different gift?" He pushed the cups under our noses without taking his eyes off of me.

"I am a lynx like our mother, and I find it very unpleasant to be called a Crossling," I said with a slightly sharp undertone.

"I'm sorry. My gift is history. It sounds just as strange as it is. The knowledge of all these books rests in my memory." He raised his arms and pointed to the books surrounding us. "My brain records every conversation. I forget nothing. I have lived thousands of lives through other people's knowledge, yet I am only just over a century old. You don't know how long I have waited for this moment."

Mr. Adrian got up, walked around the table, and

reached out his hand. "May I?" He pointed to the embroidery that covered my sleeves.

"What are you doing?" I crossed my arms in front of my chest.

Nothing of what he said made sense. Our eyes met again. Mr. Adrian wasn't a threat—his gift was knowledge. Maybe he was the person who knew more about my parents' past and could help me.

He also had spent some time with Lex and Amara, so I let myself trust him. I extended my arm.

"How did you two meet?" He ran a fingertip over the golden embroidery until he stopped at a green strand surrounded by gold.

"What?" I could hear Amara's heart racing.

"How did you two meet?"

I tilted my head to the side.

"I spoke to Cassandra in the dining room the day her parents disappeared. She was very emotional, and I had been here a few days longer, so I wanted to be there if she needed someone," Amara said with her eyes pinched. She also didn't seem to know what this had to do with me being a Crossling.

"From the day you arrived in Teviena, have you befriended other children?" He asked Amara, and a queasy feeling arose in me.

"Not really. I had my brother. Somehow, I felt responsible for Cassandra's emotions when I first saw her. But that was also the first day I could say out loud that my parents had disappeared and I might never see them again. Maybe that's why I approached her to help."

Mr. Adrian extended his hand and pointed at Amara's arm, who reluctantly extended her sleeve in his direction, shaking her head.

"You are scaring me," I whispered, reaching for

Amara's hand.

"Did you both notice you have a second color in your embroidery?"

I pulled my other hand back and hid it under the table.

"I assumed there was an error in the processing," Amara replied hesitantly, also pulling her arm away.

My eyes went to her embroidery.

A black thread was embedded in her golden stitching. How could I have missed that?

"First, there has never been a mistake in the processing of the capes. Second, fate has brought you back together after so many years. Your mother's name is Amber, isn't it?" Mr. Adrian asked, and the uneasy feeling in my gut intensified.

"How do you know that?" My voice trembled. Had he been one of my mother's instructors, like Mrs. Nerol?

"That's what I thought! Give me a minute, and I'll show you," he replied, smiling, and disappeared behind the library counter on a spiral staircase that led down into the depths.

"We should get out of here," I whispered, trying to pull Amara off her chair, who just stared at him.

"We tried to escape, and it didn't work out. I know Mr. Adrian. He is for sure no fighter material. We are far superior if it gets tough," Amara murmured back, and the blunt clicking of shoe soles made me look up.

I searched for another escape route. Large windows covered two sides of the room, but the glass was the only separation between us and the waterfall under Teviena. The steps became louder, and time ran out. I could see no other exit than the locked door.

"If he doesn't get down to business soon, I'll get us out of here by force," I growled and felt like a caged animal.

"Here it is. Usually, this book is exhibited in the Magic

Story section, but I have been restoring it, so it was down in my workshop." Mr. Adrian carefully laid a thick, black, leather-bound book in front of us and pointed at it.

Two overlapping circles were visible on the cover, the same symbol Mr. Amaeral had painted on the blackboard.

"Emmerson was a shapeshifter like you, Miss. Kayser and she fell in love with one of the most powerful magicians of her time, Norwin. His family gave her immortality as a wedding gift, with the ulterior motive of using her as the leader of all magical beings. They wanted to create hybrids between magicians and shapeshifters to stay in power. They sacrificed two magicians for her immortality. One of Emmerson's children became a hybrid, and the other possessed only the gift of magic as a Crossling. Taylor, her son, was the first hybrid in magical history. Unfortunately, none of their children inherited her immortality as the magicians had hoped, so their beloved family died, one after the other." He took a deep breath and watched us.

"Everyone knows the story of Emmerson and Norwin. My mother told me this story every night before bed," said Amara, her hand trembling in mine.

I did not know what he was talking about. "That's a great story, but I still don't understand what all this has to do with us," I replied, rubbing my temple.

"Unfortunately, I had to go back so far to make you understand. They needed two magicians for immortality," he repeated, looking at us with wide eyes as if it would become clear what he was talking about.

Amara cleared her throat. "Can't you just tell us briefly what it's all about? We need to find our friend."

I was at the end of my patience and pushed my stool back to get up.

"Listen to me carefully. There is a reason the Oblitus

broke out of Bridlio after so many years. You are precious to the Shadow Creatures. You are sisters, and to be more precise, you are twins." He searched our faces for a reaction.

I looked at him speechlessly, and a loud laugh escaped my throat. "We can't be twins! It's impossible! Lex is my brother, and I only met Amara a few days ago."

"Why don't you just tell us what it's really about?"

The tension in the air rose and was almost unbearable. I wanted to give him my opinion on his story when he raised his hand and stopped me.

"At least I have your attention now. As I've already told you, reproduction between two different gifts is possible. Amber, your mother, knew that she had to separate you two and gave Amara into the care of her sister. Then Zino, Cassandra's surrogate father, got involved in protecting you, and Amara stayed with Raylin, your aunt. Everyone assumed that your mother went mad after the misfortune with Brianna. No one has considered that there could be more behind the story. I've wondered why your mother voluntarily disappeared in the middle of the night. I knew your mother, father, aunt, and Zino. Amber was wise to follow their instincts to separate you girls. Now we know she was right about her gut feeling, but who would have thought fate would bring you back together? Your biological father also disappeared at night with your mother, and no one knows where he is."

I jumped into the air, my pores burning, and I was about to lose control. "Why do you keep telling us this nonsense? We don't have time to listen to this!"

I knew it would have consequences to talk to an instructor like that, but I had enough. I had enough of strangers calling me a Crossling. I had enough of the endless stories about my parents, who weren't even present to defend themselves. I had enough of the Magical World and its problems.

The more upset Amara and I became, the calmer Mr. Adrian got. "Guess what shapeshifter Emmerson was?" He took a dramatic break. I needed to get my emotions under control before I jumped to his throat to silence him. "Emmerson was a lynx, just like you, Cassandra. Her son Taylor also had a son, and so the bloodline of Emmerson continued down to your mother. In your veins flows the ancient blood of Queen Emmerson. However, the blood of her descendants was meaningless because Emmerson's immortality wasn't passed on to her children."

I looked at my hands; the veins were slightly pulsating under my skin. My gaze went to Amara, who did the same. My thoughts were racing, and the more he explained, the less it sounded like a fairy tale.

"So you are saying, if you mix both of our blood, it gives immortality?" Amara sounded like in a trance. "As twins, there is twice as much blood as there is from a single descendant. How do you know so much about Emmerson, and why do you think the Oblitus know we are her successors?"

Mr. Adrian clapped his hands and grinned. "Exactly! Cassandra's cloak is black with golden embroidery. Shapeshifters wear black, but the green thread in her stitching represents the cloak color of sorceress. Amara's cloak is green because she is a sorceress and her embroidery is also gold, crossed with a black strain for shapeshifting. So your capes complement each other."

He pointed to our sleeves—both capes had black, green, and gold.

"However, it becomes even more complicated. To obtain immortality from your blood, they must take three liters of blood from each of you. It has to be mixed and taken within a few minutes. Three liters of blood would cause a breakdown of the organ system, followed by death. They must sacrifice you both to attain eternal life. A situation like yours has already existed in your family, but the second embryo died in the womb and was absorbed by the stronger embryo in the uterus. When the baby was born, the hospital carried out routine blood tests with abnormal results. After further examinations, the parents were informed, and the child disappeared the same night. This find had made headlines, so other magical beings living in the Human World noticed it. Your mother has tried everything to protect you both from this fate. I am not sure how the Shadow Creatures discovered that twins were born from the Emmerson bloodline, but if they get your blood, they will be unbeatable."

"Wait a minute. You want to make us believe Cassandra is my sister and that our blood together bequeathed immortality? I was raised by my aunt and a stranger who made me believe they were my parents and that I had siblings who aren't really mine. Let's not forget that our biological father has disappeared. And, of course, ancient magical blood flows through our veins from a bloodline that goes back centuries. I think you didn't hear about the part when we were both tested and found out we're not hybrids." Amaras face turned red.

Amara stood up and walked towards the door without saying another word. She had searched in this library for answers to why the Oblitus had broken out of Bridlio after so many centuries. Now someone tried to tell us it was our fault that dozens of parents had disappeared, and each child's trauma rested on our shoulders.

Mr. Adrian cleared his throat, and Amara hesitated briefly. "Your mother was looking for a special spell that can suppress a gift until the age of eighteen, just before leaving Teviena. This spell isn't freely available to all eyes. I was the person who gave her the book with that spell because I assumed she would never use it. She was a model trainee. But if you don't believe me, please have a look at this Signum?" Mr. Adrian opened the first page of the book, and my heart stumbled.

"What does this sign mean?" My mouth became dry. My gaze fell on an old sheet of paper, which showed the same Signum I had on my grimoire and wrist.

"The star with the dots points back to the Norwin magic bloodline, while the lower part represents the shapeshifting of the Emmerson bloodline. Have you ever seen it?"

I looked at Amara, who pushed herself over the stool with a chalk-white face.

"I don't expect you to believe me, but think about my words. You won't win this fight without the other sister. There is a balance between you. You must maintain this balance to stand a chance against what is yet to come."

I heard a loud click. The door was unlocked, and Amara silently left the room and closed it behind her.

I took a deep breath to calm down and started moving. "All this information is too much for a day. Thanks for your help, but now I have to talk to Amara. We have to find our friend and the first Oblitus was discovered on the premises. It's just too much."

He just nodded and watched as I quickly proceeded to the door, tore it open, and made my way out.

I ran into Amara, who was right outside the door, surrounded by our friends. She shook her head again and again.

"What happened, Cassandra? Where have you been, and why has Viera been back for minutes, and you're just coming? We knocked on the door and tried to open it, but it was locked?" Niam asked and walked closer. He looked at me from top to bottom to make sure I was unharmed.

"I'm not sure what just happened, but we're okay. I just have to talk to Amara for a minute," I answered and pulled her aside.

Her arms wrapped around my neck, then she stepped back and looked deep into my eyes. "I would love to have you as my sister, but just because an instructor tells us we are twins who have been separated at birth doesn't mean it's true." Her eyes flickered with pain.

"How do you know the Signum? You didn't see it for the first time, did you?" I breathed so that the surrounding ears couldn't hear me.

"It's on my wrist and embedded in my grimoire. But that's not even the weirdest thing about the book. And you? You looked surprised when he opened it," Amara whispered back.

"It's also on my wrist and grimoire." A nervous shudder ran through my body. "Does your grimoire have empty pages too?"

"How do you know that?"

"Because the second half of my grimoire is blank, and we have the same Signum." I showed her the inside of my arm and waited for Amara to digest this information. I knew she couldn't see my Signum because we were in different stages, but her facial expression strengthened my suspicion.

"Can either of you tell us what's going on here?" Viera asked in surprise.

"We will explain everything, but first, we must get away from here. Amara's magic isn't enough to open the way to the crystal, and we aren't safe in the entrance hall if we get attacked. How about we find out if Miss Syryn is back?" I said.

All I needed was a little time to figure out how much truth our conversation with Mr. Adrian held.

"Let's go back to Mrs. Nerol's room and see if she's there. I would feel better if we were in the care of an instructor," Ella replied, nodding.

We set ourselves in motion.

"I'm sorry it didn't work out with the spell. I was so sure it would work!" Amara said in a low voice to Viera, who only looked at her, smiling.

"It worked. I could see the crystal, and as I stepped into the room, I found myself again in front of the locked door next to the others. Both of you were suddenly gone. We tried to break through the door, but nothing worked. We were scared that something happened to you guys."

"And we were searching for you. One moment you were standing right in front of us, and the next, you were gone. It only seemed like a few minutes to you, but believe me, it was an eternity for us," Amara replied, wiping her sweaty hands on the cape.

CHAPTER
26

For years, I tried to fit into the Human World and not stand out. It took me seventeen years to find a place I fit in. And it only took a few days until someone told me I alone was part of why an entire world stood on the brink of collapsing. It wasn't the same world I knew from an early age, but I had met so many good-natured magical beings in such a short time that this world had grown on me.

It could only be a mistake. But why would an instructor come up with a story like that, and why could I not get rid of the feeling that it was perhaps not fictitious after all?

My parents seemed happy. Could Zino really have been my mother's close friend, and I have never met my biological father? Then why did I have a brother? He was older than me, so he should have been born shortly after my mother left Teviena—if I had calculated the timing correctly. Did Lex know about this?

I wanted to scream—scream so loud to stop the thoughts from torturing me. But I remained calm.

"Isn't that your brother?" Rowan asked, ripping me out of my dream world and back into the corridor.

"What?" I asked, noting that we had already reached the fourth floor.

I looked around. Lex came up to us with waving hair.

"There's my brother," I said, louder than I should have. "You guys go ahead. I will follow soon."

Without waiting for an answer, I ran toward him. "Lex!" I screamed out at the top of my lungs, and the name echoed from one wall to the other.

He whirled around, and his face lit up when he saw me.

"Where were you? I just knocked on your door, but nobody answered. Miss Syryn told me to let all the trainees know she will hold a special meeting in the dining room tomorrow night. I wanted to start with you, and I know I'm late, but—" He stretched his arms out. "Happy birthday! I wanted to congratulate you earlier, but apparently, we always ran past each other." He wrapped his arms around me and pressed firmly.

"Wait, what?"

"You know, your birthday, the day you were born? I'm sorry I can't throw a party for you, but at least I wanted to hug you." He pushed me away from him to look me in the eye. "Did you forget your own birthday?"

Was it my birthday? That meant we had been in Teviena for five days without our parents. I had completely forgotten about my birthday. The days ran into each other without me paying attention to the day of the week. On top of that, I didn't feel like partying.

"I have never dreaded my birthday so badly," I answered truthfully and scratched my temple.

"Then I feel less bad that it took me almost all day to find you. But to be exact, you've only been eighteen for eight minutes when I remember the right time mom used to tell you. Who would have thought that the time of your birth would ever be useful to me?" He laughed and let me go. "I thought you were screaming after me because you were angry with me. But now that I know you are okay, I can continue with good conscience." He looked at his new silver watch and turned away from me.

"Can I talk to you quickly?" I said, and he paused and nodded. "I mean in private, behind closed doors?"

Lex narrowed his eyes to slits. "What is so important that we can't discuss it here?"

"I'd much rather go to one of our rooms so no one can eavesdrop on us. " Too many gifts here come with a good ear," I begged him.

"I don't have time to talk. How about we meet in an hour? I hope I'm done with my tour by then."

"It really can't wait." My begging tone, however, intensified to an order.

"Are you okay? What's wrong?"

"I'm fine," I replied, but it was more of a habit than a truthful answer. "Okay, if you don't want to come with me, we'll do it your way. Do you know anything about our parents' past? Maybe where they used to live before they bought the house together? Or have you ever seen our birth certificates?"

Lex looked at me in horror. "What are you getting at? Of course, I can't remember where we lived when I was a baby, and why are you asking for our birth certificates?" He replied indignantly, and his stern look hit my disappointed eyes.

"I've just had the most unimaginable conversation of my life. I learned a lot about our parents, and I try to understand how it all fits together." I rubbed my sweaty hands together.

"What do you mean, you learned a lot about our

parents? What is there to know? They were a happy couple who lived in the Human World. What doesn't make sense to you?"

"Have you ever wondered why we're two different shapeshifters? I mean, since we got to Teviena? Some people told me that Crosslings are forbidden."

"That's probably the reason they turned away from this world. Cassandra, I don't know where you're going with all your questions, but our family has no dark secrets. It was just too painful to talk about their past, so we know little about it. Whatever you've heard, it must be made up." Lex replied tenderly, reaching for my hand.

"You don't listen to me!" I cried, pulling away from him.

At that moment, the ground below us vibrated, and the torches which hung neatly on the wall shot up in pulsating flames. Lex jumped back, looked at a torch hanging next to us, and then at me.

"Wait, was that you?" His voice was high-pitched, and he couldn't turn his gaze away from me.

"I... I... it wasn't me!" My eyes rested on my trembling hands. I could hear the throbbing of my heart in my ears and the blood vibrating in my veins.

"What in the world was it?" Lex took a step back.

"I don't know," I replied, and a shock wave went through my body again.

"I think we're under attack! I have to tell Miss Syryn about it immediately! Come with me!" He started running in the other direction, but I couldn't move.

"Cassandra?" yelled a familiar voice behind me. It was Amara, and I could hear from the footsteps that she wasn't alone.

"I can't go with you. I have to get something out of my room. I'll find you." My voice stumbled over the lie, but

Lex didn't seem to notice.

"Take care of yourself, Cas, and hurry!" said Lex before my friends reached me.

"Are the Oblitus already here?" Niam asked out of breath, leaning against the wall.

My gaze was fixed on my trembling and numb hands—they felt like limbs that didn't belong to my body.

"Guys, that wasn't an attack," Rowan said softly and walked toward me, reaching for my hands and looking deep into my eyes. "She triggered the quake."

Niam opened his mouth repeatedly as if fishing for the right words, but he kept silent.

"I don't know… suddenly the floor shook, and the torches threw fire at the ceiling... and my brother... I mean Lex…" I couldn't get any further because Amara pushed past Rowan and buried my face in her shoulder. She hummed into my ear as if I were a baby that needed to be soothed.

"Everything is okay! There's certainly an explanation for all of this," breathed Amara.

Nothing was okay. Deep down, I knew it—I had caused the quake. I had no explanation for how I did it, but it was all my fault.

Anger was bubbling inside me when I snatched myself from Lex's grip. I knew the feeling all too well. But something new had followed the anger. My fingers tingled, and I could feel my rage vibrating in every cell of my body and bursting out of me. Usually, my pores itch to start the process of turning into a lynx, but the itch felt different.

"Happy birthday," I whispered, and Amara stepped away from me.

"How do you know that? Did you talk to my brother?" Amara asked in surprise.

"Lex just reminded me that today is my eighteenth

birthday. What a coincidence that it's also yours!" My eyes were fixed on Amara. I waited for a reaction—an outcry or an awakening. Instead, her eyes were wide open, and she hugged me again.

Suddenly, my body stopped shaking, and I snuggled up to her.

"Can anyone tell us what's going on here?" Viera busted out, and her voice fluttered with excitement.

"I'd rather show you. Come." I walked towards the Simargl Wedo, opened the door, and asked my friends to come in.

I pulled out the grimoire from under my pillows. Of course, it wasn't a very original hiding place, but I couldn't find a better spot in the morning. I walked up to Amara with the book in hand.

"Do you remember what Mrs. Nerol told us after the first training? That people with the same Signum can only read our grimoire? This is my grimoire, but—"

I held the book under Amara's arm. I sincerely hope that my assumption was correct and I didn't make a fool out of myself. Amara understood without words what I asked of her. She rolled up the sleeve of her cloak, revealing her invisible Signum. Then, with a gentle movement, she ran her wrist over my grimoire and closed her eyes.

I hesitated for a few heartbeats.

But what if the book was empty and the stories of Mr. Adrian made me hope for something that could never have been true?

I slowly opened the heavy cover and flipped to the back half, holding my breath.

"And?" Amara asked impatiently and peered over the edge.

Dizziness followed by nausea struck me, and I grabbed my stomach with one hand so I wouldn't spill the contents.

Niam came just in time to intercept Amara's fall because her knees had buckled.

"And what exactly are we looking at? I only see empty pages," said Viera, shrugging her shoulders.

"Amara and I—" I didn't know how to say it. It sounded so wrong, yet I felt an urge to complete this sentence as if this piece of truth would give me clarity about our situation. "We are twins."

Niam laughed so loud that my ears hurt. He hit his knee with his hand after releasing Amara, who was now back on her feet. "April fool's day isn't till next year. We know you come from different families", he barked, laughing.

"I know it's difficult to understand, but you must believe us. That's why it took us so long to return from the library. Mr. Adrian told us we were separated after birth. And we are apparently also the reason we are dealing with the Shadow World. But let me start from the beginning," I replied and summed up our encounter with Mr. Adrian. Everyone looked at me in disbelief. Amara added minor details here and there to help me out.

Niam shook his head while Ella's eyebrows pulled together, and Viera couldn't stop grinning. Rowan's face didn't give away what he thought.

The room filled with an unpleasant silence until Rowan spoke. "And you believe Mr. Adrian? Can there not be another reason for the outbreak of magic?"

"I didn't think it was possible, but Lex reminded me of an important detail. Mr. Adrian said that my mother inquired about a certain spell that suppresses a second gift until the eighteenth birthday. I thought little of it until Lex told me that today is my birthday. And coincidentally, today is also her birthday." I pointed at Amara.

All the puzzle pieces began to fit together and gave a

clear picture.

"It sounds so… unbelievable," said Ella, still trying to make sense of the story.

"I didn't believe it at first either, but the longer I think about it, the more it makes sense," Amara replied, curiously flipping through the grimoire. "Wait a minute. But this morning's tests would have proved that you have magic and that I can shapeshift. So why was my result negative? The crystal showed no signs of shapeshifting."

"I asked myself the same question, and Lex also answered it. My mother always said that I was born at 7:13 in the evening. She kept repeating it as if it was one of the most important pieces of information about me. Maybe she knew that this time would be important. I'm only officially eighteen since we've passed that time. Maybe that's why my test also turned out negative," I thought aloud.

"That would explain why you could make an entire floor tremble. Your second gift has unlocked," Viera added, looking at Amara. "Do you know what time you were born?"

Amara shook her head vigorously.

"And you said you couldn't see the other half of the grimoire before. How about now?" I checked and flipped through the book again, showing her the pages.

"This is the first time I have seen the part about shapeshifting," she answered hesitantly, and our eyes met. "But that would mean that I also have a second gift!"

A feeling of excitement and terror passed through my body while fear flickered in her eyes.

"Um... One of you has to get her emotions under control," Viera stammered.

A pair of shoes floated past me. I looked around the room and saw the furniture floating a few inches above the floor, followed by other loose items like a hairbrush, pillows, and a few clothes from the closet that had opened. I looked at Amara, but she was as surprised as I was.

The memory of her making objects float in my room when she had talked about her family came back into my mind. But now, I wasn't sure whether it was her or my magic that spread uncontrollably through the room.

Ella stepped in our direction. She bent down to dodge a flying pillow and stopped between us to break our eye contact. The energy that had just passed through my veins disappeared, and with a loud bang, all the objects and furniture fell to the floor.

"Focus on suppressing your feelings," Ella's voice was soft and made me calm down.

"Well… I don't think it's a good idea anymore for everyone to stay in the same room. Cassandra doesn't have her new gift under control, and Amara is a ticking time bomb," Viera said and vocalized what the others thought—but unlike her, no one dared to speak the truth.

"Amara? Do you have any more Fores that we can use?" Ella asked out of nowhere.

"I still have some in my bag in my room. Why?"

"Let's say there are two, three, or four Fores with the same sign. Would it work to teleport back and forth between the different archs, or can there only be two with the same symbol?"

Amara tilted her head as if it were an answer that everyone should know. "Of course, you can use several Fores with the same symbol to travel back and forth between different rooms. I already have connected three Fores in Teviena, One in my room, the library, and the hiding place. And I always carry one with me… just in case." A broad grin spread over her lips as she pulled a small wooden arch out of a pocket of her cloak. "I can put another one up in this room."

She placed the arch in front of the mirror without further explanation and magnified it with the same spell she had previously used in her room.

But this time, it was different. I could feel the magic she used. It felt like a light wind was blowing through the room and vanished as quickly as it had appeared.

"I think it would be better if we split up. The presence of Amara alone seems to trigger Cassandra's magic, and Amara could transform and become uncontrollable at any second. What do you guys say we take turns watching them as they try out their new powers? And if the Shadow World attacks us, we can use the Fores to disappear into the hiding place together." Ella said calmly.

I didn't think it was a good idea to break up. But I made the room float without noticing it—I was dangerous with my new gift.

What if more uncontrollable magic came out and maybe even hurt someone? And we didn't even know if Amara had another gift. It could take years to get her transformation under control if she was a shapeshifter. Of course, there were natural talents like Lex and Niam, who could transform on demand. But if Amara only had a hint of my self-discipline, then we had a problem.

"I hate to part with all of you, but Ella has a good point. Unfortunately, I cannot control magic, and I would never forgive myself if any of you were harmed," I replied after a long pause.

"I will stay with Cassandra," said Viera bravely, standing next to me.

"I appreciate your offer, but I don't think you should be in the same room as them," Rowan cut in. "We don't know what she's capable of yet, and you don't have a gift that can protect you from magic. How about I stay with

Cassandra, and Niam watches over Amara? He's a shapeshifter and can help her if she needs anything."

I still didn't know what kind of gift Rowan had, and I was too cowardly to ask him again. The foretaste of Draven's gift was more powerful than my shapeshifting, so Rowan had to assume that he, too, was superior to my magic and my other gift.

"Are you sure you can help her? When I used my magic for the first time, I almost burned down my neighbors' house," Amara warned him.

"I promise you she won't hurt me and that she will remain unharmed," he replied.

"All right! I'll keep you to that promise." Amara didn't dare to look in my direction, fearing that she would create another magical riot in me. "I will give Ella and Viera another Fores so they can put it in one of their rooms." She handed a little arch over to Ella. "And it's very simple to use it even with more than two Fores. Imagine the room you want to enter, and you will end up in the room you imagined. You can freely choose between the different Fores," Amara explained and walked toward the door.

"And what's next? Are we now waiting in separate rooms for the Oblitus to attack us?" Viera sounded scared.

Rowan shifted from one foot to the other. "We'll see you tomorrow at breakfast. I hope both of them have their gift under control by then so they can walk among people without being noticed. We can't explain to anyone what we found out tonight. If another trainee finds out that the Oblitus are only here because of Amara and Cassandra, then both of them could be in great danger," Rowan said with a firm voice, and all nodded.

Ella looked over her shoulder and gave me an encouraging smile as she followed Viera and Niam out of the room.

My stomach turned. Again, I was alone with Rowan, and he assumed I could learn to suppress my magic within a few hours. I had just accomplished to keep my shapeshifting somewhat in check, and now he demanded to hide another gift in record time.

But I had no other choice. I had to change my old train of thought. I was no longer the same person who had arrived here five days before. The last few days had proven that I had used only a fraction of my gift in the Mortal World. But I was no longer in that world. Instead, I was surrounded by other magical beings who were even more dangerous than me. Draven alone could beat me in seconds without getting his fingers dirty.

This raised the question of what gift Rowan and his brother possessed, which sounded like it was immune to magic. I fought the urge to ask him. But, even before I could make that mistake again, he set himself in motion and opened the balcony door to let fresh air in, as if there were no enemies in the outside world waiting for a weak spot.

"I don't suppose you know magic?" He asked casually and examined the messy room.

"I can assure you that none of my neighbors had magical powers." His eyebrows tightened as I spoke. It seemed as if the Human World was as unknown to him as the Magical one to me. "The only magic I have witnessed so far was from Amara and the instructors," I explained, and he nodded silently.

"Amara said that a Fores leads to the library. Do you think you can wait here for a few minutes without using magic? I could sneak into the library and see if I can find a book that can teach you at least some basic phrases."

I agreed in silence.

"You have to promise me you won't do anything while

I'm gone. Amara will kill me if something happens to you."

"Okay," was the only word I could squeak out as he disappeared into the Fores.

CHAPTER
27

Rowan really assumed that I could give him such a promise? To keep my new magic in check?

It was easy for him to say. After all, it had not taken him eighteen years to master his only gift. How could he believe I could contain this new one within hours?

I didn't even know how to access my magic; it had just flown out of me when I talked to Lex. There was no warning, like the itching of my pores. How was I supposed to know when the magic took over? My transformation seemed to be the slightest problem.

I bit my lip—maybe the slight pain I caused would distract me from thinking about magic. I closed my eyes.

It's just a bad dream. I'll finally wake up in a few minutes and start a normal day in Teviena.

A normal day in Teviena?

A *normal* day? In *Teviena?*

I laughed out loud. Nothing here was normal! Since the second I set foot on the magical ground, every day became more grotesque. And since when did I see Teviena as my refuge? I missed my room at home—my real home, in the Human World with my parents, books, and Damous.

Was Damous okay? Meanwhile, the police must have come to our home to search for us and found him. Or maybe he had run to the neighbors, and they had taken him in.

My heart hurt as thoughts rushed through my head.

What would my parents do? Were they still alive? I hoped I would see them again, just to hold on to a spark of hope? My father would tell me never to give up, that I was the most vigorous young lady he knew!

A lump spread in my throat.

My father? The man I've known since I was little; who was there when I learned how to walk; who taught me how to ride a bike and hunt and with whom I had watched movies and laughed for hours. I had never questioned whether he was my father, even though he was a wolf.

And now someone told me it was all a lie, that he was only in my life to protect me. That it was all just a show to make me believe we were a typical small family.

That couldn't be.

I got nauseous at the thought that I had been living a lie for years, and adding to it, I didn't even know my biological father. If my birth father wasn't Zino, who was he then—and where? Why didn't he attempt to see me?

The more I thought about it, the worse it became. I wrapped my arms around my stomach to suppress the uncomfortable feeling, but it didn't help.

Then, just as I thought my thoughts and remorse had calmed down, I thought of my brother. Was Lex my biological brother? He could be at least a half-brother because he had the shapeshifting form of Zino. But what if we weren't related at all? Who was he, and where was his biological mother?

I shook my head vigorously and walked up and down the room.

He had to be my brother! No one could read my mind better than him. He was always by my side, protecting me. Or did he know about my father and that we weren't related, and was he just playing dumb?

I angrily slammed my hands against my temples to stop the thought, squinting my eyes together until they hurt. Anger and grief ran through my veins.

I looked into Rowan's depressed, honey-colored eyes as I opened my eyes. I hadn't even noticed that he was back from the library.

"I can't do this anymore!" I sighed and collapsed.

Instead of helping me up, Rowan walked towards the bed, put down a pile of books he had brought from the library, and sat next to me on the floor.

"You are stronger than you think," he replied, his voice soothing. "I know this is all too much for you, but it will get easier. I promise you!"

"Get easier? The part that my mother has been lying to me since birth, or that the two men in my life aren't even related to me, or that I have a sister and a father that I didn't even know existed?"

He put his hand on my shoulder. "I understand your anger. I felt the same way years ago when it turned out my parents weren't my biological parents. Draven's not even my brother. What I'm trying to say is that just because you don't share the same blood doesn't mean you're not a family. Think of all the beautiful memories you had together. They were real. The love you felt from your parents and how much your brother cares about you can't be faked."

My throat was burning. I tried to suppress my tears and quickly wiped the sleeve of my cape over my eyes. "Do you know your birth parents?"

Rowan smiled and pressed his lips together. "That's your only question after I told you a piece of my life story?"

"I'm sorry. It was tactless of me." I lowered my head.

"I can hardly remember my biological parents. I probably wouldn't be here if the Alicens hadn't taken me in. Just like you, I didn't grow up in the Magical World. My parents told me a lot about the other world, but I had never been a part of it until I arrived here in Teviena. Draven is familiar with Teviena and the Magical World—" He took an abrupt break. "I only know little details about my parents."

"I'm sorry that you were separated from your parents. That must have been heartbreaking," I said compassionately.

"My father was very sick and passed away, and my mother couldn't live with the loss. So within a year, I had lost both parents and lived in a cabin in the middle of a forest. And that's where my new parents found me, alone, malnourished, and scared. I wouldn't have survived the winter if they hadn't found me." Rowan looked into the distance as if the wall was a projector and played the film of his life.

"I didn't want to reopen old wounds," I could feel the blood rushing out of my face.

"I didn't tell you my past to make you feel bad. I just wanted to show you that you're not alone with your feelings. Everyone here has at least one story they hate to tell—a past that hurt them—but it strengthens us. Without this pain, we wouldn't be the people we are today. And you aren't alone. Not only do you have a brother, biologically or not, but you also have a sister now. It surprised me how fast you two grew together, but now it makes sense. Although you couldn't remember your sister, your heart knew her. After all, you were together every second before being separated after birth."

Rowan was right. As I concentrated on every betrayal by the people I had blindly trusted, I had not thought about what I had gained. The second I saw Amara, my world changed. It felt like I needed her in my life. The bond between us was invisible but strong. I also had this feeling about Lex, who I saw as my brother, whether or not we had the same parents.

My thoughts wandered to Rowan's past. Was the trauma the reason he was so caring? What story brought the two boys together? If they weren't siblings and Rowan's childhood was this brutal, I didn't want to imagine what had happened to Draven.

Then I realized I had assumed their gifts were the same because I thought they were brothers, but now—there was the probability that they had different ones.

"Thank you, Rowan. I needed to hear that," I replied.

I exhaled. It was the first time since I had left the library that I had time to think without people or magic interrupting me. The painful pressure in my stomach receded, and the magic pulsing through my veins calmed down. Relaxed, I closed my eyes again.

Rowan wasn't like Draven. I am not alone. And we are getting through this night together.

I could feel a tiny box opening in my mind, and very carefully, I pressed the magic into it and closed it.

"I'm glad I could help you. But we have to start working on your magic," he said, bringing me back to reality.

I shook my head. "I don't think my magic can help me in this battle. We don't have enough time to prepare for the Oblitus, and I would rather focus on my shapeshifting instead of having two gifts and not being able to use either of them properly," I explained and stood up.

"You're doing me a favor. I don't know more about magic than you do, but I assumed we could somehow figure it out," said Rowan, smiling, still sitting on the floor.

"You offered me your help, and you don't even know magic?" I shook my head and smiled back at him.

"We would have managed somehow." He rose from the ground.

"We must go to Amara." A bad feeling grew inside of me. "I should never have left her alone."

"Amara is fine. Niam is with her. I don't know if it's a smart idea to have you both in the same room."

"But what if she needs me? Maybe I can support her. Now that I know how to suppress my magic, I'm no longer dangerous."

He scanned my face. "Just because you say you can control your magic doesn't mean you're harmless. What if your emotions get out of control?"

I didn't want to admit that he had a good point. I had to assume that I had everything under control. My sister needed me; I felt it.

"Trust me. I won't burn Teviena down. I must go to her."

His eyes shrunk, and he examined me closer. "Well! But if I feel even a spark of magic, then I push you back through the Fores into your room," Rowan warned me. A triumphant smile flashed across my lips.

We walked towards the arch and stopped, sweat running down my neck. The Fores stood right in front of the wall. What if I messed up Amara's instructions and, instead of going to another room, just ran into the stone wall?

I tried to gather courage.

"Should I start?" Rowan asked. He must have noticed my nervousness.

"Sure." Relief ran through me.

He walked calmly towards the Fores and disappeared. He made it look so easy.

"You can do it!" I said to myself, rubbing my hands together to prepare for the next step.

I leaned forward and froze in the movement. I couldn't do it. But then an energy surge ran through me, and I made another step towards the arch. The wall was only a few inches away from my face as I pressed my arms protectively in front of my face.

Amara's room. Amara's room.

I expected the impact at any moment as I tried to concentrate on where I wanted to go—but it didn't happen. Surprised, I opened my eyes and found myself in Amara's room.

CHAPTER
28

As I stepped into Amara's room, I saw Niam and Rowan, but there was no sign of Amara. Both stood a few feet away from me on the other side of the room with wide-opened eyes.

"Cassandra. Walk slowly in our direction," Niam whispered, gesturing I should come to him.

I threw my hands into the air in confusion. "Where is…" but I didn't get any further.

I could feel a pair of eyes resting on my shoulder blades. Within seconds, I turned into my lynx and landed with an elegant jump in front of the boys, their gaze directed towards the window.

It was dark outside, and the light in Amara's room was limited, but my cat's vision helped me. Metallic green eyes flash behind the bed. They were fixed on me and made a cold shiver run down my spine. I stood protectively in front of Rowan and Niam.

I didn't know what I was dealing with. It couldn't be Amara because even if she were in her new lynx's form, she would have to be at my eye level. So it could only be an Oblitus. Had they already invaded Teviena without us knowing?

"Cassandra, you're scaring her," Niam muttered, gently grabbing my shoulder to calm me down.

"Her? Who is it?" I asked softly, and a growl tore the silence apart.

My hair stood up, and all my senses were overwhelmed to find out what was attacking us.

"It's Amara," Niam whispered back, and I paused in amazement. "We all assumed that she is a lynx, like you. But no one has considered that your biological father isn't a lynx."

"She is… she's a wolf?" I exclaimed, and just as I dropped my cover, something big came at me.

A hiss escaped my throat as I jumped forward, slowly making circles around the creature. I looked into the piercing green eyes of a black wolf that was even larger than Zino's transformation. A growl drowned out my hiss—we circled each other until I stopped.

Although this wolf was more potent than anything I had ever seen, there was something comforting in the eyes of the beast. Then I realized why. I could feel the warmth in the depths of the eyes with which Amara looked at me. So slowly, I stepped closer without breaking eye contact.

"Amara, I'm here. You don't have to be afraid," I whispered, taking another step toward the wolf.

The growling grew louder, and I could see Rowan stepping in my direction out of the corner of my eye. I couldn't turn my gaze away from Amara. I had to get through to her and show her she had to fight the wolf inside her to turn back.

"Listen to me: you are a human being, not an animal. You decide when to turn and not the wolf in you. Fight it.

I know you're stronger!" I wanted to take another step toward her, but one bite of hers was enough to put me out of action.

Amara closed her eyes. The growling became quieter, and she shook her head back and forth as if wrestling with herself.

I could hear Amara's heartbeat slowing down. She was so close to defeating the wolf.

"Fight it," I repeated calmly, stepping back to give her space.

Then something happened that I didn't expect. My paw landed on an open book, and the sound of tearing paper broke the silence. This little sound was enough to interrupt Amara's concentration. She opened her eyes and jumped at me with a wide-open mouth. I froze and braced myself against the bite, which would be painful, if not fatal.

I made myself as small as possible, but even before Amara could reach me, I heard the fluttering of a cloak and found the courage to open an eye. Rowan stood before me, covering my view of Amara, bracing himself with all his might against her to divert her from her course. Amara yelped as Rowan rammed his body against her.

Both landed on the floor before the bed with a muted impact. Rowan stood up unscathed and looked down at Amara, who huddled before his feet.

"I'm sorry! I couldn't help it." Rowan's voice was filled with grief as he watched Amara finally turning back into her human form.

"Ouch, Rowan! I could have killed me," Amara replied, groaning, and she grabbed her rib.

"I would feel much worse if you had hurt your sister," added Niam, who had watched the whole thing without moving an inch.

"Wow. I didn't know you were that fast," said Amara

and tried to get up, but her legs trembled from exhaustion.

Rowan was not the only one with this ability. I had to think of his brother, who had left me in the stairwell without a trace.

Within a heartbeat, I was back in my human form and building myself up in front of Rowan with trembling nostrils. "You could have seriously hurt her!"

"And she could have killed you with one bite. You put yourself in front of us even though you didn't even know what you were dealing with." He calmly replied and helped Amara up.

It had no good argument against it; my instinct had overcome me.

Amara forced a smile on her face as Rowan put her on her bed. "But nothing happened. I'm fine. Let's talk about how much energy it takes to transform and why you two didn't stick to the plan to stay in her room." She groaned. "And how about I'm a freaking wolf, not a lynx!"

I didn't expect Amara to be a wolf. Mrs. Nerol had told me that Orion, our father, was an Amarok. His wolf's form is more prominent than an ordinary wolf. But that's all I knew about him.

"It looks like she inherited Orion's shapeshift form," I said hesitantly.

"He's an Amarok? Do you know what that means?" Niam asked, and he stiffened. I shook my head. "An Amarok is no regular wolf. When I was a child, my parents used to tell us stories. Here and there, I would sneak out at night to shapeshift because, hey, how cool is it to be a Feathered Serpent? Anyway, they told me the story of the Amarok. I always assumed that this story was only meant to frighten me so I wouldn't go out after dusk. It worked." He breathed deeply. "The story said that the Amarok is a loner and does not belong to a pack. He is taller and mightier than any wolf that has ever been sighted and that he would hunt down the people who dare to leave the house at night."

There were stories about the person who was supposed to be my father? That he was chasing innocent people during the night. My mother would never have spent time with such a person.

But how well did I know my mother? She had kept so many secrets from me that I no longer knew what was real and what was not. She had concealed my sister from me and pretended that we all had an everyday life. Maybe there was more to this story than I wanted to admit.

But I didn't want to accept a murderer as a father. I wanted to travel back in time and undo everything that had happened in the last hours and days and go back to my everyday, monotonous life with books.

"Have you ever seen an Amarok?" Amara seemed to struggle with this new information as much as I did.

"I don't think I'd be here if I'd met one," Niam replied in a small voice.

"You must not take these stories too seriously. If an Amarok is such a demonic being, they would never have allowed him into Teviena, and he would already sit in Bridlio. It's easy to paint a grim picture of beings just because they live on the edge of darkness. How many magicians sit in Bridlio? I can name some of them and the terrible deeds they have done. Have you ever heard such a scary story about them? Probably not. In your eyes, magicians are good. But when we talk about an Amarok or a Nightmare, everyone points fingers," Rowan said in an annoyed voice.

I swallowed.

"I only know a handful of inmates by name, but these are probably the most well-known creatures in Bridlio,"

Amara replied in a shameful voice.

Rowan had hit a sore spot with his statement. I felt that there was more behind his emotions about darker gifts. To me, it almost sounded like he was defending them.

I didn't know the Magical World long enough to have prejudices, but I knew I wasn't innocent. I feared Draven and Mr. Lafon, and the thought that my father could be a bloodthirsty wolf unsettled me. He was just a stranger, a figure I didn't know, but we shared the same DNA.

"I'm sorry, Rowan. It was a story that was told to me and nothing more. I didn't mean to upset you." Niam looked at the floor.

"But by spreading these stories, it only gets worse for these beings. How are they ever supposed to feel safe in the presence of other good magical beings when everyone assumes they will eventually do something bad?" Rowan's voice was deep and dark.

The oppressive air in the room almost suffocated me. Of course, I could understand Rowan's anger, but the timing for this conversation wasn't right.

Amara seemed to have the same feeling and tried to distract from the subject: "Why didn't you stay in Cassandra's room? I could have hurt you both."

"I had this queasy feeling that you needed me. And apparently, my gut was right because it didn't look like you could turn back. I've decided to focus on my shapeshifting as my defense and try to suppress the magic. As you said, it took years for you to become better, and I will certainly not learn the ins and outs of magic overnight," I explained, glad to deviate from the previous topic.

Amara nodded. "That's true. Our best chance would be to focus on our first gift. But not because we don't have enough time, but if the Oblitus find out that we have two gifts, they will probably be able to count one and one together and know that we are hybrids and have the same gifts," Amara answered.

I had forgotten about that. I was so caught up with my second gift that I had not considered that the Oblitus were after us—*the* twins. Just putting the word, *twins,* in my mouth was weird.

"What do you think about this idea?" Niam asked, tearing me back into reality.

"Excuse me?"

"I said we should tell Miss Syryn about your new gift."

"Mm... I don't know. After all, we have no evidence that it's true." I sat down beside Amara.

"No proof? You are shapeshifter and a sorceress! What else do you need to prove that you are a hybrid?" Niam scratched his head.

"But it doesn't make us twins. We can't back the story up. My mother is a shapeshifter, just like my biological father, so why is our second gift magic? Shouldn't we both be able to take two different forms instead?"

Niam paused and looked over to Rowan for an answer.

"My mother..." Amara's voice trembled as she spoke about Raylin. "She was a sorceress and must have inherited the gift of the Norwin bloodline, and Amber the gift of shapeshifting from Emmerson. Our bloodline is probably the reason we possess magic," Amara thought aloud, clapping her hands together. "Slowly, every detail gets its place. I love puzzles!"

"That would make you both hybrids," said Niam, looking at us, and with that sentence, he elicited precisely the reaction he had been waiting for.

He had said what I was so afraid of. I was just getting used to the idea that I was a Crossling. That alone was forbidden in the Magical World, just as Mrs. Nerol had made me aware of it. Hybrids were the reason that crossbreeding between beings was prohibited.

Panic set in. If anyone found out that Amara and I were hybrids, then the Saperians would be notified, and we would spend the rest of our lives in Bridlio, even though we had done nothing wrong. I couldn't risk it!

"No one should know about it!" I said sharply and corrected my high-pitch voice. "The instructors already have so much on their plate, and we don't have to add the drama of two trainees."

"But you don't understand how important it is. You two aren't just trainees—" Niam began, but my hand flew into the air in front of his face, and he fell silent.

"You don't understand what they will do to us when they figure it out. We aren't only hybrids but also the only way to eternal life. Do you really think the instructors won't let the Saperians know? I don't think so. They will probably lock us up like animals so that we aren't a threat to the Magical World anymore." My voice trembled with despair, and I felt my cheeks blushing.

"I didn't think that far," he answered softly.

"And I never thought I'd ever be in a situation like this one."

Everyone was silent for a moment. Then finally, Rowan, who had watched everything from the corner of the room, came forward. "Until we have enough evidence that Mr. Adrian's story is true, we should keep it to ourselves." He looked out of the window into the darkness. "It is getting late. We should get the others since we have established that neither Amara nor Cassandra pose a great danger to us tonight and should try to get some sleep. Who knows if the Oblitus are still attacking tonight or if only one has lost his way here?"

"I can't sleep yet because I promised Lex I'd find him to let him know I'm okay." I stood up from the bed and made my way to the door.

I couldn't forget about him again. Never had I spent so much time without him, and slowly, the feeling of loneliness spread through me, even though people surrounded me. It was a loneliness that only Lex could fill. The person I had entrusted everything to since birth, and now it seemed as if we had turned into strangers. I had so many secrets I hadn't shared with him. But how was I supposed to tell Lex the truth?

"How about you lie down, and I'll go to Lex and tell him you're alright, you've had a hectic day, and you're going to talk to him tomorrow?" Rowan asked. "I have to go to my brother, anyway. He's already waiting for me."

I held my breath for a second. "That would be helpful," I replied and was about to say something about his brother but left it at that.

"See you later," he replied, swinging out the door.

Just as my body started to relax, I stiffened. I didn't know any of the other siblings of my friends, except for Draven. My only worry was my brother and I hadn't considered that their siblings might also need our help.

"You guys must think terribly of me. Unfortunately, I had been so preoccupied with myself that I completely forgot that you also have siblings who probably need you," I muttered, rubbing my hands.

Niam grinned at me. "You don't have to worry about my sisters. Both are currently in their rebellious teenage years and know that competing against a Feathered Serpent isn't easy. They know how to defend themselves." He encouraged me with a smile and tried to find a comfortable place on the floor to rest.

"Wait, I'll help you." Amara stretched out her hands.

She focused on her bed, and out of nowhere, the mattress, blanket, and pillows began to multiply. She swung her hands towards the free floor and neatly placed the mattresses next to each other, each covered with a pillow and a blanket.

"Nothing simpler than a spell to duplicate things. And you don't have to worry about Taymon. I spoke to him this morning. A few older magicians took him under their wings. He's learned so much from them. It's easier for him not to have me around, so I can't embarrass him or remind him of our parents and siblings."

My heart calmed down.

I knew Ella and Viera didn't have any siblings, so I didn't have to bring it up again once they returned to us.

"Let me get Viera and Ella, and then we can hopefully close our eyes for a few minutes." Niam headed to the Fores.

"Thank you, Niam," we replied as one, and he smiled.

"I'll be right back!"

Silence spread through the room after Niam disappeared through the Fores.

Amara cleared her throat. "I still find it difficult to process everything. The thought that my parents and siblings don't share the same blood bothers me. But I am glad to have you in my life as a friend or twin," she said as she puffed up a pillow in her bed.

"You don't know how much I always wanted a sister, but I never thought it would come true. And now you're within my grasp, and the only thing I can think about is that I don't want to lose Lex. I can't imagine a life without him, and I'm afraid of how he'll react when he finds out that we're probably not related," I admitted, and the burning pain in my throat returned.

"You're not going to lose him. Even if he isn't your biological brother, no one can take away the connection and past you share."

A warm tear rolled over my cheek. "I don't even know how to talk to him. Every time I see him, I start a fight."

"My mother… I mean… you know, Raylin always said that we fight the most with the people we love because they keep coming back to us, no matter how humble we are. Lex will always be your brother, just like my parents and siblings will always be my family. There's nothing in the world they could do that I wouldn't forgive them."

Though there was doubt in the air that Lex was not my biological brother, I could feel his fraternal love. He was a big part of my life and one of the people who made me the person I was.

"I hope he sees it the same way," I said and laid down on a mattress next to Amara's bed.

It wasn't long before Viera, Ella, and Niam stepped through the Fores. I could hear them, but their voices seemed far away. I had no strength to open my eyes or talk to them. The more I tried to fight off sleep, the further away their voices drifted till everything around me disappeared.

CHAPTER
29

The sound of splashing water pulled me out of my sleep. I slowly opened my eyes and found myself in Amara's room.

I sat up and looked at the lifeless bodies in front of my feet and saw Viera, Niam, Ella, and one untouched empty mattress. As I turned my head to the side, I spotted Amara in her bed.

Rowan was missing. It even looked as if he hadn't come back the night before.

With a soft grunt, I maneuvered around the sleeping bodies to get to the balcony to get some fresh air. Just as I was about to step outside, I caught the sight of a figure leaning against the stone railing, looking out at the lake. I felt drowsy as I tried to focus my eyes on the person.

"You really are an early bird," Rowan said without turning in my direction. Quietly, I crept onto the balcony and locked the glass doors behind us.

"I didn't hear you come back yesterday."

Rowan smiled and continued to look at the calm lake in

front of us.

He ignored my answer. "Can you imagine that Teviena was once filled with life? Down there were hundreds of magical beings in the Quarters at home, each with a gift. Everyone was trained to get the most out of their gift, and from one day to the next, the Saperians decided that it was safer to integrate magical beings into the Mortal World so that there was no imbalance between the powers. Without this decision, we would have a fair chance against the Oblitus, but because our generation hasn't learned how to fight back, it will be a bitter fight," Rowan said dreamily, looking at the massive stone houses surrounding the lake.

As much as I tried, I couldn't imagine it. Everything below Teviena had been dead since I arrived here. "You think it was a wrong decision? Do you know when Teviena was closed?" I asked curiously. I knew the answer from Mrs. Nerol and Draven, but I wanted to hear it from him.

"Of course, it was a mistake. How many hybrids, like you, are undetected, and what's even worse, how many beings have not been classified as Oblitus since they didn't have to take the tests? I know from my parents that it was closed shortly after you were born if you just turned eighteen," he replied, and I could hear a slight hint of anger in his voice.

"But that's why we all had to take the test, right? So that we don't have black magic in our ranks."

He sighed. "What do you think they would do to the kids who have black magic? If they send them to Bridlio, they could get out because of the loophole. So even if there were Oblitus between our ranks, they are being trained, separate from the other children, because there is no safe prison for them."

My skin turned to ice. Although I tried to convince myself that we were safe, I had to admit that it was dangerous even here in Teviena. Was Draven one of the black magic trainees? Was that why he only left his room to intimidate me?

"You think we have no chance against the Oblitus?"

"There is always a spark of hope. Let's hope that the fight is still far away and that we are prepared by then. I'm really worried about the younger kids." His voice trembled with pain.

His concern was justified. I didn't understand why some children chose to stay. I didn't mean the young adults, but the younger children, some no older than seven or eight. Their courage was admirable, but the thought that something could happen to them turned my gut around.

"It's almost time for our training with Mrs. Nerol," I said and was about to open the door when Rowan put his hand on my shoulder.

"I hope you know that you and Amara need to be protected. You are the reason the Oblitus will attack, and we can't let them get their hands on you."

An icy shiver ran down my spine.

I knew I played an essential role in this fight, but no one had said that Amara and I played the main attraction in it. My whole life, I've lived in the shadow of Lex, and even though it was lonely, I enjoyed it. But now, an entire world depended on my next steps.

"I'm a normal girl from a small village," I replied indignantly and lowered my head.

"You are a Crossling between a powerful shapeshifter and the purest magical bloodline. You are a hybrid, and no one here is abnormal. Each of us is just lucky to have the privilege of growing up in two worlds."

"But I want to go back to the Human World. I was content with my life. I never wanted to get sucked into another world, even though I was searching for it."

"I don't believe you," Rowan said, staring at me tensely.

He was right. I always knew that I differed from my human classmates, and I asked myself every day why I could shapeshift and if there were more of us.

"I also have this internal struggle with my gift every day. I didn't want it. But now I'm here, and I couldn't imagine a greater honor than defending you and your sister."

The word *sister* still sounded strange. Rowan knew so much about me and my life, but I knew nothing about him except that he had a traumatizing childhood, had been adopted, and that Draven was by his side.

"Maybe I'll find out soon why you're so secretive about your gift," I replied narrowly, pushing the door open.

"Let's both hope it won't come to it," Rowan whispered so softly that I almost didn't understand him, even with my perceptive hearing.

Before us lay the rest of our group, still in a deep sleep, almost too peaceful to wake up. I reached down to shake Ella and Viera gently by their shoulders as a loud knock tore everyone out of sleep. I leaped to the door and opened it fast. In front of me stood Mrs. Nerol.

"Good morning Cassandra… and Rowan?" She paused and looked at us. Her eyes formed into slits at the sight of Rowan, who stood behind me in the doorway.

"We aren't alone," I said quickly, throwing the door open to reveal the view of Viera, Ella, Amara, and Niam, who sleepily rubbed their eyes and stretched.

"Oh… I didn't know you all were such good friends that you share a room, but that makes my job easier. I wanted to tell you that I will postpone our training. Miss Syryn gave me the order to test the last of the trainees. So you have the morning off. But I would strongly advise that you use this time wisely and maybe make use of the gym." She looked at us suspiciously. "Why, if I may ask, do you all squeeze into a room even if each of you has their own soft bed?"

"Um… I wasn't feeling too well yesterday after the encounter with an Oblitus, and they all stayed here just in case we were attacked at night, and I would still be too weak to defend myself." I tried to stay as close to the truth as I could.

"I heard about the incident. But it looks as if the Oblitus had lost its way, and it was not the announcement of an impending battle. I am glad that you have joined forces. Together, you are stronger. And now, could I borrow Viera to test her?" Mrs. Nerol said and waved Viera hastily to her.

What if Viera told her all about last night on her way to the crystal? Panicked, I looked at Viera, who walked past us with a lowered head.

"No worries. I can do it," she whispered.

"Good luck!" Amara mumbled, and I was unsure whether she meant the tests or the concealment of our secrets.

"Thank you," Viera said, just as Rowan closed the door behind her.

"Do you think she can keep our secret?" I asked anxiously and started walking up and down the room.

"Of course she can, and even if she tells Mrs. Nerol, she won't hand you over to the Oblitus. After all, she knows more about your parents than you do," Niam replied.

Relieved, I came to a standstill. Maybe it was better if an instructor knew about it. Mrs. Nerol had already indicated that she hadn't bought the story of Amber and Zion and assumed that Orion and Amber were a couple. She hadn't been wrong.

"Amara, maybe we should talk to Mrs. Nerol. She was

there when our parents met, and maybe she can help us," I said after a short while.

"But that can wait. It's more important that we don't interrupt them while testing. After all, it's finally Viera's turn," she answered.

It made me happy to think that Viera finally got tested by an instructor after we had failed the day before.

"I hope she has another gift," I replied, keeping my fingers crossed as if it could help Viera.

Another gift meant she was a hybrid, just like us. The fear of being discovered by the Saperians shot through my body. I shook the thought out of my brain. I had to deal with this matter another day if we survived the Shadow World's attack.

"How about a short workout before breakfast?" Niam asked energetically.

"On an empty stomach?" Ella frowned.

"Of course! This is the best time. We would have the hall to ourselves because everyone is eating."

"All right, all right."

I've heard about the gym, but I had never seen it. I knew that the crystal and the library were on the first floor, but I wondered how I had missed the gym.

It took us only a few minutes until we stepped out of the stairwell into the first floor and walked towards a massive iron door in front of us.

"I don't want to be a spoilsport, but my duty is calling me. I have to find Miss Syryn to see if I can help," said Rowan, scratching his head.

My heart sank because we were just about to find out what gift he had. Of course, I knew it didn't matter much what he was, but my curiosity ate me alive.

"He's not strong enough to take on a winged snake," Niam laughed, raising the mood.

"None of us can live up to your size," Amara replied, laughing, and opened the door to the training hall.

CHAPTER
30

I had expected the training hall to be equipped with all kinds of workout-related things, but I was disappointed. There were no mats, ropes to climb up on, or balls, as I was used to from the gym at my school.

Instead, this room was empty. I couldn't even see lamps. But these weren't needed because large windows illuminated the hall from two sides. The soft noise of the waterfall penetrated through the glass.

Then I noticed we weren't alone. Goosebumps ran over my arms like tiny spiders.

At the end of the hall stood... Mr. Lafon. Our laughter died the second we saw him standing there.

"Fresh meat." His lips curled into a nasty grin. "I didn't expect you to venture into this room after you seemed better at debating than fighting." His deep voice echoed through the room. "Let's see what you got!"

I turned to the door in a panic, but just as I saw it, it shut closed, and there was no way out. I could feel Amara's trembling hands clinging to my sleeve.

Black fog surrounded us. The tug on my sleeve disappeared, and I looked around and realized I was alone. The fog was so thick that I couldn't recognize my friends.

I stretched out my hands, hoping to grab a familiar arm. Instead, fear flooded my senses, and I could feel the magic in my veins vibrate. I pressed my fingernails into my palms to drown out the magic with the pain, but it didn't help. I loosened my clenched fists, and right at that moment, an energy surge shot out of me and displaced the surrounding fog.

"Transform yourself!" Ella shouted to me. I could see a glimpse of her before me.

"What?" I screamed back.

"Transform yourself," Ella repeated loudly, and I looked around to find out what we were up against.

Within seconds, I had changed. My lynx seemed to suppress the magic, and I felt grateful for Ella's advice.

Although I could now see the rest of my group in front of me, the dense black fog continued to surround us, hiding the danger ahead. I couldn't see the threat, but I knew it was there.

Niam had turned into a Feathered Serpent and was so big that he took almost the entire room to himself. Ella hesitated for a moment before lifting both palms into the air. Small rays of light gathered on her palms and transformed her skin into the same glassy substance she had turned into to give me energy. I could see through her, and behind Ella was Amara, who was visibly struggling to keep her transformation under control.

I closed my eyes to focus on my hearing. My ears were moving in all directions, but I could hear anything except the heartbeats of my friends and the feathers of Niam, who were quietly rustling as his wings were flapping up and down.

An unknown wind hit my whiskers and gave me the position of a fast-moving object. I quickly jumped over the heads of Ella and Amara into the fog and bounced against something hard. The collision made me stagger backward. I couldn't make out what I had bumped into.

Niam, who had recognized my situation, beat his wings more vigorously to whirl up the fog, and he cleared up my view. I froze.

A human-sized wooden doll stood in front of me, anchored to the ground. Other dolls were distributed throughout the room.

But that was not the reason I stopped. At the end of the hall stood our real opponent. The rattling of hooves echoed through the hall, and the pitch-black fur shimmered in the light of the flames. A large black stallion gazed in our direction with a grim look. His ears were laid back, and his nostrils flared.

This was no ordinary stallion. Fire replaced the mane and tail, and his deep black eyes pierced right through me.

I had tried to imagine Mr. Lafon as a Nightmare, but his proper form was even scarier than anything I had come up with. I tried to maintain eye contact with him, but after only a few seconds, I forced myself to look away.

The feeling of grief and fear overcame me, and for the first time in my life, I had to focus on not turning into a human again. It seemed as if the Nightmare deprived me of all my strength and thus almost made me give up my gift.

I couldn't let Mr. Lafon beat me—not in front of my friends. If I couldn't beat him, I was as good as dead when the Oblitus showed up.

I pulled all my courage together and rushed towards the Nightmare. When I looked up, I had expected that he was still standing in the same spot I had seen him, but he wasn't. Our eyes met.

He was just a few steps away from me. I had such a fast pace that I couldn't break in time to stop in front of him. His front hooves raised above my head, and I crossed my paws over my head and closed my eyes to protect my face from the collision. That moment dragged on forever... Everything happened so fast.

Frightened, I opened my eyes and lowered the crossed arms that I had held up.

The Nightmare was gone.

I could see the empty hall in front of me. I noticed I was no longer a lynx. My body shook uncomfortably. I looked over my shoulder to check on my friends' conditions.

Behind me, I could see the Nightmare attacking the rest of us. I tried to change, but I felt my lynx fighting against my demand. I wanted to help them but could neither move from the spot nor transform. My legs felt heavy.

"Watch out! He can't touch you!" My lungs hurt from screaming so loud.

I clenched my fists and tried to force my legs off the ground without success. I swung my fists around and desperately tried to lift my soles off the floor until my right fist hit something. Perplexed, I slammed my fist into the same spot next to me, and a transparent barrier stopped me. I tried again and could see small, flashing waves that seemed to flare at the same location my skin got into contact with something invisible. I panicked and tried to push my shoulder against it and had to realize that a transparent capsule surrounded me.

My scream made my ears hurt as I cried out. "Help me!"

But no one heard me. Niam and Amara had disappeared, and the Nightmare stood now between Ella and me.

Furious, I hammered my fists against the invisible barrier, and tiny sparks sprayed out under my skin. I tried to grab Mr. Lafon's attention, but he didn't seem to hear me either.

A bright beam of light illuminated the room, followed by an explosion. I sagged onto the ground to protect myself from it. But even before the blast could reach me, the inexplicable gravity that pulled my legs and anchored me to the ground gave way and made me drop to my stomach.

"I wonder why it took you so long to start training. If the Shadow World had attacked us yesterday, you would all be dead," said a deep, angry voice.

I shook my head and ran my fingers across the floor to ensure that I could still feel something and wasn't already dead.

"Get up, you pathetic pack!"

I rose quickly and saw Niam, Ella, and Amara standing beside me, all trembling. Ella embraced her upper body as if trying to hug herself to give herself comfort. Mr. Lafon's hateful gaze was on us, and neither of us dared to look up from the floor.

"Can someone please explain to me what that was? Was that all you have learned in the last few days?" Every word from Mr. Lafon's felt like a beating. Niam murmured something incomprehensible, but no one gave him a simple answer.

"And now you're all silent at once? Has no one prepared you for what's going on here in the gym?" The unpleasant silence proved that we had no clue. "Really? Okay, then I will have to explain it to you. In this room, you can use your gifts without hurting another person. If someone is eliminated, for example, by a fatal blow, this person is surrounded by a protective capsule and can neither be heard nor seen until the fight is over. This allows you to use your gifts indefinitely without getting hurt or hurting anyone." Mr. Lafon walked around us, looking at everyone from head to toe as if he were measuring us to distort us later. "I expected more from you all—the son of the famous Louis. Your father would be ashamed if he saw your fight. The daughter of Tyra, the strongest Light Fairy I have taught myself, and to see how soft her offspring has become. And then you. If you all knew what Raylin was capable of and what a fraction of magic you were using..." he scoffed. "And finally, we mustn't forget the daughter of Amber. Your parents can be glad they didn't create another weak hybrid and just a Crossling. At least your brother isn't a disappointment."

He stopped in front of me and continued to scold us. Anger was raging through me, and I imagined how satisfying it would be to attack him at that moment as a lynx. But I had to suppress this temptation.

"Did you think you would come here and I would take you by the hand and show you how beautiful the Magical World is? I knew Alysa was too soft for this job. She treats you like little children who need to be prepared slowly for this world. You would all be dead now if you had fought a real Oblitus. Bridlio's inmates have the strongest and darkest gifts there are. Do you think they will spare you because you are children? They will laugh as they tear you to pieces."

The ground around us shook.

Mr. Lafon raised an eyebrow and grinned at Amara. "You can save your strength, Miss Hazen. It's too late now." Amara looked at him, confused, and then at me. I was on the verge of losing control and unleashing my magic on him.

"I'm sorry. I'm going to work on my magic. Can we go?" asked Amara hastily, walked over to me and drilled her elbow into my side to interfere with my eye contact with Mr. Lafon. The tremor immediately stopped as I rubbed my hand over my aching side, staring at Amara angrily.

"You give up so quickly? All right. Get out of my sight, and don't dare to return until you're a real opponent," Mr. Lafon barked, and we pushed each other out of the room to bring as many doors as possible between him and us.

"Why did you interrupt me? I could have wounded him to teach him a lesson," I said to Amara, who dragged me behind her.

"Did you not listen to him? No one can be wounded in the gym. You would have made the situation much worse for us. What do you think he would have done to you if he found out you are a hybrid?" Amara calmly explained.

"I didn't think that through," I murmured, ashamed of my behavior.

Injuring him wasn't a great idea, but enduring his harsh words instead of accepting the truth was much worse than being his most hated apprentice. I did nothing to him, so why did he hate me so much?

"Who needs a break?" Niam asked bitterly and tried to put on a forced smile.

Mr. Lafon had humiliated each of us, and we knew he had spoken only aloud what we already knew. We were only shadows of our parents—afraid and heartbroken. But how could it be different? They hadn't trained us for years to master our gifts; We had been raised as people who just had gifts. I never thought I would ever need my gift to survive.

"I don't think we can afford a break just because we humiliated ourselves in the worst possible way. It doesn't mean we can rest and give up. How about we practice a little in our hiding place and then try again against Mr. Lafon?" Ella threw in. She seemed to suffer the most under the accusation of Mr. Lafon. Her eye color had changed to a light blue as if holding back tears.

"Unlike the other kids, we wasted a lot of time with dramas. We should forget for a moment what's going on in our personal lives and focus on getting our gifts under control," Ella said, and Amara agreed.

I knew she was right. I had to focus on mastering at least one gift to clear my name, which would also help me fight the Oblitus. It was up to me to improve after I had failed not once but twice in one day.

"What do you suggest?" I asked curiously.

"I'll tell you when we get to the fountain."

CHAPTER
31

Ella led us back to Amara's room, and we came to a stop in front of the Fores.

"Focus on the hiding place," Amara reminded us again before she disappeared through the arch.

There were no complications that time. Each of us had mastered the inhibitions of stepping through the Fores to get into another room the night before.

I was relieved to see the blue color of the water dancing on the walls. Someone had turned the fountain back into its original color. There was no trace of the red fluid that had frightened us.

"Okay, listen to me… we have to stop wanting to be like our parents. Of course we are their children and have the same gifts, but every one of us has more potential than we allow. We will never get stronger by reading books from other trainees. We need to train properly. Now you're probably wondering how we should do that in a small room like this. Maybe Amara can find a spell to expand this room and give us more space because Niam will need it.

You think you can do this?"

Ella addressed the last sentence to Amara, who flinched. Then she straightened herself and said with a firm voice. "I can try it. I'll be right back," as she disappeared into the Fores.

"Cassandra, I know you said you wanted to focus on your transformation, but if we teach you a bit of magic, then you have a gift that no one will see coming. Would you try it?" Ella said to me.

"I don't know…" I said hesitantly because I was afraid to use my new gift. I didn't know how to access it. But without practice, I would never get it under control, and I remembered Ella's words that we had to grow beyond our parents' heads. I nodded my head.

"And now to you, Niam. I observed your sister changing her size as a Feathered Serpent. Are you able to do that?"

"I am not surprised that she broke the rules and is showing off her shapeshifting. I guess we are siblings after all," he giggled, but his face turned serious within a second. "My parents have not used their transformation often, and this must be a new trick she learned here on Teviena. But I will do my best to figure it out."

"Don't get me wrong. It's great that you're a large shapeshifter, but that makes you an easy target. If you can change your size, I don't have to worry about you being attacked from all sides. And my task will be that I have to learn to use my new power precisely. We Light Fairies weren't created to fight, but maybe there are some tricks I can learn to defend myself."

"The explosion against Mr. Lafon was a start," Niam replied enthusiastically, dancing from one foot to the other.

"But it would have been better if I could focus on one point instead of my whole surrounding. If all of you had been standing beside me, I would have been the reason for your elimination, not Mr. Lafon." She lowered her head.

"I would have preferred that over getting trampled by him," I admitted, nudging her with my shoulder.

"What did I miss?" Amara was back with two thick books in her arms, holding them like precious babies. "Mr. Adrian asked about your well-being, Cas. I told him you were doing fine according to the circumstances."

There was my name again. *Cas.* She used it like it was the most natural thing in the world. Even though that nickname reminded me of my life before Teviena, slowly but surely, I started to accept my real ancestry and family relations.

"Ella changed my mind. Do you think you could teach me some simple spells that might be useful to me?" I asked and continued to look at the yellowed pages of the books that Amara so carefully held.

"Then you have to show me a few tricks as a shapeshifter!"

"Nothing easier than that."

A loud voice made me shriek. "There you are!" Viera busted out of the Fores and almost crashed against Amara. She was out of breath, resting her elbows on Amara's shoulder and leaning forward to gasp for air.

"And?" I asked excitedly to find out how the results of her tests were.

"As expected… I have only one gift, but…" Viera took a long break to build tension. "Mrs. Nerol found out that my grandmother was a Huntress, and… she had me test a bow, and I don't want to brag because I have never used a bow and arrow before, but I have sunk three arrows into the bullseye and then even three more blindfolded. Isn't that super exciting? And look what she gave me." Viera vanished through the Fores and came right back. She held up a wooden bow with carvings in her right and a quiver with arrows in her left.

"Stop it! You have the genes of a Huntress?" Amara grabbed Viera's hands, still holding her new weapon, and pressed it with joy.

Viera jumped up and down. "I was also surprised. I never met my grandparents. But that means I can fight beside you guys."

"But you're not going to chase us, are you? Not like in the stories... the Huntress, also called Slayer, was the enemy of magical beings," Niam said, and his smile died.

Everyone stopped and looked at Viera.

"I would never hurt you. You are my friends!" Viera said, wide-eyed.

"I just wanted to be sure," Niam replied, putting a smile back on his face.

He tried to loosen up the atmosphere between us, but the word *stories* gave me a funny aftertaste because the last two, of the twins and that of Orion, had turned out to be true. We were twins, and Orion had to be our father if Amara could turn into an Amarok.

"You don't have to worry. Even if my grandmother was a slayer of magical beings, it doesn't mean I have to follow in her footsteps," Viera assured us once again, knowing that she was telling the truth because that was her gift. "So, what were you guys doing when I was gone?"

Niam and Amara updated Viera, who had her mouth wide open as she absorbed the last hour's events.

"What did he call you?" She exclaimed after Niam had summed up the training with Mr. Lafon. She dropped her bow to the ground.

"He pretty much said that we are the most useless trainees in Teviena," Niam said, and my stomach turned again.

"I can't believe it! And he's supposed to be an instructor? How can the Saperians allow him to train children?" She picked up her bow and examined it for damages.

"I wouldn't be surprised if he was an insider for the Oblitus. He hates us profoundly and doesn't even know us. Just like Mrs. Nerol, it sounded like he trained some of our parents, if not all of them," Amara added.

This fear also plagued me. The thought had come to me that he could work with the Oblitus and was just waiting to find out who the twins were.

"That's why we must be cautious that he doesn't find out what we are." My voice was firmer than I expected.

"I don't think you have to tell us that. After today, I trust no one but myself," Ella said calmly, but something threatening lay in her voice. "And you guys, of course." She added.

"I trust Mrs. Nerol," I replied, waiting for approval, but it didn't come.

"I'm not sure who we can trust anymore. I'm afraid to tell my siblings about our secrets because I don't want to get them involved. But I can tell you one thing... the second we get attacked, I'm going to hide my sisters here to keep them safe. I cannot fight with the conscience that they are in danger," Niam answered, and I could see in his face that he was afraid.

"I'm sure no one here will object," Ella assured him, looking every one of us deep into the eyes.

"Of course, they can hide here! I am in favor of bringing as many young children as possible down here so we can protect them from the fight. Let's just hope that by then, we are strong enough to fill their place at the front," I added and was confirmed by nodding heads.

"Amara, are you able to enlarge this room?" Ella asked

energetically and pointed to the books she had brought from the library.

"I just had to make sure that I could use the same spell I used to enlarge the Fores for a room, and it turned out to work as long as there is free space around the walls. Of course, we are underground and well…" She stopped, took the first book from her pile, and opened it. "But I've found a spell that can turn the surrounding earth into crystals so we can gain space through lithium. If you don't know yet, I love stones and crystals," Amara answered proudly.

"This plan sounds super complicated, but I would like to watch you," Niam said honestly and sat down on the couch.

"The only problem is that I probably won't be strong enough to use these two spells in one day. As I explained to Cassandra, my parents disappeared before they could give me my wand, and without a magic wand, crystals, pentagrams, or candles, every spell drains me of power," Amara explained.

There was silence for a few seconds. We couldn't wait another day for the enlargement of the room because none of us dared to take another step into the training hall with Mr. Lafon, and there was no further possibility to train undisturbed.

"How about I help you?" I asked hesitantly.

"That could work." Pleased to have found a solution, she walked towards the empty wall to our right. "You can NOT break the bond between us," she said and rubbed her hands together before grabbing mine.

I felt like a fraud. I had offered my magic without knowing how to use it.

"Repeat after me," Amara whispered a phrase she had previously used for the Fores. I didn't know the language, but I sharpened my ears to pick up every syllable. Again and again, Amara repeated the same sentence until I spoke it in accordance with her.

"Focus on the earth behind these walls," Amara whispered as I repeated the foreign words.

I closed my eyes, reached out one hand to the clammy stone wall, and pressed my palm onto the icy surface. I chanted the words, but nothing happened. Then, I tried to imagine the earth behind the wall. I could feel the cool earth around me, and a fresh, earthy, musty smell rose in my nose.

Then I felt something familiar yet strange—like my veins were overrun with electricity. A warm feeling spread from my head through my chest and arms into my hands, and from there, this energy poured into the wet stone wall. The stone warmed, and it felt like a vacuum cleaner was sucking on my palms. The magic escaped through my fingertips and palms, leaving behind the feeling of numbness.

"That's enough," Amara said, pulling me out of focus.

"Did we do it?" I asked tensely, opened my eyes, and let go of Amara's hand and the wall. My hands felt cold and numb, but my body temperature returned to normal within seconds.

"You were great! Of course, we did it," Amara said in a squeaky voice. "My hands have never regenerated so quickly from magic." She kept looking at her hands with a smile.

"I remember you talking about the problem. Maybe it has something to do with you being a hybrid now?" I looked at her and prepared myself mentally for the next spell.

"You must not forget that the spell that suppressed your second gift has dissolved. Maybe part of the other gift was affected by it?" Viera asked, loud enough for us to hear. She sat on the couch next to Niam to witness the spectacle of my first spells.

"I have never noticed how loud people's voices are when you are a shapeshifter." Amara cringed as she tried to get used to her now sensitive hearing. "Are you all right? Can we do the second spell?" She held both palms in my direction.

"I've never felt better! I feel like my body has longed for this moment for years," I whispered back and grabbed my sister's hands.

Although I always saw Lex as my brother, I couldn't deny that there was total harmony between the forces of Amara and me. Our connection was so straightforward. It was as if Amara was my missing piece of the puzzle, and without her, I couldn't make my gift work. A spark of magic from Amara danced through my hands, and a feeling of familiarity and security settled in me.

"It feels so familiar," said Amara, and I could see in her warm smile that the same feelings overran her body. Then she closed her eyes and recited a new sentence, which I pronounced in no time in harmony with her.

I forgot everything that had bothered me in the last few days for a few seconds. I could feel the magic of Amara as we took a breath together simultaneously, and our voices entangled.

The energy that magic gave me filled me with warmth, even though my hands became colder. I could sense the room slowly getting bigger until I felt like a little doll in a dollhouse—a quiet noise behind the walls made me stop as we had reached the maximum size. We fell silent.

I didn't want to believe my eyes—was that me? My heart was beating faster, and for the first time in days, I felt contentment and pride.

I had mercilessly lost against my doppelgänger and Mr.

Lafon. But this room was proof that I wasn't useless—that I had the power to protect myself and that I could fight for my parents.

"If I hadn't been here, I would never have thought it possible for you to be hybrids." Niam cried with enthusiasm. He was still sitting on the couch, but unlike before, the piece of furniture looked like a little brick on a living room floor.

The space had increased several times and was now almost twice the size of the training hall.

"I think we went a little overboard. I didn't know that we could summon so much magic together." Amara spun around to examine the size of the new hideout.

My body shook with joy. "Until a few minutes ago, I didn't even know that I was capable of something like this."

I felt like hugging her. I wouldn't have made it without her guidance. Magic was just as enchanting as I had imagined.

"I don't think anyone else doubts that you are siblings," said a deep voice, and loud clapping echoed through the new hall.

My heart dropped. Since when was Rowan standing in the tunnel's passage? I had not heard him come in. With clapping hands, he walked towards the couch while his gaze still rested on Amara and me. He settled down next to Ella on the couch.

"Thank you, thank you," Amara laughed and bowed a few times as if she were on a stage and had the show of her life behind her.

"I can't put into words how I feel right now," I said and hugged her. Amara was stunned by my reaction and took a step back, but then she pressed me firmly.

"I never thought you were a person of big feelings,"

Amara admitted, slowly loosening her arms, which she had wrapped around me.

"I didn't think so either, but you helped me jump over my shadow and try something new. You see, I'm more of a creature of habit. Literally." I laughed at my choice of words. "It's hard for me to try something new."

"Any time. That's what siblings are for." Amara's smile died. "Speaking of siblings. I don't know how to explain to my brother that I'm probably not his sister."

The same fear went through me. I wasn't sure how to give this news to Lex. My body stiffened, thinking he could repel me when he discovered we couldn't even be half-siblings. Or maybe we were. But my mother would have given birth to Lex during her time in Teviena and would have been trained for another year before she left Teviena. But this timeline didn't make sense either because Mrs. Nerol had said that Zion had finished his education, which meant that there had to be another woman who was Lex's biological mother.

Then it struck me. My mother hadn't left Teviena because she had something to do with the death of Brianna. She left because she had found out she was pregnant with twins and was afraid someone would figure out her bloodline and the secret of immortality and start hunting her unborn children. I still didn't know what role Zion and Lex played in all this, but I was getting closer to the answer.

"As long as I don't have all the facts about our family constellation, I will not tell Lex about it. My mother can't be his birth mother. This raises the question, where is his mother, and why did she allow her child and husband to live with another woman? There are just too many unanswered questions before I can tell him the truth, and I would advise you to keep waiting," I said monotonously as my thoughts continued to search for the answer to Lex's mother.

"The longer I think about everything, the less I understand it," Amara said, agreeing with me. We had made our way towards the couch during the exchange of words.

"And… what do you say? Is there enough space?" I asked and threw my hands in the air to underline the size of the room.

"Now we have enough space to hide all of Teviena down here," Viera laughed, jumped up, and embraced us joyfully. "I'm so proud of you! Look what you can achieve together."

I had used up all my affection of the week for hugging Amara and tried to get out of her grip, but she was too strong that I stopped fighting it and embraced it.

"Don't think I'm going soft and need hugs every day," I smiled and tried to sound as sarcastic as possible.

"Daily hug… saved," Viera replied, laughing, and stepped away.

"I don't mind hugging," Niam grinned and came running towards us with his arms outstretched, but Amara just drilled her elbow into his side to stop his attempt. The air escaped from his lungs, and he panted. He sat back on the couch with a sad face. Amara's elbow wasn't to be trifled with. The thought alone brought back the pain in my ribs she had inflicted on me to interrupt my magic in front of Mr. Lafon.

We spent the next few hours teaching each other new tricks. Niam managed to change his size after several failed attempts until he was as small as a snake. Ella transformed the light that shone through the water's surface into lightning and small, targeted explosions. Viera showed us how accurate her aim was with a bow and arrow on a target that Amara had summoned for her. She even did it with her eyes tied. Amara helped me learn some spells. I could make things float, create fire, reduce and enlarge objects, and conjure up trifles. In return, I showed her how she could use her newly gained senses as a wolf to catch a rabbit I had summoned. I needed some attempts to conjure up an anatomically just rabbit. Everyone tried to ignore my misfired spells, but Niam kept laughing when the rabbit with two tails or the one with the colossal front teeth that were grinding over the ground hopped past him.

Only Rowan sat comfortably on the couch and flipped through some books from the bookshelves. Niam had tried several times to persuade him to train, but he refused.

Soaked in sweat, we finished our first training to go to our rooms so we could freshen up before the meeting in the dining room. We said our goodbyes in front of the Fores and, one after the other, stepped through the arch to get to our rooms.

CHAPTER
32

Istepped onto my balcony to get some fresh air and recharge. I drove my hands over the embroideries of my coat. The black color of my clothes showed I was a shapeshifter. The golden, ornate embroideries pointed to my Emmerson bloodline, and the thin, green stripe embedded in the stitching pointed to my magic.

I closed my eyes and stretched my face towards the sun that kissed my skin with warmth. A few birds chirped in the distance, but the waterfall that ran into the lake below me was the loudest noise.

My thoughts wandered to my mother and Zion—my stepfather. The thought of them put an incredible pain in my heart, and I shook my head. I had to stop thinking I'd never see them again. Instead, I had to hold on to the little spark of hope that we could find our parents and embrace them again. I didn't just want to see them; I HAD to find them because my mother and Zino were the only people who could tell me the truth about the past.

Resolutely, I clenched my fists, and an energy surge ran

through me. My job now was to ensure that a few Oblitus were captured so they could tell us about the hiding place where all our parents were. And I had to count during the meal how many young children there were in Teviena so that we could fill the hiding place with supplies that would feed them for a few days. I wasn't hoping the fight would last for days, but I wanted to play it safe.

With the new plan in mind, I went back into the room and locked the balcony door behind me. I still had a few minutes until the meeting in the dining room started, and it gave me enough time to tell Amara about my new plan.

I went towards the Fores, focused on Amara's room, and with one step, I found myself in the space of my imagination. But it was empty. I stepped onto the balcony to ensure Amara wasn't out there, but I remember her telling us she feared heights.

Where could she be? Had she already made her way to the hall?

I hurried out the door into the corridor to see if Viera was still in her room, for her room was on the same floor as Amaras. I didn't have to walk far. Between Amara's Wedo with room number 507, there was only one more room until I arrived at Viera's Wedo, which bore the number 511.

I quietly knocked on the door, but nothing moved. I forgot that not everyone had such good hearing as me, so I intensified the knocking. Viera had to be at the meeting, too.

There was no one in the corridor on the fifth floor except for me. The other children must already be gathered, and I was again one of the last.

I hurried towards the staircase, and just as I wanted to put my foot on the first step, a sound stopped me. I could hear the rattling of cloaks above me and a whisper. For a moment, I thought I had found my friends and sharpened my ears to be sure.

"We could minimize the loss of children by finding out who the twins are. Then only two children have to be sacrificed, and the rest of them would be safe." I recognized this calm voice; it was Miss Syryn. I rubbed my ears to ensure they weren't clogged and I had heard correctly.

"We're talking about children here! We can't just hand over two of them. They're innocent and have nothing to do with this fight. It's our job to protect them," replied an angry voice I made out as Mrs. Nerol.

"But you must understand that it's their destiny. Their parents could have prevented it by obeying the rules, and they didn't comply. So it is their calling," Mr. Syryn said calmly.

"Syryn, please! There must be another way to protect these children. It had been a foolish idea of the Saperians to train children for a fight they could never win. And we will be just as guilty if we allow it."

"When did you get a soft spot for children, Alysa? You know the rules. You know how dangerous the Oblitus are and what a bloodbath there will be when they get here. Don't you want to do anything about it so it doesn't happen?"

"Of course! I would do anything! But we can't just hand over the twins. We have to come up with a better plan because this would be their certain death. And what follows is much worse. We still don't know which Oblitus broke out to recruit an army from Bridlio. The Shadow World will be unbeatable if we give them the two children."

I held my breath and could taste bile in my mouth.

"Alysa, you won't be able to save the twins. Eventually, they will fall into the hands of the Oblitus. So now the question is whether we can delay it long enough and live with the fact that it probably means the death sentence for most children or whether it makes more sense to hand them over directly. Then we still have a little time to train the other children to defeat them," said a third, dark voice, and there was only one person it could belong to—Mr. Lafon.

I clenched my fists to suppress a scream.

"But that would mean that the other children will have to face the Oblitus anyway, with or without sacrifice. Why are you so sure that the twins exist? I mean, I didn't meet any trainees here who could be twins," Mrs. Nerol replied, and I could hear the tension in her voice.

"Can't you feel them? The energy that draws you to them?" I pressed myself flat against the wall as if it could stop her from feeling my presence or magic. "I can't tell who or where they are, but I can feel them. A force more powerful than anything I have ever felt in my life, and it grows with each passing day. In the beginning, it was once or twice a month, but the distances of this power became smaller and the energy stronger until the first parents disappeared, and the Saperians ordered me to reopen Teviena so that the children have a chance of survival," Miss Syryn explained with a firm voice.

"I can't feel that power you're talking about. But if they are as strong as you say, maybe we'll have a chance against the Shadow Creatures."

"We cannot dare to let the other children fight for something preventable," Miss Syryn barked sharply, and I let out a silent cry.

I had never heard this tone from Miss Syryn. Her voice sounded dark and threatening. I slapped my hands on my mouth, but I reckoned I had already given myself away. It turned out I was lucky. Nobody seems to have noticed me.

"I will personally take care of locating these two children. I mean, how hard can it be?" Mr. Lafon said, and my surprised expression about Miss Syryn's tone turned into fear.

I had to find Amara. We had to get out of here as soon as possible. We were no longer safe here. They didn't know that Amara and I were twins, but it wouldn't take long before Miss Syryn or Mr. Lafon found out.

Softly as if on velvet paws, I crept towards the doorway, but Syryn's voice stopped me, which had now returned to the soft and calm pitch I knew from her. "I know you won't disappoint me, Erebus. We have to act fast."

Silently I crept out of the stairwell until I was out of the instructor's reach, then I started running.

It did not surprise me that Mr. Lafon thought sacrificing the two children was a big deal. But never in my life had I expected this idea to come from Miss Syryn and that she, as head of Teviena, was okay with giving up two innocent people.

Was our identity still secure? Had Mr. Lafon noticed I had triggered the quake and not Amara, and he had counted one and one together?

Maybe Mrs. Nerol was sure that Amara and I were twins. But she was on our side and had rejected this absurd plan. So what could she do to help us?

I ran back to Amara's room to use the Fores to get into my room. If I hurried, I might get to the dining hall before Miss. Syryn and Mr. Lafon got there. I had to warn Amara!

I arrived in my room, slammed the door open, and ran right into Amara, who had raised her hand to knock. At lightning speed, I grabbed her collar and pulled her into the room while she let out a faint cry. Behind her stood Viera.

"Be quiet!" I whispered out of breath while Viera closed the door quietly behind us. Then, after double-checking that the door was locked from the inside, I spun around.

"Where are the others? Are they already in the dining room?"

"What's the matter with you? That hurt!" Amara answered in shock and rubbed her neck.

"Where are the others?" I repeated, and my voice shook with despair.

"I don't know. They're probably already at the meeting. What in the world is going on?" Amara asked, alarmed.

"They know about us and are looking for us! They want to sacrifice us to the Oblitus to spare the other children!" My voice broke.

"Who? Who is looking for us?" They asked, confused.

"Miss Syryn and Mr. Lafon! I overheard them making a plan to hand us over to the Oblitus. We have to leave! Now!" I was beside myself, reaching for Amara's hand to pull her away from the door.

"That doesn't sound right. But, even if it's true, where should we go?"

Yes, where should we go? We couldn't go home because we were reported missing from the Human World. And I knew nothing about Teviena. I didn't even know which continent we were on. But returning to the other world was by far safer than staying here. So we had to make a run for it.

"You guys have to believe me! We need to go!"

"But if you leave Teviena, they will know one hundred percent that you are the twins," Viera mused aloud.

"And if we stay here, they'll find out too," Amara added, settling down on the bed in a daze.

I drove my hand through my thick hair and tried to come up with a solution. "What if Miss Syryn is right? If we can put an end to this, now and here? It would spare our brothers and sisters."

Viera looked at me with a wide open mouth and then at Amara, hoping she would reject this idea. "You think the Oblitus will stop chasing other magical beings after they have you? That's absurd! They won't stop until they are the last magical beings on this planet. They have been locked away from our world like animals, and now you think they won't take revenge on the good magical beings after they have you? It will only strengthen them," Viera said, waving her hands hysterically.

"Then give me a better idea," I said helplessly, letting myself fall on the bed next to Amara.

Viera rolled her eyes. "How about—don't give up? You two are our only chance. I have seen with my own eyes how strong you are together. Without you, the Oblitus will exterminate us."

I leaned my head from one side to the other as I weighed our options.

"True, the Shadow Creatures won't give up until they are in power. But the question is, how can we disguise ourselves so that the instructors don't find out who we are?" Amara asked and rubbed her temples.

"We could ask Mrs. Nerol for advice. She was also there when Miss Syryn told him to look for us, but she refused to help them. So we could go to her. I'm sure she'll help us to get out of here," I said. It was the only plausible solution because Amara and I would never make it alone.

"Or you just hide under the fountain. Maybe none of the instructors know about the place," Viera threw in.

"And if they do? If they know about the hiding place, then we serve ourselves on a silver platter," said Amara, and Viera nodded in agreement.

"The only person who can help us now is Mrs. Nerol. We only have to maintain a normal appearance until we can talk to her." I got up and wanted to go to the door when I heard footsteps in the corridor. I turned to the others and held my index finger in front of my mouth to signal to be quiet. The steps became louder, and nausea rose in me.

According to the sound, it was two people. Had Miss Syryn already figured out that we were the twins and were on her way with Mr. Lafon to capture us against our will? I hoped the steps would simply pass our door, but the steps slowed down and stopped in front of my room.

I felt dizzy. Panic was spreading through me. I would never see my parents again. I would never get another chance to talk to Lex or escape the Magical World.

A loud knock drowned out the noise in my ears. I cringed, and none of us dared to move.

Maybe they would just leave if no one answered. I held my breath because even breathing seemed too loud. Someone turned the knob, but the door didn't open. Then the knob shook until the person gave up and stepped away from the door.

"Cassandra, I know you're in there. Open the door," Rowan called, and I breathed in relief. When I unlocked it, Rowan smiled in my direction, accompanied by Ella.

He looked at the others, and his smile turned suspicious. "What happened?"

"Did you see Miss Syryn or Mr. Lafon anywhere?" Amara shot out before anyone had the opportunity to explain what was going on.

"No. Why? And why are you acting so weird?" He took a step back.

"You didn't tell them we were hybrids, did you?" I asked, and Ella shook her head.

"Why should we? Didn't we agree to keep it between us?"

Amara breathed a sigh of relief as the tension in the air

dissipated.

"Can someone please explain what's going on?" Rowan asked and closed the door behind him.

"Have you seen Mrs. Nerol?" I didn't want to waste any more time.

"She was sitting at the dining table with the other instructors, and now tell us what's going on!" Ella begged, rubbing her hands with nervousness.

Amara ignored the confused faces of the newcomers, got up from the bed, and looked at me. "We must try not to reveal our identity for one more night."

"What are you talking about? Why another night? What happened?" Rowan asked in surprise and stared at us.

"We will explain everything to you on the way to the meeting," I said and prepared to leave.

"Where is Niam?" Viera asked, counting the people in the room with her finger.

Through all the tension, I had not noticed that he wasn't with Rowan and Ella.

"He stayed at the table. We wanted to look for you guys because the three of you are the only ones still missing," Ella explained, and the bad feeling in my stomach rose again.

How could we remain undetected if we were now the main spectacle of the meeting if we were the last to go through the door?

"This makes it difficult to remain unobtrusive," Amara admitted loudly.

"We can do it. We could say that we lost track of time while studying and just sit down with the others at the table, and as soon as the meeting is over, we find Mrs. Nerol," I assured her, grabbing her by the shoulders and trying to convince her with courage I didn't have.

"You scare me," Ella interrupted, looking back and

forth between us.

"We have to go *now*. We can't waste any more time," Viera said as she left the room.

The rest of us joined her. On the short way to the dining room, I summarized the conversation between the instructors and explained the plan to find Mrs. Nerol after the meeting and ask her for help.

"Are you sure it was Miss Syryn and Mr. Lafon? Did you see their faces?" Rowan asked in a low voice.

"Am I sure? I can make out Mr. Lafon's voice three miles against the wind. And I'm one hundred percent sure that the other voice is Miss Syryn," I assured, replaying the conversation in my head.

"How does she know about the story of the twins?" Ella asked.

A heart sank into my pants. There was another person we hadn't considered. "What if Mr. Adrian betrayed us?" I stuttered, and my hands trembled.

We were only a few steps away from the locked doors of the hall. It was the perfect time to turn around and get out of here before anyone saw us. When we stepped over that threshold, there was no going back.

"There's no way that he gave us away. If Mr. Lafon would know about us already, he would have us in his possession by now," Amara whispered, pushing herself against the door.

She froze mid-motion and turned around to stare at us.

A soul-crushing sound penetrated my ears and catapulted me back into my parents' car. Whatever was behind those closed doors—it wasn't good.

CHAPTER
33

Rowan raised his hand over his head to silence everyone. "Do you hear that?"

I sharpened my ears, and behind the door, I could hear loud noises. Not the normal sounds of children laughing and talking, but blared panicked voices, almost like screams, followed by chairs scratching over the floor. I took a deep breath and told myself everything was fine and that we were just tense because we were scared of getting caught.

"They're probably repositioning the chairs for the meeting," I said, leaning against the door. Amara rushed to my aid, but the heavy wooden wings didn't yield an inch.

"What the…" Amara exclaimed, but a loud cry silenced her.

I instantly transformed and stood on my hind paws, ready to fight.

"They are here!" Rowan exclaimed, his face petrified, and without even saying the name, each of us knew who he was talking about.

"Where are they?" Cried a shrill voice in the hall. The voice was loud enough to find its way under the door leaves, echoing through the corridor. Screams filled the air, and someone ran towards us, banging both hands against the inside of the wood in a panic.

"We have to do something!" I pushed all my weight against the door to open it.

"No! We have to get you to safety," Rowan replied calmly, grabbing Amara's and my arm and pulling us away from the door. His grip was so firm that I felt him cut off the blood supply to my hand.

"But we can't just let them die! It's our fault!" Amara yelled and tugged at her sleeve, but she was not strong enough.

"If you don't let go of me immediately, I will hurt you!" I pressed through my clenched teeth with rage.

"Try it," Rowan replied coldly, meeting my gaze, and the blood in my veins froze.

His otherwise tender, amber-colored eyes had turned into something that seemed inhuman. His bright iris had turned black-red, and his supple facial features had disappeared entirely and were replaced by something dark.

Frantically, I tried to get away from him, and I was no longer sure whether we should flee from the instructors, the Oblitus, or Rowan.

"I'm trying to help you," Rowan assured, but I didn't buy it.

It struck me like a thunderbolt.

"You're Miss Syryn's errand boy. You're going to hand us over to her, aren't you? Is that why you always followed me? To find out if I was one of the twins?" I screamed at him and could feel my world collapse.

He had been spying on me and tricked me from the first moment I arrived. Rowan wasn't looking for a friendship;

he had only followed the orders of Miss Syryn.

Rowan's dark, animalistic gaze was fixed on me, and he dragged us around the corner of the corridor before he came to a sudden halt.

I used that moment to sink my teeth into the cold skin of his arm. The taste of blood stung my tongue. Rowan let go of me as blood dripped from the fresh bite wound until suddenly, the wound began to close back up in front of our eyes.

I looked at him in disbelief to ensure he watched the same miracle, but Rowan's expression remained undisturbed.

"What are you?" I whispered in horror, but I couldn't wait for an answer. I had to get help.

I leaped forward to get into my room and use the Fores to teleport myself out of Teviena, but then I saw what made Rowan freeze.

My gaze hit the black eyes of the Nightmare. A shock went through my body and made me turn back into a human. I tried to resist the transformation, but it was too late. Without my gift, I was lost.

The warm air from the stallion's nostrils ran over my face and ruffled my hair. A heat wave swept over me, and my legs shook. I was about to faint.

This was it!

Mr. Lafon had found us and had probably heard what I had said to Rowan. Our secret was out.

"Follow me," said a familiar, dark voice that seemed to come out of the stallion's mouth. I tried to resist the request but knew I couldn't take on Mr. Lafon—with or without my gift.

"Hurry!" The Nightmare grumbled, and two hands wrapped around my upper arms.

Viera and Ella had rushed to me, looking as frightened

as I did. Amara was still fighting against Rowan's grip, but she gave up.

"We'll protect you," Ella whispered into my ear. Although I appreciated her courage, I knew her gift was not enough to deal with the Nightmare.

There was only one more thing I could do. "Spare our friends. They have nothing to do with all this!" I said, trying to sound braver than I felt.

"Be quiet and follow me!" Mr. Lafon replied coolly and turned around.

I had no strength to defend myself against him. I could probably have overcome Rowan, though I still didn't know what his gift was. The training hall had proven that we were powerless even as a team against the Nightmare.

"Come on!" Mr. Lafon called over his flank and galloped through the corridor.

If we made it to the stairwell, maybe we could escape him. My eyes met the dark pupils of Rowan. He was watching me like a hawk.

We were surrounded.

Without further resistance, I ran after the Nightmare. Behind me, I heard more trampling steps. I tried to devise an escape plan until I realized my room was right in front of us. We could use the Fores to get to another room.

As I tried to keep up with the Nightmare, I looked over my shoulder and then to the door to signal the others to run into my room. I hoped they could decipher my message. Now I just had to free Amara from Rowan's grip.

The door to my room was just a few steps away, and Mr. Lafon was about to walk past the door… when he sank his hooves into the carpet and came to a standstill.

This can't be true.

He was standing right outside my door as he turned back into his human form. "Get in," he said bluntly and opened the door.

I stumbled into the familiar room and looked around. This room had been my home since my parents disappeared. This room had comforted me when I desperately wanted to withdraw from all the new information the Magical World threw at me. And now it would be the last room I saw in Teviena.

The feeling of fear and panic disappeared, and my heart calmed down. Miss Syryn had been right. It was my destiny. I was born for this exact moment.

Numb by the overwhelming emotions, I walked to the bed, expecting Miss Syryn to wait for us, but the room was empty. Mr. Lafon threw the door into the lock and stared at us, his hand clutching the doorknob. Hot metal ran through his fingers, and as he let go of it, I saw the knob had melted and was now useless. There was no way out except through the Fores or the balcony.

"Let go of the girl," said Mr. Lafon to Rowan, who immediately removed his hand from Amara's arm. She made her way to me and embraced me.

"Who would have thought that the two of you are the twins?" said Mr. Lafon with a gloomy voice, and the corners of his mouth slipped into an unpleasant smile.

Ella stepped toward him to attack him, but I grabbed her by the shoulder and held her back.

"It's all right," I replied calmly.

"Save your strength," Amara agreed, straightening her back.

"Which is the nearest Fores to the garden?" Asked Mr. Lafon, as if he hadn't heard Ella's attempt to harm him.

I didn't think he knew what a Fores was. But he was an instructor and probably knew magic objects better than any of us.

I considered lying to him or playing dumb, but then I

chose the truth. "The library," I said briefly, and Viera looked at me indignantly.

Of course, the hiding place was much closer to the garden, but the last thing I could do was to protect it. It wasn't much, but at least they could still hide children down there and bring them to safety.

"We don't have much time," Mr. Lafon replied, stepping closer to us.

I looked at our friends. Tears rolled over Ella's cheeks while Viera held on to her.

Then my gaze went to Rowan, who had his normal eye color back and sadness flickered in his eyes. That was the Rowan I knew, not the emotionless monster that had dragged us through the corridor.

Finally, with a heavy heart, I looked over to Amara, who was just as willing to say goodbye to our friends.

"Thank you for everything," I said before Mr. Lafon pulled us through the arch behind him.

Amara had placed a Fores between the last bookshelves on a wall in the library, making it look like it belonged to it.

Again, Mr. Lafon made sure that no one could follow us. Small flames shot out of his hands, and the wooden arch turned to ashes within seconds.

He walked past us. I trotted after him, and for a moment, I hoped we might come across Mr. Adrian so he could save us, but then I discarded that thought. We had already involved enough people in this, and a historian would be even more powerless against a Nightmare than I am with my gift, which currently refused to show.

We had made it into the entrance hall without interruption.

I tried to stay calm as hundreds of thoughts rushed through my head, each plan as useless as the other. But then an idea stuck, something I hadn't thought about before.

No, I couldn't do that, could I?

What if Mr. Lafon couldn't deliver us both if one of us were to get hurt? Then the other twin's blood would be useless. But even this idea was not helpful because the Oblitus didn't need us alive to get to our blood.

"Can't you walk a little faster?" Mr. Lafon barked. He was several steps away from us and broke through the front door. "If you two keep this pace, she will find us."

I frowned. Who would find us? Was the head of the Oblitus a woman?

"Who are they talking about?" Amara asked faintly.

I didn't expect an answer and was surprised when Mr. Lafon said, "Miss Syryn wants to hand you over to the Oblitus. We need to get you out of here."

My mouth opened, and I had to fight my limbs to keep going. Had I understood it correctly? Did he want to take us away from here? I had heard him in the stairwell. He tried to find the twins—us—and hand us over.

"But…" I stammered. "You promised Miss Syryn that you would take us to her. I heard everything!"

He slowed his step. "So that I have two innocent children on my conscience? You think I don't have a soul because I'm a Nightmare?" He murmured loudly, and small flames shot out of his hands.

"No, of course not…" But yes, that was precisely what I had thought of him. My face burned.

"The moment Miss Syryn told me her plan, I realized she was not the person she claims to be. Weeks ago, she recruited me on behalf of the Saperians to return to Teviena. Normally, the council takes over this task personally, but I didn't think about it until yesterday. Have you noticed that many children here pretend their parents never existed?"

Immediately, my thoughts went to Lex, who acted like a completely different person. He seemed emotionless every time I mentioned our parents. I knew that something was wrong, but I had blamed it on the fact that he was grieving.

"What are you talking about?" Asked Amara and hurried after him.

"I've watched a handful of children disappear as a pile of misery with Miss Syryn. Then, shortly afterward, I met two of these children in the hallway, being cheerful. I asked them why they had cried a few minutes earlier, and they couldn't remember spilling a single tear. Questionable, isn't it?"

"Maybe they weren't the same children," I said.

"Are you accusing me of not knowing my trainees?" Mr. Lafon grumbled angrily, and she pressed her lips together in shame. "I don't know what she did to them, but I'll figure it out. At that time, I knew something wasn't right. I'm obligated to ensure you're safe until I hear from the Saperians what's happening here."

I couldn't believe it. I've assumed Mr. Lafon hated us, and now he was trying to save us from Miss Syryn, of all people? She had helped my brother with a healer. Whenever she had time, she assisted trainees while she searched for our parents. She was the head of Teviena and pure perfection. I tried to make sense of his accusation.

We passed the enormous tree behind the fountain, and Mr. Lafon was about to set foot in the garden when a loud sound behind us caught our attention. I turned to see where the noise came from as Mr. Lafon threw himself protectively in front of us and turned into the Nightmare. At first, I couldn't see where the crashing sound came from because the Nightmare blocked my view, but then I saw the culprit.

The head of a vast Feathered Serpent had broken through the ceiling of Teviena, almost twice the size of Niam's form. My eyes tried to focus on the creature that looked like an oversized clown jumping out of a box, and I could tell by the color and appearance that it was indeed Niam.

He floated above the roof where the dining room had to be and rippled through the air. At least he had managed to escape, but instead of flying away, he shrunk and disappeared back into the hole he had created.

CHAPTER
34

"Run!" Mr. Lafon yelled.

We ran into the garden without questioning him.

I didn't know where to run to or where we were safe, but I knew we had to get away as far from Miss Syryn and the Oblitus as possible.

I tried to transform myself, and for a moment, my lynx resisted. It was a silent battle between us until the lynx gave up. Next to me, I could see Amara struggling to take on her wolf form.

A loud hiss tore the air. Even before I could react and warn my sister, she was lifted into the air by a black cloud of fog and was thrown back. I pushed myself with all my strength into the ground to turn around. I couldn't leave her behind.

"What are you doing?" Mr. Lafon said with a raised voice, who had been close on my heels.

"She needs me!"

I ran past him towards Teviena, tears building up as the

cooling wind burned my eyes. My heart skipped a beat as I caught her lifeless body in front of the big tree. I gritted my teeth and ran faster than ever before.

Finally, I reached the garden entrance and was only a few leaps away from Amara when I was hit by the same dark cloud that had appeared out of nowhere. The force was so strong that I was lifted from my paws and catapulted against a small tree. I gasped as I hit the ground.

"Well, well, well… Who allowed you to leave?" Asked a voice I knew only too well.

The numbing smell of rotten eggs rose into my nose. I held my breath, but I wasn't sure if it was because of the stench or my injuries.

How have I not noticed that her perfume was only to overshadow the sulfur smell a Shadow Creature brought with it or that she was surprised about the early appearance of an Oblitus because she didn't give the order? Or all the time she spent away from Teviena to train her own army of dark gifts and magic. Or her walk through the aisles to find the twins on her own. All the clues were there, and I was just too blind to see them.

"Leave her alone!" Mr. Lafon screamed as he stepped between Amara and me, looking around disoriented.

I couldn't see the location of where the voice had come from because my eyes were blurred by tears caused by the pain of the impact. I tried to stand up, my arms shaking like aspen leaves as I tried to apply pressure on them.

"Who would have thought the good old grump would come to their aid? But even you can't stop me." A barking laugh made me tremble.

Dry dust from the earth below me found its way into my nostrils and replaced the poisonous stench. I tried to rise from the ground again. My head was throbbing with pain, and my back felt like it had been whipped several times—I couldn't give up. With all my strength, I drove my arms into the ground, lifting myself up, and stood staggering behind Mr. Lafon, whose flames crackled menacingly. The warmth of his fire ran through my clothes.

"You want us? Then finish it, but spare the other children. They are innocent!" I shouted, trying to stabilize my posture.

"Innocent? Everyone with a gift bears the same guilt," the voice roared back, and I could trace the origin.

High above the tree was Miss Syryn.

Her hair stood out in all directions, her face disfigured with anger, and her otherwise bright eyes were dark as the night sky.

The dark opal attached to a chain around her neck floated in the air, just like her. The stone was glowing and threw off tiny white sparks.

"Let them go!" I screamed again and rubbed the tears from my cheeks.

"I can't let them live. They're just as dangerous as you and your sister. I knew I couldn't trust anyone here. It was a matter of time before someone found you two and tried to sneak you away from me."

"Please," I begged and tried to ignore the movement in the corner of my eye so I wouldn't draw attention to it.

Amara moaned loudly. To my relief, she wasn't dead.

"We can end this here right now," Mr. Lafon's deep voice startled me.

"If it would only be that simple."

The surrounding air got heavier. I could feel the tension increasing that had settled on my shoulders over the last few days.

"I'm doing you all a favor." Miss Syryn gently lowered herself to the floor.

"By becoming immortal?" I couldn't suppress the sarcastic undertone.

"I should have known you would make me the villain. You think I want immortality, you foolish child?" Her eyes sparkled with hatred. "I know the tragedy that followed the last person who was granted immortality. Oh no, I don't want to become immortal. I want to correct the mistakes that followed her story—hybrids. Emmerson was the reason my bloodline was crossed. Without her, the balance between the gifts would still exist. But no, she had to birth the first Crossling. There wouldn't be black magic without her. Without her, countless magical beings wouldn't rot in Bridlio just because they are a hybrid or have a hint of black magic. Without her, I would be a sorceress and not a hybrid. My bloodline was destroyed, and I must fix this mistake and start over."

If Miss Syryn's bloodline was crossed by Emmerson, which also ran through my veins, that meant she was a descendant from Nerol's family—which would make us related. Suddenly I felt dizzy.

This can't be!

Even Mr. Lafon didn't know what to say. I knew now Miss Syryn wasn't after our blood any longer—her actual plan was even worse.

"This is insane!" Mr. Lafon called and took a step towards her, but the ground below us trembled, and he withdrew.

I held out my arms to keep my balance as I waited for the quake to stop. I knew it wasn't my doing, so it had to come from her.

"Syryn, don't do it!" Mr. Lafon's voice broke.

"Syryn here, Syryn there." She rolled her eyes and smiled. "I should have known that even YOU don't even recognize me."

"What are you saying?"

"You heard me. You were the one who handed me over to the Saperians when I needed help the most with my black magic."

"I don't understand."

"Syryn? Siren? I was the only Siren you ever trained and didn't find good enough." I could hear an undertone of pain in her quivering voice.

"Aurora?" Mr. Lafon said, astonished.

"Give the dog a bone! That took you a long time to figure out."

Aurora? The same Aurora whose diary we found? The Aurora that spent her time with my mother in Teviena? Did my mother know they were related?

"Our mother was your friend," I called and held onto the only silver lining I could find. Maybe she would spare us if she knew we were more than just some random kids.

"Your mother?" She asked, amused.

"Amber? I heard you two were friends." I didn't want to add that I knew we had the same ancestors.

"Friends? Do you want to know how many times she inquired about me in Bridlio? Not once!" Aurora's nostrils shook, and she strolled toward us. "If my plan had worked then, she would have drowned, not the other girl."

I swallowed. I knew she was talking about Brianna. I assumed my parents had something to do with her death through all the stories. I had forgotten entirely that Aurora was locked away shortly afterward.

"But… you were friends… even more than that," I repeated. I could feel my hope slipping through my hands.

"I must admit, she was the only one who wasn't afraid of me. She took me into her circle of friends, and I started to feel comfortable when I discovered she was a Crossling like me. But unlike me, she had no black magic and no other gift. It took me a few months to realize that we were related. My bloodline goes back to the brother of Norwin, while hers goes back to Emmerson. I wanted to tell her, but she was too busy with Orion to listen to me. I did some research and found out her ancestor was the reason for Crossings. Because Emmerson mated with another gift, other beings followed her example. Without her, I wouldn't be the monster I am now. Without her, a Siren and a magician would have never thought about falling in love." Aurora took a deep breath.

"I'm sorry." I lowered my head.

I could understand her pain. I, too, had been afraid to put my hand on the crystal to find out if I had black magic.

Mr. Lafon shook his head slowly. "We gave you a choice. If you had kept to your training, you would have become a phenomenal Siren. You were on the right track, and suddenly—"

Aurora interrupted him. "You think I didn't give it my all so I wouldn't end up in Bridlio? I was searching day in and day out for good in me. I knew I had a good heart somewhere in there. But do you know how mean other kids can be to you if you're different? They teased me. A boy even threw stones at me." She was now standing right before us, her dark eyes sparkling with rage.

"But why Brianna?" My heart ached at the thought that she had been after my mother and that Brianna was just in the wrong place at the wrong time.

"Your mother had everything; a family, friends. She was popular and had her gift under control. Even though some of the same blood flowed through our veins, she was all I wasn't. When she made a move on Orion, it was enough for me. She reminded me every day that I would never be enough and that more Crosslings would be born in the next generation! Black magic pulsed through my veins every time she was around me. I wanted to put an end to it and make it look like it was an accident, but she didn't even find it necessary to show up at our meeting point."

My stomach turned. I didn't want to hear what she had done to Brianna, but I couldn't stop her.

"It was dark, and I was swimming in the lake of Teviena when I saw a figure approaching me. I thought it was Amber and started singing, but then I recognized Brianna right before she plunged herself into the lake's depths. I wanted to save her…" She didn't need to say more to make me understand. A sad twinkle flitted across her eyes, but then her face turned back to a stone facade.

I didn't need to be raised in the Magical World to know a Siren's abilities. They were pretty women who, with their enchanted songs, lured sailors to steer their ships into dangerous waters and to their death.

I shook my head. "And then my father found her, and everyone thought it was him," I added, and my legs were about to cave in.

Aurora nodded. "Your mother fled in panic when she found out I sang my song for her. The guilt drove me insane. Brianna was innocent, a sorceress through and through, and the grief for her finally unleashed my black magic to its full potential."

"We can't undo the past. But you can turn over a new leaf by letting the children go. They can't be harmed for the deeds of their ancestors," said Mr. Lafon gently, who had turned back to his human form and slowly walked towards Aurora with his hands raised. "Tell us where their parents are, and we can fix everything. We will speak to the Saperians and ensure they release Bridlio's inmates."

"The parents…" She clasped her necklace with a firm grip. "I still need them." My gaze fell onto the stone on her chain, and even Mr. Lafon had noticed her movement.

"And the Saperians won't help us. The human sage had been so kind as to give me access to their palace, and he could hardly wait to help me with my plan."

Mr. Lafon lowered his arms. I couldn't see his face, but I knew he was shaking with rage because of his trembling hands.

Aurora stared at him. "There is no other alternative. We have to start all over again... The sage had been quite pleased to eliminate these powerful beings."

"What have you done?" Mr. Lafon asked in horror.

"Only what I was born to do." She waved her hand, and before I could even blink, Mr. Lafon flung through the air and landed on the ground near Amara with a muffled impact.

Aurora's gaze followed him. I used this second, jumped towards her, wrapped my palm around the black stone on her chain, and pulled on it. The chain broke with a loud snap. A stabbing pain cut into my hand, and I wanted to drop the stone, but I was sure this rock had something to do with my parents.

Clenching my teeth in pain, I turned around and ran around various bushes scattered in the garden.

There was no plan on what to do next. I knew I had to lead Aurora away from the wounded and Teviena and bring the stone to safety. I didn't know what was behind the garden, but I would find out soon.

A shrill cry cooled the blood in my veins. It was not a human cry; it sounded as if several people were screaming in unison.

I didn't look back. Instead, I zigzagged between the bushes, stuffing the broken chain into my coat pocket to ease the burning pain of my hand, and transformed myself. As far as the eye could see, there were only plants.

The stench of rotten eggs struck me like an invisible fist.

My stomach was about to empty itself until a black mist caught my attention and distracted me from my nausea.

The same dark circle the Oblitus had used at the fountain appeared before me. Before I could turn and dive around the next bush, an oversized man stepped out of the circle and grinned at me. Half of his teeth were brown and rotten. He stretched out his massive hand at me as I tried to stop. He was about to grab me by the neck when his arm disappeared from my view, and an angry scream ripped through the air.

A silver pair of eyes stared back at me, where the voluminous Oblitus had been just a heartbeat before. The Shadow Creature had been pushed back into the circle, and the man had vanished, as well as his portal.

The silver eyes rested on me, and I took a step back to get a more accurate picture of my savior. I exhaled.

It was my Wedo.

This beautiful Simargl had rushed to my rescue—as Amara had explained. I had noticed the various mythical creatures when I had walked through the corridors, but I hadn't expected that they were real protectors.

The silver wolf turned his gaze away from me, lowered his head in a graceful movement, and opened his silver wings wide to show his back. Although I wanted to take the time to thank and examine him, I had no time to lose.

I understood his offer. I jumped and found myself on his narrow waist, holding on to the metallic peacock feathers covering his neck and shoulder blades. Even before I could give an order, the Simargl straightened up, rushed forward, and flapped his wings. I looked down at the bushes racing past us and getting smaller and smaller. Finally, we were off the ground.

I looked up into the sky covered with black clouds, and with every stroke of his wings, we increased the distance to the ground. We were high enough that I could see the garden's dimensions and realized that I would never have made it out without help.

The garden stretched over three football fields and was cut off at the end of the island. Teviena lay on an island surrounded by a large river, which turned into a waterfall and formed a lake in front of the Quarters.

We were on an isolated piece of land without access to the outside world.

Below me, black circles cut the air from which Shadow Creatures streamed like ants from their burrows.

I strengthened my grip around the feathers. I had jumped on the back of the Wedo without thinking about how to steer it. Hesitantly I tugged at the feathers, but that didn't take the Simargl off course.

I looked over my shoulder and saw Teviena surrounded by darkness.

We have to go back! I have to help them!

As if the Wedo had read my thoughts, he turned to the left and headed for the courtyard.

"Thank you," I whispered, trying to cling to him to emphasize my words.

Just as I exhaled in relief to have a few seconds to think about my next moves, we were hit by something.

The impact tore me off the Wedo, and I staggered uncontrollably through the air until my breath was squeezed out of my lungs. Panicked, I looked for support when I found myself on his back again.

While I was flipping through the air, the Simargl must have dived after me and positioned itself below me to catch my fall.

How many times could I thank a statue? It was the second time he saved me within a few minutes.

"You can't escape!" Aurora's loud voice made my ears

hurt.

"I don't want to," I screamed back and searched the ground for her.

Below me, I could see children bravely fighting back against the Shadow Creatures. From magic spells that ran through the air to shapeshifters who defended themselves with their animalistic powers.

I looked up and recognized Aurora. She wasn't on solid ground. She floated in the air in front of me and whirled her hands around each other in circular motions. Blackness formed between her palms, and she sent the darkness in our direction with a graceful hand movement. The cloud rushed towards us, but the Wedo sucked it in with a breath instead of hitting us.

"What?!" Aurora screamed, and two more black masses flew towards us. The Simargl had no problem inhaling them, and I could have sworn that he grew bigger with every breath.

"This is impossible!" She yelled and let go of her attempts to hit us with her black magic.

I didn't understand what had happened either. Her magic should have hit us, but it didn't.

"I have to go to my sister," I whispered as I noticed he couldn't only fly but could also protect us from her spells.

He turned towards the tree and tucked his wings in. I prepared myself that the metallic feathers would cut into my legs, but the silver mass melted around my body to give me better support. Bent forward, I clasped his neck to avoid the chilly wind hitting my face.

Amara was only a few heartbeats away from us when I saw Lex stepping out of the door of Teviena.

My heart stopped.

Beside him, two black circles swirled, announcing the arrival of more Oblitus.

Amara leaned against the tree, messaging her forehead in sorrow. A silver Griffin stood next to her with outstretched wings and served as a barrier between her and the space in front of her. I couldn't find a Shadow Creature near her.

My gaze went back to Lex, who had recognized the threat and was fighting in his wolf form against one of the Oblitus, while the other was stalking up on him from behind. Both were wrapped in black hooded cloaks.

I had to make a decision.

CHAPTER
35

My heart broke as I made a decision.

"To Lex!" I said in a quivering voice, and my Wedo redirected his course and was still on time at the stairs before the Oblitus could attack Lex from behind. I let myself fall off his back and landed precisely on the Shadow Creature that hit the ground and gave me a soft landing.

I startled Lex with my unannounced arrival. He had let go of the Oblitus, who took this opportunity to form a magical aura in the palm of his hand. I tried to grab Lex to get him out of the way. But, as I stretched out my paw, a red fireball released from my paw pad and hit the dark figure in the abdominal area. He staggered back and fell backward over the barrier of the stairs.

My body froze. I wasn't aware that I could use my magic as a lynx.

Lex's eyes widened as he looked at the spot where the Oblitus had been and then at my paw.

I knew what he was thinking. After all, I had concealed

from him that I was both a shapeshifter and a sorceress. He was a Crossling, but I was a hybrid. I had so many secrets from him. How could I expect my parents to tell me the truth if I couldn't even bring it over myself to tell my brother about mine?

I wanted to say something, but this was not the time to explain everything to him. "Later," I hissed and pulled him towards my Wedo as a silver Centaur broke through the wall next to us and stopped in front of Lex.

"You took your sweet time!" Lex snarled, looking at the Wedo's flaring nostrils.

My gaze ran over the Centaur's muscular chest and the hole he had left in the wall with no problems.

"You have to trust me! Collect as many children as possible, go to my room to the wooden arch, and focus on a hiding place when you step through. I have no time to explain everything to you, but you must save the children!" I said, looking into his wounded eyes.

He knew that there were so many unspoken things between us. He knew that after this fight, nothing would be the same. I could see it in his eyes.

"You come with me!" He said with a firm voice and reached for my paw.

I clasped his paw with my other and looked into his beautiful, light brown eyes. "Amara needs me," I said, my voice trembling with pain.

I didn't want to choose between my siblings. Lex and Amara were my lifeblood. I had to get Lex to safety, so I could take care of Amara so that we could get out of here together. "Your Wedo can help you open my door. You have to hurry!"

I wanted to hug, comfort, and tell him everything that had happened, but my heart broke with his expression. I Ignored his orders—that I had to stay with him—I swung myself on the back of the Simargl, and together we climbed into the air towards Amara.

I searched both the sky and the ground for Aurora. The sun was covered with thick, dark clouds. It seemed like it was nighttime. The battle was going on to the fullest below me. I tried to shoot more fireballs out of my paws to disable some of the Shadow Creatures to help the children—without success.

My Wedo arrived with a metallic click on the ground next to the tree, and I ran towards Amara, who was now standing shakily on her feet. I wrapped my paws around her and pressed her to me.

"You are okay," I whispered as I fought against tears yet again.

"And you tickle," said Amara, grinning, pushing my whiskers out of her face. "Be careful!"

Amara pushed me away from her, and I fell to the ground. A black cloud flew towards us and was about to hit Amara when her Griffin stepped in front of her and absorbed the magic. I exhaled and jumped on all fours.

Aurora's devilish laughter echoed across the courtyard. But I was not afraid this time. She had gone too far. Talking wouldn't deter Aurora from her plan. We had to fight! But even with magic, I was no match for her.

Aurora hovered over the garden entrance, and her gaze drove over us. "I'm at the end of my patience! Surrender before the blood of these children clings to your hands," she said in a sweet voice. Her face was disfigured with anger, and her lips curled up.

"Never!" Amara barked back and grabbed my paw, her Griffin, and my Simargl shielding us. "She can't use her dark magic. Wedos can absorb black magic and transform it into energy," Amara quietly explained without taking her gaze off Aurora.

That was the reason she couldn't hurt me in the air. Apparently, Aurora had not followed me because she had to come up with a new strategy.

Black circles formed between Aurora and us, and I realized what strategy she had chosen. Dozens of Shadow Creatures appeared before us and looked up to her as if they were waiting for their orders.

"If you don't give up voluntarily, I will have to force you." A big smile stretched over her face.

She opened her mouth and began to sing. Goosebumps shot over my body. I had heard the melody before. It had soothed me when I sat on the mountain cliff looking down on the village the night my parents had disappeared.

Before I knew it, I looked at the woman who had welcomed me to Teviena. Aurora had turned back into her pure form, her singing wrapping around me like warm honey, pulling me towards her.

I only had eyes for her.

I clumsily walked past my Wedo, and Amara also seemed to follow her call.

Large silver paws encircled my chest and tried to hold me back, but I wiggled myself free of them and walked further into my sweet ruin.

I had no control over my body. My desire to follow this woman was too great.

Darkness closed in around me, blocking the view of Aurora, and the song became quieter and quieter until it fell silent. I shook my head and looked into complete darkness.

"Cas?" I heard Amara calling.

I groped through the thick fog to find her. Something had stirred the darkness up to my right, and a wine-red trouser leg stepped out of the darkness, followed by the rest of the body.

Rowan's arms were outstretched on both sides, and a dark aura ignited his hands and snuggled around him like a cat begging for touch. His eyes were black, and I gasped for air.

He walked towards me in all his glory. I wanted to retreat and get to safety far away from him, but his darkness drew me to him like a magnet.

"Cas!" Amara's voice penetrated my subconscious and pulled me out of my trance. She stepped between Rowan and me, not knowing he was behind her.

I threw my arms around her and looked over her shoulder at Rowan, who was only a few steps away from us. I mentally armed myself against his attack—until I saw Ella and Niam walking past him. They ran towards us and pulled us apart.

"You're all right!" Niam said, wrapping himself around us.

"We have no time for sentimentality," growled Rowan, who stopped beside us, my gaze resting on him. He seemed to both absorb and radiate the darkness around us.

"How did you find us?" Amara choked out, squeezing Ella's hand.

"Rowan and I fled through the Fores to the hiding place to find you guys. On the way, Shadow Creatures attacked us, but with his help, it was a breeze to get past them," Ella said.

"And I found them in the yard after I put as many children as I could under the fountain through the Fores in Amara's room," Niam added. "Viera is doing her best to hold the line with her bow and arrows."

"My brother?" Amara asked breathlessly.

"He's safe and with my sisters," Niam assured.

"I can feel Miss Syryn trying to get through my barrier," Rowan said, his hands shivering.

"Rowan is a Shadow, as it turns out," Ella said casually and shrugged.

I didn't know what a Shadow was and what abilities this gift brought with it. But it seemed like Rowan could summon darkness that could protect us from attacks.

"Miss Syryn is Aurora. She's a Siren and a sorceress," I said briefly to bring everyone up to speed.

"THE Aurora?" Niam asked in horror.

"EXACTLY that one," Amara stressed, standing next to me.

"But there is even more to it," I whispered.

Rowan's voice was raw, and he looked at the spot where Aurora had floated before. "We only have a few seconds left."

"Let's do this." Niam turned into a miniature version of his Feathered Serpent.

I grabbed Ella's and Amara's hands. My heart was racing. We had no tactic, no powers to fight Aurora. But we would fight, aware that it was our downfall.

The surrounding darkness subsided, and I could see Aurora's silhouette through the fog.

"At last," she said, letting herself down to the floor. "None of you thought you had a person with black magic in your ranks, did you?"

My breath stopped. At first, I was confused, but then I knew she could only speak of Rowan. As a Shadow, he had to be able to access black magic.

"Come to me," she said.

"Over my dead body," Niam exclaimed, standing next to Ella. Then, even before I realized what was going on, Rowan walked towards her through the thin layer of fog.

I wanted to scream, grab his arm, and pull him back to us, but my body didn't move. Anger spread within me.

How could I have trusted him again? He had been her

errand boy, her recruit, her spy.

"What are you doing?" Niam shouted.

"He can't help it being ruled by darkness. It's in his nature. Do you know now why Crosslings are dangerous?" Aurora grinned and extended her hands wide to receive Rowan. "He delivered you all together, as promised."

I didn't dare to move and didn't want to admit that Rowan had betrayed us. He had delivered us like a beautifully wrapped gift, knowing that we were inferior to Aurora.

"That's not true!" I screamed, and Rowan slowed his step for an eye-blink, then he walked on. "It's not true! I know him! I know he's good!"

Aurora's laugh broke my heart.

How could I have been so naive? I had seen what his brother was capable of. Had I really assumed that Rowan was different?

Ella withdrew my grip and threw her hands forward to produce light, but her hands remained empty, and she looked around in panic. "There is no light here! Only darkness! My gift cannot help us!" Her voice failed. Thick clouds covered the sky and made it look like nighttime.

Niam shot toward Aurora and Rowan, and a movement of her hand was enough to hit him with a black aura. Niam slumped to the ground and shifted back into a human.

I looked at Rowan, whose eyes rested on us. He didn't move as he stood beside Aurora, surrounded by Shadow Creatures.

I strengthened my grip around Amara, trying to pull on her magic and create enough to free us from the danger. But there was no magic I could tap into. Amara's power was depleted.

Where were our Wedos? And the instructors? Someone had to come to our aid. I was too afraid to turn my eyes away from our opponents.

"We have to do something," Ella hissed.

But what? My transformation was not enough, and my magic was uncontrollable. I had defeated the last Oblitus by chance.

"Destroy them," Aurora said impatiently, waiting for a reaction from us, expecting us to fight back. Now she had lost patience in her deadly play, like a child with a defective toy.

Rowan's black eyes studied me. I tried to beg him with my gaze to spare us, but he looked right through me. He raised his hands, and darkness flowed out of them like ink, swirling around him before it rushed purposefully at us.

I held my breath; my body froze. We could have run away, but Amara was powerless, and Ella's gift was useless without light.

The darkness embraced us and pressed us together, coldness running over my body like freezing water. I could hear Ella scream softly as the darkness engulfed us.

"Use fire," a voice echoed through my head.

"What?"

"Your fire!"

My fire? What could it be good for? Fire couldn't bring an end to the darkness.

I thought about what it could mean, concentrating on my hands, which I couldn't see through the dense dark mass.

Please, please, please, please!

It had previously worked on using my magic to form a flame in my hand. I had done it again and again in the hiding place and against an Oblitus that threatened Lex.

Something red flickered in the darkness, and the cold that penetrated my clothes into my bones lessened.

"Light!" Ella's voice echoed in my ears.

Of course!

Ella needed light to use her gift. The flame grew bigger as if my body understood her desire.

But not only was my fire getting bigger, something bright in the corner of my eye made me look away from my hands—Ella had used my fire to metamorphose. Her glassy figure pushed away the surrounding nothingness.

"I need a little more," Ella demanded.

I had no more to give. My magic came and went as it desired.

A hand grabbed my wrist, and an energy surge ran through my body. The flame shot up and almost burned my face. Amara had gathered a magic spark in her and passed it on to me.

"Now," Ella whispered, and the darkness around us fell to the ground like a curtain.

The next few seconds went by too fast. A white ball of light shot through the falling darkness and hit Aurora in the chest, followed by a glaring explosion.

I tried to keep my eyes open.

Black specks shot from the center of the explosion in all directions. I wanted to protect myself from them, but a speck of darkness hit me in the chest and threw me backward.

"No!" Amara's voice sounded distorted.

My ears roared, and my heart stood still—for a beat. I remained on the ground, the surface trembling as someone ran toward me. I looked up at the sky, which had instantly reverted to the previous blue before Aurora had used her magic. Exhausted, I closed my eyes.

"We need a healer! Quick!"

I tried to open my eyelids, but they were too heavy, and my surroundings became quiet—too quiet.

CHAPTER
36

Whispers pulled me back out of the void. I thought of my parents.

If I opened the door, I would see them sitting together on our couch. They were within my grasp. I just had to lean into the door and...

I opened my eyes to see them. My vision needed a moment to focus.

"She is awake!"

Amara's face appeared in my field of vision, my heart breaking—it wasn't my parents I had heard.

"Cas!" Niam threw himself at me to hug me.

A burning pain penetrated my chest and made me gasp.

"Be more careful with her." Rowan's voice ran through my body like a knife.

I wanted to shapeshift and tear him into little pieces because he had delivered us to Aurora, which was why we almost died. He had betrayed us, not once but twice.

A hiss left my throat, but I had no energy for more.

"Everything is alright. Rowan saved us," Ella said

calmly and sat down beside me. I wasn't aware of who else was surrounding me.

"Saved?" My voice was scratchy. "He brought us to her like animals to slaughter!"

"He gave us time to beat Aurora. He used his gift to give us time to attack," Amara said softly, running her hand over mine.

Fragments of the confrontation came back to me— *Rowan approaching Aurora. His pause. Darkness shot out of his hands and surrounded us. Coldness. A voice that spoke in my consciousness directed me to create a fire.*

"It was you." My voice sounded smoother. "You wanted me to use my magic."

"I didn't know if the plan would work, but it was worth a try," Rowan answered and appeared over me. His warm eyes radiated sadness.

A ray of light. The explosion. A speck of darkness. I was thrown to the ground.

"Have we destroyed them?"

An unpleasant silence followed, and Amara gazed at Niam and Rowan to look for an answer.

I sat up, panting, and looked around. I was back in my room in Teviena. My eyes fell on Mrs. Nerol, who was standing next to the bed someone had placed me on. Her face was friendly but withered with pain.

"We know that most of the Shadow Creatures have disappeared with her, but we aren't sure whether the light has only scared them away or whether they are gone for good. We captured a few Oblitus, and Mr. Lafon is trying to get information from them with the help of Viera. Her gift is beneficial."

I had noticed that Viera was missing, but I had resisted thinking of the worst.

"And Lex?" My voice broke.

The last time I saw him, I had stirred all my secrets up with a single fireball. I hadn't had time to tell him the truth and instead had ordered him to hide the children.

He stepped out of the shadow of Mrs. Nerol. I wanted to hug him.

"I have to tell you something..." I began, but he interrupted me.

"You were in a coma for three days. I thought you'd never wake up again." He walked towards me. "These three days were the longest of my life and gave me enough time to learn about all your secrets."

Tears formed in my eyes. His disappointed face tore my heart apart. It was my fault; I should have trusted him. His eyes ran over my face.

"Oh, I'm not mad you didn't tell me. I was under a spell by Aurora. Her spell lifted the moment she disappeared."

"I should have told you, anyway. You're my brother!"

His face softened, and he hugged me. It hurt, but I didn't flinch.

"And you'll always be my sister, no matter what!"

Warm tears rolled down my face as I embraced him with a firmer grip.

I had been so afraid of this moment that he would repel, ignore, or even laugh at me.

Lex let go of me and sat beside Amara on the bed. I stretched my hand out to grab him but stopped when I saw a bandage around my palm.

My hand.

I had burned my hand on Aurora's stone. I frantically scanned my clothes, but I was no longer wearing the same cloak as before. Instead, I was dressed in a linen dress.

Mrs. Nerol moved into my view. "The opal is in Mr. Adrian's care, and he discovered the stone is linked to the souls of your parents and other family members the

Shadow Creatures had claimed. Aurora was able to harvest the energy of their gifts using the Opal. Mr. Adrian is trying to find a way to free your families, so far unsuccessfully."

Relaxed, I leaned back. I had not been crazy. I had not imagined Aurora's behavior when she wrapped the opal protectively in her hand when I asked about our parents.

"So my intuition was right. I hoped her necklace had something to do with them."

"Apart from the fact that none of the trainees were fatally injured, possessing the opal is our true victory. Now the only question is how to get them out of the crystal unscathed. Mr. Adrian hopes to find an answer within the next few days." Mrs. Nerol scanned me and then my friends. "I wish I would have known sooner that you two are the twins. I could have helped you."

I wanted to say something, but there were no right words.

"You did it. You found our parents," Niam said happily, breaking the awkward silence.

"With the help of all of you," I said. Every bone in my body hurt, and I let out a quiet sigh.

"The healer couldn't tell what was wrong with you," Ella said, who had noticed my discomfort. "I have also tried to heal you, but your body refused my light."

The thought of the warmth of her gift reminded me of how good it had felt.

"I just have to heal like a normal person. That's fine. We are all just people with gifts," I whispered, closing my eyes to save my strength.

"We should let her rest. Cassandra will be back on her feet in a few days." Mrs. Nerol opened the door. "Tomorrow, we'll inform you about everything that has happened in the last 72 hours, but until then, you need to regain your strength."

Lex leaned down for another hug before he stepped away. Both Amara and Niam gave me a warm smile. Ella stroked a strand of hair out of my face before joining them.

"I'm so glad you're okay," Rowan said softly, and his cold hand rested on mine before he turned away and closed the door behind him.

I had so much to say to each of them, but I needed time to sort my thoughts. I had to get back on my feet because I had wasted three days sleeping.

We had to find a way to remove our families from the opal so I could embrace them and never let go of them. I also had to ask my mother about her past—maybe that would lead to meeting my biological father for the first time.

But as of now, we were safe and sound.

A sharp pain shot through my body as I put my feet on the floor. I wanted to give up, but my limbs needed movement.

Wobbly and in pain, I stood up and walked around the bed to get to the balcony.

My reflection in the mirror caught my attention. I pressed my hand on the glass to lean against it and take a quick break.

My light brown hair fell ruffled over my face and shoulders. I looked at the dark circles under my eyes and let out a little scream as I looked into my eyes.

Something animal, inhuman even, looked back. My green iris was flooded with something dark that looked like black ink. Before I could bend over to focus on it, the darkness in my eyes was gone.

Something was seriously wrong.

ABOUT THE AUTHOR

C.K. Franziska's debut novel, A Speck of Darkness, is the first book in her duology series. She is the wife of a traveler, as well as the mother of two mini versions of herself and way too many pets. In her spare time, she is also a photographer, traveler, full-time entertainer, and animal lover. She does her best writing at night, at the beach listening to the waves, or while camping. C.K. loves to play make-believe, transporting readers to a place where the heroes have to step out of the seemingly endless cycle of family curses, where the magic is as beautiful and untamable as we think, and where every person deserves to be celebrated.